The Dragon Done It

Baen Books by Eric Flint

Ring of Fire series:
1632 by Eric Flint
1633 by Eric Flint & David Weber
1634: The Baltic War by Eric Flint & David Weber
Ring of Fire ed. by Eric Flint
1634: The Galileo Affair by Eric Flint & Andrew Dennis
1635: The Ram Rebellion by Eric Flint and Virginia DeMarce et al.
1635: The Cannon Law by Eric Flint & Andrew Dennis
1634: The Bavarian Crisis by Eric Flint & Virginia DeMarce
Grantville Gazette ed. by Eric Flint
Grantville Gazette II ed. by Eric Flint
Grantville Gazette III ed. by Eric Flint
Grantville Gazette IV ed. by Eric Flint
Ring of Fire II ed. by Eric Flint

Joe's World series:
The Philosophical Strangler
Forward the Mage (with Richard Roach)

Standalone titles:
Mother of Demons
Crown of Slaves (with David Weber)
The Course of Empire (with K.D. Wentworth)
Mountain Magic (with Ryk E. Spoor, David Drake & Henry Kuttner)

With Mercedes Lackey & Dave Freer:
The Shadow of the Lion   *This Rough Magic*

With Dave Freer:
Rats, Bats & Vats   *The Rats, The Bats & The Ugly*

Pyramid Scheme   *Pyramid Power*

With David Drake:
The Tyrant

The Belisarius Series with David Drake:
An Oblique Approach   *In the Heart of Darkness*
Destiny's Shield   *Fortune's Stroke*
The Tide of Victory   *The Dance of Time*

Edited by Eric Flint
The World Turned Upside Down (with David Drake & Jim Baen)
The Best of Jim Baen's Universe
The Best of Jim Baen's Universe II

The Dragon Done It

edited by **Eric Flint**
and **Mike Resnick**

THE DRAGON DONE IT

This is a work of fiction. All the characters and events portrayed in this book are fictional, and any resemblance to real people or incidents is purely coincidental.

Introduction copyright © 2008 by Eric Flint & Mike Resnick. "The Long and Short of It" copyright © 2008 by Mike Resnick. "The Witch's Murder" copyright © 2008 by Dave Freer and Eric Flint. See also acknowledgements page for further copyright information.

A Baen Books Original

Baen Publishing Enterprises
P.O. Box 1403
Riverdale, NY 10471
www.baen.com

ISBN 10: 1-4165-5528-5
ISBN 13: 978-1-4165-5528-5

Cover art by Bob Eggleton

First printing, March 2008

Distributed by Simon & Schuster
1230 Avenue of the Americas
New York, NY 10020

Library of Congress Cataloging-in-Publication Data

The dragon done it / edited by Eric Flint and Mike Resnick.
    p. cm.
  A cross-genre collection of stories by popular writers.
  ISBN-13: 978-1-4165-5528-5 (hc)
  ISBN-10: 1-4165-5528-5 (hc)
 1. Detective and mystery stories, American. 2. Fantasy fiction, American. I. Flint, Eric. II. Resnick, Michael D.

PS648.D4D73 2008
813'.087208—dc22
                                                        2007051120

10 9 8 7 6 5 4 3 2 1

Pages by Joy Freeman (www.pagesbyjoy.com)
Printed in the United States of America

Contents

Editors' Introduction

IT WAS SIMPLY A FORTUNATE CONFLUENCE OF EVENTS. MIKE HAD just edited a pair of science fiction mystery anthologies—*Down These Dark Spaceways* and *Alien Crimes*—for the Science Fiction Book Club. Not too long ago Eric had edited a massive collection of Randall Garrett's beloved Lord Darcy stories, the first edition in history that puts all the stories together.

In short, both of us were thinking along the same lines: science fiction, fantasy, mystery. And it occurred to us that, to the best of our knowledge, no one has yet put together an anthology of fantasy detective stories, as opposed to science fiction mysteries. It seemed hard to believe, since there are certainly enough examples out there, going back at least to the works of Poe and to the hinted-at but never-written Sherlock Holmes tale of "The Giant Rat of Sumatra." So we got together, approached Jim Baen with the idea, and got a contract—one of the very last he issued before his untimely death.

Probably the two most famous fantasy sleuths are Lord Darcy, and Seabury Quinn's Jules de Grandin, who appeared in 121 stories in the old *Weird Tales* magazine. We were very familiar with the Darcy stories, but hadn't read the Quinn stories in decades. So Eric read half of them and Mike read the other half, and we came to the unhappy conclusion that they're a little too dated and a little too clumsily written.

Having anchored the volume with one of the best Lord Darcy stories, we went a-hunting—and came up with stories by such

1

superstars as Neil Gaiman, Harry Turtledove, Gene Wolfe, and David Drake. We resurrected a story by William Hope Hodgson, recent winner of the Cordwainer Smith Rediscovery Award, which was as old as the Jules de Grandin stories but read a lot better. Agatha Christie proved long ago that the detective story is not the private property of male writers, and we picked up fine stories from Esther Friesner, Tanya Huff, and Laura Resnick, then rounded out the book with another seven stories.

We then looked at what we had. We felt they were a fine batch of stories but that perhaps something was missing. Since we each had written our own series of fantasy detective tales over the years, we decided to make this an even more unique collection by writing brand-new novelettes featuring our detectives, and start and finish the book with those two brand-new stories.

So Mike wrote a new John Justin Mallory story, which is now the sixth novelette to go along with the original Mallory novel, *Stalking the Unicorn*. Those have been published in *The Magazine of Fantasy and Science Fiction* and *Black Gate Magazine*, and the anthologies *Newer York*, *A Christmas Bestiary*, and *Masters of Fantasy*. He's still negotiating the contract as we write these words, but he will be writing at least two more Mallory novels in the very near future. Eric and Dave Freer wrote a new novelette in the Heirs of Alexandria fantasy series they're doing with Mercedes Lackey (*Shadow of the Lion*, *A Mankind Witch*, *This Rough Magic*, *Much Fall of Blood*—with at least three more novels coming).

We hope you enjoy the anthology. We think the most interesting thing about it is that, given the rules of each magical venue, the authors play as fair with the reader as Dashiell Hammett or Rex Stout ever did. Which is harder than you think in a universe filled with witches, goblins, and dragons.

Eric & Mike
December, 2006

The Long and Short of It
A John Justin Mallory Story

➤ MIKE RESNICK ◄

JOHN JUSTIN MALLORY WAS HAVING A BAD DAY.

He'd gone out to Jamaica and picked the wrong horse six races in a row, a feat made even more remarkable by the fact that his favorite, Flyaway, who had lost fifty-four consecutive races, wasn't even entered.

When he'd stopped by Joey Chicago's for a drink on the way home, he found out they were all out of Old Peculiar and that some irate mage had hexed the tap on the Old Washensox.

He decided to eat at Morgan the Gorgon's 2-Star Diner and Hardware Store, made what he thought was a funny crack about wanting to eat Can't Miss, who had just missed by sixty-three lengths with Mallory's twenty dollars riding on him, and got a steak so rare that he could still see the jockey's whip marks.

Finally he went back to the office, where with his partner Winnifred Carruthers he plied his trade as a private detective. Winnifred had gone home for the night, and he plopped down wearily in his chair, briefly looked at the Playmate he'd pinned up on the wall (and on which Winnifred had meticulously drawn undergarments), and considered taking a hit from the office bottle, which shared a drawer with his collection of old *Racing Forms* and garish pulp magazines.

"Welcome back," said Perriwinkle, his magic mirror. "How much did you lose today? You *did* lose, didn't you? I mean, I

3

haven't noticed the stars stopping in their courses or anything like that."

"If there's one thing I hate, it's a lippy mirror."

"I have no lips."

"Details, details," muttered Mallory.

"Let me show you something to relax you," suggested the mirror.

"An old Bettie Page striptease might be nice," said Mallory.

"Mundane," said Perriwinkle contemptuously. "But if you must see a stripper, how about Tassle-Twirling Tessie Twinkle, the Lizard Girl? She removes her skin four times a night, and five on Saturdays."

"Please," said Mallory. "I almost just ate."

"Okay, hurt my feelings, spit on my offerings," said the mirror. "See if I care."

It fell silent, and began displaying a 1934 Southwest Association game between the Phoenix Pompadours and the Great Falls Geldings.

"Wonderful," said Mallory. He spent the next half hour opening his mail, which consisted entirely of unpaid bills, except for an ad to eat at Cannibal Joe's new all-night diner, which moved to a new location each day (or oftener if necessary). He finally finished, made a paper plane out of the heating bill, and gently tossed it toward the fireplace on the far wall. It got halfway there when a graceful figure that at first seemed human but was definitely feline launched itself from its perch atop the refrigerator in the next room and snared the bill in her mouth.

"If you like it, I have a dozen more," said Mallory dryly. "I'll even pour a little mustard on them for you."

"I thought it was a little white bird," said the cat person, spitting the bill onto the floor. "A fat little white bird. A fat helpless little white bird. A delicious fat helpless . . ."

"Spare me the catalog of its virtues."

"All right," she said, hopping lightly onto his desk and lying on her stomach. "Skritch between my shoulder blades."

"I've been meaning to ask you for some time now, Felina," said Mallory. "What exactly is the difference between scratching and skritching?"

Felina reached out a hand, extended her fingers, and suddenly a two-inch claw shot out of each. "*I* scratch," she said. "*You* skritch."

He reached out and skritched her back. Then suddenly she sat up.

"Let me guess," he said. "I did it wrong."

"Shhh!" she hissed. "They're arguing."

Mallory looked around the empty office. "Who's arguing?"

"Them."

"I don't see anyone."

"Me neither," said Perriwinkle, the game vanishing long enough for it to look around the room.

"They're outside the door," said Felina.

"What are they arguing about?" asked Mallory.

"You."

Mallory slid open his desk drawer and made sure his pistol was in it.

"They're arguing about how much they're willing to pay you," continued Felina.

"Are they now?" said Mallory, closing the drawer.

Felina nodded. "One of them is saying that if you cost too much they should just forget about it, and the other says it doesn't matter what you charge because you almost certainly won't survive to collect it."

"So there are two of them," said Perriwinkle.

"You must have been the brightest one in your class," said Mallory sardonically.

"That's it!" snapped Perriwinkle. "No more Rita Hayworth movies for you!"

"Is that a promise?" said Mallory.

"Bah!" said the mirror, reverting to the second inning of the baseball game in a grainy black and white.

"Are they still arguing?" asked Mallory.

Felina shook her head. "No, now they both agree that you'll die a horrible death before they have to pay you." She shot him an innocent, ingratiating smile. "Can I watch?"

Mallory didn't know whether to ignore her or throw something at her. While he was making up his mind, the door opened and a pair of men walked in. Each wore a dark, ill-fitting suit; one was too tight and the sleeves and cuffs were too short, while the other was too loose, with sleeves and cuffs held back by thick rubber bands. The men were each about six feet tall, with wild black hair, clear blue eyes, and shaggy mustaches. Mallory's first thought was that they were twins, or at least brothers. His second was that they needed a good barber and a better haberdasher.

"Mr. Mallory?" said the one on the left.

"That's right."

"We are in desperate need of your services," said the one on the right. "Mallory and Carruthers is said to be the best detective agency in all New York."

Mallory decided not to mention that it was the only one in New York, gestured for them to sit down, and simply waited for them to explain the nature of their problem.

"Have you ever gone to the circus, Mr. Mallory?" asked the one on the left.

"Not since I was a kid."

"Then you probably don't remember us," said the one on the right.

"Probably not," agreed Mallory. "Are you jugglers?"

"Certainly not!" they said in unison.

"Trapeze artists?"

"No!"

"I could sit here guessing all night, or you could tell me and we could get on with the case," suggested Mallory.

"Have you ever heard of Macro, the ten-foot-tall giant?" asked the one on the left.

"You?" asked Mallory.

The man shook his head. "No," he said, gesturing toward his companion. "*He* is."

"And have you ever read about Micro, the smallest human in the world, the Nineteen-Inch Dynamo?" Macro jerked a thumb toward the one on the left. "Him."

"This is a joke and you guys are here for the heating bill, right?" asked Mallory.

"I assure you this is no joke, Mr. Mallory," said Micro.

"We are in desperate need of your help," added Macro.

"I don't think I provide the kind of help you need," said Mallory.

"Only you *can* provide it!" said Micro desperately. "We have lost what makes us unique!"

"You've lost your grip on reality," observed Mallory. "*That* makes you pretty unique."

"We didn't come here to be insulted!" snapped Macro.

"Fine," said Mallory. "You pick up the tab, and I'll be happy to insult you down the street at the Emerald Isle Pub."

"Why won't you listen to us?"

"Because you're the same size as me, give or take an inch here and a pound there, and even when I've had a snootful I've never thought I was a ten-foot giant or a nineteen-inch midget."

"But that is precisely why we have sought you out!" insisted Macro. "Will you at least hear us out?"

"It's been a long, hard day," said Mallory.

"Would two thousand dollars suffice as a retainer?" asked Micro, pulling out the money and laying it on the detective's desk.

"On the other hand, the night's a pup," said Mallory. Suddenly Felina hissed. "Or a kitten, anyway."

"It began about two weeks ago," said Macro. "At first I thought I was losing a little weight, because my clothes were just a bit loose. I didn't mention it to anyone, because, to be honest, I could do with a little less weight."

"And at the same time," chimed in Micro, "I noticed that my shoes were getting tight, and that my pants seemed a little shorter."

"It took us almost a week to understand the full magnitude of what was happening," said Macro. "Some fiend has been making me shrink down to normal size . . ."

". . . and me grow up to it," said Micro.

"You have to help us, Mallory!" Macro implored the detective. "All we've ever been is a giant and a midget. We have no other skills. What do I know about tightrope walking or lion taming?"

"There *are* other occupations," noted Mallory.

"We don't want any other occupations!" shouted Micro. "We want you to find the bastard who did this to us and make him restore us to our former glory."

"We'll pay you a thousand dollars a day and a bonus if you succeed," said Macro.

"Of course," added Micro, "you'll have to succeed in four days or less. We're just about tapped out, what with buying new clothes every day."

"I'll do what I can," said Mallory. "Now, who do you think might have a grudge against you?"

"We're the salt of the earth," replied Macro. "You could look far and wide and not find two more lovable souls. Everybody knows that."

"So no one you know has any reason to do this to the pair of you?"

"Well, there's Atlas, the Strong Man," said Micro. "He found out that we were having a little fun with his wife."

"Both of you?" asked Mallory.

"We're a team."

"So I should start by questioning the strong man?"

"And the lion tamer," added Macro. "And the tightrope walker. Oh, and two of the bareback riders."

"Don't forget the clowns," said Micro.

"How could they know?" asked Macro. "After all, we were wearing clown make-up the whole time."

"There aren't a lot of ten-foot clowns in the circus," said Micro. He turned back to Mallory. "And probably you should ask two of the jugglers. Don't bother with the one in the middle; he's a bachelor."

"I think what you're telling me is that if it works for the circus and has a wife or a girlfriend, it has a grudge against you," said Mallory.

"In essence," admitted Macro.

"What about the sideshow acts?"

"Well," said Micro, "there's the sword swallower. And of course the fire eater. And the contortionist's husband."

"Oh my goodness yes!" said Macro, a blissful smile. "The contortionist!"

"I'm surprised you guys had time to go on display," said Mallory dryly.

"We never missed a show," said Macro.

"Or a woman," added Micro.

"Anyone not connected with the circus got a grudge against you?" asked Mallory. "After all, there are probably three or four million husbands wandering around Manhattan."

"No, we always keep it in the family."

"I can't tell you how many filthy puns spring to mind," replied Mallory.

"If you'll tell them to me as soon as these two leave, I'll tell you the one about the explorer and the three belly dancers," said Perriwinkle.

"What was that?" ask Macro.

"My magic mirror," said Mallory. "Say hello to the gentlemen, Perriwinkle."

"Hi, guys," said Perriwinkle.

"It talks!" exclaimed Micro.

"Of course I talk."

"I don't think I ever saw a talking mirror before," said Micro.

"That's your loss," said Perriwinkle. "I come from a long line of magic mirrors, so don't you go acting as if I'm a mere *object*. I have hopes and fears and sexual needs, just like anyone else."

"Not like these two, I hope," interjected Mallory.

"How did you get such a wondrous thing?" asked Macro.

"I kind of inherited it," said Mallory.

"He gave me to the army, but I was bored there," added Perriwinkle. "All they wanted were battle scenes, so I came back here. At least John Justin enjoys black-and-white movies and baseball games."

"Isn't that amazing!" said Micro, still staring at the mirror. "A talking mirror! Why, the next thing you know, that catlike statue will speak."

"Skritch my back," said the catlike statue.

"Not now, Felina," said Mallory.

"This place is getting a little weird for us," said Macro. "Maybe we should think about going and letting Mr. Mallory get to work."

"It's weirder for me," said Mallory. "At least you two were born here."

"Weren't you?" asked Macro.

Mallory shook his head. "No, I've only been here a couple of years."

"Where are you from?"

"Manhattan."

"But *this* is Manhattan."

"This is the Manhattan that people in *my* Manhattan can sometimes see out of the corner of their eye, but when they turn to face it it's not there."

"So how did you get here?"

"It's a long story.* I assume I can contact you at the circus?"

Macro shook his head unhappily. "We've been fired. You can find us at Joyful Jessie's Bulgarian Pizzaria and Flophouse."

"Third room on the right," added Micro. "Knock first."

"Why bother?" said Macro unhappily. "There's no door."

---

*Author's note: but it's a good story. It's currently out of print, but scour your second-hand stores. Or better still, nag this publisher to bring it back.

"It kind of makes up for all the boards over the window," said Micro.

"It's on the corner of Sloth and Despair," said Macro.

"I'm sure I can find it," said Mallory. "I'll be in touch as soon as I learn anything."

"*Almost* anything," said Perriwinkle. Mallory turned to the mirror. "After all," it continued, "you're going to learn the story of the explorer and the three belly dancers. I'm sure that these gentlemen couldn't care less about it."

"I don't know about that," said Macro, stopping at the door. "Is it dirty?"

"Filthy."

Macro slipped another five dollars to Mallory. "Remember to tell it to me next time we meet," he said, and then he and Micro walked out into the night.

"So what do you think?" said Mallory as he finished explaining the case to his partner.

Winnifred Carruthers brushed a wisp of gray hair back from her pudgy face. "The circus is clearly the place to start," she replied. "Our clients seem to have been so busy making enemies there I wouldn't think they've had time to make them anywhere else." She looked at him suspiciously. "Why do you have that strange expression on your face, John Justin?"

"There's a circus filled to overflowing with suspects, and we've only got four days," he replied. "I was thinking that we might enlist a little outside help."

"Who did you—?" Suddenly Winnifred frowned. "Oh, no!" she exclaimed. "Not the Grundy!"

"He'd be able to tell us who knows enough magic to pull this off," said Mallory.

"He's the most powerful demon on the East Coast—and in case it's slipped your mind, he's your mortal enemy!"

"Maybe he doesn't like someone else practicing magic," suggested Mallory. "Maybe we can make a deal. He may be Evil Incarnate, but he's got his own sense of honor. He's never broken his word to me."

"His last word was that he was going to disembowel you slowly and painfully," she reminded him.

Mallory shrugged. "A poetic metaphor."

"From a demon who never breaks his word?"

"All right," he said with a sigh. "I won't talk to the Grundy. What do you suggest?"

"Our obvious first step is to go to the circus and look around," said Winnifred. "I'm not without my contacts there."

"You have contacts at the circus?" said Mallory, surprised.

"I was a white hunter for forty years before I retired and you saved me from a life of boredom," she reminded him. "I'm the one who captured half the beasts in the circus."

"I don't suppose any of them practice magic?"

"Don't be silly, John Justin," she said. "They're just dumb brutes."

"Lions and tigers and the like?" asked Mallory.

"Nothing so mundane," she said. "I brought back every gorgon, gryphon, dragon and harpy you'll see there, as well as some of the more exotic creatures."

Mallory stared at her with open admiration. "I'm suddenly remembering why I wouldn't let you say No when I offered to make you my partner." He got to his feet. "We might as well get started."

Ninety pounds of feminine muscle and fur launched itself through the air and landed on his back.

"I'm going too!" said Felina.

"I don't think so," said Mallory. "We'll probably be there more than five minutes, and I've never seen you behave yourself for five minutes at a time."

"But I'm your friend, John Justin."

"Only when you're hungry," said Mallory. "You'll just be a nuisance."

"No, I won't," Felina assured him. "Oh, I'll desert you when the going gets rough—but in the meantime I'm your devoted friend."

"I don't suppose you could devote yourself to getting off my back," said Mallory.

"Yes, John Justin," she purred, leaping lightly to the floor.

"You're going to listen to orders and do exactly as I say, right?"

"Yes, John Justin," she purred.

"And you'll behave yourself?"

"Yes, John Justin," she purred.

"Why don't I believe you?" he said.

"Yes, John Justin," she purred.

Mallory and Winnifred exchanged looks. "Okay," he said, "let's get this show on the road."

Winnifred walked through the doorway. Mallory was about to follow her when Felina leaped onto his back again.

"Prove your love," she purred. "Carry me."

The Ringling & Bailey Barnum Brothers Circus was ensconced in an abandoned hockey stadium. Here and there were small crosses commemorating where various hockey players had died in fights, or from minor infractions like high-sticking, knifing, mugging, or shooting with an unregistered handgun.

The main arena now housed three rings, plus rigging for all the high-wire and trapeze acts. It was midmorning, and some of the performers were running through their routines. Winnifred seemed to know her way around, so Mallory fell into step behind her. Finally, after greeting a number of old friends, she stopped and turned to him.

"I think we can cover a lot more ground if we split up, John Justin," she said. "I'll start interviewing the performers, and you can concentrate on the sideshow."

"Sounds good to me," said Mallory. "Come along, Felina."

"Look at those juicy birds!" whispered Felina, pointing above the center ring.

"Those are trapeze artists," said Mallory. "Come on now."

He reached out, grabbed her hand, and began walking off toward the sideshow.

"I wonder how much white meat they have?" mused Felina.

"I never knew you to be that fussy about what you ate before," noted Mallory.

She pointed to the three flyers and the catcher. "I never had that many to choose from before."

They walked out of the main area and into the broad corridor, some sixty feet wide, that circled it. The corridor was lined with sideshow attractions and kiosks offering everything from beer to protection against deadly spells. One man was selling nothing except umbrellas guaranteed to protect the buyer from rains of toads.

"The all-seeing all-knowing Madame Nadine will guess your time of death for a dollar," offered a woman in glowing robes as Mallory and Felina passed by.

"I'm still alive," said Mallory.

"I meant your first death," explained Madame Nadine, as if speaking to a child. "For another dollar, I'll guess your height, weight, and political affiliation."

"What if you're wrong?"

"Then you'll feel smug and superior all day long."

"But I'll also feel two dollars poorer," said Mallory.

"What do you want for two dollars, Mac?" she said irritably. "For twenty bucks I'll do an Irish jig and sing 'The Ring Dang Doo,' if that's more to your taste."

Mallory pulled a hundred dollar bill out of his wallet and held it up.

"For *that*," said Madame Nadine, "you get three sexual perversions and a player to be named later."

"Not interested," said Mallory.

"That's odd," she said. "You don't *look* like some kind of sicko."

"This is my cat," said Mallory, indicating Felina.

"You want a threesome, it'll be a hundred and fifty."

"Why don't you just listen to me?" said Mallory in annoyed tones.

"It's two hundred for listening to you talk dirty," she said.

"Do you want to earn this money, or do you want to tell me all the things you won't do for it?"

"You talk, I'll listen," said Madame Nadine.

"Like I said, this is my cat," said Mallory. "I'm moving to a smaller place. I want to find someone who can shrink her down to two or three feet in height. Let me know who can do it and the hundred is yours."

"Just for that?" she asked suspiciously.

"Just for that."

"No sexual perversions, no threesomes with animals, no wild orgies with totally disgusting sex toys?"

"Nope."

"Damn!" said Madame Nadine unhappily. Then: "Okay, the man you want to see is Marvin the Mystic."

"Where do I find him?"

"I seem to remember that the deal was a hundred bucks for his name," she said. "Nobody said anything about telling you where you could find him."

Mallory reached into his pocket and pulled out a ten dollar bill.

Madame Nadine frowned. "Five hundred."

"I already know his name," said Mallory. "I'll just ask one of the others where to find him. Come on, Felina."

"Wait!" said Madame Nadine.

Mallory stopped and turned to her.

"You say ten, I say five hundred," she said. "Let's split the difference. Four hundred seventy-five and I'll tell you."

"Let's split the difference," replied Mallory. "Eleven dollars and I won't ask someone else."

"All right," she said, holding out her hand. Mallory gave her a ten and a one. "If you'll go around the corner you'll come to the Visitors' Locker Room. Marvin has appropriated the coach's office, which is just off to the right."

"Thanks," said Mallory. He studied her face. "You only got eleven dollars. Why do you look so happy?"

"You'll find out," promised Madame Nadine. A maintenance man walked by, carrying a shovel and a pail. "Hey, Mac," she said, all interest in Mallory gone now that the deal was completed, "guess your fourteen favorite Andrews Sisters for a dollar?"

"There were only three," said Mallory.

"Depends which Andrews family you're talking about, doesn't it?" Madame Nadine shot back, never taking her eyes off her new mark.

"Let's go," said Mallory to Felina, heading off toward the locker room and hoping he wouldn't pass anyone rehearsing a trained bird act along the way.

They reached their destination, and Mallory looked around for the coach's office. It took only a moment to locate the door, but a goblin, an elf, a troll and a leprechaun were lounging in front of it.

Mallory took a step toward the door, and suddenly all four of them turned to face him, shoulder to shoulder.

"Take a hike, buddy," said the goblin.

"I want to see your boss," said Mallory.

"Our boss left orders," said the troll. "Nobody disturbs him."

"Right," chimed in the leprechaun. "So just take off before we lose our tempers. I haven't killed anyone since breakfast, and I'm getting restless."

"Right," said the goblin. "You take one more step in this direction and we'll dispatch you with such skill and dexterity that they'll award us both ears and the tail."

"Right," added the elf. "There won't be enough of you left to bury!"

"Uh . . ." said the troll nervously. "I don't want to be presumptuous or anything, but what's the hideous creature behind you?"

"That's Felina," said Mallory. "Say hello to the boys, Felina."

Felina offered them a toothy grin and extended a hand. An instant later shining two-inch claws jutted forth from each finger.

"Now," said Mallory, "you were saying something about not disturbing Marvin the Mystic?"

"Well," said the troll, backing up a step, "when you get right down to it, I don't see how a friendly little visit could actually *disturb* him."

"What's the matter with you?" demanded the elf.

"Trolls are afraid of cat people," said the troll. "Everyone knows that."

"Well, elves aren't afraid of cat people," said the elf, making no attempt to hide his contempt for his companion.

Felina took a step toward the elf.

"Now let's not have any misunderstandings here!" said the elf. "Call her off!"

"I thought elves weren't afraid of cat people," said Mallory.

"We aren't!" said the elf nervously. "But we're desperately afraid of dying!"

"Wimps!" snarled the leprechaun. "It's just a cat person!"

"Then you plan to stand your ground?" asked Mallory.

"Let's set the rules of engagement first," said the leprechaun. "Best two out of three falls. No biting. No scratching. No rolling pins. No weapons larger than .45 caliber. No kidney punches." He paused. "I'm sure I'm forgetting something." He turned to the goblin. "What town are we in, Harry?"

"New York," said the goblin.

"Right," said the leprechaun. "No kissing in the clinches, and no reading *New York Times* editorials over a fallen foe for more than an hour." He looked Felina in the eye. "Is that acceptable to you?"

She grinned and nodded.

"It is?" said the leprechaun. "I mean, once you've been humiliated and battered into senselessness, I don't want it said that the fight wasn't according to Hoyle."

Felina replied with an eager purr.

The leprechaun turned to Mallory. "Just to make it official: we have an agreement, right?"

"Right," said Mallory.

"You're sure, now? No backing down."

"I'm sure."

"Okay," said the leprechaun, stepping back a few feet. "Take her, Harry."

"*Me?*" said the goblin, surprised.

"Well, I negotiated the rules," said the leprechaun. "I knew you'd want to do *something*."

"I kind of thought I'd pull out a bible and read over the corpse," said Harry.

"What makes you think she's religious?" asked the leprechaun.

"What makes you think I'd be reading over *her*?" Harry shot back.

"This is ridiculous!" said the leprechaun. "I function best in an advisory capacity. Now stop arguing and go tear her limb from limb."

"Yeah, go get her, Harry," said the troll. "We'll cheer you on to victory!"

"And if you lose we'll always honor your memory," added the elf.

"Gee, guys," said Harry, staring almost hypnotically at Felina's claws, "I'd love to, really I would, but my lumbago's been acting up lately."

"You don't *have* lumbago," said the leprechaun.

"It's adult onset," said Harry defensively. "It began about twenty seconds ago. One of you will have to step in and take my place."

"Can't be me," said the elf. "My rheumatiz just flared up not half a minute ago."

"My arthritis is bothering me," said the troll. "You wouldn't want to fight me if I wasn't at my best."

"I guess it's you, then," said Mallory to the leprechaun.

"What the hell," said the leprechaun. "If no one else will kill her, I'll do it myself." Suddenly he began looking around in panic. "Omygod!" he cried. "I forgot about my prostate problem! Where's the john?"

He raced out into the hall.

"The poor guy's going to have an accident," said Harry, running toward the exit. "I'd better go after him and help clean up."

"He might have *two* accidents!" shouted the elf, joining Harry.

"Or three!" cried the troll, racing off after them.

"I never get to have any fun!" complained Felina, her claws vanishing back into her fingers.

"Come on," said Mallory, walking toward the office door. "When we're done here I'll buy you a hot dog."

"They're no fun to play with after they're dead," said Felina unhappily.

Mallory reached out for the doorknob, but the door opened before he could touch it, and he stepped into an office that was decorated with football trophies, crystal balls, a blackboard filled with X's and O's and another filled with magic spells scribbled in a foreign tongue and strange symbols. Sitting at a desk was a small, wiry man with a very sparse white beard and shaggy white eyebrows. He wore a robe of spun gold and a triangular hat with signs of the zodiac on it.

"Marvin the Mystic?" said Mallory.

"Of course."

"My name is—"

"John Justin Mallory, I know," said Marvin. "The great Marvin sees all and knows all."

"Not bad," admitted Mallory.

"Besides, Nadine called me on her cell phone and told me you were coming over, so I prepared a little greeting for you."

"I've seen better security forces," said Mallory.

"Good help is hard to find these days," complained Marvin. "Still, all they were required to do was delay you for a minute so I could prepare my defenses."

"And are they all prepared now?" asked Mallory.

"Absolutely," said Marvin. "You could pull a gun out and shoot me at point-blank range and the bullet would never reach me."

"Really?" asked Mallory.

"Uh . . . just a minute," said Marvin nervously. "Don't pull a gun and test it out. The spell works in theory, but I've never actually put it into practice. I mean, it *should* work. But I also created a spell for blackjack. I play with my computer, and I win every single hand . . . but for some reason the spell doesn't work in Vegas or Jersey, or even at Creepy Conrad's over on 34th Street." He frowned as he considered the problem, then shrugged. "All right, Mallory. What can I do for you?"

"You know Micro and Macro, right?"

"The giant and the midget, right."

"The former giant and the former midget," said Mallory. "These days they look just like you and me."

"Even including the beard?" said Marvin. "Remarkable."

"No, not the beard—the height. I'm told that you have the skills to have done that to them."

"I certainly do," said Marvin. "My magic can stop the world from spinning, can halt the stars in their courses, can make Time run backwards. Of course, it can't get Thelma the kootch dancer into the sack, but I'm working on it."

"What do you have against Micro and Macro?" asked Mallory.

"Nothing," said Marvin. "Why?"

"So you're not carrying a grudge?"

"Certainly not. They were two of my best friends."

"Just for the record: did you put a spell on them?"

"I did not."

"Who else has the skill to make Macro smaller and Micro bigger?"

"Well, there's always the Grundy."

"The Grundy probably doesn't even know they're alive."

"Yeah, I suppose when you're Evil Incarnate you take more of an interest in them after they're dead." Suddenly he looked very nervous. He turned his face to the ceiling and said in a loud clear voice: "That was just a figure of speech. Actually, the Grundy is the salt of the earth, the most noble of demons, and he would never listen in on a private conversation or misinterpret an expression of enormous respect."

"I'm starting to understand why he and I have a mutual respect for each other," said Mallory with a grimace. "Neither of us has much tolerance for bullshit." He paused. "Who else could do it?"

"Shrink and grow them?" said Marvin. "Well, there's Morris the Mage, and Big-Hearted Milton, and they say Dead End Dugan is pretty good at hexing ever since he came back."

"Came back from where?" asked Mallory, curious in spite of himself.

"The cemetery over in Queens," answered Marvin. "He's a zombie now. And then there's—"

"Just a minute," said Mallory. "I don't really need a list of every magician in the city. Do any of them work for the circus?"

"No, not since Spellsinger Slim accidentally left his wand in Backbreaker Bennie's bed."

"Backbreaker Bennie. Isn't he the wrestler?"

"He used to be. Now he's our strong man."

"Why would he care if Spellsinger Slim left a wand in his bed?"

"Because Slim left Mrs. Backbreaker there too." Marvin shook his head. "Poor Slim. I still miss him."

"Does anyone around here ever think of anything besides sex?" asked Mallory.

"At least twice a day I think of eating."

Mallory walked to the door. "I've heard enough for one morning," he said. "I may want to speak to you again. Tell the troops to let me pass next time."

"They let you pass this time," noted Marvin. "Your cat did terrible things to their self-confidence."

"Just tell them," repeated Mallory. "Next time she may do terrible things to their bodies."

"Where are we going now?" asked Felina as they left the locker room.

"To find Winnifred and see if she had any better luck than we did."

They began walking toward the arena. Along the way they passed Madame Nadine again.

"Hey, Buddy," she said, not looking up at him, "for a dollar the all-seeing all-knowing Madame Nadine will name three rock stars who haven't been busted on drug charges in the past year. Well, two anyway."

Mallory just walked past her without a word, and a moment later entered the arena. He had to step aside while a pair of eight-ton dragons pulled a chariot filled with scantily-clad warrior women back to the dressing area, then spotted Winnifred speaking with a man who stood inside a large cage containing half a dozen gorgons. He held a whip in one hand and a chair in the other, but the gorgons, gathered on the far side of the cage, looked half-asleep.

"Yes," he was saying, "they had a restless night, what with all that crying and carrying on."

"The poor dears," said Winnifred. "By the way, I'd feed the one on the left a little extra meat each morning. I think he's showing the early stages of pellagra."

"Do gorgons *get* pellagra?"

"Oh, yes," she assured him. "Gorgons can get pellagra, mumps, measles, any number of diseases. Although," she added thoughtfully, "I've never known one to come down with *chracksmir*."

"*Chracksmir?*" repeated the man nervously. "What is that?"

"It's a relatively rare disease that causes serious softening of the bill in the Three-Toed Blue-Eyed Central African Woodpecker." Winnifred paused thoughtfully. "No, I've never known a gorgon to come down with it." She stared at the gorgon in question. "I still remember his mother," she continued. "She was a handful. There were times I thought I'd never get her back to the States in one piece."

"How did you manage?"

"I set up a turntable just outside her cage on the boat and played a Rolling Stones record."

"And that soothed the savage breast?"

"No," said Winnifred. "It practically drove her berserk. I told her if she misbehaved again I'd play it for a whole day." She smiled. "You couldn't have asked for a better-mannered gorgon from that moment forward."

The man laughed. "I'll keep that in mind the next time one of the krakens starts getting delusions of grandeur." He turned to Mallory. "Are you waiting to see me?"

Mallory shook his head. "Her," he said, nodding toward Winnifred.

"John Justin," said Winnifred, "I'd like to you to meet an old friend—Sam Ramar."

"Of the jungle?" asked Mallory.

"How did you know?" replied Ramar.

"A shot in the dark."

One of the gorgons suddenly began roaring.

"Watch your tongue, Mr. Mallory!" said Ramar sternly.

"What did I say?"

"One of his brothers was killed by"—Ramar lowered his voice to a whisper—"a shot in the dark."

"I apologize."

"Not to *me*," said Ramar. "To *him*."

"You're kidding, right?" said Mallory.

"Am I smiling?"

Mallory shrugged and turned to the gorgon. "I'm sorry."

"Now walk over and let him smell the back of your hand," said Ramar.

"Some other time."

"You'll never be an animal trainer at this rate," said Ramar.

"I suppose I can learn to live with that," replied Mallory. He turned to Winnifred. "Learn anything?"

"Yes, John Justin," she said. "Thank you for your help, Ramar." She began walking toward the box seats, where they couldn't be overheard.

"Well?"

"All the animals in the circus are on edge," she said.

"Why?" asked Mallory. "Are the crowds making them nervous?"

"That's the interesting part," said Winnifred. "It's not the crowds, it's not the venue, it's not even the food." She paused. "They're not getting any sleep at night."

"I heard Ramar mention something about crying?"

"That's right. Evidently almost every woman in the circus is crying her heart out every night and keeping the animals awake."

"Let me guess," said Mallory dryly. "They miss our clients."

"Yes," said Winnifred. "But here's the interesting part, John Justin: the animals haven't had a good night's sleep for the past month."

Mallory frowned. "That doesn't add up," he said. "Micro and Macro only started shrinking and growing two weeks ago, so why should all the women be crying for a month?"

"I don't know," answered Winnifred. "But once we find out, I think we'll be well on the road to cracking the case."

"Hey, fella!" said a loud voice. "Either put your damned cat on a leash or get her out of here!"

Mallory turned and found himself confronting a bald, red-faced man. "What's the problem?" he asked.

"I've got a seal and walrus act," said the man angrily. "And every time I toss one of them a fish as a reward, your cat catches it and eats it. Now they've gone on strike—no fish, no performance."

"All right, keep your shirt on," said Mallory, walking over to where Felina was crouching, waiting to spring through the air when the next fish was thrown to a seal. He grabbed her by the arm and started pulling her away, while she hissed at him and displayed her claws. "You touch me with those and I'll pull 'em out one by one!" he snapped.

"Without anesthetic?" said Felina. "What kind of fiend are you?"

"An angry one," said Mallory. "Now come with me before I really lose my temper."

He began leading her back to Winnifred when he suddenly realized that a hush had fallen across the entire area. The hustle and bustle had stopped, and he could have heard a pin drop at twenty paces. Gradually he became aware that all heads had turned to the north end of the arena, where the most beautiful woman he had ever seen was preparing to practice her bareback routine atop a chestnut centaur.

"Close your mouth, John Justin," said Winnifred. "You never know what might fly into it at a circus."

"Do you see her?" whispered an awestruck Mallory. "She makes Sophia Loren look like a boy! She's like . . . like jelly on springs!"

"Don't be vulgar," said Winnifred.

"I'm not being vulgar, I'm being honest," said Mallory. "I've never seen anything like her. She's enough to make an atheist believe in God."

"I don't think I want to hear any more of this, John Justin. I'd like to continue respecting my partner."

Mallory suddenly shook his head vigorously, as if to clear it. "Don't go disrespecting your partner too soon," he said. "I think he just solved the case."

Winnifred looked confused. "What are you talking about?"

"Look around you," he said. "Every man in the arena is looking at her the same way I was. Hell, if you're a man and alive you can't help but look at her that way."

"I assume you are making your way laboriously to the point?"

"Micro and Macro went to bed with anything that twitched, right?"

"Poor choice of words, but yes," said Winnifred.

"They spread themselves around, so everyone seemed content," continued Mallory. "Or at least, none of their ladyfriends made any waves." He smiled. "But I'll bet you four thousand dollars that *she* started working here a month ago, and once our boys saw her, there were suddenly a lot of lonely ladies in the circus. Lonely, unhappy—and maybe vengeful."

"That presupposes that they actually were able to . . . to . . ." Winnifred searched for an inoffensive word.

"To score with her?" suggested Mallory. "There's an easy way to find out."

"I agree," said Winnifred. "Let's go ask her."

"*I'll* ask her," said Mallory. "You watch the cat."

"But—"

"It'll be good for me to practice some self-restraint."

"You're not getting off to a very good start," noted Winnifred.

Mallory never took his eyes off the girl. "Just look at her bouncing up and down on that centaur!"

"If you make a comment about how she could bounce up and down like that on you, I'm dissolving our partnership," said Winnifred distastefully.

"I'd never say something like that to you," said Mallory. Then: "But I can think it, can't I?"

"Just go and ask her what you have to ask."

"Right," said Mallory, starting to walk across the arena. When he came to the ring where the centaur was cantering in a circle, he stopped and stood there, admiring the sight.

After a few moments he became aware of a sudden sharp pain in his shin and realized that Felina had just kicked him.

"Goddammit!" he bellowed. "What the hell are you doing?"

"Winnifred sent me over to make sure you were still alive," answered the cat-girl pleasantly. "I'll go tell her you are."

Felina returned to Winnifred as the centaur, startled by Mallory's yell, came to a stop. The girl jumped lightly to the ground before fifty sets of appreciative male eyes, and Mallory walked up to her.

"Excuse me," he said. "I wonder if I might have a word with you."

"All right," she said in the most melodic voice he'd ever heard. "But I should tell you up front that I'm not a doctor."

"I never thought you were," said Mallory, surprised.

"Oh," she said. "I thought you wanted to consult with me about your palsy."

"I don't have any palsy."

"I wouldn't bet on that," she said dubiously. "You're shaking like a leaf."

"I'm just chilly," he lied.

She flashed him a smile. "I've very glad to hear it."

"Allow me to introduce myself. My name is John Justin Mallory."

"What a strong, masculine name," she said. Mallory resisted the urge to bay at the moon, which he was sure wasn't out at eleven in the morning. "And I am Circe." She extended her hand. "I'm very pleased to meet you."

He took her hand and had to remind himself that it was

attached to the rest of her and that sooner or later he'd have to let go of it, much as he hated the thought.

"How long have you been with Ringling and Bailey circus?" he asked.

"Five weeks next Wednesday," she said. "Why?"

"Just a routine question," he said, wondering how his throat could become so dry in such a short time. "I'm a detective."

"Like Sam Spade and Philip Marlowe?"

"More like John Justin Mallory," he answered. "My clients are Micro and Macro. I believe you know them?"

"Yes, I do," replied Circe. "Such sweet boys. I was wondering what had happened to them. Have they left the show?"

"Temporarily," said Mallory. "I'm afraid I have to ask you a rather delicate question, ma'am," he continued uneasily.

"Circe."

"Circe," he repeated. "This is a little awkward. Did you ever . . . I mean, did they . . . that is . . . ?"

"You want to know if I ever slept with them?" she asked pleasantly.

"Yes."

"They were very unique, you know," she said. "The world's tallest giant and the world's smallest midget. And they had a wonderful sense of humor. Also, no one could mix a drink like Macro. And you should have heard Micro play the nose-flute!"

"I'm sure that's all true," said Mallory. "But I need to know if you—"

"They were very attractive," said Circe.

"So you *did* sleep with them?"

"I went to bed with them," she said. "I don't think sleeping was ever on the agenda," she added with a giggle.

"Was this a one-night stand, or did you—"

"Oh, eight or ten times a day once we got to know one another."

"Eight or ten times a day?" he repeated, trying not to look shocked.

"They had a lot of spare time," she explained with a smile. "They didn't have to rehearse being tall or being short." She paused. "Do you have any other questions?"

"No," said Mallory. "Thank you, Circe. You've been a great help."

"I really miss them. Do you think they'll be coming back soon?"

"It's a possibility," he replied. "I'm sorry to have disturbed you. You can go back to rehearsing."

"Mr. Mallory?"

"Yes?"

"May I have my hand back now?"

"Eight or ten times a *day*?" said Winnifred. "The mind boggles!" Her eyes narrowed. "I wonder if she's lying. I hope she is. I hate to think of anyone having so much fun while we're out risking life and limb."

"Somebody's been lying, all right," said Mallory with conviction, "but it isn't her."

"What now?" asked Winnifred.

"Now we confront the real culprit, and then we figure out what to do about it."

He headed off toward the locker room, followed by Winnifred and Felina.

"Guess your social security number, blood pressure, and outstanding back taxes for a dollar?" offered Madame Nadine as he passed her.

He ignored her and continued walking. When he arrived the four guards were there waiting for him.

"Go right in," said Harry the goblin with an evil grin.

"He's waiting for you," said the elf nastily.

"I hope you have a nice cemetery plot picked out," added the troll.

"He didn't say anything about the fat broad, though," said the leprechaun. "Maybe we'll just have a little fun with her."

Suddenly he was looking down the barrel of a .45 Magnum.

"You're a cute little fellow," said Winnifred, her finger on the trigger. "I wonder how you'd look stuffed and mounted in my den?"

"You don't want me!" said the leprechaun. "You want my brother! He's much better-looking! You could stand him on his head and grow flowers out of his nostrils."

"Oh, don't be such a sissy!" said Harry. "She's just a fat wrinkled old broad. Go up and take the gun away from her."

Suddenly the Magnum was aimed right between Harry's eyes.

"What did you call me?" asked Winnifred.

"It was a term of endearment!" cried Harry. "My wife's a fat wrinkled old broad, and I love her with a passion that knows no bounds."

"Or loyalty," put in the leprechaun.

"You shut up!" snapped Harry. "You're her target! I'm just a distraction."

The elf looked at his bare wrist. "My, my," he said. "Eleven twenty-six and forty seconds already. Time for me to clock out."

"What are you talking about?" demanded the leprechaun. "We don't punch a clock!"

"I have three personal days and two weeks of vacation coming to me," said the elf stubbornly. "I'm taking them right now."

The troll sidled over to Mallory. "Pathetic, aren't they?" he said. "They just don't know how to deal with new situations."

"How would *you* deal with it?" asked Mallory.

"Easy," said the troll. He pulled out a five-dollar bill and slipped it to Mallory. "When you go in to see the boss, tell him we scared the shit out of you."

Mallory returned the bill. "I don't think so."

"What kind of demented fiend won't accept an honestly-offered bribe?" demanded the troll.

"A fiend who's getting tired of trolls, elves, goblins and leprechauns," said Mallory.

"Did you hear that?" shrieked the troll. "Tired of *us*? You're *sick*, Mallory! Sick! I'll see you later!"

He started walking away.

"Where do you think you're going?" asked Winnifred.

"To file a complaint with the union," said the troll.

"I'd better go with you," said the leprechaun, quickly joining him. "They may want corroborative testimony."

"Good point!" chimed in the elf, falling into step. "I'll support both of your stories."

"What about you?" Mallory asked Harry the goblin.

"I'm just a spear carrier in the vast tapestry of the fat old broad's life," replied the goblin with a sudden show of confidence. "She doesn't care about me."

"What makes you think so?" asked Winnifred, lining him up in her sights.

"Mallory, tell her it's not sporting to shoot someone with glasses!"

"You're not wearing any glasses," said Winnifred.

"I left them at home," said Harry. "But if I'd known what kind of tempers you fat old broads had, I'd have worn them to work."

"Get out of here," said Winnifred.

"No offense intended," said Harry quickly.

"Now!" said Winnifred, firing a shot into the concrete just in front of his feet.

Harry proceeded to run the fastest fifty yards on record, and was threatening Secretariat's time for the mile and a half when he raced out of sight.

Mallory turned to Felina. "Thanks for your help," he said sardonically.

"I'm sulking," said the cat-girl. "You wouldn't let me kill any of them, but you let the fat old broad shoot at them."

"Watch it, cat," said Winnifred ominously.

"Shall we get to work?" said Mallory. Winnifred nodded, and Mallory turned to Felina. "You stay out here until you learn how to behave." She turned her back on him and concentrated on licking her forearm. Then, as he opened the door, he felt ninety pounds leap onto his back.

"I forgive you, John Justin," purred Felina.

"Welcome back," said Marvin the Mystic, standing up to greet them. "I had a feeling you'd be returning."

"Well, you *did* lie to me before," said Mallory.

"It was privileged information," said Marvin. "A matter of mage/client confidentiality."

"Call it what you will," said Mallory. "You lied."

"I prefer to think that I refused to betray a sacred trust."

"Do you know how many years in the slammer you could get for not betraying that particular sacred trust?"

"I was mostly truthful," replied Marvin. "You asked me if I had any grudge against Micro and Macro, and I told you truthfully that I didn't, that they were my good friends."

"Then why did you put a spell on them?" asked Mallory.

"They're my friends, and the salt of the earth and all," answered Marvin, "but friends come and go. Money stays."

"Not when John Justin goes to the track, it doesn't," said Felina helpfully.

"Who paid you to do it?" asked Mallory.

"You're the detective," said Marvin. "Can't you guess?"

"How many women in the show?"

"Seventy-three."

"That narrows it down to seventy-two suspects," said Mallory.

"It doesn't really matter. We're not cops, and we're not here to arrest anyone, but my money's on Madame Nadine."

"Why her?" asked Marvin.

"She's the one who warned you I was coming."

"Well, you're partly right," said Marvin. "That's not bad for one morning's work. If I ever need a detective, you're the man I'll come to."

"Reverse the spell or you're going to need an intensive care unit long before you need a detective," said Winnifred, who hadn't put her Magnum away.

"You don't have to return the money," said Mallory. "Like I said, we're not cops. All our clients want is for you to reverse the spell."

"That's all *my* clients want too," said Marvin with a sigh.

"Explain," said Winnifred.

"It wasn't just Madame Nadine," said the magician. "She delivered the money, but *all* the women were jealous of Circe. They offered to pay me to turn her into a sea slug, or a fat old wrinkled broad"—he missed Winnifred's outraged glare—"or something like that. But no red-blooded man would ever do that to anything as perfect as—" a deep sigh "—Circe, so I told them no. Then the women decided that if they couldn't have Micro and Macro, they'd take up a collection—Madame Nadine paid me, but they all chipped in—and fix it so they would have to leave the show and Circe couldn't have them either."

"Okay, that's about what I figured once I saw Circe," said Mallory.

"Isn't she something?" said Marvin enthusiastically. "You get the feeling that if you live an absolutely perfect life, she'll be waiting for you at the end of it."

"I don't think I want to hear any more of this," said Winnifred irritably.

"Let's have the rest of it, Marvin," said Mallory.

"It turned out that the women missed Micro and Macro so much they decided half a loaf—well, actually, about an eighth of a loaf once Circe arrived—was better than none. So they offered me double what they'd paid me to reverse the spell."

"Then why didn't you?"

"I *can't*!" Marvin said miserably. "This spell can only be stopped. It can't be reversed."

"You're sure?"

"They're my friends. Why would I do this to them? And more to the point, the money was twice as good."

"So if you stop it today, they'll each be six-footers for the rest of their lives?" said Mallory.

"That's right."

"Could you make me big enough to kill and eat a gorgon?" asked Felina hopefully.

"Certainly," said Marvin. "After all, I *am* Marvin the Mystic." He frowned. "But I couldn't make you small again."

"I'd be too big to sleep on top of the refrigerator," said Felina. "Maybe you could shrink one of the gorgons instead. They look so tasty!"

"John Justin," said Winnifred, "you suddenly have the strangest expression on your face."

"Felina just gave me an idea," said Mallory. "Marvin, can I borrow your cell phone for a minute?"

The magician muttered a chant and snapped his fingers, and suddenly Mallory found a Louisville Slugger in his hand.

"Oops, wrong spell," said Marvin apologetically. He tried again, and this time Mallory wound up with a phone.

"I'm just going to step out into the locker room for a couple of minutes to make a private call," he said. "I'll be right back."

He left the office, and Felina spent the next few minutes naming every monster in the circus and asking Marvin if he could shrink it to the point where she could play with it a bit before killing and eating it.

"Okay," said Mallory, reentering the office. "I've spoken to our clients, and I've come up with a solution that's acceptable to them—and, I think, to all parties involved."

"What is it?" asked Marvin and Winnifred in unison. Felina, who wanted to ask about still more animals, turned her back and stared intently at a wall.

"They both agree that they're a little long in the tooth to retrain. They *like* doing nothing but being short and tall—and being irresistible to women, of course."

"But I can't put them back the way they were," said Marvin. "I've already explained that."

"You can do the next best thing," said Mallory.

"I don't follow you."

"You said you can stop the spell, you just can't reverse it, right?"

"That's right."

"Then let Macro keep shrinking until he's nineteen inches tall, and stop him there. And let Micro keep growing until he's ten feet."

"They don't mind?" asked Marvin, surprised.

"They'll still be the world's tallest giant and smallest midget, and they'll still have more girlfriends than they know what to do with."

"Oh, they knew what to do with them," said Marvin. "That's why the women tried to pay me to reverse the spells." Suddenly his eyes widened. "I could accept their fee now, couldn't I? I mean, they wanted a big one and a little one, and that's what they're going to get." He turned to Mallory. "Of course, I'd slip you ten percent for keeping your mouth shut. And ten percent for the fa— for the lovely lady with the gun. Maybe I'll even shrink a three-headed dragon down for your cat."

"It's not necessary," said Mallory. "We're getting paid enough by our clients."

"And we don't think much of your business practices," added Winnifred harshly.

"I thought fat people were supposed to be jolly," said Marvin.

He hit the floor a fraction of a second before the bullet passed through the spot where he'd been and tore into the wall behind him.

Felina refused to speak to Mallory all the way home, and announced her intention of never saying another word to him until he went back and let Marvin shrink a dragon for her. Her resolve lasted almost half an hour, when she decided to forgive him and let him skritch between her shoulder blades.

Micro and Macro returned to the circus the next morning. Just before dinnertime a week later there was a knock at the office door. Mallory opened it and stepped aside as a uniformed delivery man brought in seventy-three long-stemmed roses, each with a scented thank-you note.

Winnifred decided to burn the notes before Mallory could answer them. Especially the one with the faint odor of a centaur still on it.

Dead Wolf in a Hat

> **➤ GRAHAM EDWARDS ◄**

THE MAN IN THE HAT BURST THROUGH MY OFFICE DOOR, CLOSELY followed by the bullet that killed him.

Don't you just hate that?

Me, I kept my feet up on the desk. Sometimes it just doesn't do to move too fast. All the same, even before the big guy hit the floor I was reaching for the desk holster. I didn't release it though, not yet. I just held my finger over the lever and stared out the open door into the rain.

It's hard to see much through the rain. Of course, it's always raining here, which is why I never use the door. There's more than one way in and out of this office. It's ten years now since I took over the business and I've already found eighty-nine exits. I figure that's around half. I use whichever one suits the case. The door I leave to the clients.

So there I was, feet on top of the desk, fingers itching underneath it, with rain lashing in and a man with a hat on, breathing his last on the floor. I kept one eye on the rain and flicked the other towards my visitor.

"You all right, buddy?" I said.

What came out of the guy's mouth was muffled, on account of his face being buried in the carpet. But I did catch two words: "... *hilfe* ..." and "... *knock* ..."

Another bullet cut through the rain. Whining like a mosquito, it struck the steel sole of my left shoe and ricocheted into the coffee-machine. Like I said, it doesn't always do to move too fast.

With a shriek, the machine shattered, spraying hot coffee up the wall. I ground my teeth in fury—that coffee-machine and I went back a long, long way. But still I didn't move.

I let the next four bullets hit my feet before pulling the lever. The desk holster launched the little pistol into my hand. *Then* I moved.

Rolling off the chair, I jumped the man in the hat and shouldered the door shut. Just in time: the invisible shooter had already reloaded. Six fresh bullets bounced off the glass, just below my nameplate. I told the door to stay shut, no matter what, and heard the satisfying clicking sounds as it dead-bolted itself into the floor.

Knowing I was safe, I knelt down beside my visitor. The carpet he'd buried his face in was now soaked in blood as well as rainwater. Each time he breathed out he made little red bubbles. He made three more bubbles before giving up for good.

Great. Now I had a corpse on my hands, my office was a crime scene and I had to get my carpet cleaned—again.

And things just kept getting better.

I was about to roll the stiff on to his back, so as to get a good look at his face, when he started to twitch. *Undead*, I thought at once. It was the obvious conclusion. Feeling in need of a little extra protection, I tucked the pistol into my shoulder holster and grabbed my coat off the wall. Some folk might think it odd that a guy like me should turn to his coat in times of trial but, trust me, that coat and I go back even further than the coffee-machine.

I turned the coat inside-out four times until its lining was made of titanium (chain links, herringbone weave) and put it on.

When I turned back to look at the dead man in the hat, he was already halfway through changing into a wolf.

Okay, a word about werewolves. You've seen it all before. We all have. Feet stretching out to become enormous paws, fur exploding everywhere, this great, fanged muzzle punching out from inside the guy's jaw . . . all accompanied by a sound like a championship knuckle-cracking team making popcorn in a fireworks factory. Yeah, there was all that—there always is—but what most folk don't realize is that there's this weird kind of *beauty* to it all. No really, trust me, there is.

It roots me to the spot, is what I'm trying to say. Always has done. Seeing a body change like that, whether it's alive or dead, is like getting a glimpse of something you're not meant to see. Not that I want to get all sappy about it—it just gets to me, you know?

The thing is, it's not like it's really the body that's doing the changing. It's like the body is *being changed from outside*. Like there's this invisible sculptor picking things up and molding them into something else, rearranging them, whittling them like soft wood and pressing them like warm clay, only it's happening inside as well as outside. But, get this: it's *gentle*. The noise is moderately alarming, no question, but to look at . . . it's like poetry. And whenever I'm privileged enough to witness it, I get to thinking about who that sculptor might be, and where he might be, and what else he might get up to in his spare time . . .

Enough already. The changeover routine got to me a little, that's all you need to know. I stood like a tree while the dead guy in a hat turned into a dead wolf in a hat. When it was over, I snapped myself out of it and went over to examine the remolded corpse.

The first thing I did was check the beast's pulse. The last thing I wanted in my office was a gun-shot werewolf waking up and deciding lunch was served. I held my breath until I was happy the werewolf didn't have any of its own left to hold, then I set about working out what pack it belonged to.

They all belong to a pack, you see. Like a clan—it's a family thing. There are hundreds of packs scattered, mostly across Europe, although there's a big cluster in Siberia too. Each pack has its own badge. The badges are a kind of uniform, but they have a more important function too: without its badge, a werewolf can't change.

Another little-known fact here.

A werewolf needs the full moon to change, sure, but it also needs its badge. Without the badge: no cracking bones, no explosion of fur, no mystical sculptor doing the muzzle-stretch thing. Oh, and while I'm revealing trade secrets, I'll bet you didn't know that a werewolf is not a human who turns into a wolf. It's the other way round. So, when they die, it's different than what most folk expect. The old cliche of the werewolf melting back to human form the instant it's killed is all backwards. If you don't believe me, just remember what happened to the man in the hat when he finally breathed his last red bubble on my office carpet.

So: pack badges. They vary. There's the *Halskettewolfen* pack, for example. They have to put on a gold necklace before they can change (they're closely related to the infamous *Boxenwolfen*, who use special belts). In Italy you have the *Lupo-guanto* with their metal gloves, in England the cravat-wearing *Tyedogs*, in Spain the *Lobolengua*, who can only change their form when they put in these crazy tongue-piercings. That's just grotesque, if you ask me.

I set to work trying to identify the wolf on my floor.

The words the man had spoken before he died had sounded German, and even through the carpet I knew I'd heard an eastern Bavarian accent. Which narrowed it down to three: my visitor was either a *Ringhund*, a *Glasaugewolf* or a *Knopfwolf*. I checked: there were no rings on any of the beast's paws and both its eyes looked natural enough. *Knopfwolf*, then.

I checked every button on that damned beast—trenchcoat, cuffs and, yes, even its fly—and every single one came up blank. Not a *Knopfwolf* then.

I sat back, careful to avoid the red stain on the floor, and scratched my head. Then I had an idea.

I took the hat off the dead wolf's head, looked inside the lining and saw the official seal of a werewolf pack I'd never heard of in my life: the *Helmwolf Bruderschaft*.

I've had many strange visitors come out of the rain and into my office, but never a werewolf in a hat.

I took time out then to clear up the mess the shooter had made of my coffee-machine. It wasn't as bad as I'd thought. The glass jug was history but the rest of the workings looked in good shape. The coffee had stripped the paint where it splattered up the wall, but I'd never really liked that wall in the first place. And at least now it looked like the other walls. Some folk call my office shabby; me, I call it my office.

"You'll be okay, buddy," I whispered to the coffee-machine as I set it straight on the filing cabinet again. "New jug, fresh grounds, you'll be right as rain in no time."

It burped wearily and I turned my attention back to the dead werewolf.

"Okay, buddy," I said to the corpse. "Some questions. One. What brought you through my door? Two. Who shot you and why? Three. *Hilfe* I understand—that means *help*, but what did you want to knock? Four. Why have I never heard of the *Helmwolfen*?"

In truth, I was feeling rattled. I'd thought I knew everything there was to know about werewolves. Call it pride if you like—I just call it knowing my trade. Not knowing about the *Helmwolfen* bugged me even more than having a corpse on my floor so, even though I knew I should be calling the cops, I did the next best thing: I started looking through the Big Dictionary.

All the books on my shelf are for show except one: the Big Dictionary. *Naked Singularities and Their Application to the Law* I know by heart and *Self-Defense in Dimensionally Unstable Environments* is just for beginners. You'll occasionally catch me leafing through *What to Look for in a Femme Fatale* but, if I'm honest, that's only for the pictures. But the Big Dictionary . . . well, it's my Bible.

I cracked the spine backwards until the cover read *V to X*, then turned it to *W*. All the werewolf packs were listed alphabetically but, surprise surprise, no mention of the *Helmfwolfen*. The list went straight from *Hatchet-wolf* to *Hosenhund* without taking a breath.

I closed the book and cracked the spine again until it was an atlas. A quick scan of Bavaria gave me no clues, so I closed and cracked it a third time until it was a history of shapeshifters. Still nothing.

I sighed, put the Big Dictionary back on the shelf and went to pick up the phone. What I saw outside my office door stopped me in my tracks.

It was a *femme*, and she sure was looking *fatale*.

She was tall—tall enough so I'd have had to stand on a box to meet her eye. A long, white sweater, soaked through by the rain, clung to her curves all the way down to her knees. Beneath it there was nothing but her. Water on the glass obscured her face. One hand was perched on her hip, the other was holding a handgun—a big one—up against the door. As I watched, she fired a bullet at point-blank range into the glass.

The door rang like a bell and I saw the bullet ricochet, carving a thin trail of vapor through the rain. It missed the dame's left ear by an inch, maybe two.

"Hey, lady . . ." I began. Then she fired again.

This time, when the bullet ricocheted, it took a chunk out of the sidewalk. It also took a chunk out of the glass.

"Hey," I said again, "what's with the—?"

Another bullet. Another sliver of glass.

The dame fired four more bullets, reloaded quickly and calmly, then started firing again.

The door was tough enough to take this kind of punishment for a while, but not forever. I shot a glance at the filing cabinet—I have my own arsenal of weapons in the second drawer up—but something made me slide my gaze up to the drawer above.

Another bullet hit the door, then she wiped the glass clean and peered inside, showing me her face for the first time. As a rule I don't gasp. Not unless somebody gives me good reason. She did.

"Of all the dames!" I gasped. "It had to be you."

I picked up the hat. Then, without thinking, I strode over to the filing cabinet and did something I hadn't done for nearly ten years: I opened the top drawer, folded myself in half and fell inside.

It was just as bad as I remembered.

I was falling through dark, bitter air. Icy winds tried to grab me with angry fingers. Way in the distance I could see flashes of what looked like lightning, but what sounded like a giant clearing its throat.

I fell like this for what felt like a day. During that time I only blinked my eyes once.

Then, slowly, something began to materialize out of the gloom: a pair of parallel silver lines, writhing like two snakes that had been shackled together but which hated each other's guts. They weren't snakes, of course; they were railroad tracks.

The tracks came closer. The lightning still flashed, but now there was another light smearing its way towards me. It was centered on the tracks, and followed their jitterbug routine like it was glued to them. Which, in a way, it was.

Soon I heard a rumbling sound, more metallic than the throat-clearing, twice as loud and getting louder all the time. The wind gusted, blasting into me from the same direction as the approaching smear of light. Then I heard a whistle, long and glutinous, and suddenly it was on me, an immense iron lobster with two hundred wheels, all interconnected with rods and dripping sinews and sprung cables and grinding cylinders. Brakes engaged and the mammoth train screeched to a halt. Steam erupted from a thousand greasy sphincters, oil oozed through toothsome grilles, chains with links as thick as my arm cracked like whips and flaming coals spilled from a great brazier perched high behind the funnel, half a mile above my head.

And there I stood, just as amazed and daunted as I had been the first—and last—time, before the Search Engine.

There was a sudden movement, halfway up, right behind the boiler. Something emerged, a little like a head, a little like a shadow.

"You comin' up?" The voice rolled down to me like syrup, with an afterbite of cheap bourbon.

A ladder made from what looked like human thighbones rattled down in its wake. Reluctantly, I started to climb.

"I need to find something," I shouted when I was nearly at the top.

"Don't they all!" screamed the shadow. Inside the great cylindrical boiler, something crashed like an ocean liner hitting an iceberg.

The Search Engine started to move again, quickly, all at once. The ladder was hurled backwards; grimly I clung on, crawling hand-over-hand along the last few rungs until something like a claw grabbed my shoulder and hauled me inside the cab.

The thermometer dangling outside the cab read ten degrees shy of absolute zero. I watched as a tiny bird made from cosmic string perched briefly on the bracket before darting off into the void. Inside the cab it was hot as a furnace.

The driver turned to me and spoke with something like a mouth.

"So, pilgrim, what ya searchin' for?"

I shivered. If I'd stuck the thermometer into that voice the mercury would have dropped another six degrees.

I held up the hat.

"I need to know where this came from," I said, working hard to keep my voice level. I am a professional, after all.

The driver threw me something like a grin and bore down on a lever the size of a small crane. The Search Engine barrelled left, towards a nearby darkness.

"That everything ya want to know, pilgrim?" shouted the driver, standing suddenly tall on something like legs. With a mighty inhalation the Search Engine plunged into the blackness of the Tunnel of All Ends.

Okay, so I'd seen the dame before. We went back a long way, she and I. Not as far as the coffee-machine, and she couldn't even compete with the filing cabinet. But it was a long way, all the same.

It was seven years ago she first walked into my office. Same curves, different sweater. She must have seen the look on my face because the first thing she'd done was flash me the ring on her left hand, warning me off. But she'd also flashed me her legs when she sat down. And all through the conversation her eyes had bored into mine. Sometimes you just know, you know?

The case had been simple enough. Her husband, who'd spent most of their marriage using her as a punching bag, had gotten himself locked away for his part in one of the biggest vault heists this side of the River Lethe. I knew his gang—everyone in the business did. They'd knocked off a score of places before finally coming unstuck at the Silverlode. The Silverlode is just the other side of the street from the Still Point of the Turning World, which is why they wanted to get into it so bad. A haul from the Silverlode is a good enough haul, but nobody's ever broken their way into the S.P.T.W.—I mean *nobody*. This gang figured if they could break into the Silverlode, maybe they could tunnel their way across the street into the S.P.T.W. Nobody knows what they might have come out with if they'd succeeded but one thing's for certain, they'd have been treated like gods. Well, maybe not gods. Titans, at the very least.

They didn't even make it as far as the end of the street.

All these places are on the Street of Fools and there's not many get past a Fool. No sooner had Cerberus started barking (and barking, and barking) than the tall guy who puts down pennies on the sidewalk sniffed them out and called down the thunder-birds. After that, they practically handed themselves in. Cerberus you probably know, but there's not many have heard of the guy with the pennies. I'll tell you about him another time; suffice it to say, if *you* ever see a penny lying on the sidewalk, my advice is to ignore the old rhyme and cross to the other side of the street. Preferably move to another town. Don't, whatever you do, pick it up.

But I was telling you about the dame, the getaway driver's wife. He got life in Wulan Pen, naturally, but she told me he'd found a loophole, a way of getting to her at weekends. She couldn't prove anything because it was a temporal loophole, so he always managed to leave her apartment and get back to the pen fifteen minutes before he'd arrived, which meant he never showed up on any of the security cameras. But the bruises he gave her showed up all right. All the way up her legs, right up to her pantyhose. I never forgot those bruises.

So I staked out the apartment, caught the husband and closed the loophole. Closed the case too. Open and shut, just the way I liked it.

She liked it the same way as me, so we spent the night in the sack. Okay, maybe it was unprofessional, but a guy's got needs, right?

Next morning, while she was making chicory coffee, I saw something under the mattress. It looked like a photograph, and here's one thing you should know about me: I'm never off-duty. Call it dedication, call it a curse. In this case, call it trouble.

The picture showed the getaway car on the day of the heist. The guy behind the wheel wasn't the husband. It wasn't even a guy. It was the dame.

She came through with the coffee, saw me with the photo and laughed.

"You can't prove anything," she said.

"You framed your own husband," I replied.

"My alibi's cast-iron."

"What about the photo?"

"A sentimental reminder," she said, drawing a tiny gun from the garter around her right thigh. She wasn't wearing anything else so there was nowhere else she could have hidden a weapon.

The gun held one bullet and she used it to shoot a hole in the photo, right where her face was. I tossed the ruined photo aside through a cloud of gunsmoke and chicory.

"You used me," I said. "Now that loophole's closed your husband's never getting out of there. And you're walking around free as a bird."

"As an eagle," she laughed.

As I brushed past her she pulled me close and kissed me once, brutally.

"See you around, mister," she whispered.

And she did. Most years she came to me with some scam or other. Every time I told myself I wouldn't get involved. Every time I told myself she was a ruthless, heartless dame on the lookout only for herself. And every single time I fell for it. And her.

Except this time.

This time, I told myself, things were going to be different.

The Tunnel of All Ends is the place to go when you want to find something out. Everything's down there, and I mean everything. Everything that ever happens gets recorded and filed away in some or other side alley and it stays there forever. Don't ask me how it works—something to do with a quantum inseparability link to a place called *Stone*—but the paperwork must be catastrophic because *everything's* there, categorized and cross-referred and waiting to be found. You just have to know where to look.

Which is where the Search Engine comes in. It's ugly and terrifying but it's fast and it never fails.

Unfortunately, the fare can be on the high side.

"There," said the driver, pointing out a long, shabby passage with something like a finger. At the far end, a tired-looking station platform sagged beneath flickering fluorescents. "Lycanthropia Terminus."

Then the driver turned towards me, brandishing something like a hole punch, but more like a surgical instrument, and said the words I'd dreaded hearing this whole trip: "Tickets, please."

By the time I folded myself back out of the filing cabinet, the dame had shot herself a neat, round hole in the door. She was about to reach through the hole to undo the latch. Dropping the hat, I marched over and did it for her. Her fingers brushed mine and our eyes met through the rain-streaked glass. Her lips parted and, so help me, I felt my heart do that familiar high-wire plunge.

I pulled away from the door and slumped myself down behind the desk.

"You can let yourself in," I growled.

"I already did," she replied, her voice husky, maybe from the cold, maybe not. "May I sit down?"

I shrugged. "Please yourself. You usually do."

She sat down, smoothing her soaked sweater over her knees. I tried not to watch her doing this, without much success.

"I'll come straight to the point," she began. "This man . . ." she pointed to the corpse on the floor, ". . . I mean, this *creature*, has been blackmailing me."

I kept my eyes fixed on hers. It wasn't hard. "Looks like he just stopped," I said.

"Are you going to turn me in?" She leaned across the desk and clasped her hands around mine. Her touch was cold and electric. "Are you?"

"Is that why you shot your way in here? To plead your innocence before I figured it was you?"

"How long would it have taken you to find out?"

I shrugged. "Would have taken me a minute or two to get the slug out of the stiff. As for tracing it—that depends who I went to."

"Give me a for instance."

"Deke the Rip could do it in a half hour. Twenty minutes to get to his place and back."

"So you'd have been knocking on my door within the hour."

Again I shrugged. "It's what I do."

"You think I don't know that?"

"You know it. So why shoot the werewolf on my doorstep? Why not choose somewhere more discreet? And why was he blackmailing you?"

She pressed her shoulders back in the chair and crossed her legs. Water squeezed from the soaked fabric and puddled beneath the desk. "You're asking a lot of questions—no, you don't need to tell me: it's what you do."

I raised my eyebrows. "You got that right. So, you want to answer some of them?"

Lowering her eyes, she began her story.

"I hooked up with him a couple of months ago. He was kind of mysterious and that fascinated me. He only let me see him two nights a week and never at all around the full moon. I suppose I should have guessed his secret but . . . well, with some folk, just being around them makes you blind to the obvious, you know what I mean?"

"Yes, ma'am," I murmured, watching what was left of the rain trickling through her hair. "I know."

"He was big on casinos so we did the strip. He won a lot of dough; he was lucky that way."

"Not so lucky now," I said, eyeing the corpse. "So, why the blackmail, if he was on such a winning streak?"

"Because his luck ran out. He ran himself up a tab he couldn't pay off and got the heavies on his back—I'm talking about the real heavies now. He owes a lot of money to a lot of very ugly people. I mean owed, I guess."

"The Tartarus Club?" I hazarded. She nodded her head and shuddered. The movement did remarkable things to the curves beneath that damned sweater. "Are you telling me the Titans were after him?"

"Yes. Only I got to him first."

"So what did you have that he wanted?"

"Money, what else? I inherited a packet from my third husband."

"How did *he* die?"

"In tragic circumstances."

"I'll bet."

"Are you cross-examining me?"

"Is that an invitation?"

"Since when did you wait to be invited?"

"Stick to the story, ma'am."

By now her eyes were locked back on mine. That was just the way I liked them.

"I'm a rich widow these days," she went on, "and that's all you need to know. So, the wolfman got wind of my billions . . ."

"Pardon me—did you say *millions*?"

"No. Now where was I? Oh yes, he found out I was rich and decided I was the one to pay off his debts and buy his ticket out of hell. Only I'd already found out he was cheating on me, so it was no deal. That's when I got the first blackmail note."

"What did he have on you?"

She held my gaze and said quietly, "There were two photos taken that day."

I closed my eyes and all at once I was back in that apartment. Damn it all, I could even smell the gunsmoke and chicory.

"Why didn't you destroy all the evidence?" I said. "You were quick enough to shoot a hole in the photo I found."

I could sense this whole thing was getting out of hand, maybe even getting dangerous. The dame still had a gun in her hand, after all. I knew I had to keep her talking. Besides, I was curious: why had she kept the one piece of evidence that could have put her away for life? Why run the risk?

To my astonishment, a tear was spilling from between her perfect black lashes.

"Sentimental reasons," she said. "My first husband—the one they locked away, the one I framed, the one who spent every spare hour of the day beating the bright blue hell out of me . . . I . . ."

"You still love him," I said. "Sweet mother of mercy! Now I've heard it all."

I rocked back in the chair and reminded myself there are two things man was never meant to know: what happened before the big bang singularity and why dames do what they do.

"So," I said heavily, "your boyfriend, the werewolf, stole the photo and used it to blackmail you, to pay off his gambling debts."

Wide, tear-filled eyes trembled in her pale, cold face as she nodded, her bottom lip trembling.

"It's just a coincidence we were in your neighborhood when I finally got him cornered. And that's the honest truth," she said, her voice breaking.

Rising from my chair, I slammed both fists down on the desk and lunged towards her, my own lips pulled back from my teeth, and with the most ferocious growl I could muster I said, "Liar!"

Her tears stopped abruptly. I held my breath and waited for the gunshot. I wished I'd put my feet up on the desk—that would at least have given me a fighting chance. But no, I faced her down, knowing my only hope was to outstare her.

Only when she looked away did I allow myself to breathe again. How much time had I bought myself? I didn't know. What I did know was I'd knocked her off-balance. I had to keep her that way, so I went over to the wolf's corpse and picked up the hat.

"Interesting badge," I said, fingering the lining. "The *Helmwolfen Bruderschaft*. Not a very well-known pack."

"I wouldn't know," she said listlessly. The big handgun lay on her lap; her fingers lay on the big handgun.

"It's not well-known for one very simple reason," I continued. "It isn't a wolf pack at all."

"Isn't it? But I thought all werewolves belonged to packs."

"They do. But our friend here isn't a werewolf."

I whipped off my coat and made ready to turn it inside-out.

The intense heat of the Search Engine's cab had prompted me to turn it into comfortable but penetrable sealskin. Right now it was about as bulletproof as a wet paper towel. I was quick, but the dame was quicker. Throwing back the chair, she stood in a lithe, economical movement and pointed the big handgun right at the center of my head. Since that's a part of my anatomy I'm particularly fond of, I froze.

"Drop the coat," she hissed.

"It's just a coat."

"Drop it!"

I dropped the coat.

"What do you know?" she snapped.

"I'd never heard of the *Helmwolfen*. There was no mention of any such pack in the book. But not everything gets into the Big Dictionary." I smiled. "You're not in there, for instance, but you exist all right."

"You can be sure of it. Go on."

"When I dug a bit deeper I discovered there's a secret society called the *Helmwolfen*, but they're not werewolves."

"They're not?"

"No, ma'am, although they move in similar circles. Turns out the *Helmwolfen* are gamblers. What they do is kind of weird: they take ordinary articles of clothing and lace them with *lycanthropia* . . ."

"*Lycanthropia*? What's that?" She looked puzzled, but I wasn't convinced the expression was genuine.

"Essence of werewolf. Musk. Distilled hound-juice. Whatever. It's intense stuff, very, very powerful. You don't even want to think about how they get their hands on it. Anyway, it does pretty much what a werewolf badge does to its owner."

"What do you mean?"

"Put it this way, you put on an outfit laced with *lycanthropia* and it won't be your own face you see next time you check the mirror."

"It can turn anybody into a werewolf?"

"Not necessarily a wolf. Could be anything. Tiger, bear, stoat, you name it. It's usually a mammal, usually a carnivore. But not always. There's records of wereparrots. One poor bastard turned into a wereshark and suffocated in his own front room."

"So where does the gambling come in?"

"The *Helmwolfen* bet on what the victim—and these *are* victims, make no mistake—will turn into. Big money changes hands. It's not a game for the squeamish. Wereism isn't a stable condition. Unless you're born to it, chances are the transformation will only be successful one way."

"One way?"

"Yeah. When you change back, all the different parts of your body go back in the wrong order."

"How do they get the . . . victims . . . to do it?"

"Gambling again. There are *Helmwolfen* behind most of the big casinos in most of the big towns. Including the Tartarus Club. They see some poor sucker laying down more than he can afford and make him an offer he can't refuse. 'Try this game,' they say. 'Survive, and we'll wipe the slate clean.'"

The gun wavered in her hand.

"You're the one who owes the money," I said, seizing the advantage, "aren't you? I'm just telling you what you already know. Because the truth is that *you're* the one they made the offer to, not this poor schmuck."

For a moment I didn't know which way she'd tip. Then she collapsed like a bunch of wet noodles into the chair, bent her head to the desk and sobbed her wretched little heart out.

Me, like the poor sap I am, wrapped my arm around her shoulders. Beneath the sodden sweater she felt hot and alive. I told myself to keep my mind on the job.

"I'm s-sorry," she wept. "I didn't know w-what else to do. I w-was so d-desperate. Can you forgive me?"

"I don't know," I said. "I'll need to get it all straight in my head first. Without a guy like me on the case this could all get mighty confusing."

"You can work it out," she said, touching my cheek with ten thousand volts of fingertip. "I know you're the man for the job."

"Okay," I said. "Let me see. You start visiting the Tartarus Club, maybe thinking you'll get hooked up with some rich widower, maybe just to kid yourself you still got a life. Instead you get hooked on the gaming tables—blackjack's my guess. Am I right so far?"

Sniffling, she nodded.

"So, you run yourself deep into debt. You go to the management, flash them your legs, maybe a little more. They decline your offers and make you one of their own. 'Just try this hat on for size,' they tell you. 'We got ourselves a little game going back here. Big Iapetos thinks you just might be a swan.' 'Can I think about it?' you say. 'Sure,' they say. And again, when you ask if you can keep the hat while you chew it over, they say, 'Sure.' Because they know you won't dare get rid of it, for fear of what they'll do to you. And you won't dare try it on. You'll just stare at it and stare at it until you run back to them screaming to get it over with. Am I still on the eight ball here?"

Her eyes had glazed a little and she looked ready to cry again. I felt bad, like I was rubbing her nose in it, but if I was going to help her . . .

Was I going to help her? Sweet mother of mercy!

"Am I right?" I repeated.

"Huh? Oh, yes. On the button."

"So, tell me where you found the dog."

She drew the back of her hand across her mouth, sat up and stared into at the rain. "At the pound," she said. "I picked the one that looked most like a wolf—German shepherd it said on the cage. I told the superintendent I was going to give it a good home, then I brought it here."

"Did you know what would happen when you put the hat on it?"

"No. I was guessing. Luckily for me I guessed right."

"Not so lucky for the German shepherd."

"The hat turned him into a wereman."

"Most dangerous werebeast of all. So it's said."

"I did it in the alley that runs down the side of your office. Once the transformation was complete, it was easy enough to herd the wretched creature into your doorway and . . . and . . ."

"And shoot it in cold blood at point-blank range."

She buried her face in her hands. "It was just a dog," she sobbed.

"Not a werewolf at all," I mused, "but a wereman. An Alsatian in a *lycanthropia* hat. Now I've seen it all. All you need to tell me now is why."

"I told you, I was desperate. If I go back to the Titans they'll turn me into something horrible and I'll never get back in one piece. If I try to run they'll track me down and kill me anyway. You don't know what those Titans are like."

I stopped rubbing her shoulders for a moment. An old scar on the back of my hand throbbed suddenly. *Remember me*, it seemed to be saying.

"Oh yes," I muttered, "oh yes I do."

"You do?" she looked at me curiously.

"Another story," I said. "Another time. You were telling me why you shot the dog."

"So you could get me put away," she said. Then she added, "Could you rub my shoulders again? It feels kind of nice."

Dumbstruck, I obliged.

"You?" I said when I could speak again. "The woman who framed her own husband to avoid the clink . . . and now you're framing yourself!"

"It was the hat that gave me the idea. I sat there staring at it, just like you said, when the idea came to me. If I could commit what looked like a murder on the doorstep of someone I could trust, I could get myself into safe custody before the Titans even got a sniff of what was going on. Nobody can touch you once they put you in Wulan Pen, not even the Titans. But only a murder would guarantee me a life sentence. I could never kill anyone, not for real, and that's when I thought up the trick with the dog."

"And when the dead body turned back into what looked like a wolf, everyone would assume you'd killed a shapeshifter. Even me. Making it, in the eyes of the law, first degree murder."

"I really thought you'd believe the blackmail story," she said sulkily. "The whole thing would have worked if you hadn't been so damned keen on following up the clues."

I adopted my best hurt expression.

"Ma'am," I said, "it's what I do."

Pressing herself into my embrace, she said softly, "Now you know the truth. So what are you going to do? Take me back to the Titans? Or turn me over to the cops?"

Her eyes flashed, once, twice, and my heart did the high-wire thing again. Then, so help me, I said, "Hold tight, lady. I got a better idea."

We stood beside the dancing railroad tracks: me, the dame and three Titans. Winter wind howled into our flesh. Lightning flashed above us, beneath us, inside our heads. In the far, far distance, a familiar smear of light came galloping out of the gloom.

The great lobster shape of the Search Engine crashed to a halt just inches from our faces, spilling its load of noxious gases and lubricants into the noisome filth of its wake. Even the Titans had the good grace to look impressed.

Something like a head emerged from the cab. Following it out, moving with sidewinder speed, came something like a body. This time, instead of inviting us up, the driver was coming down.

We backed away. Even the Titans backed away. We had to, to give the driver room to stand.

The Titans, I noticed, had dipped their massive, horned heads in respect.

"Which one of you's brought it?" said the driver, with something like anticipation.

The dame took one step forward and handed it over. When she stepped back, I slipped an arm around her waist and pulled her close.

"Don't worry," I whispered in her ear. "It'll all work out."

Raising something like an arm, the driver put on the hat.

We sat in my office: me, the dame and the two remaining Titans.

"I'd offer you coffee," I said, "only the machine's busted."

Hyperion, the bigger of the two, waved away the offer with one gargantuan hand.

"Who'd have thought it?" he rumbled in a voice like boulders in a tumble-dryer.

"Ah well," drawled Oceanus. "We lost a bet. So what?"

"We lost Iapetos, is what we did. We shouldn't have bet him."

"He was noisy. You never liked him."

"Yah."

Then Hyperion turned to me and said, "We got you to thank for showing us that place, buddy."

"Interesting place," Oceanus put in.

"Sure enough. Strange fellow though, that driver. Who'd have thought he'd turn into something with so many teeth?"

"Yah. Poor Iapetos."

"Who'd have thought it?" I agreed. "So you didn't mind my, er, client making the substitution? Not putting the hat on herself."

"Nah," said Oceanus, picking a piece of driftwood from between his teeth. "It can get pretty dull, you know, being a Titan. Everything's smaller than you are. Even most worlds."

"Especially most worlds," put in Hyperion.

"Yah. And it isn't every day we get to see a place we've never seen before."

"Especially one that's bigger than we are."

"And that driver."

"One weird character."

"Yah. And just a little . . . would you say . . . ?"

"Scary?" I put in.

"Yah. Scary. We don't get scared much."

They sat silent for a minute or two, considering fear with eyes like turning worlds.

"So," I said, "my client's debt?"

"All paid," said Hyperion, swiping that mighty hand again. "No bother. You guys, you did something today nobody's done for a long time."

"An eon," put in Oceanus.

"An eon," Hyperion agreed.

The dame pressed some of my favorite parts of her body close to me. I relaxed back in the chair and said, "What did we do?"

"You surprised us."

"It's a long time since I surprised a god," I said when the Titans had left.

"They aren't gods," said the dame.

"Next best thing," I replied. I pointed to the footmarks on the carpet. "The size they are, they might as well be."

"You know, that's always puzzled me. They must be, what, a thousand miles high? But they always manage to fit in an ordinary room. How do they do that?"

"Search me," I said. "I still don't know how we got them inside that filing cabinet. I never folded a Titan before."

We both stared at the cabinet.

"Is the world inside that top drawer bigger than this one?" she asked.

"Bigger than all of them put together," I said. "At least, that's what the guy in the market said when he sold it to me. I've only been inside it three times now but, from what I've seen so far, I think he may be right."

"It impressed the hell out of the Titans."

"That was the idea."

"What about the one who, um, stayed behind? What do you think will happen to him?"

"Iapetos? Search me. I'm just glad I got him down there in the first place. I promised the driver I would, you see. That was the ticket price we agreed on, you see, when I was down there hunting werewolves. That was the fare: one Titan."

"What does the Search Engine driver want with a Titan? Especially one in so many pieces."

"Who knows? Maybe they burn well."

Slithering off my lap, she danced across the office. The Titans had been good enough to clear away both the corpse of the poor Alsatian and the mess it left behind, so she had room to pirouette. She'd taken off the sweater and hung it over the stove to dry, which improved the view no end.

"You knew all along, didn't you?" she said, reaching a breathless halt. "All that time you were just keeping me talking and watching me dig myself deeper and deeper."

Enjoying the sight of her chest rising and falling, I nodded.

"I didn't work it out all at once," I said. "The information I gathered at Lycanthropia Terminus just confirmed the hunch I got when I worked out what that pooch had really said while it was dying on the carpet."

"And what was that?"

"When the poor critter turned into a man, it absorbed just enough human vocabulary to ask for help; of course, being a German shepherd, it came out as *hilfe*. After that, I thought it said *knock*."

"Knock?"

"Yeah. Only I think what it was really trying to say *Knochen*."

"What does that mean?"

"Brush up your German, sweetheart. It means *bone*. The poor mutt was just looking for his lunch."

"You're so clever, my own little poor mutt. Have you got a bone?"

"Why don't you come over here and find out for yourself?"

She came over and, funny, all that German went right out of my head. Like I said: *femme*, yes; *fatale*, most definitely. Ooh la la.

This Town Ain't Big Enough

➤ TANYA HUFF ◄

"OW! VICKI, BE CAREFUL!"

"Sorry. Sometimes I forget how sharp they are."

"Terrific." He wove his fingers through her hair and pulled just hard enough to make his point. "Don't."

"Don't what?" She grinned up at him, teeth gleaming ivory in the moonlight spilling across the bed. "Don't forget or don't—"

The sudden demand of the telephone for attention buried the last of her question.

Detective-Sergeant Michael Celluci sighed. "Hold that thought," he said, rolled over, and reached for the phone. "Celluci."

"Fifty-two division just called. They've found a body down at Richmond and Peter they think we might want to have a look at."

"Dave, it's . . ." He squinted at the clock. ". . . one twenty-nine in the A.M. and I'm off duty."

On the other end of the line, his partner, theoretically off duty as well, refused to take the hint. "Ask me who the stiff is?"

Celluci sighed again. "Who's the stiff?"

"Mac Eisler."

"Shit."

"Funny, that's exactly what I said." Nothing in Dave Graham's voice indicated he appreciated the joke. "I'll be there in ten."

"Make it fifteen."

"You in the middle of something?"

Celluci watched as Vicki sat up and glared at him. "I was."

51

"Welcome to the wonderful world of law enforcement."

Vicki's hand shot out and caught Celluci's wrist before he could heave the phone across the room. "Who's Mac Eisler?" she asked as, scowling, he dropped the receiver back in its cradle and swung his legs off the bed.

"You heard that?"

"I can hear the beating of your heart, the movement of your blood, the song of your life." She scratched the back of her leg with one bare foot. "I should think I can overhear a lousy phone conversation."

"Eisler's a pimp." Celluci reached for the light switch, changed his mind, and began pulling on his clothes. Given the full moon riding just outside the window, it wasn't exactly dark and given Vicki's sensitivity to bright light, not to mention her temper, he figured it was safer to cope. "We're pretty sure he offed one of his girls a couple weeks ago."

Vicki scooped her shirt up off the floor. "Irene Macdonald?"

"What? You overheard that too?"

"I get around. How sure's pretty sure?"

"Personally positive. But we had nothing solid to hold him on."

"And now he's dead." Skimming her jeans up over her hips, she dipped her brows in a parody of deep thought. "Golly, I wonder if there's a connection."

"Golly yourself," Celluci snarled. "You're not coming with me."

"Did I ask?"

"I recognized the tone of voice. I know you, Vicki. I knew you when you were a cop, I knew you when you were a P.I. and I don't care how much you've changed physically, I know you now you're a . . . a . . ."

"Vampire." Her pale eyes seemed more silver than grey. "You can say it, Mike. It won't hurt my feelings. Bloodsucker. Night-walker. Creature of Darkness."

"Pain in the butt." Carefully avoiding her gaze, he shrugged into his shoulder holster and slipped a jacket on over it. "This is police business, Vicki, stay out of it. Please." He didn't wait for a response but crossed the shadows to the bedroom door. Then he paused, one foot over the threshold. "I doubt I'll be back by dawn. Don't wait up."

Vicki Nelson, ex of the Metropolitan Toronto Police Force, ex private investigator, recent vampire, decided to let him go. If he could joke about the change, he accepted it. And besides, it was always more fun to make him pay for smart-ass remarks when he least expected it.

She watched from the darkness as Celluci climbed into Dave Graham's car. Then, with the taillights disappearing in the distance, she dug out his spare set of car keys and proceeded to leave tangled entrails of the Highway Traffic Act strewn from Downsview to the heart of Toronto.

It took no supernatural ability to find the scene of the crime. What with the police, the press, and the morbidly curious, the area seethed with people. Vicki slipped past the constable stationed at the far end of the alley and followed the paths of shadow until she stood just outside the circle of police around the body.

Mac Eisler had been a somewhat attractive, not very tall, white male Caucasian. Eschewing the traditional clothing excesses of his profession, he was dressed simply in designer jeans and an olive-green raw silk jacket. At the moment, he wasn't looking his best. A pair of rusty nails had been shoved through each manicured hand, securing his body upright across the back entrance of a trendy restaurant. Although the pointed toes of his tooled leather cowboy boots indented the wood of the door, Eisler's head had been turned completely around so that he stared, in apparent astonishment, out into the alley.

The smell of death fought with the stink of urine and garbage. Vicki frowned. There was another scent, a pungent predator scent that raised the hair on the back of her neck and drew her lips up off her teeth. Surprised by the strength of her reaction, she stepped silently into a deeper patch of night lest she give herself away.

"Why the hell would I have a comment?"

Preoccupied with an inexplicable rage, she hadn't heard Celluci arrive until he greeted the press. Shifting position slightly, she watched as he and his partner moved in off the street and got their first look at the body.

"Jesus H. Christ."

"On crutches," agreed the younger of the two detectives already on the scene.

"Who found him?"

"Dishwasher, coming out with the trash. He was obviously meant to be found; they nailed the bastard right across the door."

"The kitchen's on the other side and no one heard hammering?"

"I'll go you one better than that. Look at the rust on the head of those nails—they haven't been hammered."

"What? Someone just pushed the nails through Eisler's hands and into solid wood?"

"Looks like."

Celluci snorted. "You trying to tell me that Superman's gone bad?"

Under the cover of their laughter, Vicki bent and picked up a piece of planking. There were four holes in the unbroken end and two remaining three-inch spikes. She pulled a spike out of the wood and pressed it into the wall of the building by her side. A smut of rust marked the ball of her thumb but the nail looked no different.

She remembered the scent.

Vampire.

". . . unable to come to the phone. Please leave a message after the long beep."

"Henry? It's Vicki. If you're there, pick up." She stared across the dark kitchen, twisting the phone cord between her fingers. "Come on, Fitzroy, I don't care what you're doing, this is important." Why wasn't he home writing? Or chewing on Tony. Or something. "Look, Henry, I need some information. There's another one of, of us, hunting my territory and I don't know what I should do. I know what I want to do . . ." The rage remained, interlaced with the knowledge of another. ". . . but I'm new at this bloodsucking undead stuff, maybe I'm overreacting. Call me. I'm still at Mike's."

She hung up and sighed. Vampires didn't share territory. Which was why Henry had stayed in Vancouver and she'd come back to Toronto.

Well, all right, it's not the only reason I came back. She tossed Celluci's spare car keys into the drawer in the phone table and wondered if she should write him a note to explain the mysterious emptying of his gas tank. "Nah. He's a detective, let him figure it out."

Sunrise was at five twelve. Vicki didn't need a clock to tell her that it was almost time. She could feel the sun stroking the edges of her awareness.

"It's like that final instant, just before someone hits you from

behind, when you know it's going to happen but you can't do a
damn thing about it." She crossed her arms on Celluci's chest and
pillowed her head on them adding, "Only it lasts longer."
"And this happens every morning?"
"Just before dawn."
"And you're going to live forever?"
"That's what they tell me."
Celluci snorted. "You can have it."

Although Celluci had offered to light-proof one of the two
unused bedrooms, Vicki had been uneasy about the concept. At
four and a half centuries, maybe Henry Fitzroy could afford to be
blasé about immolation but Vicki still found the whole idea terrifying and had no intention of being both helpless and exposed.
Anyone could walk into a bedroom.

No one would accidentally walk into an enclosed plywood box,
covered in a blackout curtain, at the far end of a five-foot-high
crawl space—but just to be on the safe side, Vicki dropped two-
by-fours into iron brackets over the entrance. Folded nearly in
half, she hurried to her sanctuary, feeling the sun drawing closer,
closer. Somehow she resisted the urge to turn.

"There's nothing behind me," she muttered, awkwardly stripping
off her clothes. Her heart slamming against her ribs, she crawled
under the front flap of the box, latched it behind her, and squirmed
into her sleeping bag, stretched out ready for the dawn.

"Jesus H. Christ, Vicki," Celluci had said squatting at one end
while she'd wrestled the twin bed mattress inside. "At least a coffin
would have a bit of historical dignity."
"You know where I can get one?"
"I'm not having a coffin in my basement."
"Then quit flapping your mouth."

She wondered, as she lay there waiting for oblivion, where
the other was. Did they feel the same near panic knowing that
they had no control over the hours from dawn to dusk? Or had
they, like Henry, come to accept the daily death that governed an
immortal life? There should, she supposed, be a sense of kinship
between them but all she could feel was a possessive fury. No
one hunted in her territory.

"Pleasant dreams," she said as the sun teetered on the edge of
the horizon. "And when I find you, you're toast."

Celluci had been and gone by the time the darkness returned.

The note he'd left about the car was profane and to the point. Vicki added a couple of words he'd missed and stuck it under a refrigerator magnet in case he got home before she did.

She'd pick up the scent and follow it, the hunter becoming the hunted and, by dawn, the streets would be hers again.

The yellow police tape still stretched across the mouth of the alley. Vicki ignored it. Wrapping the night around her like a cloak, she stood outside the restaurant door and sifted the air.

Apparently, a pimp crucified over the fire exit hadn't been enough to close the place and Tex Mex had nearly obliterated the scent of a death not yet twenty-four hours old. Instead of the predator, all she could smell was fajitas.

"God damn it," she muttered, stepping closer and sniffing the wood. "How the hell am I supposed to find . . ."

She sensed his life the moment before he spoke.

"What are you doing?"

Vicki sighed and turned. "I'm sniffing the door frame. What's it look like I'm doing?"

"Let me be more specific," Celluci snarled. "What are you doing here?"

"I'm looking for the person who offed Mac Eisler," Vicki began. She wasn't sure how much more explanation she was willing to offer.

"No, you're not. You are not a cop. You aren't even a P.I. anymore. And how the hell am I going to explain you if Dave sees you?"

Her eyes narrowed. "You don't have to explain me, Mike."

"Yeah? He thinks you're in Vancouver."

"Tell him I came back."

"And do I tell him that you spend your days in a box in my basement? And that you combust in sunlight? And what do I tell him about your eyes?"

Vicki's hand rose to push at the bridge of her glasses but her fingers touched only air. The retinitis pigmentosa that had forced her from the Metro Police and denied her the night had been reversed when Henry'd changed her. The darkness held no secrets from her now. "Tell him they got better."

"RP doesn't get better."

"Mine did."

"Vicki, I know what you're doing." He dragged both hands up through his hair. "You've done it before. You had to quit the force. You were half blind. So what? Your life may have changed but you were still going to prove that you were 'Victory' Nelson. And it wasn't enough to be a private investigator. You threw yourself into stupidly dangerous situations just to prove you were still who you wanted to be. And now your life has changed again and you're playing the same game."

She could hear his heart pounding, see a vein pulsing framed in the white vee of his open collar, feel the blood surging just below the surface in reach of her teeth. The Hunger rose and she had to use every bit of control Henry had taught her to force it back down. This wasn't about that.

Since she'd returned to Toronto, she'd been drifting; feeding, hunting, relearning the night, relearning her relationship with Michael Celluci. The early morning phone call had crystallized a subconscious discontent and, as Celluci pointed out, there was really only one thing she knew how to do.

Part of his diatribe was based on concern. After all their years together playing cops and lovers she knew how he thought; if something as basic as sunlight could kill her, what else waited to strike her down. It was only human nature for him to want to protect the people he loved—for him to want to protect her.

But, that was only the basis for part of the diatribe.

"You can't have been happy with me lazing around your house. I can't cook and I don't do windows." She stepped towards him. "I should think you'd be thrilled that I'm finding my feet again."

"Vicki."

"I wonder," she mused, holding tight to the Hunger, "how you'd feel about me being involved in this if it wasn't your case. I am, after all, better equipped to hunt the night than, oh, detective-sergeants."

"Vicki . . ." Her name had become a nearly inarticulate growl.

She leaned forward until her lips brushed his ear. "Bet you I solve this one first." Then she was gone, moving into shadow too quickly for mortal eyes to track.

"Who you talking to, Mike?" Dave Graham glanced around the empty alley. "I thought I heard . . ." Then he caught sight of the expression on his partner's face. "Never mind."

Vicki couldn't remember the last time she felt so alive. *Which, as I'm now a card carrying member of the bloodsucking undead, makes for an interesting feeling.* She strode down Queen Street

West, almost intoxicated by the lives surrounding her, fully aware of crowds parting to let her through and the admiring glances that traced her path. A connection had been made between her old life and her new one.

"You must surrender the day," Henry had told her, *"but you need not surrender anything else."*

"So what you're trying to tell me," she'd snarled, *"is that we're just normal people who drink blood?"*

Henry had smiled. *"How many normal people do you know?"*

She hated it when he answered a question with a question but now, she recognized his point. Honesty forced her to admit that Celluci had a point as well. She did need to prove to herself that she was still herself. She always had. The more things changed, the more they stayed the same.

"Well, now we've got that settled . . ." She looked around for a place to sit and think. In her old life, that would have meant a donut shop or the window seat in a cheap restaurant and as many cups of coffee as it took. In this new life, being enclosed with humanity did not encourage contemplation. Besides, coffee, a major component of the old equation, made her violently ill—a fact she deeply resented.

A few years back, CITY TV, a local Toronto station, had renovated a deco building on the corner of Queen and John. They'd done a beautiful job and the six-story, white building with its ornately molded modern windows, had become a focal point of the neighborhood. Vicki slid into the narrow walkway that separated it from its more down-at-the-heels neighbor and swarmed up what effectively amounted to a staircase for one of her kind.

When she reached the roof a few seconds later, she perched on one crenellated corner and looked out over the downtown core. These were her streets; not Celluci's and not some out-of-town bloodsucker's. It was time she took them back. She grinned and fought the urge to strike a dramatic pose.

All things considered, it wasn't likely that the Metropolitan Toronto Police Department—in the person of Detective-Sergeant Michael Celluci—would be willing to share information. Briefly, she regretted issuing the challenge then she shrugged it off. As Henry said, the night was too long for regrets.

She sat and watched the crowds jostling about on the sidewalks below, clumps of color indicating tourists amongst the Queen

Street regulars. On a Friday night in August, this was the place to be as the Toronto artistic community rubbed elbows with wanna-bes and never-woulds.

Vicki frowned. Mac Eisler had been killed before midnight on a Thursday night in an area that never completely slept. Someone had to have seen or heard something. Something they probably didn't believe and were busy denying. Murder was one thing, creatures of the night were something else again.

"Now then," she murmured, "where would a person like that— and considering the time and day we're assuming a regular, not a tourist—where would that person be tonight?"

She found him in the third bar she checked, tucked back in a corner, trying desperately to get drunk, and failing. His eyes darted from side to side, both hands were locked around his glass, and his body language screamed: I'm dealing with some bad shit here, leave me alone.

Vicki sat down beside him and for an instant let the Hunter show. His reaction was everything she could have hoped for.

He stared at her, frozen in terror, his mouth working but no sound coming out.

"Breathe," she suggested.

The ragged intake of air did little to calm him but it did break the paralysis. He shoved his chair back from the table and started to stand.

Vicki closed her fingers around his wrist. "Stay."

He swallowed and sat down again.

His skin was so hot it nearly burned and she could feel his pulse beating against it like a small wild creature struggling to be free. The Hunger clawed at her and her own breathing became a little ragged. "What's your name?"

"Ph . . . Phil."

She caught his gaze with hers and held it. "You saw something last night."

"Yes." Stretched almost to the breaking point, he began to tremble.

"Do you live around here?"

"Yes."

Vicki stood and pulled him to his feet, her tone half command half caress. "Take me there. We have to talk."

Phil stared at her. "Talk?"

She could barely hear the question over the call of his blood. "Well, talk first."

"It was a woman. Dressed all in black. Hair like a thousand strands of shadow, skin like snow, eyes like black ice. She chuckled, deep in her throat, when she saw me and licked her lips. They were painfully red. Then she vanished, so quickly that she left an image on the night."

"Did you see what she was doing?"

"No. But then, she didn't have to be doing anything to be terrifying. I've spent the last twenty-four hours feeling like I met my death."

Phil had turned out to be a bit of a poet. And a bit of an athlete. All in all, Vicki considered their time together well spent. Working carefully after he fell asleep, she took away his memory of her and muted the meeting in the alley. It was the least she could do for him.

The description sounded like a character freed from a Hammer film; The Bride of Dracula Kills a Pimp.

She paused, key in the lock, and cocked her head. Celluci was home, she could feel his life and if she listened very hard, she could hear the regular rhythm of breathing that told her he was asleep. Hardly surprising as it was only three hours to dawn.

There was no reason to wake him as she had no intention of sharing what she'd discovered and no need to feed but, after a long, hot shower, she found herself standing at the door of his room. And then at the side of his bed.

Mike Celluci was thirty-seven. There were strands of grey in his hair and although sleep had smoothed out many of the lines, the deeper creases around his eyes remained. He would grow older. In time, he would die. What would she do then?

She lifted the sheet and tucked herself up close to his side. He sighed and without completely waking scooped her closer still.

"Hair's wet," he muttered.

Vicki twisted, reached up, and brushed the long curl back off his forehead. "I had a shower."

"Where'd you leave the towel?"

"In a sopping pile on the floor."

Celluci grunted inarticulately and surrendered to sleep again.

Vicki smiled and kissed his eyelids. "I love you too."

She stayed beside him until the threat of sunrise drove her away.

"Irene Macdonald."

Vicki lay in the darkness and stared unseeing up at the plywood. The sun was down and she was free to leave her sanctuary but she remained a moment longer, turning over the name that had been on her tongue when she woke. She remembered facetiously wondering if the deaths of Irene Macdonald and her pimp were connected.

Irene had been found beaten nearly to death in the bathroom of her apartment. She'd died two hours later in the hospital.

Celluci said that he was personally certain Mac Eisler was responsible. That was good enough for Vicki.

Eisler could've been unlucky enough to run into a vampire who fed on terror as well as blood—Vicki had tasted terror once or twice during her first year when the Hunger occasionally slipped from her control and she knew how addictive it could be—or he could've been killed in revenge for Irene.

Vicki could think of one sure way to find out.

"Brandon? It's Vicki Nelson."

"Victoria?" Surprise lifted most of the Oxford accent off Dr. Brandon Singh's voice. "I thought you'd relocated to British Columbia."

"Yeah, well, I came back."

"I suppose that might account for the improvement over the last month or so in a certain detective we both know."

She couldn't resist asking. "Was he really bad while I was gone?"

Brandon laughed. "He was unbearable and, as you know, I am able to bear a great deal. So, are you still in the same line of work?"

"Yes, I am." Yes, she was. God, it felt good. "Are you still the Assistant Coroner?"

"Yes, I am. As I think I can safely assume you didn't call me, at home, long after office hours, just to inform me that you're back on the job, what do you want?"

Vicki winced. "I was wondering if you'd had a look at Mac Eisler."

"Yes, Victoria, I have. And I'm wondering why you can't call me during regular business hours. You must know how much I enjoy discussing autopsies in front of my children."

"Oh God, I'm sorry Brandon, but it's important."

"Yes. It always is." His tone was so dry it crumbled. "But since you've already interrupted my evening, try to keep my part of the conversation to a simple yes or no."

"Did you do a blood volume check on Eisler?"

"Yes."

"Was there any missing?"

"No. Fortunately, in spite of the trauma to the neck the integrity of the blood vessels had not been breached."

So much for yes or no; she knew he couldn't keep to it. "You've been a big help, Brandon, thanks."

"I'd say any time, but you'd likely hold me to it." He hung up abruptly.

Vicki replaced the receiver and frowned. She—the other—hadn't fed. The odds moved in favor of Eisler killed because he murdered Irene.

"Well, if it isn't Andrew P." Vicki leaned back against the black Trans Am and adjusted the pair of nonprescription glasses she'd picked up just after sunset. With her hair brushed off her face and the window-glass lenses in front of her eyes, she didn't look much different than she had a year ago. Until she smiled.

The pimp stopped dead in his tracks, bluster fading before he could get the first obscenity out. He swallowed, audibly. "Nelson. I heard you were gone."

Listening to his heart race, Vicki's smile broadened. "I came back. I need some information. I need the name of one of Eisler's other girls."

"I don't know." Unable to look away, he started to shake. "I didn't have anything to do with him. I don't remember."

Vicki straightened and took a slow step towards him. "Try, Andrew."

There was a sudden smell of urine and a darkening stain down the front of the pimp's cotton drawstring pants. "Uh, D...D...Debbie Ho. That's all I can remember. Really."

"And she works?"

"Middle of the track." His tongue tripped over the words in the rush to spit them at her. "Jarvis and Carlton."

"Thank you." Sweeping a hand towards his car, Vicki stepped aside.

He dove past her and into the driver's seat, jabbing the key into the ignition. The powerful engine roared to life and with one last panicked look into the shadows, he screamed out of the driveway, ground his way through three gear changes, and hit eighty before he reached the corner.

The two cops, quietly sitting in the parking lot of the donut shop on that same corner, hit their siren and took off after him.

Vicki slipped the glasses into the inner pocket of the tweed jacket she'd borrowed from Celluci's closet and grinned. "To paraphrase a certain adolescent crime-fighting amphibian, I love being a vampire."

"I need to talk to you, Debbie."

The young woman started and whirled around, glaring suspiciously at Vicki. "You a cop?"

Vicki sighed. "Not any more." Apparently, it was easier to hide the vampire than the detective. "I'm a private investigator and I want to ask you some questions about Irene Macdonald."

"If you're looking for the shithead who killed her, you're too late. Someone already found him."

"And that's who I'm looking for."

"Why?" Debbie shifted her weight to one hip.

"Maybe I want to give them a medal."

The hooker's laugh held little humor. "You got that right. Mac got everything he deserved."

"Did Irene ever do women?"

Debbie snorted. "Not for free," she said pointedly.

Vicki handed her a twenty.

"Yeah, sometimes. It's safer, medically, you know?"

Editing out Phil's more ornate phrases, Vicki repeated his description of the woman in the alley.

Debbie snorted again. "Who the hell looks at their faces?"

"You'd remember this one if you saw her. She's . . ." Vicki weighed and discarded several possibilities and finally settled on, ". . . powerful."

"Powerful." Debbie hesitated, frowned, and continued in a rush. "There was this person Irene was seeing a lot but she wasn't charging. That's one of the things that set Mac off, not that the shithead needed much encouragement. We knew it was gonna happen, I mean we've all felt Mac's temper, but Irene wouldn't stop. She said that just being with this person was a high better than drugs. I guess it could've been a woman. And since she was sort of the reason Irene died, well, I know they used to meet in this bar on Queen West. Why are you hissing?"

"Hissing?" Vicki quickly yanked a mask of composure down over her rage. The other hadn't come into her territory only to kill Eisler—she was definitely hunting it. "I'm not hissing. I'm just having a little trouble breathing."

"Yeah, tell me about it." Debbie waved a hand ending in three-inch scarlet nails at the traffic on Jarvis. "You should try standing here sucking carbon monoxide all night."

In another mood, Vicki might have reapplied the verb to a different object but she was still too angry. "Do you know which bar?"

"What, now I'm her social director? No, I don't know which bar." Apparently they'd come to the end of the information twenty dollars could buy as Debbie turned her attention to a prospective client in a grey sedan. The interview was clearly over.

Vicki sucked the humid air past her teeth. There weren't that many bars on Queen West. Last night she'd found Phil in one. Tonight; who knew.

Now that she knew enough to search for it, minute traces of the other predator hung in the air—diffused and scattered by the paths of prey. With so many lives masking the trail, it would be impossible to track her. Vicki snarled. A pair of teenagers, noses pierced, heads shaved, and Doc Martens laced to the knee, decided against asking for change and hastily crossed the street.

It was Saturday night, minutes to Sunday. The bars would be closing soon. If the other was hunting, she would have already chosen her prey.

I wish Henry had called back. Maybe over the centuries they've— we've—evolved ways to deal with this. Maybe we're supposed to talk first. Maybe it's considered bad manners to rip her face off and feed it to her if she doesn't agree to leave.

Standing in the shadow of a recessed storefront, just beyond the edge of the artificial safety the streetlight offered to the children of the sun, she extended her senses the way she'd been taught and touched death within the maelstrom of life.

She found Phil, moments later, lying in yet another of the alleys that serviced the business of the day and provided a safe haven for the darker business of the night. His body was still warm but his heart had stopped beating and his blood no longer sang. Vicki touched the tiny, nearly closed wound she'd made in his wrist the night before and then the fresh wound in the bend of his elbow. She didn't know how he had died but she knew who had done it. He stank of the other.

Vicki no longer cared what was traditionally "done" in these instances. There would be no talking. No negotiating. It had gone one life beyond that.

"I rather thought that if I killed him you'd come and save me the trouble of tracking you down. And here you are, charging in without taking the slightest of precautions." Her voice was low, not so much threatening as in itself a threat. "You're hunting in my territory, child."

Still kneeling by Phil's side, Vicki lifted her head. Ten feet away, only her face and hands clearly visible, the other vampire stood. Without thinking—unable to think clearly through the red rage that shrieked for release—Vicki launched herself at the snow-white column of throat, finger hooked to talons, teeth bared.

The Beast Henry had spent a year teaching her to control, was loose. She felt herself lost in its raw power and she reveled in it.

The other made no move until the last possible second then she lithely twisted and slammed Vicki to one side.

Pain eventually brought reason back. Vicki lay panting in the fetid damp at the base of a dumpster, one eye swollen shut, a gash across her forehead still sluggishly bleeding. Her right arm was broken.

"You're strong," the other told her, a contemptuous gaze pinning her to the ground. "In another hundred years you might have stood a chance. But you're an infant. A child. You haven't the experience to control what you are. This will be your only warning. Get out of my territory. If we meet again, I will kill you."

Vicki sagged against the inside of the door and tried to lift her arm. During the two and a half hours it had taken her to get back to Celluci's house, the bone had begun to set. By tomorrow night, provided she fed in the hours remaining until dawn, she should be able use it.

"Vicki?"

She started. Although she'd known he was home, she'd assumed—without checking—that because of the hour he'd be asleep. She squinted as the hall light came on and wondered, listening to him pad down the stairs in bare feet, whether she had the energy to make it into the basement bathroom before he saw her.

He came into the kitchen, tying his bathrobe belt around him, and flicked on the overhead light. "We need to talk," he said grimly as the shadows that might have hidden her fled. "Jesus H. Christ. What the hell happened to you?"

"Nothing much." Eyes squinted nearly shut, Vicki gingerly probed the swelling on her forehead. "You should see the other guy."

Without speaking, Celluci reached over and hit the play button on the telephone answering machine.

"Vicki? Henry. If someone's hunting your territory, whatever you do, don't challenge. Do you hear me? Don't challenge. You can't win. They're going to be older, able to overcome the instinctive rage and remain in full command of their power. If you won't surrender the territory . . ." The sigh the tape played back gave a clear opinion of how likely he thought that was to occur. ". . . you're going to have to negotiate. If you can agree on boundaries there's no reason why you can't share the city." His voice suddenly belonged again to the lover she'd lost with the change. "Call me, please, before you do anything."

It was the only message on the tape.

"Why," Celluci asked as it rewound, his gaze taking in the cuts and the bruising and the filth, "do I get the impression that it's 'the other guy' Fitzroy's talking about?"

Vicki tried to shrug. Her shoulders refused to cooperate. "It's my city, Mike. It always has been. I'm going to take it back."

He stared at her for a long moment then he shook his head. "You heard what Henry said. You can't win. You haven't been . . . what you are, long enough. It's only been fourteen months."

"I know." The rich scent of his life prodded the Hunger and she moved to put a little distance between them.

He closed it up again. "Come on." Laying his hand in the center of her back, he steered her towards the stairs. Put it aside for now, his tone told her. We'll argue about it later. "You need a bath."

"I need . . ."

"I know. But you need a bath first. I just changed the sheets."

✳   ✳   ✳

The darkness wakes us all in different ways, Henry had told her. We were all human once and we carried our differences through the change.

For Vicki, it was like the flicking of a switch; one moment she wasn't, the next she was. This time, when she returned from the little death of the day, an idea returned with her.

Four hundred and fifty-odd years a vampire, Henry had been seventeen when he changed. The other had walked the night for perhaps as long—her gaze had carried the weight of several lifetimes—but her physical appearance suggested that her mortal life had lasted even less time than Henry's had. Vicki allowed that it made sense. Disaster may have precipitated her change but passion was the usual cause.

And no one does that kind of never-say-die passion like a teenager.

It would be difficult for either Henry or the other to imagine a response that came out of a mortal not a vampiric experience. They'd both had centuries of the latter and not enough of the former to count.

Vicki had been only fourteen months a vampire but she'd been human thirty-two years when Henry'd saved her by drawing her to his blood to feed. During those thirty-two years, she'd been nine years a cop—two accelerated promotions, three citations, and the best arrest record on the force.

There was no chance of negotiation.

She couldn't win if she fought.

She'd be damned if she'd flee.

"Besides . . ." For all she realized where her strength had to lie, Vicki's expression held no humanity. ". . . she owes me for Phil."

Celluci had left her a note on the fridge.

Does this have anything to do with Mac Eisler?

Vicki stared at it for a moment then scribbled her answer underneath.

Not anymore.

It took three weeks to find where the other spent her days. Vicki used old contacts where she could and made new ones where she had to. Any modern Van Helsing could have done the same.

For the next three weeks, Vicki hired someone to watch the

other come and go, giving reinforced instructions to stay in the car with the windows closed and the air conditioning running. Life had an infinite number of variations but one piece of machinery smelled pretty much like any other. It irritated her that she couldn't sit stakeout herself but the information she needed would've kept her out after sunrise.

"How the hell did you burn your hand?"

Vicki continued to smear ointment over the blister. Unlike the injuries she'd taken in the alley, this would heal slowly and painfully. "Accident in a tanning salon."

"That's not funny."

She picked the roll of gauze up off the counter. "You're losing your sense of humor, Mike."

Celluci snorted and handed her the scissors. "I never had one."

"Mike, I wanted to warn you, I won't be back by sunrise."

Celluci turned slowly, the TV dinner he'd just taken from the microwave held in both hands. "What do you mean?"

She read the fear in his voice and lifted the edge of the tray so that the gravy didn't pour out and over his shoes. "I mean I'll be spending the day somewhere else."

"Where?"

"I can't tell you."

"Why? Never mind." He raised a hand as her eyes narrowed. "Don't tell me. I don't want to know. You're going after that other vampire, aren't you? The one Fitzroy told you to leave alone."

"I thought you didn't want to know."

"I already know," he grunted. "I can read you like a book. With large type. And pictures."

Vicki pulled the tray from his grip and set it on the counter. "She's killed two people. Eisler was a scumbag who may have deserved it but the other . . ."

"Other?" Celluci exploded. "Jesus H. Christ, Vicki, in case you've forgotten, murder's against the law! Who the hell painted a big vee on your long johns and made you the vampire vigilante?"

"Don't you remember?" Vicki snapped. "You were there. I didn't make this decision, Mike. You and Henry made it for me. You'd just better learn to live with it." She fought her way back to calm. "Look, you can't stop her but I can. I know that galls but that's the way it is."

They glared at each other, toe to toe. Finally Celluci looked away.

"I can't stop you, can I?" he asked bitterly. "I'm only human after all."

"Don't sell yourself short," Vicki snarled. "You're quintessentially human. If you want to stop me, you face me and ask me not to go and then you remember it every time you go into a situation that could get your ass shot off."

After a long moment, he swallowed, lifted his head, and met her eyes. "Don't die. I thought I lost you once and I'm not strong enough to go through that again."

"Are you asking me not to go?"

He snorted. "I'm asking you to be careful. Not that you ever listen."

She took a step forward and rested her head against his shoulder, wrapping herself in the beating of his heart. "This time, I'm listening."

The studios in the converted warehouse on King Street were not supposed to be live-in. A good seventy-five percent of the tenants ignored that. The studio Vicki wanted was at the back on the third floor. The heavy steel door—an obvious upgrade by the occupant—had been secured by the best lock money could buy.

New senses and old skills got through it in record time.

Vicki pushed open the door with her foot and began carrying boxes inside. She had a lot to do before dawn.

"She goes out every night between ten and eleven, then she comes home every morning between four and five. You could set your watch by her."

Vicki handed him an envelope.

He looked inside, thumbed through the money, then grinned up at her. "Pleasure doing business for you. Any time you need my services, you know where to call."

"Forget it," she told him.

And he did.

✶   ✶   ✶

Because she expected her, Vicki knew the moment the other entered the building. The Beast stirred and she tightened her grip on it. To lose control now would be disaster.

She heard the elevator, then footsteps in the hall.

"You know I'm in here," she said silently, "and you know you can take me. Be overconfident, believe I'm a fool and walk right in."

"I thought you were smarter than this." The other stepped into the apartment then casually turned to lock the door. "I told you when I saw you again I'd kill you."

Vicki shrugged, the motion masking her fight to remain calm. "Don't you even want to know why I'm here?"

"I assume, you've come to negotiate." She raised ivory hands and released thick, black hair from its bindings. "We went past that when you attacked me." Crossing the room, she preened before a large ornate mirror that dominated one wall of the studio.

"I attacked you because you murdered Phil."

"Was that his name?" The other laughed. The sound had razored edges. "I didn't bother to ask it."

"Before you murdered him."

"Murdered? You are a child. They are prey, we are predators— their deaths are ours if we desire them. You'd have learned that in time." She turned, the patina of civilization stripped away. "Too bad you haven't any time left."

Vicki snarled but somehow managed to stop herself from attacking. Years of training whispered, *Not yet*. She had to stay exactly where she was.

"Oh yes." The sibilants flayed the air between them. "I almost forgot. You wanted me to ask you why you came. Very well. Why?"

Given the address and the reason, Celluci could've come to the studio during the day and slammed a stake through the other's heart. The vampire's strongest protection, would be of no use against him. Mike Celluci believed in vampires.

"I came," Vicki told her, "because some things you have to do yourself."

The wire ran up the wall, tucked beside the surface-mounted cable of a cheap renovation, and disappeared into the shadows that clung to a ceiling sixteen feet from the floor. The switch had been stapled down beside her foot. A tiny motion, too small to evoke attack, flipped it.

Vicki had realized from the beginning that there were a number of problems with her plan. The first involved placement. Every living space included an area where the occupant felt secure—a favorite chair, a window . . . a mirror. The second problem was how to mask what she'd done. While the other would not be able to sense the various bits of wiring and equipment, she'd be fully aware of Vicki's scent on the wiring and equipment. Only if Vicki remained in the studio, could that smaller trace be lost in the larger.

The third problem was directly connected with the second. Given that Vicki had to remain, how was she to survive?

Attached to the ceiling by sheer brute strength, positioned so that they shone directly down into the space in front of the mirror, were a double bank of lights cannibalized from a tanning bed. The sun held a double menace for the vampire—its return to the sky brought complete vulnerability and its rays burned.

Henry had a round scar on the back of one hand from too close an encounter with the sun. When her burn healed, Vicki would have a matching one from a deliberate encounter with an imitation.

The other screamed as the lights came on, the sound pure rage and so inhuman that those who heard it would have to deny it for sanity's sake.

Vicki dove forward, ripped the heavy brocade off the back of the couch, and burrowed frantically into its depths. Even that instant of light had bathed her skin in flame and she moaned as for a moment the searing pain became all she was. After a time, when it grew no worse, she managed to open her eyes.

The light couldn't reach her, but neither could she reach the switch to turn it off. She could see it, three feet away, just beyond the shadow of the couch. She shifted her weight and a line of blister rose across one leg. Biting back a shriek, she curled into a fetal position, realizing her refuge was not entirely secure.

Okay, genius, now what?

Moving very, very carefully, Vicki wrapped her hand around the one-by-two that braced the lower edge of the couch. From the tension running along it, she suspected that breaking it off would result in at least a partial collapse of the piece of furniture.

And if it goes, I very well may go with it.

And then she heard the sound of something dragging itself across the floor.

Oh shit! She's not dead!

The wood broke, the couch began to fall in on itself, and Vicki, realizing that luck would have a large part to play in her survival, smacked the switch and rolled clear in the same motion.

The room plunged into darkness.

Vicki froze as her eyes slowly readjusted to the night. Which was when she finally became conscious of the smell. It had been there all along but her senses had refused to acknowledge it until they had to.

Sunlight burned.

Vicki gagged.

The dragging sound continued.

The hell with this! She didn't have time to wait for her eyes to repair the damage they'd obviously taken. She needed to see now. Fortunately, although it hadn't seemed fortunate at the time, she'd learned to maneuver without sight.

She threw herself across the room.

The light switch was where they always were, to the right of the door.

The thing on the floor pushed itself up on fingerless hands and glared at her out of the blackened ruin of a face. Laboriously it turned, hate radiating off it in palpable waves and began to pull itself towards her again.

Vicki stepped forward to meet it.

While the part of her that remembered being human writhed in revulsion, she wrapped her hands around its skull and twisted it in a full circle. The spine snapped. Another full twist and what was left of the head came off in her hands.

She'd been human for thirty-two years but she'd been fourteen months a vampire.

"No one hunts in my territory," she snarled as the other crumbled to dust.

She limped over to the wall and pulled the plug supplying power to the lights. Later, she'd remove them completely—the whole concept of sunlamps gave her the creeps.

When she turned, she was facing the mirror.

The woman who stared out at her through bloodshot eyes, exposed skin blistered and red, was a hunter. Always had been really. The question became, who was she to hunt?

Vicki smiled. Before the sun drove her to use her inherited sanctuary, she had a few quick phone calls to make. The first to Celluci; she owed him the knowledge that she'd survived the night. The second to Henry for much the same reason.

The third call would be to the 800 line that covered the classifieds of Toronto's largest alternative newspaper. This ad was going to be a little different than the one she'd placed upon leaving the force. Back then, she'd been incredibly depressed about leaving a job she loved for a life she saw as only marginally useful. This time, she had no regrets.

Victory Nelson, Investigator: Otherwordly Crimes a Specialty.

The Case of the
Four and Twenty Blackbirds

➤ NEIL GAIMAN ◄

I SAT IN MY OFFICE, NURSING A GLASS OF HOOCH AND IDLY
cleaning my automatic. Outside the rain fell steadily, like it seems
to do most of the time in our fair city, whatever the tourist
board says. Hell, I didn't care. I'm not on the tourist board. I'm
a private dick, and one of the best, although you wouldn't have
known it; the office was crumbling, the rent was unpaid and the
hooch was my last.

Things are tough all over.

To cap it all the only client I'd had all week never showed up
on the street corner where I'd waited for him. He said it was
going to be a big job, but now I'd never know: he kept a prior
appointment in the morgue.

So when the dame walked into my office I was sure my luck
had changed for the better.

"What are you selling, lady?"

She gave me a look that would have induced heavy breathing
in a pumpkin, and which shot my heartbeat up to three figures.
She had long blonde hair and a figure that would have made
Thomas Aquinas forget his vows. I forgot all mine about never
taking cases from dames.

"What would you say to some of the green stuff?" she asked,
in a husky voice, getting straight to the point.

75

"Continue, sister." I didn't want her to know how bad I needed the dough, so I held my hand in front of my mouth; it doesn't help if a client sees you salivate.

She opened her purse and flipped out a photograph. Glossy eight by ten. "Do you recognize that man?"

In my business you know who people are. "Yeah."

"He's dead."

"I know that too, sweetheart. It's old news. It was an accident."

Her gaze went so icy you could have chipped it into cubes and cooled a cocktail with it. "My brother's death was no accident."

I raised an eyebrow—you need a lot of arcane skills in my business—and said "Your brother, eh?" Funny, she hadn't struck me as the type that had brothers.

"I'm Jill Dumpty."

"So your brother was Humpty Dumpty?"

"And he didn't fall off that wall, Mr. Horner. He was pushed."

Interesting, if true. Dumpty had his finger in most of the crooked pies in town; I could think of five guys who would have preferred to see him dead than alive without trying.

Without trying too hard, anyway.

"You seen the cops about this?"

"Nah. The King's Men aren't interested in anything to do with his death. They say they did all they could do in trying to put him together again after the fall."

I leaned back in my chair.

"So what's it to you. Why do you need me?"

"I want you to find the killer, Mr. Horner. I want him brought to justice. I want him to fry like an egg. Oh—and one other little thing," she added, lightly. "Before he died Humpty had a small manila envelope full of photographs he was meant to be sending me. Medical photos. I'm a trainee nurse, and I need them to pass my finals."

I inspected my nails, then looked up at her face, taking in a handful of waist and Easter-egg bazonkas on the way up. She was a looker, although her cute nose was a little on the shiny side. "I'll take the case. Seventy-five a day and two hundred bonus for results."

She smiled; my stomach twisted around once and went into orbit. "You get another two hundred if you get me those photographs. I want to be a nurse real bad." Then she dropped three fifties on my desktop.

I let a devil-may-care grin play across my rugged face. "Say, sister, how about letting me take you out for dinner? I just came into some money."

She gave an involuntary shiver of anticipation and muttered something about having a thing about midgets, so I knew I was onto a good thing. Then she gave me a lopsided smile that would have made Albert Einstein drop a decimal point. "First find my brother's killer, Mr. Horner. And my photographs. Then we can play."

She closed the door behind her. Maybe it was still raining but I didn't notice. I didn't care.

There are parts of town the tourist board don't mention. Parts of town where the police travel in threes if they travel at all. In my line of work you get to visit them more than is healthy. Healthy is never.

He was waiting for me outside Luigi's. I slid up behind him, my rubber-soled shoes soundless on the shiny wet sidewalk.

"Hiya, Cock."

He jumped and spun around; I found myself gazing up into the muzzle of a .45. "Oh, Horner." He put the gun away. "Don't call me Cock. I'm Bernie Robin to you, Short-stuff, and don't you forget it."

"Cock Robin is good enough for me, Cock. Who killed Humpty Dumpty?"

He was a strange-looking bird, but you can't be choosy in my profession. He was the best underworld lead I had.

"Let's see the color of your money."

I showed him a fifty.

"Hell," he muttered. "It's green. Why can't they make puce or mauve money for a change?" He took it though. "All I know is that the Fat Man had his finger in a lot of pies."

"So?"

"One of those pies had four and twenty blackbirds in it."

"Huh?"

"Do I hafta spell it out for you? I . . . Ughh . . ." He crumpled to the sidewalk, an arrow protruding from his back. Cock Robin wasn't going to be doing any more chirping.

Sergeant O'Grady looked down at the body, then he looked down at me. "Faith and begorrah, to be sure," he said. "If it isn't Little Jack Horner himself."

"I didn't kill Cock Robin, Sarge."

"And I suppose that the call we got down at the station telling us you were going to be rubbing the late Mr. Robin out. Here. Tonight. Was just a hoax?"

"If I'm the killer, where are my arrows?" I thumbed open a pack of gum and started to chew. "It's a frame."

He puffed on his meerschaum and then put it away, and idly played a couple of phrases of the *William Tell* Overture on his oboe. "Maybe. Maybe not. But you're still a suspect. Don't leave town. And Horner . . ."

"Yeah?"

"Dumpty's death was an accident. That's what the coroner said. That's what I say. Drop the case."

I thought about it. Then I thought of the money, and the girl. "No dice, Sarge."

He shrugged. "It's your funeral." He said it like it probably would be.

I had a funny feeling like he could be right.

"You're out of your depth, Horner. You're playing with the big boys. And it ain't healthy."

From what I could remember of my school days he was correct. Whenever I played with the big boys I always wound up having the stuffing beaten out of me. But how did O'Grady—how could O'Grady have known that? Then I remembered something else.

O'Grady was the one that used to beat me up the most.

It was time for what we in the profession call "legwork." I made a few discreet enquiries around town, but found out nothing about Dumpty that I didn't know already.

Humpty Dumpty was a bad egg. I remembered him when he was new in town, a smart young animal trainer with a nice line in training mice to run up clocks. He went to the bad pretty fast though; gambling, drink, women, it's the same story all over. A bright young kid thinks that the streets of Nurseryland are paved with gold, and by the time he finds out otherwise it's much too late.

Dumpty started off with extortions and robbery on a small scale—he trained up a team of spiders to scare little girls away from their curds and whey, which he'd pick up and sell on the black market. Then he moved onto blackmail—the nastiest game. We crossed paths once, when I was hired by this young society kid—let's call him Georgie Porgie—to recover some compromising snaps of him kissing the girls and making them cry. I got the snaps, but I learned it wasn't healthy to mess with the Fat Man. And I don't make the same mistakes twice. Hell, in my line of work I can't afford to make the same mistakes once.

It's a tough world out there. I remember when Little Bo Peep first came to town . . . but you don't want to hear my troubles. If you're not dead yet, you've got troubles of your own.

I checked out the newspaper files on Dumpty's death. One minute he was sitting on a wall, the next he was in pieces at the bottom. All the King's Horses and all the King's Men were on the scene in minutes, but he needed more than first aid. A medic named Foster was called—a friend of Dumpty's from his Gloucester days—although I don't know of anything a doc can do when you're dead.

Hang on a second—Dr. Foster!

I got that old feeling you get in my line of work. Two little brain cells rub together the right way and in seconds you've got a 24-carat cerebral fire on your hands.

You remember the client who didn't show—the one I'd waited for all day on the street corner? An accidental death. I hadn't bothered to check it out—I can't afford to waste time on clients who aren't going to pay for it.

Three deaths, it seemed. Not one.

I reached for the telephone and rang the police station. "This is Horner," I told the desk man. "Lemme speak to Sergeant O'Grady."

There was a crackling and he came on the line. "O'Grady speaking."

"It's Horner."

"Hi, Little Jack." That was just like O'Grady. He'd been kidding me about my size since we were kids together. "You finally figured out that Dumpty's death was accidental?"

"Nope. I'm now investigating three deaths. The Fat Man's, Bernie Robin's and Dr. Foster's."

"Foster the plastic surgeon? His death was an accident."

"Sure. And your mother was married to your father."

There was a pause. "Horner, if you phoned me up just to talk dirty, I'm not amused."

"Okay, wise guy. If Humpty Dumpty's death was an accident and so was Dr. Foster's, tell me just one thing: Who killed Cock Robin?"

I don't ever get accused of having too much imagination, but there's one thing I'd swear to. I could hear him grinning over the phone as he said: "You did, Horner. And I'm staking my badge on it."

The line went dead.

My office was cold and lonely, so I wandered down to Joe's Bar for some companionship and a drink or three.

Four and twenty blackbirds. A dead doctor. The Fat Man. Cock Robin . . . Heck, this case had more holes in it than a Swiss cheese and more loose ends than a torn string vest. And where did the juicy Miss Dumpty come into it? Jack and Jill—we'd make a great team. When this was all over perhaps we could go off together to Louie's little place on the hill, where no one's interested in whether you got a marriage license or not. The Pail of Water, that was the name of the joint.

I called over the bartender. "Hey. Joe."

"Yeah, Mr. Horner?" He was polishing a glass with a rag that had seen better days as a shirt.

"Did you ever meet the Fat Man's sister?"

He scratched at his cheek. "Can't say as I did. His sister . . . huh? Hey—the Fat Man didn't have a sister."

"You sure of that?"

"Sure I'm sure. It was the day my sister had her first kid—I told the Fat Man I was an uncle. He gave me this look and says, 'Ain't no way I'll ever be an uncle, Joe. Got no sisters or brother, nor no other kinfolk neither.'"

If the mysterious Miss Dumpty wasn't his sister, who was she?

"Tell me, Joe. Didja ever see him in here with a dame—about so high, shaped like this?" My hands described a couple of parabolas. "Looks like a blonde love goddess."

He shook his head. "Never saw him with any dames. Recently he was hanging around with some medical guy, but the only thing he ever cared about was those crazy birds and animals of his."

I took a swig of my drink. It nearly took the roof of my mouth off. "Animals? I thought he'd given all that up."

"Naw—couple weeks back he was in here with a whole bunch of blackbirds he was training to sing 'Wasn't that a dainty dish to set before Mmm Mmm.'"

"Mmm Mmm?"

"Yeah. I got no idea who."

I put my drink down. A little of it spilt on the counter, and I watched it strip the paint. "Thanks, Joe. You've been a big help." I handed him a ten-dollar bill. "For information received," I said, adding, "Don't spend it all at once."

In my profession it's making little jokes like that that keeps you sane.

I had one contact left. Ma Hubbard. I found a payphone and called her number.

"Old Mother Hubbard's Cupboard—Cake Shop and licensed Soup Kitchen."

"It's Horner, Ma."

"Jack? It ain't safe for me to talk to you."

"For old time's sake, sweetheart. You owe me a favor." Some two-bit crooks had once knocked off the Cupboard, leaving it bare. I'd tracked them down and returned the cakes and soup.

". . . Okay. But I don't like it."

"You know everything that goes on around here on the food front, Ma. What's the significance of a pie with four and twenty trained blackbirds in it?" She whistled, long and low. "You really don't know?"

"I wouldn't be asking you if I did."

"You should read the Court pages of the papers next time, sugar. Jeez. You are out of your depth."

"C'mon, Ma. Spill it."

"It so happens that that particular dish was set before the King a few weeks back . . . Jack? Are you still there?"

"I'm still here, ma'am," I said, quietly. "All of a sudden a lot of things are starting to make sense." I put down the phone.

It was beginning to look like Little Jack Horner had pulled out a plum from this pie.

It was raining, steady and cold. I phoned a cab.

Quarter of an hour later one lurched out of the darkness.

"You're late."

"So complain to the tourist board."

I climbed in the back, wound down the window, and lit a cigarette.

And I went to see the Queen.

✳   ✳   ✳

The door to the private part of the palace was locked. It's the part that the public don't get to see. But I've never been public, and the little lock hardly slowed me up. The door to the private apartments with the big red heart on it was unlocked, so I knocked and walked straight in.

The Queen of Hearts was alone, standing in front of the mirror, holding a plate of jam tarts with one hand, powdering her nose with the other. She turned, saw me, and gasped, dropping the tarts.

"Hey, Queenie," I said. "Or would you feel more comfortable if I called you Jill?"

She was still a good-looking slice of dame, even without the blonde wig.

"Get out of here!" she hissed.

"I don't think so, toots." I sat down on the bed. "Let me spell a few things out for you."

"Go ahead." She reached behind her for a concealed alarm button. I let her press it. I'd cut the wires on my way in—in my profession there's no such thing as being too careful.

"Let me spell a few things out for you."

"You just said that."

"I'll tell this my way, lady."

I lit a cigarette and a thin plume of blue smoke drifted heavenwards, which was where I was going if my hunch was wrong. Still, I've learned to trust hunches.

"Try this on for size, Dumpty—the Fat Man—wasn't your brother. He wasn't even your friend. In fact he was blackmailing you. He knew about your nose."

She turned whiter than a number of corpses I've met in my time in the business. Her hand reached up and cradled her freshly powdered nose.

"You see, I've known the Fat Man for many years, and many years ago he had a lucrative concern in training animals and birds to do certain unsavory things. And that got me to thinking . . . I had a client recently who didn't show, due to his having been stiffed first. Doctor Foster, of Gloucester, the plastic surgeon. The official version of his death was that he'd just sat too close to a fire and melted.

"But just suppose he was killed to stop him telling something that he knew? I put two and two together and hit the jackpot. Let me reconstruct a scene for you: You were out in the garden—probably hanging out some clothes—when along came one of Dumpty's trained pie-blackbirds and pecked off your nose.

"So there you were, standing in the garden, your hand in front of your face, when along comes the Fat Man with an offer you couldn't refuse. He could introduce you to a plastic surgeon who could fix you up with a nose as good as new, for a price. And no one need ever know. Am I right so far?"

She nodded dumbly, then finding her voice, muttered: "Pretty much. But I ran back into the parlor after the attack, to eat some bread and honey. That was where he found me."

"Fair enough." The color was starting to come back into her cheeks now. "So you had the operation from Foster, and no one was going to be any the wiser. Until Dumpty told you that he had photos of the op. You had to get rid of him. A couple of days later you were out walking in the palace grounds. There was Humpty, sitting on a wall, his back to you, gazing out into the distance. In a fit of madness, you pushed. And Humpty Dumpty had a great fall.

"But now you were in big trouble. Nobody suspected you of his murder, but where were the photographs? Foster didn't have them, although he smelled a rat and had to be disposed of—before he could see me. But you didn't know how much he'd told me, and you still didn't have the snapshots, so you took me on to find out. And that was your mistake, sister."

Her lower lip trembled, and my heart quivered. "You won't turn me in, will you?"

"Sister, you tried to frame me this afternoon. I don't take kindly to that."

With a shaking hand she started to unbutton her blouse. "Perhaps we could come to some sort of arrangement?"

I shook my head. "Sorry, your majesty. Mrs. Horner's little boy Jack was always taught to keep his hands off royalty. It's a pity, but that's how it is." To be on the safe side I looked away, which was a mistake. A cute little ladies' pistol was in her hands and pointing at me before you could sing a song of sixpence. The shooter may have been small, but I knew it packed enough of a wallop to take me out of the game permanently.

This dame was lethal.

"Put that gun down, your majesty." Sergeant O'Grady strolled through the bedroom door, his police special clutched in his hamlike fist.

"I'm sorry I suspected you, Horner," he said drily. "You're lucky I did, though, sure and begorrah. I had you trailed here and I overheard the whole thing."

"Hi, Sarge, thanks for stopping by. But I hadn't finished my explanation. If you'll take a seat I'll wrap it up."

He nodded brusquely, and sat down near the door. His gun hardly moved.

I got up from the bed and walked over to the Queen. "You see, Toots, what I didn't tell you was who did have the snaps of your nose job. Humpty did, when you killed him."

A charming frown crinkled her perfect brow. "I don't understand . . . I had the body searched."

"Sure, afterwards. But the first people to get to the Fat Man were the King's Men. The cops. And one of them pocketed the envelope. When any fuss had died down the blackmail would have started again. Only this time you wouldn't have known who to kill. And I owe you an apology." I bent down to tie my shoelaces.

"Why?"

"I accused you of trying to frame me this afternoon. You didn't. That arrow was the property of a boy who was the best archer in my school—I should have recognized that distinctive fletching anywhere. Isn't that right," I said, turning back to the door, ". . . 'Sparrow' O'Grady?"

Under the guise of tying up my shoelaces I had already palmed a couple of the Queen's jam tarts, and, flinging one of them upwards, I neatly smashed the room's only light bulb.

It only delayed the shooting a few seconds, but a few seconds was all I needed, and as the Queen of Hearts and Sergeant "Sparrow" O'Grady cheerfully shot each other to bits, I split.

In my business, you have to look after number one.

Munching on a jam tart I walked out of the palace grounds and into the street. I paused by a trash can, to try to burn the manilla envelope of photographs I had pulled from O'Grady's pocket as I walked past him, but it was raining so hard they wouldn't catch.

When I got back to my office I phoned the tourist board to complain. They said the rain was good for the farmers, and I told them what they could do with it.

They said that things are tough all over.

And I said. Yeah.

The Whistling Room

> **WILLIAM HOPE HODGSON** <

CARNACKI SHOOK A FRIENDLY FIST AT ME, AS I ENTERED, LATE. Then, he opened the door into the dining room, and ushered the four of us—Jessop, Arkright, Taylor and myself—in to dinner.

We dined well, as usual, and, equally as usual, Carnacki was pretty silent during the meal. At the end, we took our wine and cigars to our usual positions, and Carnacki—having got himself comfortable in his big chair—began without any preliminary:

"I have just got back from Ireland, again," he said. "And I thought you chaps would be interested to hear my news. Besides, I fancy I shall see the thing clearer, after I have told it all out straight. I must tell you this, though, at the beginning—up to the present moment, I have been utterly and completely 'stumped.' I have tumbled upon one of the most peculiar cases of 'haunting'—or devilment of some sort—that I have come against. Now listen.

"I have been spending the last few weeks at Iastrae Castle, about twenty miles northeast of Galway. I got a letter about a month ago from a Mr. Sid K. Tassoc, who it seemed had bought the place lately, and moved in, only to find that he had bought a very peculiar piece of property.

"When I got there, he met me at the station, driving a jaunting-car, and drove me up to the castle, which, by the way, he called a 'house-shanty.' I found that he was 'pigging it' there with his boy brother and another American, who seemed to be half-servant and half-companion. It seems that all the servants had left the place, in a body, as you might say; and now they were managing among themselves, assisted by some day-help.

"The three of them got together a scratch feed, and Tassoc told me all about the trouble, whilst we were at table. It is most extraordinary, and different from anything that I have had to do with; though that Buzzing Case was very queer, too.

"Tassoc began right in the middle of his story. 'We've got a room in this shanty,' he said, 'which has got a most infernal whistling in it; sort of haunting it. The thing starts any time; you never know when, and it goes on until it frightens you. All the servants have gone, as you know. It's not ordinary whistling, and it isn't the wind. Wait till you hear it.'

"'We're all carrying guns,' said the boy, and slapped his coat pocket.

"'As bad as that?' I said; and the older boy nodded. 'It may be soft,' he replied; 'but wait till you've heard it. Sometimes I think it's some infernal thing, and the next moment, I'm just as sure that someone's playing a trick on me.'

"'Why?' I asked. 'What is to be gained?'

"'You mean,' he said, 'that people usually have some good reason for playing tricks as elaborate as this. Well, I'll tell you. There's a lady in this province, by the name of Miss Donnehue, who's going to be my wife, this day two months. She's more beautiful than they make them, and so far as I can see, I've just stuck my head into an Irish hornet's nest. There's about a score of hot young Irishmen been courting her these two years gone, and now that I'm come along and cut them out, they feel raw against me. Do you begin to understand the possibilities?'

"'Yes,' I said. 'Perhaps I do in a vague sort of way; but I don't see how all this affects the room?'

"'Like this,' he said. 'When I'd fixed it up with Miss Donnehue, I looked out for a place, and bought this little house-shanty. Afterwards, I told her—one evening during dinner—that I'd decided to tie up here. And then she asked me whether I wasn't afraid of the Whistling Room. I told her it must have been thrown in gratis, as I'd heard nothing about it. There were some of her men friends present, and I saw a smile go round. I found out, after a bit of questioning, that several people have bought this place during the last twenty-odd years. And it was always on the market again, after a trial.

"'Well, the chaps started to bait me a bit, and offered to take bets after dinner that I'd not stay six months in the place. I looked once or twice to Miss Donnehue, so as to be sure I was "getting the note" of the talkee-talkee; but I could see that she didn't take it as a joke, at all. Partly, I think, because there was a bit of a sneer in the way the men were tackling me, and partly because she really believes there is something in this yarn of the Whistling Room.

"'However, after dinner, I did what I could to even things up with the others. I nailed all their bets, and screwed them down hard and safe. I guess some of them are going to be hard hit, unless I lose; which I don't mean to. Well, there you have practically the whole yarn.'

"'Not quite,' I told him. 'All that I know, is that you have bought a castle with a room in it that is in some way "queer," and that you've been doing some betting. Also, I know that your servants have got frightened and run away. Tell me something about the whistling?'

"'Oh, that!' said Tassoc. 'That started the second night we were in. I'd had a good look round the room, in the daytime, as you can understand; for the talk up at Arlestrae—Miss Donnehue's place—had made me wonder a bit. But it seems just as usual as some of the other rooms in the old wing, only perhaps a bit more lonesome. But that may be only because of the talk about it, you know.

"'The whistling started about ten o'clock, on the second night, as I said. Tom and I were in the library, when we heard an awfully queer whistling, coming along the East Corridor—The room is in the East Wing, you know.

"'"That's that blessed ghost!" I said to Tom, and we collared the lamps off the table, and went up to have a look. I tell you, even as we dug along the corridor, it took me a bit in the throat, it was so beastly queer. It was a sort of tune, in a way; but more as if a devil or some rotten thing were laughing at you, and going to get round at your back. That's how it makes you feel.

"'When we got to the door, we didn't wait; but rushed it open; and then I tell you the sound of the thing fairly hit me in the face. Tom said he got it the same way—sort of felt stunned and bewildered. We looked all round, and soon got so nervous, we just cleared out, and I locked the door.

"'We came down here, and had a stiff peg each. Then we got fit again, and began to think we'd been nicely had. So we took sticks, and went out into the grounds, thinking after all it must be some of these confounded Irishmen working the ghost-trick on us. But there was not a leg stirring.

"'We went back into the house, and walked over it, and then paid another visit to the room. But we simply couldn't stand it. We fairly ran out, and locked the door again. I don't know how to put it into words; but I had a feeling of being up against something that was rottenly dangerous. You know! We've carried our guns ever since.

"'Of course, we had a real turnout of the room next day, and the whole house-place; and we even hunted round the grounds; but there was nothing queer. And now I don't know what to think; except that the sensible part of me tells me that it's some plan of these Wild Irishmen to try to take a rise out of me.'

"'Done anything since?' I asked him.

"'Yes,' he said, 'watched outside of the door of the room at nights, and chased round the grounds, and sounded the walls and floor of the room. We've done everything we could think of; and it's beginning to get on our nerves; so we sent for you.'

"By this time, we had finished eating. As we rose from the table, Tassoc suddenly called out: 'Ssh! Hark!'

"We were instantly silent, listening. Then I heard it, an extraordinary hooning whistle, monstrous and inhuman, coming from far away through corridors to my right.

"'By G–d!' said Tassoc 'and it's scarcely dark yet! Collar those candles, both of you, and come along.'

"In a few moments, we were all out of the door and racing up the stairs. Tassoc turned into a long corridor, and we followed, shielding our candles as we ran. The sound seemed to fill all the passage as we drew near, until I had the feeling that the whole air throbbed under the power of some wanton Immense Force—a sense of an actual taint, as you might say, of monstrosity all about us.

"Tassoc unlocked the door; then, giving it a push with his foot, jumped back, and drew his revolver. As the door flew open, the sound beat out at us, with an effect impossible to explain to one who has not heard it—with a certain, horrible personal note in it; as if in there in the darkness you could picture the room rocking and creaking in a mad, vile glee to its own filthy piping and whistling and hooning. To stand there and listen, was to be stunned by Realization. It was as if someone showed you the mouth of a vast pit suddenly, and said: That's Hell. And you knew that they had spoken the truth. Do you get it, even a little bit?

"I stepped back a pace into the room, and held the candle over my head, and looked quickly round. Tassoc and his brother joined me, and the man came up at the back, and we all held our candles high. I was deafened with the shrill, piping hoon of the whistling; and then, clear in my ear, something seemed to be saying to me: 'Get out of here—quick! Quick! Quick!'

"As you chaps know, I never neglect that sort of thing. Sometimes it may be nothing but nerves; but as you will remember, it was just such a warning that saved me in the 'Grey Dog' Case, and in the 'Yellow Finger' Experiments; as well as other times. Well, I turned sharp round to the others: 'Out!' I said. 'For God's sake, *out* quick.' And in an instant I had them into the passage.

"There came an extraordinary yelling scream into the hideous whistling, and then, like a clap of thunder, an utter silence. I slammed the door, and locked it. Then, taking the key, I looked round at the others. They were pretty white, and I imagine I must have looked that way too. And there we stood a moment, silent.

"'Come down out of this, and have some whisky,' said Tassoc, at last, in a voice he tried to make ordinary; and he led the way. I was the back man, and I know we all kept looking over our shoulders. When we got downstairs, Tassoc passed the bottle round. He took a drink himself, and slapped his glass down on to the table. Then sat down with a thud.

"'That's a lovely thing to have in the house with you, isn't it!' he said. And directly afterwards: 'What on earth made you hustle us all out like that, Carnacki?'

"'Something seemed to be telling me to get out, quick,' I said. 'Sounds a bit silly-superstitious, I know; but when you are meddling with this sort of thing, you've got to take notice of queer fancies, and risk being laughed at.'

"I told him then about the 'Grey Dog' business, and he nodded a lot to that. 'Of course,' I said, 'this may be nothing more than those would-be rivals of yours playing some funny game; but, personally, though I'm going to keep an open mind, I feel that there is something beastly and dangerous about this thing.'

"We talked for a while longer, and then Tassoc suggested billiards, which we played in a pretty half-hearted fashion, and all the time cocking an ear to the door, as you might say, for sounds; but none came, and later, after coffee, he suggested early bed, and a thorough overhaul of the room on the morrow.

"My bedroom was in the newer part of the castle, and the door opened into the picture gallery. At the east end of the gallery was the entrance to the corridor of the East Wing; this was shut off from the gallery by two old and heavy oak doors, which looked rather odd and quaint beside the more modern doors of the various rooms.

"When I reached my room, I did not go to bed; but began to unpack my instrument trunk, of which I had retained the key. I intended to take one or two preliminary steps at once, in my investigation of the extraordinary whistling.

"Presently, when the castle had settled into quietness, I slipped out of my room, and across to the entrance of the great corridor. I opened one of the low, squat doors, and threw the beam of my pocket searchlight down the passage. It was empty, and I went through the doorway, and pushed-to the oak behind me. Then along the great passageway, throwing my light before and behind, and keeping my revolver handy.

"I had hung a 'protection belt' of garlic round my neck, and the smell of it seemed to fill the corridor and give me assurance; for, as you all know, it is a wonderful 'protection' against the more usual Aeiirii forms of semi-materialization, by which I supposed the whistling might be produced; though, at that period of my investigation, I was quite prepared to find it due to some perfectly natural cause; for it is astonishing the enormous number of cases that prove to have nothing abnormal in them.

"In addition to wearing the necklet, I had plugged my ears loosely with garlic, and as I did not intend to stay more than a few minutes in the room, I hoped to be safe.

"When I reached the door, and put my hand into my pocket for the key, I had a sudden feeling of sickening funk. But I was not going to back out, if I could help it. I unlocked the door and turned the handle. Then I gave the door a sharp push with my foot, as Tassoc had done, and drew my revolver, though I did not expect to have any use for it, really.

"I shone the searchlight all round the room, and then stepped inside, with a disgustingly horrible feeling of walking slap into a waiting Danger. I stood a few seconds, waiting, and nothing happened, and the empty room showed bare from corner to corner. And then, you know, I realized that the room was full of an abominable silence; can you understand that? A sort of purposeful silence, just as sickening as any of the filthy noises the Things have power to make. Do you remember what I told you about that 'Silent Garden' business? Well, this room had just that same *malevolent* silence—the beastly quietness of a thing that is looking at you and not seeable itself, and thinks that it has got you. Oh, I recognized it instantly, and I whipped the top off my lantern, so as to have light over the *whole* room.

"Then I set to, working like fury, and keeping my glance all about me. I sealed the two windows with lengths of human hair, right across, and sealed them at every frame. As I worked, a queer, scarcely perceptible tenseness stole into the air of the place, and the silence seemed, if you can understand me, to grow more solid. I knew then that I had no business there without 'full protection'; for I was practically certain that this was no mere Aeiirii development; but one of the worst forms, as the Saiitii; like that 'Grunting Man' case—you know.

"I finished the window, and hurried over to the great fireplace. This is a huge affair, and has a queer gallows-iron, I think they are called, projecting from the back of the arch. I sealed the opening with seven human hairs—the seventh crossing the six others.

"Then, just as I was making an end, a low, mocking whistle grew in the room. A cold, nervous pricking went up my spine, and round my forehead from the back. The hideous sound filled all the room with an extraordinary, grotesque parody of human whistling, too gigantic to be human—as if something gargantuan and monstrous made the sounds softly. As I stood there a last moment, pressing down the final seal, I had no doubt but that I had come across one of those rare and horrible cases of the *Inanimate* reproducing the functions of the *Animate*. I made a grab for my lamp, and went quickly to the door, looking over my shoulder, and listening for the thing that I expected. It came, just as I got my hand upon the handle—a squeal of incredible, malevolent anger, piercing through the low hooning of the whistling. I dashed out, slamming the door and locking it. I leant a little against the opposite wall of the corridor, feeling rather funny;

for it had been a narrow squeak. . . . 'Theyr be noe sayfetie to be gained bye gayrds of holieness when the monyster hath pow'r to speak throe woode and stoene.' So runs the passage in the Sigsand ms., and I proved it in that 'Nodding Door' business. There is no protection against this particular form of monster, except, possibly, for a fractional period of time; for it can reproduce itself in, or take to its purpose, the very protective material which you may use, and has the power to '*forme* wythine the pentycle'; though not immediately. There is, of course, the possibility of the Unknown Last Line of the Saaamaaa Ritual being uttered; but it is too uncertain to count upon, and the danger is too hideous; and even then it has no power to protect for more than 'maybee fyve beats of the harte,' as the Sigsand has it.

"Inside of the room, there was now a constant, meditative, hooning whistling; but presently this ceased, and the silence seemed worse; for there is such a sense of hidden mischief in a silence.

"After a little, I sealed the door with crossed hairs, and then cleared off down the great passage, and so to bed.

"For a long time I lay awake; but managed eventually to get some sleep. Yet, about two o'clock I was waked by the hooning whistling of the room coming to me, even through the closed doors. The sound was tremendous, and seemed to beat through the whole house with a presiding sense of terror. As if (I remember thinking) some monstrous giant had been holding mad carnival with itself at the end of that great passage.

"I got up and sat on the edge of the bed, wondering whether to go along and have a look at the seal; and suddenly there came a thump on my door, and Tassoc walked in, with his dressing gown over his pajamas.

"'I thought it would have waked you, so I came along to have a talk,' he said. '*I* can't sleep. Beautiful! Isn't it!'

"'Extraordinary!' I said, and tossed him my case.

"He lit a cigarette, and we sat and talked for about an hour; and all the time that noise went on, down at the end of the big corridor.

"Suddenly, Tassoc stood up:

"'Let's take our guns, and go and examine the brute,' he said, and turned towards the door.

"'No!' I said. 'By Jove—*no!* I can't say anything definite, yet; but I believe that room is about as dangerous as it well can be.'

"'Haunted—*really* haunted?' he asked, keenly and without any of his frequent banter.

"I told him, of course, that I could not say a definite *yes* or *no* to such a question; but that I hoped to be able to make a statement, soon. Then I gave him a little lecture on the False Re-Materialization of the Animate-Force through the Inanimate-Inert. He began then to see the particular way in the room might be dangerous, if it were really the subject of a manifestation.

"About an hour later, the whistling ceased quite suddenly, and Tassoc went off again to bed. I went back to mine, also, and eventually got another spell of sleep.

"In the morning, I went along to the room. I found the seals on the door intact. Then I went in. The window seals and the hair were all right; but the seventh hair across the great fireplace was broken. This set me thinking. I knew that it might, very possibly, have snapped, through my having tensioned it too highly; but then, again, it might have been broken by something else. Yet, it was scarcely possible that a man, for instance, could have passed between the six unbroken hairs; for no one would ever have noticed them, entering the room that way, you see; but just walked through them, ignorant of their very existence.

"I removed the other hairs, and the seals. Then I looked up the chimney. It went up straight, and I could see blue sky at the top. It was a big, open flue, and free from any suggestion of hiding places, or corners. Yet, of course, I did not trust to any such casual examination, and after breakfast, I put on my overalls, and climbed to the very top, sounding all the way; but I found nothing.

"Then I came down, and went over the whole of the room—floor, ceiling, and walls, mapping them out in six-inch squares, and sounding with both hammer and probe. But there was nothing abnormal.

"Afterwards, I made a three weeks' search of the whole castle, in the same thorough way; but found nothing. I went even further, then; for at night, when the whistling commenced, I made a microphone test. You see, if the whistling were mechanically produced, this test would have made evident to me the working of the machinery, if there were any such concealed within the walls. It certainly was an up-to-date method of examination, as you must allow.

"Of course, I did not think that any of Tassoc's rivals had fixed up any mechanical contrivance; but I thought it just possible that there had been some such thing for producing the whistling, made away back in the years, perhaps with the intention of giving the room a reputation that would ensure its being free of inquisitive folk. You see what I mean? Well, of course, it was just possible, if this were the case, that someone knew the secret of the machinery, and was utilizing the knowledge to play this devil of a prank on Tassoc. The microphone test of the walls would certainly have made this known to me, as I have said; but there was nothing of the sort in the castle; so that I had practically no doubt at all now, but that it was a genuine case of what is popularly termed 'haunting.'

"All this time, every night, and sometimes most of each night, the hooning whistling of the Room was intolerable. It was as if an intelligence there, knew that steps were being taken against it, and piped and hooned in a sort of mad, mocking contempt. I tell you, it was as extraordinary as it was horrible. Time after time, I went along—tiptoeing noiselessly on stockinged feet—to the sealed door (for I always kept the Room sealed). I went at all hours of the night, and often the whistling, inside, would seem to change to a brutally malignant note, as though the half-animate monster saw me plainly through the shut door. And all the time the shrieking, hooning whistling would fill the whole corridor, so that I used to feel a precious lonely chap, messing about there with one of Hell's mysteries.

"And every morning, I would enter the Room, and examine the different hairs and seals. You see, after the first week, I had stretched parallel hairs all along the walls of the room, and along the ceiling; but over the floor, which was of polished stone, I had set out little, colorless wafers, tacky-side uppermost. Each wafer was numbered, and they were arranged after a definite plan, so that I should be able to trace the exact movements of any living thing that went across the floor.

"You will see that no material being or creature could possibly have entered that room, without leaving many signs to tell me about it. But nothing was ever disturbed, and I began to think that I should have to risk an attempt to stay the night in the room, in the Electric Pentacle. Yet, mind you, I knew that it would be a crazy thing to do; but I was getting stumped, and ready to do anything.

"Once, about midnight, I did break the seal on the door, and have a quick look in; but, I tell you, the whole Room gave one mad yell, and seemed to come towards me in a great belly of shadows, as if the walls had bellied in towards me. Of course, that must have been fancy. Anyway, the yell was sufficient, and I slammed the door, and locked it, feeling a bit weak down my spine. You know the feeling.

"And then, when I had got to that state of readiness for anything, I made something of a discovery. It was about one in the morning, and I was walking slowly round the castle, keeping in the soft grass. I had come under the shadow of the East Front, and far above me, I could hear the vile, hooning whistle of the Room, up in the darkness of the unlit wing. Then, suddenly, a little in front of me, I heard a man's voice, speaking low, but evidently in glee:

"'By George! You chaps; but I wouldn't care to bring a wife home in that!' it said, in the tone of the cultured Irish.

"Someone started to reply; but there came a sharp exclamation, and then a rush, and I heard footsteps running in all directions. Evidently, the men had spotted me.

"For a few seconds, I stood there, feeling an awful ass. After all, *they* were at the bottom of the haunting! Do you see what a big fool it made me seem? I had no doubt but that they were some of Tassoc's rivals; and here I had been feeling in every bone that I had hit a real, bad, genuine Case! And then, you know, there came the memory of hundreds of details, that made me just as much in doubt again. Anyway, whether it was natural, or abnatural, there was a great deal yet to be cleared up.

"I told Tassoc, next morning, what I had discovered, and through the whole of every night, for five nights, we kept a close watch round the East Wing; but there was never a sign of anyone prowling about; and all the time, almost from evening to dawn, that grotesque whistling would hoon incredibly, far above us in the darkness.

"On the morning after the fifth night, I received a wire from here, which brought me home by the next boat. I explained to Tassoc that I was simply bound to come away for a few days; but told him to keep up the watch round the castle. One thing I was very careful to do, and that was to make him absolutely promise never to go into the Room, between sunset and sunrise.

I made it clear to him that we knew nothing definite yet, one way or the other; and if the room were what I had first thought it to be, it might be a lot better for him to die first, than enter it after dark.

"When I got here, and had finished my business, I thought you chaps would be interested; and also I wanted to get it all spread out clear in my mind; so I rung you up. I am going over again tomorrow, and when I get back, I ought to have something pretty extraordinary to tell you. By the way, there is a curious thing I forgot to tell you. I tried to get a phonographic record of the whistling; but it simply produced no impression on the wax at all. That is one of the things that has made me feel queer, I can tell you. Another extraordinary thing is that the microphone will not magnify the sound—will not even transmit it; seems to take no account of it, and acts as if it were nonexistent. I am absolutely and utterly stumped, up to the present. I am a wee bit curious to see whether any of your dear clever heads can make daylight of it. *I* cannot—not yet."

He rose to his feet.

"Good night, all," he said, and began to usher us out abruptly, but without offense, into the night.

A fortnight later, he dropped each of us a card, and you can imagine that I was not late this time. When we arrived, Carnacki took us straight into dinner, and when we had finished, and all made ourselves comfortable, he began again, where he had left off:

"Now just listen quietly; for I have got something pretty queer to tell you. I got back late at night, and I had to walk up to the castle, as I had not warned them that I was coming. It was bright moonlight; so that the walk was rather a pleasure, than otherwise. When I got there, the whole place was in darkness, and I thought I would take a walk round outside, to see whether Tassoc or his brother was keeping watch. But I could not find them anywhere, and concluded that they had got tired of it, and gone off to bed.

"As I returned across the front of the East Wing, I caught the hooning whistling of the Room, coming down strangely through the stillness of the night. It had a queer note in it, I remember—low and constant, queerly meditative. I looked up at the window, bright in the moonlight, and got a sudden thought to bring a ladder from the stableyard, and try to get a look into the Room, through the window.

"With this notion, I hunted round at the back of the castle, among the straggle of offices, and presently found a long, fairly light ladder; though it was heavy enough for one, goodness knows! And I thought at first that I should never get it reared. I managed at last, and let the ends rest very quietly against the wall, a little below the sill of the larger window. Then, going silently, I went up the ladder. Presently, I had my face above the sill and was looking in alone with the moonlight.

"Of course, the queer whistling sounded louder up there; but it still conveyed that peculiar sense of something whistling quietly to itself—can you understand? Though, for all the meditative lowness of the note, the horrible, gargantuan quality was distinct—a mighty parody of the human, as if I stood there and listened to the whistling from the lips of a monster with a man's soul.

"And then, you know, I saw something. The floor in the middle of the huge, empty room, was puckered upwards in the centre into a strange soft-looking mound, parted at the top into an ever-changing hole, that pulsated to that great, gentle hooning. At times, as I watched, I saw the heaving of the indented mound, gap across with a queer, inward suction, as with the drawing of an enormous breath; then the thing would dilate and pout once more to the incredible melody. And suddenly, as I stared, dumb, it came to me that the thing was living. I was looking at two enormous, blackened lips, blistered and brutal, there in the pale moonlight. . . .

"Abruptly, they bulged out to a vast, pouting mound of force and sound, stiffened and swollen, and hugely massive and clean-cut in the moonbeams. And a great sweat lay heavy on the vast upper lip. In the same moment of time, the whistling had burst into a mad screaming note, that seemed to stun me, even where I stood, outside of the window. And then, the following moment, I was staring blankly at the solid, undisturbed floor of the room—smooth, polished stone flooring, from wall to wall; and there was an absolute silence.

"You can picture me staring into the quiet Room, and knowing what I knew. I felt like a sick, frightened kid, and wanted to slide *quietly* down the ladder, and run away. But in that very instant, I heard Tassoc's voice calling to me from within the Room, for help, *help*. My God! but I got such an awful dazed feeling; and I had a vague, bewildered notion that, after all, it was the Irishmen who had got him in there, and were taking it out of him. And then the call came again, and I burst the window, and jumped in to help him. I had a confused idea that the call had come from within the shadow of the great fireplace, and I raced across to it; but there was no one there.

"'Tassoc!' I shouted, and my voice went empty-sounding round the great apartment; and then, in a flash, *I knew that Tassoc had never called.* I whirled round, sick with fear, towards the window, and as I did so, a frightful, exultant whistling scream burst through the Room. On my left, the end wall had bellied in towards me, in a pair of gargantuan lips, black and utterly monstrous, to within a yard of my face. I fumbled for a mad instant at my revolver; not for *it*, but myself; for the danger was a thousand times worse than death. And then, suddenly, the Unknown Last Line of the Saaamaaa Ritual was whispered quite audibly in the room. Instantly, the thing happened that I have known once before. There came a sense as of dust falling continually and monotonously, and I knew that my life hung uncertain and suspended for a flash, in a brief, reeling vertigo of unseeable things. Then *that* ended, and I knew that I might live. My soul and body blended again, and life and power came to me. I dashed furiously at the window, and hurled myself out head-foremost; for I can tell you that I had stopped being afraid of death. I crashed down on to the ladder, and slithered, grabbing and grabbing; and so came some way or other alive to the bottom. And there I sat in the soft, wet grass, with the moonlight all about me; and far above, through the broken window of the Room, there was a low whistling.

"That is the chief of it. I was not hurt, and I went round to the front, and knocked Tassoc up. When they let me in, we had a long yarn, over some good whisky—for I was shaken to pieces —and I explained things as much as I could, I told Tassoc that the room would have to come down, and every fragment of it burned in a blast furnace, erected within a pentacle. He nodded. There was nothing to say. Then I went to bed.

"We turned a small army on to the work, and within ten days, that lovely thing had gone up in smoke, and what was left was calcined, and clean.

"It was when the workmen were stripping the panelling, that I got hold of a sound notion of the beginnings of that beastly development. Over the great fireplace, after the great oak panels had been torn down, I found that there was let into the masonry a scrollwork of stone, with on it an old inscription, in ancient Celtic, that here in this room was burned Dian Tiansay, Jester of King Alzof, who made the Song of Foolishness upon King Ernore of the Seventh Castle.

"When I got the translation clear, I gave it to Tassoc. He was tremendously excited; for he knew the old tale, and took me down to the library to look at an old parchment that gave the story in detail. Afterwards, I found that the incident was well-known about the countryside; but always regarded more as a legend, than as history. And no one seemed ever to have dreamt that the old East Wing of Iastrae Castle was the remains of the ancient Seventh Castle.

"From the old parchment, I gathered that there had been a pretty dirty job done, away back in the years. It seems that King Alzof and King Ernore had been enemies by birthright, as you might say truly; but that nothing more than a little raiding had occurred on either side for years, until Dian Tiansay made the Song of Foolishness upon King Ernore, and sang it before King Alzof; and so greatly was it appreciated that King Alzof gave the jester one of his ladies, to wife.

"Presently, all the people of the land had come to know the song, and so it came at last to King Ernore, who was so angered that he made war upon his old enemy, and took and burned him and his castle; but Dian Tiansay, the jester, he brought with him to his own place, and having torn his tongue out because of the song which he had made and sung, he imprisoned him in the Room in the East Wing (which was evidently used for unpleasant purposes), and the jester's wife, he kept for himself, having a fancy for her prettiness.

"But one night, Dian Tiansay's wife was not to be found, and in the morning they discovered her lying dead in her husband's arms, and he sitting, whistling the Song of Foolishness, for he had no longer the power to sing it.

"Then they roasted Dian Tiansay, in the great fireplace—probably from that selfsame 'galley-iron' which I have already mentioned. And until he died, Dian Tiansay ceased not to whistle the Song of Foolishness, which he could no longer sing. But afterwards, 'in that room' there was often heard at night the sound of something whistling; and there 'grew a power in that room,' so that none dared to sleep in it. And presently, it would seem, the King went to another castle; for the whistling troubled him.

"There you have it all. Of course, that is only a rough rendering of the translation of the parchment. But it sounds extraordinarily quaint. Don't you think so?"

"Yes," I said, answering for the lot. "But how did the thing grow to such a tremendous manifestation?"

"One of those cases of continuity of thought producing a positive action upon the immediate surrounding material," replied Carnacki. "The development must have been going forward through centuries, to have produced such a monstrosity. It was a true instance of Saiitii manifestation, which I can best explain by likening it to a living spiritual fungus, which involves the very structure of the aether-fibre itself, and, of course, in so doing, acquires an essential control over the 'material-substance' involved in it. It is impossible to make it plainer in a few words."

"What broke the seventh hair?" asked Taylor.

But Carnacki did not know. He thought it was probably nothing but being too severely tensioned. He also explained that they found out that the men who had run away, had not been up to mischief; but had come over secretly, merely to hear the whistling, which, indeed, had suddenly become the talk of the whole countryside.

"One other thing," said Arkright, "have you any idea what governs the use of the Unknown Last Line of the Saaamaaa Ritual? I know, of course, that it was used by the Ab-human Priests in the Incantation of Raaaee; but what used it on your behalf, and what made it?"

"You had better read Harzan's Monograph, and my Addenda to it, on Astral and Astral Coordination and Interference," said Carnacki. "It is an extraordinary subject, and I can only say here that the human vibration may not be insulated from the astral (as is always believed to be the case, in interferences by the Ab-human), without immediate action being taken by those Forces which govern the spinning of the outer circle. In other words, it is being proved, time after time, that there is some inscrutable Protective Force constantly intervening between the human soul (not the body, mind you,) and the Outer Monstrosities. Am I clear?"

"Yes, I think so," I replied. "And you believe that the Room had become the material expression of the ancient Jester—that his soul, rotten with hatred, had bred into a monster—eh?" I asked.

"Yes," said Carnacki, nodding, "I think you've put my thought rather neatly. It is a queer coincidence that Miss Donnehue is supposed to be descended (so I have heard since) from the same King Ernore. It makes one think some curious thoughts, doesn't it? The marriage coming on, and the Room waking to fresh life. If she had gone into that room, ever . . . eh? *It* had waited a long time. Sins of the fathers. Yes, I've thought of that. They're to be married next week, and I am to be best man, which is a thing I hate. And he won his bets, rather! Just think, *if* ever she had gone into that room. Pretty horrible, eh?"

He nodded his head, grimly, and we four nodded back. Then he rose and took us collectively to the door, and presently thrust us forth in friendly fashion on the Embankment and into the fresh night air.

"Good night," we all called back, and went to our various homes. If she had, eh? If she had? That is what I kept thinking.

Doppelgangster

> **LAURA RESNICK** <

IT WASN'T NO SURPRISE THAT SKINNY VINNY VITELLI GOT RUBBED out. I mean, hey, I'd nearly whacked him myself a couple of times. So had most guys I know. Not to speak ill of the dead and all that, but he was an *irritating* bastard. Vinny could pick an argument with a plate of pasta. He could piss off the Virgin Mother. He could annoy the dead—so it wasn't exactly a big shock when he *became* one of them.

A couple of nuns taking a cigarette break found his body in an alley early one morning. He'd been done with four slugs straight to the chest. Which was a little strange, actually, because Vinny always wore the bulletproof vest he got the time he whacked that Fed.

It's not what you're thinking. It was personal, not business. Vinny caught the guy in bed with his underage daughter. The vest was lying right there on the floor, and after Vinny impulsively emptied a whole clip into the guy's torso, he decided the vest was A Sign. (Did I mention he was a pretty religious guy?) See, Vinny had always been afraid of dying exactly the way he'd just killed the Fed who'd been stupid enough to take off his bulletproof vest while humping a wiseguy's seventeen-year-old daughter right there in her father's house. (Feds. They breed 'em dumb.)

So Vinny picked the vest up off the floor, put it on, and never took it off since. I mean *never*. Just ask his wife. Well, if you can find her. She hot-tailed it straight down to Florida before the

103

corpse was cold and ain't been seen since. She was making plans for her new life right there at Vinny's funeral, yakking on her cell phone with her real estate agent while the casket was being lowered into the ground.

"It's a funny thing," I said to Joey (the Chin) Mannino while the grieving Mrs. Vitelli kicked some dirt into her late husband's open grave with the toe of her shoe while telling her real estate agent she expected to be in Florida by nightfall.

"Huh?" Joey didn't really hear me. He was stroking his scarred chin as he stared lovesick at the Widow Butera. She was glaring back at him. A very beautiful woman, even at forty-five, but bad news for any guy.

"Give it up, Joey," I advised.

"I can't." He shook his head. "I've asked her to marry me."

I slapped my forehead. "Are you nuts?" One of the mourners frowned at me, so I lowered my voice. "She's had three husbands, and they're all dead. Don't that tell you something?"

"She's been unlucky."

"Her *husbands* have been unlucky. All three of them. So I'll lay odds that number four is gonna be real unlucky, too."

"It's not her fault, Vito."

"No, but being married to her is so unlucky it crosses over into dumb."

Her first husband got hit just because he was having dinner with Big Bobby Gambone at Buon Appetito the night Little Jackie Bernini decided to kill Bobby and didn't feel too particular about who else he sprayed with his Uzi. That was the start of the first Gambone-Bernini war. Well, a beautiful woman like that couldn't stay widowed forever. So three years later, during the second Gambone-Bernini war, she married a hit man from Las Vegas who the Gambones brought into town to teach the Berninis a lesson. But then the Berninis brought in their own hit man from Boise to deal with him, and ain't *nobody* tougher than those Boise guys. So the Widow was widowed again. Then, maybe because she was tired of marrying Gambones who got whacked out, the Widow shocked everyone by marrying Bernini Butera, who was everybody's favorite pick to head the Bernini family next . . . until Joey clipped him last year. That hit pretty much ended the third Gambone-Bernini war. But from the way the Widow Butera was glaring at Joey across Skinny Vinny Vitelli's grave now, it didn't look like she had forgiven Joey for stuffing her third husband into a cement mixer in New Jersey.

"What'd she say when you asked her to marry you?" I asked Joey.

"She told me she'd rather fry in hell." He shrugged. "She'll come round."

I shook my head. "Joey, Joey, Joey . . ."

He gave a friendly little wave to the Widow Butera. She hissed at him. The priest, Father Michael, smiled vaguely at her and said, "Amen."

So, to take Joey's mind off the Widow, I said, "Anyhow, like I was saying before, it's a funny thing."

"What's a funny thing?"

"About Vinny."

"No, no," Connie Vitelli was saying into her cell phone as she shook Father Michael's hand, "the condo's got to have an ocean view, or no deal. Understand?"

"Funny?" Joey said. "Oh! You mean about the vest, right?"

"Yeah." I shook my head when Father Michael gestured to me to throw some dirt onto the coffin. Hey, I didn't kill Vinny, so no way was I doing the work of deep-sixing him. Not my problem, after all. "Why'd Vinny take off that vest for the first time in five years? It ain't like him. He was a religious bastard."

"I think you mean superstitious." Joey's an educated guy. Almost read a book once.

"Okay, superstitious. Vinny always thought he'd get killed if he ever took that thing off. And, sure enough, look what happened. So why'd he take it off? It don't make sense."

"You mean you didn't hear, Vito?"

"Hear what?"

Connie was shouting into her cell phone, "Speak up! Are you driving through a tunnel or something? I'm getting tons of static!"

Vinny's daughter, now twenty-two years old and reputedly still a virgin, stepped up to the grave, made a face at her father's coffin, and then spit on it.

"Poor Vinny," said Father Michael, who looked like he'd taken a fistful of Prozac before coming here. "He will be missed."

"Not by anybody I ever met," muttered Joey.

I said to Joey, "What is it that I didn't hear?"

"Oh! The strange thing is, Vito, Vinny was still wearing his vest when they found his body."

"Huh? So how'd four slugs wind up in his chest?"

Joey shrugged. "It's a mystery. No holes in the vest. No marks at all, like it was never even hit. But as for Vinny's chest..." Joey grimaced.

While I thought about this, Connie Vitelli said, "But how big is the master bathroom?"

"So, Joey, you're saying that someone clipped Vinny, then put that vest back on him? For what? A joke?"

Joey shook his head. "That vest never came off him, Vito."

"Of course it did. How else did four bull—"

"The cops said the fasteners on Vinny's vest were rusted and hadn't been disturbed for years."

"Jesus. So it's true what Connie said. Vinny even *showered* in that thing!"

"Uh-huh."

I frowned at Joey. "But what you're saying... I mean, how did the bullets get past the vest and into Vinny's chest?"

"That's what's got the cops stumped."

"And why'd the cops tell *you* this?" Cops don't usually say nothing to guys like us besides, "I'll get you into the Witness Protection Program if you cooperate."

"I don't think they meant to tell me," Joey said. "It just sort of slipped out somewhere during the seven straight hours they spent interrogating me yesterday."

"Oh, *that's* why you weren't at the wake."

Joey nodded wearily. "I'm thinking of suing them for the emotional trauma caused by missing a dear friend's wake, as well as the stain they have placed on my good reputation."

"How come they think you're the one who whacked him?"

"Well, you know, I had that argument with Vinny last week at Buon Appetito."

"So what?"

"So it turns out there were three undercover Feds in the place at the time, and they took it the wrong way when I held a steak knife to Vinny's throat and said I'd kill him if I ever saw him again."

"Man," I said, sick at how unfair it all was. "You just have to be so careful these days. Watch every damn little word."

"Tell me about it."

"Whatever happened to the First Arraignment?" I said.

"Amendment."

"Whatever."

"I admit," Joey said, "I thought about whacking Vinny."

"Sure."

"Who didn't?"

"You said it."

"But it's not like he didn't deserve it," Joey said.

"Absolutely," I said as Vinny's son opened his fly and pissed on his father's grave.

"So I don't see why the cops have to get so bent out of shape just because someone finally *did* whack Vinny."

"Me, neither."

"And just because I'm the last guy anyone saw threatening to kill him, the cops ruin my whole day. Now is that fair? Is that the American way?"

"It really stinks." I patted Joey on the back. "Just out of curiosity, *did* you kill him?"

"No. I was proposing to the Widow Butera at the estimated time of death."

"Did she alibi you to the cops?"

"No."

Women.

"So I wonder who did it?" I said.

"Could've been any one of a hundred guys," Joey said.

"More," I said.

"Yeah."

The Widow Butera stepped up to Vinny's grave and looked down at it for a long moment. Then she crossed herself, glared once more at Joey, and started walking to her car.

When Connie Vitelli got off the phone for a split second, Joey and I paid our respects so we could get the hell out of there.

"Such a shame," Joey said politely to Vinny's widow. "Him being so young and all."

"Not that young." Connie shook her head. "And I think dementia was setting in already. He was seeing things."

"Seeing things?" Joey said. "Then 'dementia' probably isn't the right word, because that's when—"

"Oops! I gotta take this," Connie said as her cell phone rang.

"Wait a minute," I said. "What things was Vinny seeing? Feds stalking him? Hitters from the Bernini family coming after him?" If we knew, we might be able to figure out who'd whacked him.

Connie rolled her eyes. "Himself, if you can believe it."

"Huh?"

"The day before Vinny died, he came home in a cold sweat, babbling about how he had just bumped into the spitting image of himself on the street outside Buon Appetito. The guy was even dressed like Vinny. Right down to the bulletproof vest. Go figure." Connie shrugged off the idea that her husband's perfect double was out there somewhere and added, "Now I've really got to take this call. Thanks for coming, fellas." She turned away and said into her cell phone, "Hello? Oh, good! Thanks for getting back to me today. Yes, I'll be out of the house by tonight, so put it on the market right away."

"So Vinny was losing his mind," I said.

Joey nodded towards Connie and the kids. "And you're surprised by this?"

"No, I guess not."

Which is why I didn't think any more about it. Not then, anyhow. Not until three days later, which was when a dinner-and-dance cruise accidentally found Johnny Be Good Gambone's body floating in the Hudson River.

"But it can't be Johnny," I said to Joey Mannino when he told me about it.

"It is. Positive ID, no doubt about it."

"No, it can't be, because—"

"Vito, pull yourself together," Joey said. "Two of our guys dead in one week. We're going to the mattresses."

"It can't be Johnny, because I saw him alive at the same time they were fishing that corpse out of the river."

"It must be the Berninis doing these hits. Who else would have the nerve? Those bastards! Well, if they want another war, we'll give them another w—"

"Joey, are you listening to me? I'm telling you, whoever they found in the Hudson, it wasn't Johnny Gambone, because I had dinner with him last night!"

Joey stared at me. "Are you losing your mind, too?"

"No! They're just putting the wrong name on the corpse."

But when we showed up at the mortician's to inspect the body,

I saw there'd been no mistake. That was Johnny Gambone lying on that slab, no doubt about it. Who else in the world had a purple tattoo of a naked broad on his shoulder with the word "Mom" written across it?

"So you're not still denying that's Johnny?" Joey prodded.

"Couldn't be anyone else, but . . ."

"But?"

"But, I'm telling you, I was having dinner with him that evening. We talked about Vinny's death. Johnny told me that, no matter how much we hated Vinny, it was our job to find out who'd clipped him, because we can't just let people go around killing made guys without even asking first. Especially not *our* made guys."

"Vito, that's impossible. According to the cops, Johnny had already been dead for thirty-six hours by the time you had dinner with . . . with . . ."

"Something's not right," I said.

And whatever was not right became even more wrong a couple of days later when Danny (the Doctor) Bardozzi, best known for chopping up four members of the Gambone family and passing them off as ground ostrich meat at an East Village restaurant which went out of business soon after Danny was indicted, was found dead.

I know what you're thinking, but we didn't do it. We didn't even *know* who did it, just like we didn't know who'd clipped Johnny and Vinny. We were knee-deep in bodies by now, and we had no idea who was stacking them up.

"And the *way* the doctor was killed," Joey told me as we walked along Mott Street, "is really strange."

"You mean compared to the normal way Vinny was killed, with four bullets pumped into his chest and not a scratch on the bulletproof vest he was wearing at the time? Or the normal way Johnny Gambone was found floating in the river while I was watching him eat linguine and bitch about his indigestion?" Okay, I was feeling irritable and got a little sarcastic.

Joey said, "Listen, Danny showed up at Bernini's Wine and Guns Shop in a panic, armed with two Glocks and a lifetime supply of ammo, and locked himself in the cellar. There's no way in or out of the cellar except through the one door he'd locked, and—because Danny was acting so crazy—there were a dozen Berninis standing right by that door trying to convince him to come out."

"And?"

"Next thing they know, they hear a few shots go off. So they break down the door and run downstairs. Danny's alone. And dead." Joey grimaced. "Shotgun. Made a real mess."

"But you said he had two Glocks."

"That's right. And, no, there wasn't a shotgun down there. Not before Danny locked himself in . . . and not when the Berninis found him there."

"Then it wasn't a shotgun. He blew his own head off with a Glock."

"No. His guns hadn't even been fired, and there was buckshot everywhere. Just no shotgun."

"In a locked cellar with no windows and no other door? That's impossible."

"Like it was impossible for you to be eating dinner with a guy whose two-day-old corpse was floating in the Hudson River at the time?"

"We're in trouble," I said. "We've got something going on here that's bigger than another war with the Berninis."

"That's what they think, too."

"What? You mean they ain't blaming us for Danny's death?"

"How could they? I just told you what happened. They know we're not invisible, and neither are our guns. In fact, they knew something strange was happening even before we did, because they knew they didn't kill Johnny Gambone."

"We've got to have a sit-down with the Berninis."

"I've called one for tonight. At St. Ignazio's. I gotta have dinner at my mother's in Brooklyn first, but I'll be there."

St. Ignazio's was dark and shadowy, lit only by candles. The whole place smelled of incense and lingering perfume . . . The Widow Butera's perfume, I realized, as I saw her kneeling before a statue of Saint Paula, patron saint of widows.

Father Michael and two guys from the Bernini family were waiting for me in an alcove on the other side of the church.

"Is Joey here yet?" I asked the Widow Butera.

"What do I care? What do I care about any of you fiends?" She rose to her feet and came towards me. "I hate you all! Every single one of you! I spit on you! I spit on your mothers' graves!"

"So you haven't seen him?"

She shook her fist at me. "Stay away from me!"

"Hey, I'm not the one trying to make you a widow for the fourth time. So don't yell at *me*, sister. And..." I frowned as wispy white things started escaping from the fist she shook at me. "Are those feathers? Whatever happened to praying with rosary beads?"

She made a really nasty Sicilian gesture and stomped towards the main door in a huff just as Joey entered the church. The poor guy's face brightened like he'd just met a famous stripper.

He asked her, "Have you thought any more about my proposal? I mean, take all the time you need, I just wond—"

"Get out of my way!" she shrieked. "Don't ever come near me again! Don't even look at me!"

"Maybe we'll talk later?" Joey said to her back.

She paused to look over her shoulder at him. "Amazing," she said in a different tone of voice. Then she left.

"You're late," I said to Joey.

"Sorry. Couldn't be helped."

"Gentlemen," said Father Michael, smelling strongly of sacramental wine as he came close to us, "the Berninis are eager to begin this summit, so if you—"

"Summit?" I repeated.

"Sit-down," said Joey.

"Oh."

"So if you'll just take your seats..."

"You're fucking late," said Carmine Bernini. He was Danny (the Doctor) Bardozzi's cousin by marriage, and also the world's biggest asshole.

"But we haven't been waiting too long," added Tony Randazzo. He was a good-looking kid who'd been a soldier in the Bernini family for a few years. A stand-up guy, actually, and I'd let him date my daughter if I didn't think I'd probably have to kill him one day.

"Would anyone care for some chips and dip?" Father Michael asked. "Maybe some cocktails?"

"We ain't here to fucking socialize," said Carmine.

"Don't curse in church," said Joey.

"Well, please fucking excuse *me*."

Like I said—the world's biggest asshole. "Never mind the refreshments, Father," I said. "This'll just take a few minutes." I looked at Carmine. "Let's lay our cards on the table."

So we did. And what these guys told me about Danny Bardozzi's death got my full attention.

"He said *what*?"

Tony said, "Danny came into the shop that day and said he'd just seen his perfect double, his spitting image."

"His doppelgänger?" said Father Michael.

"Yeah, his doppelgangster," said Carmine. "He was fucking freaking out. In a cold sweat, shaking like a virgin in a whorehouse, babbling like a snitch with the Feds. Scared out of his mind."

"Because he'd seen this doppelgangster?" I said.

"Yeah. He said it meant he was gonna die."

"He was right," I said. "But how did he know?"

"Perhaps he knew that, traditionally," said Father Michael, "seeing your doppelgänger portends your own death."

"No shit?" said Carmine.

"No sh— Um, yes, really," said Father Michael.

"But we got more than people *pretending* their deaths here, Father," I said.

"No, *portending*," the priest said. "Seeing your doppelgänger is, in popular folklore, a sure sign that you're going to die."

"Weird shit," said Carmine.

"Even weirder," I said, "Danny ain't the only one around here who's seen a doppelgangster." I told them about Skinny Vinny telling Connie he'd seen his own perfect double the day before he died.

"Johnny Gambone did, too!" said Father Michael, swaying a little. "My God! I didn't realize . . ." He wiped his brow. "Just a few days before his body was found, Johnny told me after Mass that he'd seen a man who looked very much like himself, dressed the same, even bearing the same tattoo—but nowhere near as handsome."

"He always was a vain sonofabitch," said Carmine.

"So he saw his double, too, then," I said. "All three of these guys died after seeing their doubles."

"And died in such strange ways," Tony added.

"Yes," said Father Michael. "Almost as if meeting the doppelgänger doesn't just presage death, it actually curses the victim, making him utterly defenseless against death when it comes for him."

"So once you see this fucking thing, that's it?" said Carmine. "You're as good as whacked?"

"That would explain how bullets somehow got past or around Vinny's vest," I said.

"And how someone walked past all of us without being seen," said Tony, "and got through a locked door to kill Danny."

"So we're dealing with . . . what?" I said. "Witchcraft? Some kind of curse? The Evil Eye?"

"It's some weird fucking shit," said Carmine.

Father Michael fumbled behind the skirts of the shrine of the Virgin and pulled out a bottle of wine. He uncorked it, gulped some down, and then said, "Black magic. What else could it be?"

"Fucking creepy."

"And whoever is doing it is damn good," I said. "I had dinner with Johnny Gambone's doppelgangster and didn't even know it wasn't the real guy."

"But no one has seen Vinny, Johnny, and Danny since they were found dead, right?" said Father Michael. "I mean . . . no one has seen their doubles since then?"

I hadn't even thought about that. "No," I said. "That's right. The last time I saw Johnny's double—the last time anyone saw it, as far as I know—was before his body was found."

"So . . ." Father Michael took another swig. "So whoever is doing this sends a doppelgangst . . . doppelgänger after the victim to curse him with inevitable death. And then, after the victim is dead, the perfect double continues carrying on the victim's normal life until the death is discovered."

"And then what?"

"Then it . . ." Father Michael shrugged. "It probably disintegrates into whatever elemental ingredients it was originally fashioned from."

"So if you hid the fucking body well enough, it would be years before anyone even knew you'd made the hit. Hey, this black magic is some fucking great stuff! If I could learn to do it—"

"Whoever *has* learned to do it," I said, "is out to kill all of us. Get it? We've got to stop him before we're all dead!"

"Vito's right," said Joey. "We're all in danger."

My cell phone suddenly rang, making us all jump a little. (Hey, if you thought someone was about to kill you that way, wouldn't you be a little jumpy, too?) I pulled the phone out of my pocket. "Hello?"

"Vito?" said Joey at the other end. "I'm coming from my

mother's, and I'm still in Brooklyn. Stuck in traffic. You'd better start the sit-down without me. I'll get there as soon as I can."

My blood ran cold as I stared at the Joey sitting here with me, absently stroking his chin the way the real one often did. Choosing my words carefully, I said, "Seen anything strange lately?"

"Huh?"

"Anyone familiar?"

"Well . . . my mother, obviously."

"No one else?"

"What are you talking about?"

"Okay, good," I said with relief. I liked Joey, I'd miss him if he was the next one to die. "Listen to me very carefully. *Stay right where you are.* Call me back in an hour."

"But Vito—"

"Just do it!" I hung up.

"Who was that?" asked Joey.

I jumped him, took him to the floor, and started banging his head against the stone. "Vito!" he screamed. "Vito! *Stop!* What are you doing? *Ow!*"

"Vito!" cried Father Michael "Stop!"

"Fucking maniac," said Carmine.

"Thought you'd get Joey Mannino, did you?" I shouted at the doppelgangster. "Well, think again, you bastard!"

"This is one of them?" the priest shrieked.

"Yes!" I kept banging its head against the floor. "And it's gonna tell me who's behind these hits!"

Its eyes rolled back into its head, it convulsed a few times, and then its head shattered like dry plaster.

"Whoa!" said Tony.

I looked down at the mess. Nothing but crumbled dust, lumps of dirt, and feathers where the thing's head had been. Then its body started disintegrating, too.

"I think you whacked it, Vito," said Tony.

Father Michael poured the whole rest of the bottle of wine down his throat before he spoke. "Well . . . I guess this means that Joey is safe now?"

"Not for long," I said. "Whoever did this will make another one the moment he knows this one has been . . . Wait a minute!"

"Vito? What is it?" said Tony.

"Maybe it's not a *he*," I said.

"Huh?"

"Think about it! Who would hit the Berninis *and* the Gambones? Who hates *both* families that much? Who wants all of us dead?"

"You saying the fucking Feds are behind this?"

"No, you asshole! I'm saying the one person who hates both families equally is behind this!" I grabbed a handful of the crap that had been Joey's doppelgangster a minute ago and waved it at these guys. "*Feathers!*"

"Vito, this is a very serious accusation," said Father Michael, slurring his words a little. "Are you absolutely sure?"

"Huh?" said Tony.

"Just fucking follow him," said Carmine as I ran for the same exit that the Widow Butera had taken.

I kicked in the door of her apartment without knocking. I'd figured out her scam by now, so I expected the feathers, the blood sacrifices, the candles, the chanting, and the photos of Bernini and Gambone family members.

I just didn't expect to see my own perfect double rising out of her magic fire like a genie coming out of a lantern. I pulled out my piece and fired at it.

"*Noooo!*" screamed the Widow Butera. She leapt at me, knocked my gun aside, and started clawing at my face.

"Kill it! Kill it!" I shouted at the others.

Carmine said, "I always wanted to do this to you, Vito," and started pumping bullets into my doppelgangster while I fought the Widow. Father Michael ran around the room praying loudly and drenching things in holy water. Tony took a baseball bat—don't ask me where he got it—and started destroying everything in sight: the amulets and charms hanging everywhere, the jars of powders and potions stacked on shelves, the cages containing live chickens, and the bottles of blood. My perfect double shattered into a million pieces in the hail of Carmine's bullets, and the pieces fell smoldering into the fire. Then Tony kicked at the fire until it was scattered all over the living room and started dying.

"It's a fucking shame about the carpet," Carmine said as chickens escaped the shattered cages and started running all over the room.

". . . blessed are thou, and blessed is the fruit of thy womb . . ." Father Michael was chanting.

"What else can I break? What else can I break?" Tony shouted.

"I'll kill you all!" the Widow screamed. "You're all dead!"

"Too late, sister, we're onto you now. You've whacked your last wiseguy," I said as she struggled in my grip.

"Three husbands I lost in your damned wars!" she screamed. "I told them to get out of organized crime and into something secure, like accounting or the restaurant business, but would they listen? *Noooo!*"

"Secure? The fucking restaurant business? Are you kidding me?"

"The Berninis and Gambones ruined my life!" the Widow Butera shrieked. "I will have vengeance on you all!"

"Repent! Repent!" Father Michael cried. Then he doused her with a whole bottle of holy water.

"*Eeeeee!*" She screamed something awful . . . and then started smoking like she was on fire.

I'm not dumb. I let go of her and backed away.

The room filled with smoke and the Widow's screams got louder, until they echoed so hard they made my teeth hurt . . . then faded. There was a dark scorch mark on the floor where she'd been standing.

"Where'd she go?" I said.

"She'll never get her fucking security deposit back now," said Carmine, looking at the floor.

Tony added, "No amount of buffing will get that out."

"What the hell happened?" I said, looking around the room. The Widow had vanished.

Father Michael fell to his knees and crossed himself. "I don't think she was completely human. At least, not anymore. She had become Satan's minion."

"Huh. I wondered how she kept her good looks for so fucking long."

"That's it?" I asked Father Michael. "She's just . . . gone?"

He nodded. "In Hell, where she belongs." After a moment, he added, "Mind you, that's only a theory."

"Either way," I said, "I'm kinda relieved. I know we couldn't just let her go. Not after she'd hit three guys and tried to hit me and Joey, too. But I really didn't want to whack a broad."

"What a fucking pussy you are, Vito."

"Carmine, you asshole," I said, "the sit-down was successful. We found out who's behind these hits, we put a stop to it, and there ain't gonna be no new war. So now get outta my sight before I forget my manners and whack you just for the hell of it."

"Did I mention how much fun it was pumping a whole clip into your fucking doppelgangster?"

My cell phone rang, making Father Michael jump.

"Damn." I knew who it was even before I answered it. "Hello?"

"Vito," said Joey, "I've been sitting here in my car, not going anywhere, just like you said, for a whole hour. Now do you want to tell me what the hell is going on?"

I looked at the scorched spot the Widow had left in the floor and tried to think of the best way to break the news to him. "So, Joey . . . would you still want to marry the Widow Butera if you knew she'd been trying to whack you and everyone you know?"

Claus of Death

> MICHAEL M. JONES <

IT BEGAN, AS THESE THINGS ALWAYS DO, WITH A WOMAN. SHE strolled into the dingy, cramped room I laughingly call an office these days, pausing at the door to cast a contemptuously dubious look around at the mix-and-match Salvation Army decor. I could just imagine how it all looked through her eyes: the scarred mahogany desk overflowing with papers and empty coffee mugs, the dented green file cabinet on which sat a single fern barely clinging to life, bare wooden floor, the couch with its assortment of stains and old cigarette burns, the mismatched wooden chairs, and the faded paint on the door that read, NICHOLAS ST. CLAUS, PRIVATE INVESTIGATOR. Yeah, I knew just how this lady would look upon her surroundings and despair. I knew her tastes, and this was as far away from them as you got. I couldn't even imagine what she made of me, so I slammed the door on that line of thought immediately.

In fact, before I even looked directly at my visitor, I opened the minifridge I kept behind the desk, and pulled out some liquid courage, a half-empty bottle of spiked eggnog which had kept me company through the long Christmas nights. Splashing a liberal amount into the nearest coffee mug, I drained it quickly. I needed it. Courage was all I had left. Like some bizarre reverse Wizard of Oz, the lady'd stolen my heart, messed with my head, and caused me to leave home once and for all. My hand shook, and I took that as a sign to pour another shot. The lady started to speak, but I held up my free hand, stopping her words in their tracks. I tossed back the drink, and slammed the mug down on the table, pinning down an overdue electricity bill. "Hello, Ginny," I said. Where my ex-wife is concerned, I wanted the first word, and whenever possible, the last.

"Hello, Nick," she replied, not waiting for an invitation before settling down gingerly on the seat closest to my desk. She crossed her legs, her little black skirt riding up to grant me a highly enjoyable view of smooth, pale skin. My hand tightened around the empty mug. No, two shots was already pushing it on an empty stomach. She went on before I could find the right words to ask her what the hell brought her down from her ivory tower to my hole in the wall, the hole I'd crawled into five years ago and hoped never to emerge from again. Ginny was by far the last person I'd ever expected to see in here. "I need your help," she said. Words I'd never thought to hear, followed by words I'd often heard only in my most bitter fantasies: "Jack's dead, Nick. He was murdered. And I need you to find out who did it."

Jack Frost. The guy who'd been nipping at more than Ginny's nose since I left, and some time before that. My former protege turned rival. My replacement, in more ways than one. Funny. I'd always thought I'd feel a lot better with him dead, but Ginny's cold, matter-of-fact words left me feeling just a little emptier inside, like someone'd taken an ice pick to my heart. I looked up to meet her eyes, truly seeing her for the first time in half a decade, and my power instinctively rose to the occasion, telling me everything I needed to know about her. Within a heartbeat, I knew exactly how she'd been nice, and how she'd been naughty. I knew if she'd been bad or good, and what she'd have gotten in her stocking if I still filled stockings on that one magical night of the year. I thought of peaches to go with the cream of her skin, a gold necklace to match her hair, and sapphire earrings to match her eyes. I thought of—aw, Hell, I had to stop thinking along those lines. But it had been a long time, and I was still a man. I looked closer, and within another heartbeat, I could read between the lines, and see the true anguish in those eyes. She was keeping it together for appearances' sake. Calm, cool, and collected, like an ice sculpture, but brittle. She was going to tell me everything she knew, take advantage of our shared history and the embers of my love for her, and then she was going to go home and shatter with grief. Her presence here meant that she had no one else she could turn to. I sighed mentally, took all of those old feelings and desires and bitter memories, shoved them all into a tiny box in the back of my mind, and locked it. Leaning forward, I tried to sound professional as I said, "Tell me everything, Ginny."

And she did. Her recitation of the facts was mechanical, her voice controlled tightly, and I watched her knuckles grow white as she clutched the arms of her chair. There wasn't much to tell, really. He'd been melted with a heating spell, a very focused, very personalized bit of magic that hit the guy where it counted, counteracting the magic that had brought him to life and granted him human form in the first place. Ginny, no expert when it came to spellwork, could only tell me that it had been long-range, possibly even delayed release, something that struck out of the blue while they were in bed. I read between the lines, and gathered that they hadn't exactly been asleep at the time. God, what a mental image. One I didn't need. But anyway, no muss, no fuss, exit Jack Frost as a puddle of water, stage left. With a little better timing, it might have taken days for someone to notice his absence. I wondered if the killer'd wanted Jack's demise to be noticed immediately.

Once Ginny'd finished telling me what little she knew, we haggled briefly, over terms of payment and compensation. We both knew I was doing this as a favor, in memory of what we'd once shared, but neither of us were foolish enough to say so. Things between us were . . . complicated on both sides. She'd broken my heart, but in the end, I wasn't entirely blameless. There was plenty of pain and anger to go around, but real feelings still existed also. It was a mess. My payment for this case, though, would keep me in rent and 'nog for a while. It was a relief when she left and I could lock the door behind her and shut out the world.

It took an hour or so, but finally, I felt ready to get to work. I grabbed my overcoat (still bemoaning the recent loss of the old red-and-white parka, but that fur trim had proven way too flammable for my own good, and that's another long story) and left the office. Going down two flights of stairs and out the front door put me out on the streets of Holiday, and onto the case of Jack Frost's murder.

Holiday, Alaska. Sitting right on the border between where

the mundane world ended and the magical one began, it was a frontier town where the Northern Lights cast dark shadows, and beings both mundane and supernatural ended up when they had nowhere else to go. It was the ends of the Earth for people like me, a refuge for the weary of heart and heavy of soul. It was also the closest island of civilization to the realm I'd once ruled, and saw a lot of traffic from the North Pole's inhabitants. Somehow, I just couldn't see myself living in warmer, sunnier, more pleasant climates. Everyone in Holiday had their reasons for being here. Everyone had their secrets, most of them dirty and sordid and downright unpleasant. Lucky me, I knew most of them already.

My first stop was The Confessional, which, while not the only bar in town, was the only bar worth visiting for people in the know. I'd been drinking there for a very long time, which made me as much of a regular as anyone ever got in a place like this. The Confessional was a dark little place, an afterthought shoved up against the back of St. Peter's, an old church of indefinite denomination that catered to just about anyone willing to believe in a Christian god. In one of those strange twists that so characterized Holiday, the priest at St. Peter's and the bartender at the Confessional were one and the same, with Father Aaron saving souls one day a week, and serving spirits the other six, and you had to be careful what you let him know and under what circumstances, for while he respected the sanctity of the church's confessional, anything else he heard was fair game.

This early in the day, the place was fairly empty; in Holiday, most people don't get down to serious drinking until after sunset. I bellied up to the bar, parking my butt on my usual stool down at the end. Father Aaron finished polishing a glass, and came over to check on me. We exchanged our usual snappy repartee, acknowledging that yeah, we were both still alive and kicking, and yeah, that life of celibacy was still working out for him, which I found amusing since rumor has it that before he put on the collar, he was quite the ladies' man. We weren't what you'd call friends; I had a rather dubious relationship with the whole Christian faith, and my roots were all too pagan. But we had an understanding, and got along fine for all that. He was one of my best sources of information in town. Over a stiff eggnog, I outlined the problem.

"Yeah," allowed the good Father, nodding thoughtfully and

scratching at his chin. "I seem to remember hearing something of a hitter here in town. Supposedly one of the Mysteries," he added somewhat disparagingly. He wasn't too big on the mystic, for all that many of his patrons came from one supernatural tradition or another. "Didn't pay it much mind, on account of not my business." That, we both knew, was patented bullshit. Father Aaron remembered everything, assigning it a value in his mental bank, and all it took to get him to share was knowing his prices.

"A hundred bucks to the poor box," I said thoughtfully, "would go a long way, right?"

"Two hundred would buy a lot of hot soup and blankets," agreed Father Aaron, amiably.

We settled on one-fifty, which I wrote off as expenses, and Father Aaron agreed to arrange a meeting for me with the hitman, an out-of-towner called Mr. Tuesday. On my way out, I stuffed my "donation" into the box Aaron'd helpfully set out by the Confessional's door. "Thank you. Thank you very much," Father Aaron recited as I left.

Next stop was the factory itself, a place I returned to with an extreme reluctance. I'd built it from the ground up, and nurtured it for a long time, and just thinking about it tore the scabs from my heart. The good memories had all been overlaid with bad ones, such as me catching Ginny in bed with Jack and too much tinsel. Yeah. Not a very merry Christmas, or a happy New Year.

It didn't take me long at all to get there; one of the little magic tricks I still possessed was an ability to get where I wanted to go without actually crossing any distance. I hated it; these days, it made me queasy and reminded me of happier days. Walking was better for me anyway. But short of a magic sleigh, there weren't many other ways to get where I was going. The factory doesn't exist in the real world.

Suffice it to say, nosing around the place was a mistake. There was nothing new to be learned there. Everyone loved Jack. He'd brought modernization to the factory, and it hummed like a well-oiled machine. Things had changed drastically since the old days, had been changing well before I left. It had become impossible to manufacture all the toys kids would get on Christmas. Hell, you couldn't even fill up the stockings with fruit and baubles anymore. The population explosion in the past century combined with the rise of an industrialized, consumer-oriented society meant that our

role in the holiday had become almost entirely ornamental. Ironi-
cally, the more I'd become a cultural icon, the less I was actually
needed. The world wanted the image, not the man. Ultimately,
we'd abandoned the old system. Now the factory worked to gather
magic from all over the world year-round, distilling it into "the
Christmas spirit," which was then infused into little objects and
ornaments and redistributed to spread the cheer. Warm fuzzies,
Christmas miracles, happy family reunions, that sort of thing.
Random acts of kindness and senseless acts of beauty.

Yeah. Pretty abstract, I know. I never could wrap my mind
around it. That's about the time I brought Jack on board and let
him handle business matters along with Ginny. I was a hands-on
kind of guy, clinging to the old ways, such as actual gift-giving
and the annual Christmas Eve Ride. Is it any surprise I let my
attention slide on the other matters? It's certainly no surprise
that I missed what Jack and Ginny were up to behind my back.
I think, on some level, I didn't want to know.

I nosed around the factory long enough to be made profoundly
uncomfortable. I conducted a few half-hearted interviews with
some of the senior staff, the elves that had been with me since
the early days, the ones who'd moved up in the ranks and success-
fully weathered the transition of methods and management. The
longest of those interviews was with Gunter, one of the Germanic
tribe who'd first come to work for me back when I needed skilled
craftsmen and dedicated laborers. These days, he had an office all
his own, and an official position as head of Magic Distillation,
making him one of the busiest, most important people there. All
courtesy of Jack's restructuring of the company's internal workings.
I spent fifteen, maybe twenty minutes with him, all of it forced
and awkward. As I finished the interviews, I allowed myself to
admit that in some ways, I was hurt that so many had stayed on
despite the change in regime; I'd half-hoped more would have left
with me. But why risk a good job in a dwindling market?

Just for old times' sake, I poked my head in the reindeer quarters, which were pretty much ceremonial these days, and then I
called it a day. I had enough. Everyone'd liked Jack. Great guy, very
charismatic, very hip. Knew all the latest slang and fads. The more
I heard, the more I felt like an old fossil, one who'd overstayed
his welcome by a century or two. The more I was confronted by
the radical changes brought about in recent years, the more it

twisted in my gut. People were doing just fine without me. Any hope I'd had that they'd all been pining for my return was dashed. Sure, they were polite and welcoming, but . . . It wasn't the same anymore. Honestly though, I didn't know what I'd hoped to learn here anyway. I hadn't stumbled across any books entitled *Melting People For Fun and Profit,* at any rate. It looked like my best bet was to meet with Mr. Tuesday, and see what he had to tell me, willing or no. With any luck, he'd be the link I needed to get to the heart of things.

I departed the factory weighed down by my thoughts, the suspicion that I'd missed something nagging at the back of my mind. I wanted to dismiss it, call it the disconcerting feeling of being back in old surroundings and finding everything changed, the familiar turned unfamiliar. Such was my mood that when I exercised my little spatial twist to transition back to Holiday, I accepted my stomach's lurching as just another attempt by the world to make me miserable. Of course, there was no rest for the weary; a message waited for me on my answering machine. Father Aaron had come through for me. Mr. Tuesday was willing to meet me tonight, at eight. According to my clock, that gave me just enough time to clean up and trudge on over.

That's how I ended up back at The Confessional, this time tucked away in one of its tiny booths, nursing yet another spiked eggnog and nibbling unenthusiastically on a plate of freshly-baked chocolate chip cookies, one of Aaron's house specialties. I'd arrived just a few minutes early, wanting to get settled in before my "guest" arrived. I'd dug up a little about the man who called himself Mr. Tuesday, rummaging through my files. Like me, he was one of the old gang, a Mystery fallen upon hard times and forced to find another line of work to keep from vanishing altogether. Probably Norse, if his pseudonym was any clue to his original identity.

Lost in my thoughts, still puzzling over who had the motive to want Jack out of the picture, I wasn't paying attention when Tuesday slipped into the seat across from mine, silently. He was a sharp man, both in features and in clothing, well-dressed and almost painful to look at. Hard angles and cold eyes made his face one I'd never forget. As he rested his arms on the table, I couldn't help but notice the way his right sleeve draped loosely, calling attention to his missing hand. Yeah. I offered my left hand to shake, trying to downplay how his arrival had startled me. He shook it, and then leaned back in his seat. "Nick St. Claus. I have to admit, your request surprised me. I can't even imagine how naughty someone must have been to require my services."

I was glad he didn't waste any time. After the way today had beat me down emotionally, and kicked me where I'd be sure to feel it, I wasn't in a mood to beat around the bush anymore. Leaning forward over the table, I replied, "I didn't call you because I want someone killed. I called you because someone's already dead, and you were in town when it happened."

Tuesday arched an eyebrow, and watched me, evenly. "Is that so?" He took a cookie, and bit into it, fiercely. Once he'd swallowed, he continued. "And this concerns me why?"

Screw it. I knew how he wanted to play this, but I was in no mood to play cat and mouse with an old-god-turned-professional-killer. I steepled my fingers, and met his icy eyes with my own, once again unlocking that coil of magic deep within my mind. With a familiar mind, it's easy and gentle, my power slipping right on it. Mortals are even easier, their minds defenseless, and children practically scream their secrets to any who'll listen. No, with Tuesday, it was hard and focused and violent, like a drill going through concrete, and later I'd feel ashamed of myself for it. I broke through his barriers before he caught on, and read his soul mercilessly, finding every stain and secret. Who he'd killed, how, why, all the sordid details. I discovered that while he was in town to eliminate a problem, it wasn't Jack Frost. I dug just deep enough to discover he was contracted to knock off a local Mystery-turned-drug lord, and then I retreated. I didn't care what happened to Frosty; that icy bastard and I had history as well, none of it good. The important thing was that Tuesday knew nothing at all about Jack's murder, and I was back to square one.

The abuse of my power left me exhausted and dirty inside, too tired to react with anything other than grudging acceptance when Tuesday responded by sticking a gun in my face. Hell, I'd earned it.

"What the hell?" he exclaimed, features turned ugly with rage. Yeah. Serves me right for pissing off an old war god. "You've got three seconds to explain before I ventilate your skull, you ass. You've got some nerve, rummaging through my head. I should empty yours for it."

Eyes closed, trying to banish the new headache and erase the image of the cold metal oblivion positioned inches from my face, I explained as succinctly as possible. "My ex-wife's lover got killed, and she hired me to investigate. I was an idiot to take the case, and it's been eating me up inside ever since. I'm done, Tyr. I'm all torn up, and tired of the whole thing. Go ahead and shoot. Hell, let's do this outside, so Aaron doesn't have to clean up the mess."

There was a long pause, and the metallic clunk of a gun being placed on the table. "Relax," he ordered. I opened my eyes, and caught him watching me with pity in his eyes. "You're a mess, Nick. But believe it or not, I understand you. I'm not happy about what you did, but . . ." He shrugged. "We all do stupid shit from time to time. Look, obviously I didn't kill your guy. You're barking up the wrong tree here. If this is your idea of detective work, you need a new job." No kidding. I never claimed to be a great detective. I fell into the job when I first came to Holiday. But Tuesday wasn't done. "My advice to you is simple: Ask yourself 'who benefits?' Who gains from having your guy out of the way?"

"I've already done that," I protested, knowing what I said was a lie. I hadn't thought that deep, because honestly, I didn't want to be here, doing this, and it showed. I'd gone about this like a drunken man in the dark, stumbling through the motions sloppily, picking my angles of investigation almost at random, and had gotten nowhere. If I wanted to see this thing through, I'd have to go back, try harder, look deeper, and most likely, learn something I didn't want to know about someone I liked.

Tuesday looked disappointed. "Don't lie. Nick, you're a decent guy who's made a few really bad choices. But you could make a good detective, if you actually tried, rather than wallowing in self-pity and stupidity. I remember you from the old days. You were one of the greats until you let it all slide. Don't be a loser." He stood up, grabbing his gun. "I have to work to do. So do you." A pause. "Oh, by the way. If you ever try that shit with me again," and here he tapped his forehead, "I'll make sure your death is slow and painful."

"Hold on," I said quickly, my mind racing. "One last piece of business."

"Shoot," he said curiously.

I told him what I needed, and though surprised, he was will-ing to oblige, fairly cheaply. Then he was gone, the bar seeming empty in his wake. Father Aaron watched the door shut behind Tuesday, before glaring at me in disapproval. I mumbled my apologies, not wanting to hear his thoughts on the matter, and left as well. I had to return to the factory, one last time, and put an end to things.

As I closed the distance between myself and the factory, letting the cold crunch of frozen snow underfoot punctuate my thoughts, I ran through the list of suspects, thinking about what I'd seen, heard, and learned during my first visit. I threw in all the niggling suspicions and gut instincts, some of them going back years, and let it all simmer. By the time I twisted through space and arrived at the factory, I knew where I had to go, and who to find.

Gunter was in his office, like a good little workaholic, a quality which had led to his current success.

"Evening, Gunter," I greeted him, entering and closing the door behind me.

"Mister Claus!" he replied, clearly startled. He jerked a hand across his desk, sweeping a pile of papers into an open drawer, slamming it quickly. "What are you doing back? Do you need something? Have you found out who killed Mister Frost yet?"

I nodded, sadly. "Yeah. I know who did it. What I don't know is why, Gunter. Why'd you go and kill Jack Frost?"

Just like that, the cards were on the table. He'd known he was busted the second I entered, and looked almost relieved to have it out in the open. "For you, boss," he said promptly. "I did it so we'd get you back. I knew that if Mister Frost was killed, Miss Virginia would go to you, and you'd take the case, and then you'd have to come back here, and maybe we could go back to how things were before. You don't understand, it's just not the same without you."

"Oh, I understand completely," I agreed. "I know things have changed. But you really couldn't have expected it to work, could you? It seems a bit . . . well, simplistic. Kill Jack so I'll return?"

"I knew once you and Miss Virginia saw each other again, you'd patch things up. Especially with her in need of comfort," he explained earnestly, eyes wide and hopeful. "Please, boss. We all want you back."

There it was. It was too easy, too pat. Too much like what I wanted to hear. He was trying too hard. "It's not that simple, Gunter. You can't heal the past so easily."

He continued to cajole me, half desperate, half pathetic, and I watched him lie to my face, his eyes flickering back and forth rapidly. I knew he was hiding something, and while he talked, I reached deep with my power, uncoiling it like a snake in the sun, slow and subtle. It was easy; I'd known Gunter for centuries, and the only reason I hadn't done this earlier was because, well, it was Gunter. I didn't want to suspect him. I hadn't wanted to see into his heart. We'd worked together for so long. But I probed, and unraveled the threads of his soul, letting his sins spill out for my perusal. He'd been very, very naughty. "Oh, Gunter," I said, suddenly bone-weary and ready to cry. "I wish you hadn't been so obvious."

He blinked. "I—what?"

"I know everything, now. How you've been embezzling magic from the factory for years. Abusing your position. It was easy when I was here, I gave you free rein and things were simpler. Jack, though, he liked paperwork and checked up on things. He found something, didn't he? Noticed some discrepancies and dug until he found your secret stash. So you killed him, but you were too hasty, and things didn't go as planned. Sloppy. Impatient." I recited the facts dully, taking no joy in how his expression went from indignant to resigned. "You didn't expect Ginny to turn to me and drag me back into this mess. You thought you'd have more time to clean up your tracks with someone who didn't know you. Another day, and you'd have been in the clear, I bet. And here I am, stumbling through your half-assed coverup, and whoops, it's all over."

"Like you even cared about Jack Frost?" snapped Gunter. "Come on, boss, you wanted him dead as much as anyone. You should be dancing on his grave, not pointing fingers at me! Merry early Christmas! Jack's dead, and you didn't have to do a damned thing!" His tone turned agreeable, wheedling. "And you know, you could walk away. I know you want to. For old times' sake. We split the magic, you turn your back, and you never see me again. You're happy, I'm happy, end of story."

"You're right," I agreed reluctantly. "I wanted Jack dead. I really thought it would make me happy. He stole Ginny, took the company, replaced me, and did better than me in every regard.

I hated him with a passion, especially at first." I jammed my hands deep into my pockets, shaking my head. "But I don't feel satisfied. Just hollow inside."

"So what now? Arrest me? Come on, Nick, we could all come out on top if you take the deal!" insisted Gunter. I could tell he was getting antsy, especially with me blocking the only exit. I saw his fingers twitch, and felt magic stirring in the air. Yeah, he was desperate, and lord, I was tempted to take the offer. Walk away from this train wreck and never look back.

"What it boils down to," I said slowly, "is that I hated Jack, but dammit, he made Ginny happy, and when you killed him, you hurt her, and that's the one thing I can't stand. It's why I left in the first place. You made Ginny cry, Gunter. You killed Jack, stole from the company, and made me walk waist-deep in the shit of my life. You've been extremely naughty." And before he could finish whatever spell he had on tap, I pulled Tuesday's gun from my pocket. I was all out of coal, so I filled Gunter with lead, instead, in the twinkling of an eye. He dropped before the last shot finished echoing in the small room, and I tossed the gun onto his corpse, done with it.

Just like that, it was over. I left the room, and went to go find Ginny and tell her how it had all gone down. I was going to get my money, and then I was taking a long vacation to somewhere warm and far away.

I was tired of being cold.

McNamara's Fish

➤ RON GOULART ◄

THE BEACH ON THE OTHER SIDE OF THE FENCE SLOPED DOWN
slowly to the quiet ocean. Max Kearny waited but no one came
to warn him about trespassing. He braced himself with one hand
against the redwood boards of the fence and took off his shoes
and socks. He tied the laces together and hung the shoes around
his neck.

The sand was warm, streaked with bright pebbles and broken
seashells. Max walked down beyond the scrub-topped dunes and
then kept parallel with the ocean. A seagull came walking toward
him, then angled away as though it were crossing a street to avoid
him. The surf hissed in and then slid away and the clam holes
popped all along the wet sand.

Standing in a windless cove between low sand hills was a
painter's easel. An empty canvas chair fluttered gently in front of
the easel and a wooden paint box sat open on the ground near
it. Max crossed the sand and looked at the painting. The small
canvas showed several men in red mackinaws doing something
to rows of trees. Max leaned closer. The men were hanging up
syrup buckets probably. In the background among the stick-straight
trees a horse and buggy was passing.

Max turned from the picture and lit a cigarette. He'd seen a
whole wall of pictures like this yesterday in Hollywood at one
of the newer art galleries. They were by somebody who signed
herself Aunt Jenny and would cost you $1,000 each. Aunt Jenny's

favorite motif was sap buckets, with an occasional snow storm thrown in.

"Hello, Max."

Max turned again. Standing next to the painting was Joan McNamara. She was a tall blonde girl, deeply tanned now, wearing white shorts and a blue denim shirt. "I saw an easel," Max said. "I thought maybe it was yours."

Joan frowned. "What made you think that?"

"You still are an artist, aren't you?"

"Yes," she said, smiling. "It's good to see you, Max. What is it—two years?"

"Since you and Ken moved down here from San Francisco."

"You're still with the same agency and all up there?" Joan sat down in the canvas chair, angling it to face Max.

"Yeah. That's why I'm down here. To watch them tape some commercials I did the storyboards for." He dropped his shoes down on the sand. "You said you had a problem."

"I was so glad when you phoned us and said you were down for a week. You still do have your hobby?"

"The occult business," said Max. "Yes."

A gate slammed and then two people appeared, coming toward Max and Joan. One was a tall young man in white duck pants and a pullover cablestitch sweater. With him was an old woman in a flowered silk dress. Her hair was tinted pale blue and she wore an L.A. Dodgers baseball cap over it.

"Mrs. Willsey and Val," Joan said to them. "This is our friend, Max Kearny. He's an artist, too. Max, Mrs. Willsey and her son, Val Willsey."

Max shook hands with Val.

"Mother is Aunt Jenny," Val said, grinning at the half-done painting.

"I've seen her work," said Max.

"Do you paint also?" asked Mrs. Willsey, taking the canvas chair Joan stood to give her.

"No," said Max. "I'm just an art director in an ad agency."

"Sold out?" said Val.

"We didn't have maple trees where I grew up," said Max.

"I didn't touch a brush until I was past forty-three," said Mrs. Willsey. "That was more years ago than I'd care to have you guess. Now I do at least three canvases a week."

"Mother's having a one-man show at the Alch Gallery on LaCienega next month."

"At first I simply copied colored photos from the magazines," said Mrs. Willsey. "Once I even copied the creation of the world from *Life* magazine. Now, of course, I utilize my own girlhood for subject matter. Paint what you know."

Joan caught Max's arm. "Max will be staying with Ken and me over the weekend. I imagine you'd like a drink or something, Max, after driving all the way from Hollywood to Osodoro Beach."

"Fine," said Max.

They said goodbye to Aunt Jenny and her son and started back across the beach toward the house Joan and Ken McNamara were living in.

"The place is awful, isn't it?" Joan said.

"No. But it's big as hell."

"At least it's not Moorish."

"It's whose house? Ken's dad's?"

"Ewen McNamara himself, yes. He's retired from the movie business and is living in Arizona. He gave us the damn place more or less."

"What's Ken doing?"

Joan shrugged. "He doesn't have a job right now. I'm doing pretty well. Freelancing ad stuff and selling a painting now and then."

"I thought Ken had somebody to finance the boat."

"Boat?"

"You wrote he was going to prove Heyerdahl wrong and do something in the Pacific with a raft."

"Oh, yes. No, Ken decided not to. All the bomb tests out there and all. He thought he'd be arrested as a pacifist." Joan stopped and pointed at the driftwood log. "Let's sit there for a minute. I take it you didn't find Ken back at the house?"

"No. Nobody. I decided to look for you on the beach."

Joan sat on the log and stretched her legs straight out in front of her. "Now, Max, you've made a lifetime study of the supernatural."

"No," said Max, sitting beside her. "Only the past couple of years."

"Well, you know enough." She spread her fingers wide and slid her hands down her legs to her knees. Rocking slightly she said, "Living by the ocean has been quite a thing."

"You've picked up quite a tan."

"Ken, too. Wait till you see him. No, but, what I mean is that especially at night there's something about the ocean. You know. You've read all the stuff about the mysteries of the deep and the poems what's-his-name Arnold and John Masefield wrote."

"I like Popeye, too. Is what's bothering you the ocean?"

"You mustn't talk to Ken about this."

"Okay, I guess."

"We have separate bedrooms now, you know."

"It wasn't in the papers."

"I mean we've been having all sorts of disagreements and such."

"I'm sorry."

"When Ken was doing the masks he got the idea he'd like to work nights and it developed into his using one of the spare bedrooms as a workshop and finally just sleeping there, too."

"Masks?"

"He met a fellow in Caliente who sold him two hundred masks, the kind they make down there, for fifty dollars. Ken had the idea he'd make lamps out of them. With sombreros for shades. The lightbulbs made them catch fire, though, and he gave it up."

"And the trouble?"

"He's having an affair with a mermaid."

Max stood up, dropping his shoes. "This isn't one of his projects? This is something he's actually doing?"

Joan said, "Yes, I'm afraid so." She put one hand over her eyes like a visor. "I thought maybe you could investigate."

"Like Peekaboo Pennington and get flash pictures?" Max knelt in the sand. "What gave you these suspicions about a mermaid?"

"Well," said Joan. "About two months ago I became aware that Ken was slipping out at night. He didn't take the car and if anyone picked him up I'd hear that, too. He'd be gone sometimes for hours. When I'd get his clothes ready to wash I'd find sand in the cuffs and seaweed smears. I know he goes down to the beach in the middle of the night, Max."

"If he goes with you in the daytime couldn't that be how he gets the sand and stuff?"

"All right. I made a special point of checking. He wears warmer clothes at night and in the morning there's sand all over them."

"And how come it's got to be a mermaid he's meeting?"

"You know Ken's father had a lot of the things from his movie studio moved here when it closed down," Joan said. "In fact, we have all those outbuildings full of stuff. But in the house there's a library. All kinds of obscure books that McNamara Studios had in their research department. A whole wall of books on the occult. I know Ken's been reading them lately. I found out which books he's been taking off the shelves. The books are all on the subject of mermaids."

"Whole books on mermaids?"

"And related subjects," said Joan. "He's involved with some sea woman."

"You've never tried to follow him? Or asked him about it?"

"I'm afraid to follow him," Joan said. "And asking him outright would only lead to a great debate."

"I didn't know you and Ken were," began Max.

"Growing apart? Since we moved in here it's been advancing. This place and Ken's not having a job. You're sure going to have a fun-filled weekend." Joan shook her head. "These past two months, though, Max, it's been different. The way Ken's acting. I know it's not just some other woman. It's a mermaid."

Max put his hands in his pockets and watched the seagulls skim along over the water.

"Max?"

"Yes?"

"If Ken asks say I came out here with you. Don't mention the Willseys unless you have to."

"I don't have to."

Joan smiled hopefully at him. "You'll figure everything out, Max. I know."

"Sure," Max said. He didn't smile back at her.

The tapestries that hung stiffly down between the shelves in the library were faded and cryptic.

"What?" Ken McNamara said to Max.

"I was wondering what battle the tapestries represent," Max said, casually moving near the shelf Joan had nodded at earlier.

"I don't know," said Ken. "Something that Tyrone Power fought in. They're all props from one of my dad's pictures."

Things fell over in the kitchen.

Ken put his drink on a gargoyle-legged table and went to the doorway. "You okay out there, Joan?"

"Where'd you put the wine vinegar?" his wife called.

Ken hesitated. "We're all out," he called back finally.

Max lit a cigarette and looked up at the rows of occult books.

"Listen, Max," said Ken.

"Yeah?"

"Wait." Ken closed the cherub-covered door. "You do detective work, don't you?"

"Only occult stuff. As a hobby."

"No hard-boiled things?"

"I beat a werewolf two falls out of three last fall."

"I mean the usual sleazy private op work."

"Divorce and motel?"

"Joan's having an affair," Ken said, walking by the row of German Renaissance beersteins on the mantel and tapping each one with his forefinger.

"Oh, so?" Max looked around for an ashtray.

"Use the mummy case over there," said Ken. "She sneaks out at night."

Max lifted the lid of the flat-lying case that rested on a wrought-iron stand near the fireplace. "The mummy does?" The case was half filled with cigarette butts. He added his and dropped the lid.

"No, for Christ sake, Joan. She's slipping around. And you know where she goes?"

"Sleeping around is the phrase."

"Whatever. You know where she goes?"

"Down to the beach?"

"No. Over to visit this guy named Val Willsey. A beach-boy type. Lives in the estate next door with his mother. I'm sure Joan's seeing him." He stopped and scowled at Max. "What's the matter with you anyway? This is serious."

Max lit a new cigarette. "What's the matter with you? Back in San Francisco you and Joan always looked like *House Beautiful*'s couple of the month."

"Do they have a couple of the month?"

"I'll check with media. Now what the hell is wrong?"

Ken sat down in a leather chair. "I don't know. The last year things have been going wrong. Since I lost the Orange Rupert concession."

"Orange Rupert?"

"The soft drink they sell along the highways in stands that look like oranges with a window in them. I had one two miles from here, on 101 just outside of Osodoro. But they took it away from me. I was showing a profit, too."

"Why?"

"The orange started to peel."

"Come on."

"The paint did. Kept coming off the damn thing. All the other damn Orange Rupert oranges were orange. Mine was rusty silver. It wouldn't stay orange."

Max took a book from a shelf. "Have you seen Joan over there with this Willsey guy?"

"No. I'm not a sneak, Max."

"But you've got a hunch, huh?"

"Right."

"*Mermaids And Other Creatures Encountered By A Norwegian Whaling Captain*," Max said, reading the title of the weathered book. "You read any of these?"

Ken blinked. "No. No, I don't. That's more your kind of crap." He rose. "Now about Joan."

The door of the library swung open. "Well," said Joan, "there's no vinegar. But, such as it is, dinner's ready. Okay?"

"Sure," said Ken. "See if you recognize the dining room table, Max. They used it in a picture my dad made with Douglas Fairbanks."

Max put the mermaid book back on the shelf and followed Joan and Ken down the high shadowy corridor to the dining room.

Everything was white with moonlight. The untended shrubs, the vast unclipped lawns and the great unclassifiable McNamara house. Max was sitting in a clump of damp ferns with his hands cupped over the bright tip of his cigarette. Far downhill the ocean made low tumbling sounds.

The gabled part of the house roof had a clock steeple stuck on one of its peaks. The clock showed one A.M. The darkness in among the shrubbery was dotted with frog calls and cricket chirps. Max felt his eyes start to close. He exhaled smoke and then took several deep breaths of the cold night air. He shook his head and widened his eyes. Finally he got himself almost awake again.

A dark figure appeared on the wide marble steps that wound down from the Dutch door at the side of the house. The figure moved off down the driveway, heading for the outbuildings. It was Ken.

This didn't seem right. Max ground his cigarette into the dirt. He'd picked this side of the house to watch because it faced the ocean.

But Ken wasn't heading for the beach. Max followed, keeping off the driveway gravel as much as he could.

There were a half-dozen dissimilar buildings on the grounds behind the main house. One looked like a Gothic cathedral built to the scale of a motel cottage. Another was a large two-story building that looked something like a Midwest bank. Between these two was an Arabian Nights sort of building, the size of a tract home. Ken went into this one. Max had the impression that Ken was carrying a package carefully in front of him.

Cutting down a flagstone path Max edged along the side of the Arabian structure. Flickering light showed at its horseshoe-shaped windows.

Directly behind this building was one that resembled an airplane hangar. Piled in front of it was a tangled assortment of chairs. Max picked three that seemed still in fair shape, hoping they weren't some of the McNamara's breakaway furniture. In among the nest of Georgian dining room chairs Max found some spare table boards.

Back under the arched window he put a board between two chairs and put the third chair on top of the board. He climbed up on the whole thing.

A lantern and brass lamp were burning in the room below. The whole place was full of props from old McNamara's Eastern pictures. Piles of wrought-iron doors and stacks of gilt trellises. Scatterings of peacock feathers and patterned silks, brass gongs and silver censers. In the center of all the confusion of worn out background pieces was an actual pool. It was large, its water a filmy green. Bordering it was real sand and jungle shrubbery. On a prop rock at the pool's edge was Ken, sitting with a salad bowl in his lap.

Ken dipped his hand into the bowl and brought out a handful of what seemed to be shrimp salad.

"I got the wine vinegar for it this time, LJ," Ken said.

"Mr. LJ is in conference," said a rasping voice. "He suggests you make an appointment."

"You're still on this kick, LJ?"

"Mr. LJ."

"Anyway, I made an appointment this afternoon. Remember?"

"We'll consult our appointment pad."

Max strained to see what it was that was talking from the pool.

"I can't wait around here all night, LJ. Come off it."

"Do you good to cool your heels in the waiting room for a while. We can find no record of your appointment. What was the nature of your business with Mr. LJ?"

"You're supposed to fix things up between Joan and me."

"Full names please. Last name first and please print."

"How can I print when I'm talking?"

"Perhaps you'd like to take your business to one of our competitors?"

"I'll take the shrimp, too, if you don't shape up," said Ken. "What kind of a water spirit are you if you can't even do any magic?"

There was a splashing at the darkest end of the pool and something swam toward Ken. "Who said I was a water spirit?" A fat blue fish nearly a foot and a half high pulled itself up on the rock with Ken. The pulling was easy because the fish had arms and legs. "You sure it's wine vinegar?"

"Yes."

LJ jabbed a blue hand into the salad bowl and began eating. "Not as good as a commissary, but it'll do."

"If you aren't a water spirit, what are you?"

"Mr. LJ is all you have to know."

"I've looked through all my dad's damned books on this sort of thing. And I can't quite pin you down."

"McNamara was strictly a shlep," said LJ, finishing the salad.

"And how come you're talking like this lately?"

"So why shouldn't I?" said LJ. "I've been all up and down the coast here."

"You didn't talk that way when I found you on the beach."

"So I should be consistent just to impress a third-rate creep like you."

"Okay, forget it, LJ," said Ken. "I know you have magic powers."

"How else did I get so far? Besides sheer guts, I owe the rest to magic. Out in the ocean it's dog eat dog. You don't stay on top for three hundred years just on luck."

"Isn't one of your powers the ability to tell what's going on?"

"Sure. Like now I'm sitting here with you."

"In places other than here. You can tell me where Joan goes when she sneaks off."

"It's possible I could," said LJ, more or less sitting down and crossing his legs.

"And you could work some kind of spell to make her stop her affair."

"So why not."

"It's been over seven weeks since I brought you here. And the results haven't been much so far."

"I tell you, Ken baby, Rome wasn't built in a day. Not even by DeMille. So don't be anxious. We'll work us out something. Meanwhile, before you make an appointment for tomorrow you should locate some lobsters for yours truly." The blue fish stood up and stretched its arms. "Excuse it, I've had a tough day."

"Lobsters?"

"I can maybe see you tomorrow morning around eleven, Ken sweetie. See you around the lot." LJ dived back into the pool.

Max let himself silently down to the ground. He waited until the lights went out and he saw Ken cutting back toward the house. Then he put the chairs and boards back.

The front door of the house clicked quietly and Joan, with her hands tight in the pockets of a gray belted raincoat, came out into the night. Max stopped moving. He had been coming around from the outbuildings and he halted now in a scattering of lemon trees.

Joan ran across the tangled grounds and vanished in among a blurred labyrinth of hedges at the far end of the place.

Dropping his cigarette butt into the Grecian urn near the sundial, Max followed Joan.

The hedges gave way finally to a spike-topped iron fence. Up across a half acre or more of close-cropped lawn sat the Willsey house. Max spotted Joan, a black silhouette bobbing, moving toward the house.

Max wiped his palms on his pants and got a grip on the black wrought-iron bars. He got himself over, tearing only one cuff.

Joan went down an arbored path and into a Spanish-style guest house. Its lights came on.

Max came up and looked in the window. Joan had taken off her coat and was putting on a smock. She had a canvas set up on an easel and, as Max watched, she started painting.

Max went away finally, puzzled. For some reason Joan was

ghosting paintings for Aunt Jenny. She even had a real sap bucket up to use as a model.

Max bent a match folder open and snapped it between the pages of the thick book. He set it aside and opened another book. He had a hunch what LJ was and he hoped the occult books in the McNamara collection would provide him with more specifics.

The morning sun was right at the library windows now and the chill of the room was lifting. There was a soft knock on the door and Joan came in. Her hair was tied back and she had on a blue robe. "Did you see her?"

"Who?" said Max, making another bookmark.

"The mermaid," Joan said, sitting across from him.

The mantel clock struck eleven and a team of allegorical figures popped out. Max waited until they'd gone indoors again and then he said, "Are you working for the Willseys?"

"Who said that?"

"I saw you over there last night. Painting one of those god-awful Aunt Jenny abortions."

"Your bloodhound instincts really ran wild. It's Ken you're supposed to watch."

"The sea air keyed me up. I got such a kick out of following him I decided to track you, too."

"There's nothing supernatural about what I'm doing," Joan said. The lace of her slip showed along the robe edge and she traced its pattern with her finger. "I wanted to get some kind of money ahead. So we wouldn't have to depend on Ken's father. Mrs. Willsey asked me to help her on one of her paintings. That was four or five months ago. Aunt Jenny likes the fun of painting. Laying it out and finishing it up tire her. I've painted at least part of all her things. Lately I ghost whole paintings."

"Then it's you who's responsible for the Aunt Jenny boom down here."

"Probably. Anyway I get forty percent of everything I do. I opened an account in a bank in Santa Monica." Joan noticed her moving hand and stopped it. She dropped both hands in her lap. "But what did you find out about Ken?"

"Is he around?"

"No. He drove off early. He's not back yet. Didn't you trail him this morning?"

"I overslept," said Max. "There is something."

"Something?"

"A fish."

"Ken's having an affair with a fish?"

"No, he's trying to get advice from the fish."

Joan turned toward the window. "That's the car coming back. What fish? What sort of advice? He's not still worried about the lighthouse business? The company said they'd refund the deposit because you can't get to the island except by autogiro."

"Let's just limit it to this fish. No other projects."

"Is the fish in the ocean? Does Ken visit it there?"

"No. It's in that Arabian-looking building out back. In the pool."

"What sort of fish is it, Max? A shark or something dangerous?"

"A little blue fish with arms and legs. It talks and does magic."

Joan shook her head. "I don't understand. I've never heard of . . ." There was a great cloud of yellow smoke suddenly around Joan. Then a loud explosion.

"Joan." Max jumped for her chair.

The chair teetered and slammed over sideways. Joan was gone.

Max spun around. The room was empty, the door still closed.

Max opened it and ran out into the hall. The house was quiet. Max went out the side door that led back to the outbuildings.

Coming down the path toward him was Ken.

"Did you give the lobster to LJ?" Max said, pulling up.

"Had to drive all the way to Santa Monica for it but I—who told you about LJ?"

"Joan just vanished."

"Off with Val Willsey probably. Or maybe just shopping," said Ken. "I'm willing to admit she could be just shopping."

"She doesn't usually vanish in a puff of yellow smoke, does she?"

"No, she takes the Volkswagen. Max? You mean Joan's disappeared by magic?"

"Why not? You've been goading LJ into doing something. Apparently you've finally succeeded in bringing him into action."

Ken said, "This isn't the sort of solution I expected."

Someone said, "Yoo hoo."

"Max, I think I heard something strange."

"Yoo hoo," called a woman's voice.

"Is that some magic phrase, Max?"

"Sounds more like yodeling." Max turned.

Coming from the front of the house was Aunt Jenny. She waved her Dodgers cap at them. "Did Val happen to stop by here?" she called.

"See?" said Ken. "It's an open secret."

"Is he missing?" asked Max.

"I'm beginning to think so," said the old woman as she joined them. "He vanished in a cloud of ugly smoke. That isn't like Val at all."

"LJ again," said Max.

"Beg pardon?"

"We'll tell Val you were asking after him," Max said. "I'm pretty sure he'll be back by this afternoon."

"Will there be any more smoke? We did settle out here to get away from the smog. If Val's going to take to coming and going in enormous gusts of smoke I don't think we'll have gained much."

"No more smoke," said Max, smiling and guiding Aunt Jenny around to the front of the house.

Ken followed. He waited until the old woman was into the hedges. Then he said, "Damn it. What's happening? Are Joan and Val shacked up in the fourth dimension someplace?"

"You can't get in without luggage," said Max. "Look, where did you find LJ?"

"That bastard. Here I butter him up for weeks and he does this." Ken hit his fist into his palm. "He washed in down at the beach a couple months ago. He seemed like an out-of-the-ordinary sort of fish and I put him in the old pool. When it turned out he was probably magic I decided to get him to help out with Joan. I had to turn to somebody. With Joan having an affair."

"You should have tried Abigail Van Buren first," said Max. "And Joan isn't having an affair."

"What makes you say that?"

"I looked through some windows and peeked over some shrubs. She's ghosting Aunt Jenny pictures to make extra money."

"It could be I've screwed up some then."

"That's a possibility."

"I'll fix LJ, Max. I'll stand up to him and tell him to knock it off and tell me what's become of Joan." Ken stopped. "Max, she'll come back somehow, won't she?"

Max nodded. "She'll come back." He shook out a cigarette and lit it. "Did he talk like a Hollywood type when you found him?"

"No, that's only lately. In fact, he had some vague European accent when I found him."

"I think he's some kind of old world elemental spirit," said Max. "We have to have some weapon before we talk to him."

"A water spirit," said Ken. "I thought so, too. But none of the pictures in the reference books look like LJ."

"Maybe the guy who did the illustrations never saw one like LJ."

"That's right. Before television they went on hearsay a lot more than now."

"A spell to control a water elemental should work on LJ," said Max. "Even if he's only probably a second-string water spirit."

"There's a couple of good spells in one of the books."

"I know," said Max. "Let's see what we can work out."

They ran back into the house.

Ken looked over Max's shoulder into the kitchen sink. "We sprinkle him with that stuff and that's all?"

Max looked from the book of spells to the gray-green liquid in the sink. "According to this. It's not the top magic fluid, but it's the best we can do with household ingredients."

"How would a siphon be? A seltzer bottle to spray the junk at him with."

"You have one? I thought they only used those in comedies."

"That's where this one came from. A picture of my dad's." Ken went to the white-doored cabinet at the kitchen end and felt inside. "That book is over three hundred years old. Suppose the spell is stale."

Max checked through the drawers and found a ladle and a funnel. "LJ is over three hundred years old, too. It should fit."

Ken put the bottle on the drain board and Max filled it with the fluid. "Don't spill any, Max."

"There's enough."

"I mean Joan'll get mad if we make a mess in her kitchen."

"There."

"If we get her back."

Max tightened the siphon on the bottle. "We should. Come on."

"Mr. LJ's in conference, sweetie," said the voice at the end of the pool.

"Tell him to get his ass down here," said Ken.

"So is this how you talk to somebody who has solved your

problems?" LJ swam to them and pulled himself up on the rock. "Who's the creep with you?"

Max squatted and said, "What did you do with Joan McNamara?"

"Leave your card with my secretary, chum. You I don't even know."

"The bottle," said Max.

Ken brought it out from behind his back. "Ready."

"Bribes won't help you," said LJ. "Anyway I fixed up your problem swell for you, honey. This clown, Val Willsey, will never get his hands on your little lady now. Believe you me."

"Tell us what you did with them," said Max. "Or we'll use some of this anti-elemental spray on you."

"So who's an elemental?" LJ laughed. "Why are you boys so stewed up? I fixed things good. That's what you wanted."

"You didn't fix things good at all," said Ken. "You made the same stupid mistakes I did about Joan. It was Max here who..."

"Max, that's a nice name," said LJ. "If he noses around too much in my affairs I'll fix him, too. Him I'll cast as Cupid with a dolphin if he don't watch it."

"We don't want to hurt you," said Max.

"So how could you?" LJ put his hands behind his scaly blue back and paced. Then he closed one eye and turned. Pointing at Max he said, "You I'll fix right now."

Ken sprayed the fluid at LJ. "Damn you."

"How typical," said LJ, toppling over. He fell and lay still with his legs up stiff in the air.

"It works," said Ken.

"Works great." Max watched LJ.

LJ popped and disintegrated into blue dust. "I had to use the stuff to save you, Max. It worked too good."

Max stood up, watching the spot where LJ had been. "In all the props and stuff that're stored here, is there much statuary?"

"Sure," said Ken. "In the big warehouse back of here. All sorts of birdbaths and fountains and lawn statues. Greek stuff and so on." He put the bottle down. "Hey. And that's where a lot of my dad's old files and clippings and letters are stored."

"Could LJ get in there?"

"The pipes from here run back to the warehouse," said Ken. "That's probably where he picked up his Hollywood material."

"Let's take a look," said Max. "He threatened to turn me into a decorative piece for a fountain. Maybe he did the same with Joan."

Ken found her. "Hey, Max. Over here."

Joan and Val Willsey were on a pedestal, turned to stone. "Very funny," said Max.

"This used to be a satyr chasing a nymph."

"And never getting his hands on her," said Max. "LJ was a whimsical guy." Max looked at the rows of stone figures.

"It just occurred to me," said Ken. "I was so happy finding Joan I forgot. LJ's destroyed and Joan is turned to stone. How do we break this spell?"

Max walked once around the two figures and then leaned back against a stone Venus. "Try kissing her. That works sometimes."

"What about Val."

"Try Joan first."

Ken pulled a stool over and reached up. He leaned out and kissed the statue Joan. "Once enough?" he asked.

"Once enough for what?" said Joan, stepping down off the pedestal. "Ken, what happened?" She glanced at the stone Val Willsey. "Is that Val?"

Ken hesitated. "Kiss him."

"The statue?"

"Go ahead."

Joan did. It brought Val back. "What an odd thing to have happen over breakfast," he said. "Excuse me. Mother's probably having eight kinds of fits." He nodded at them and hurried away.

"I guess I misunderstood you," said Ken.

"Me, too, with you," said Joan.

Ken looked at Max. "I bet lots of people would be interested in that spray we made to use on LJ. There are probably other elementals around."

"LJ?" Joan asked.

"Tell you back at the house," Ken said, taking her hand. "Coming, Max?"

"In a minute. You go ahead."

"Thanks, Max," said Joan as she and Ken walked out of the warehouse.

Max lit a cigarette. He watched the stone Venus over his shoulder. Not a bad-looking girl.

When he finished the cigarette Max walked down the row of statues and out into the daylight.

Gunsel and Gretel

> ESTHER M. FRIESNER <

IT WAS A HOT, HUMID, L.A. AFTERNOON, A DAY WHEN THE CEILING
fan just stirs the air around slow, like a witch's brew, the kind of
day that makes me ask myself why I ever left the cool shade of
the German forests for this city, this office, this job. Lucky for
me, all I had to do to find the answer was open the paper and
see Hitler's smiling face. There are worse things in this world than
muggy weather, hard-nosed cops, and overdue dentist bills.

I was about to meet another one.

I knew she was trouble the minute she ankled into my office.
They always are, if they're coming to see me. Somehow I never
seem to attract the sweet young things trying to get their own
back from some kiss-and-tell toad or the frumpy *hausfraus* out
to nail Prince Charming for getting horizontal in someone else's
glass coffin; just the dames.

This dame I knew. I watched her baby blues go wide when she
recognized me. I kind of enjoyed it. Yeah, we had a past, and if
they ever wrote it up in the history books it'd make Waterloo,
Pearl Harbor, and Custer's Last Stand read like *The House at
Pooh Corner*.

"Hello, gorgeous," I said, taking my feet off the desk. I accidentally stepped on the cat's tail. He screeched, but things are
tough all over. "It's been a long time. What's a nice kid like you
doing in a dump like this?"

She had the class to lower her eyes. You come face-to-face

with the person you think you bumped off years ago and a little embarrassment's only good manners. That's what I always say.

"I'm—I'm sorry," she mumbled. "When I saw the name on the door, I never thought—"

"—that it was me? Why should you? Give your mind the five-cent tour down Memory Lane, sweets. Aside from shacking up with me, leading me on, running out on me and leaving me for dead, you didn't once think to ask my name. Never formally introduced, and us nearly a lifetime item. Tsk-tsk, what would Emily Post say?" I grinned until I could feel the tip of my nose touch the tip of my chin.

She gave me a hard stare. "Like *that* would make a difference." She always was feisty, more snap to her than a box of rubber bands. That's okay: I like them feisty. "That's a *man's* name on your door."

"It's a man's world, sugar."

"You're operating under false pretenses."

"You should feel right at home." The cat jumped into my lap. I petted him until he started shedding, then I dropped him to the floor. I don't give a damn what they say: Black fur *does* show on a black dress. "So, now you know it's me, I guess you'll be going. Drink before you leave? For old times' sake?" I opened the bottom drawer and took out the bottle and a pair of glasses.

She shook her head.

"Mind if I indulge?" I didn't wait for an answer; I poured a tall one and knocked it back fast and smooth.

She gave me the fish-eye. "How can you drink that stuff?"

"In case you haven't noticed, cupcake, I'm sitting down. You can do the same, or you can leave. The door works both ways."

She sat down on the only other chair in my office, looking about as comfortable as a beautiful princess at a wicked stepmothers' convention. Her hands closed tight over the clasp of a cheap red plastic pocketbook balanced on her nyloned knees. Her whole outfit screamed two-bit canary with a sideline in grifting. I gave her the once-over, saw how she'd changed. The years had been pretty good to her. Last time I saw her, she was a skinny little piece of cheesecake; *too* skinny for my taste.

Tastes change; so had she. She'd filled out nice, real nice. She was still trying to play the innocent, though. That was a laugh. If there was ever a tough cookie, she was it, and believe me, I know tough cookies.

She finally found her tongue. It was right there in her own mouth. For a change.

"I'm not going to lie to you," she said. I managed not to laugh. "Even if you are . . . who you are, I still want you to take my case. I came here because a friend of mine—one of the other girls down at the La Zazz Club—gave me your name. The one on your door, I mean."

"The La Zazz Club," I repeated. The name rang a bell—it was a notorious jive joint—but that was all. I tried to think if I ever had a client who worked there.

I get quiet when I'm thinking. My visitor didn't like things quiet. She started yakking to fill up the silence: "My friend said you helped her out of a tough bind. She said you got the job done and you didn't ask the wrong kind of questions to do it. She said she'd trust you with her life, that you're the best in the business."

"Flatterer."

"I mean it!" She slammed a fist down on my desktop so hard it made my glass clink against the bottle. I took this as a sign to fill it up so it wouldn't make too much noise and upset the neighbors. "I've got a real problem. I need help."

This time I sipped my drink slow. "Keep talking."

"It's my brother. He's disappeared."

I thumbed back the brim of my hat and set down the empty glass. "Some reason the cops can't handle this?"

She didn't say anything. That said it all. "In case it's slipped your pretty little mind, sweets, my past association with your family hasn't exactly been a romp in the forest. I wasn't looking for you to show up on my doorstep, but Destiny's a funny dame. She's got a way of giving you the brass ring with one hand and ripping your heart out with the other. You want me to go out there, pound shoe leather and get my Sunday-go-to-meeting broom all dusty looking for your brother? *Trying* to find him? I'm about as interested in finding that scrawny little bastard as Japan is in giving back Mongolia. Find yourself another sucker."

That was when she turned on the faucets. I watched her smear her mascara into skid marks for a while, and when I saw she was crying real tears I reached up my sleeve and tossed her a handkerchief.

"Please, don't turn me down," she begged, dabbing at her eyes. "You can't; you're my last hope."

"That so?" I thumbed my hat back again, only this time I pushed it too far. It fell off my head and rolled around on its point until the cat jumped on it and crushed the brim. I lost my patience and turned him into a toad. He gave me this ominous croak that as good as told me he was going to accidentally-on-purpose use my shoes for a litter box as soon as I turned him back. I've lived with worse threats.

"Your last hope, well, well," I repeated as I grabbed my hat off the floor and put it back on. The toad hopped away to sulk in a corner. "And here you were just now, saying I was your first choice. Either the honeymoon's over already, or you're not playing it square with me, sugar. I wouldn't recommend that."

"I'm sorry." She took a deep breath. It did things. "I lied."

"I'd like to say I'm surprised, cupcake, but since it's you . . ." I shrugged. "Tell you what, you give me the facts in the case, I listen, and maybe I take it. Maybe not. No promises. Okay, one: You lie to me again, you're out of here on your cute little bustle. Got it?"

"Got it." She sniffled one last time, but the fire was back in her eyes. She got out her compact and started repairing the damage while she told me the whole story:

"It's been two weeks since I heard from Hansel. That's not normal; we're close. Usually he calls me every other day, or I call him. We get together on the weekends, catch a movie, maybe take a drive up the coast."

"With the war on?" I gave her a warning look. "What's your car run on, Coca-Cola? Even I can't make gasoline out of thin air."

She shrugged, but she didn't backpedal. "It's his car. I guess I never thought to ask him where he got the fuel for it. It's a fancy ride, powder blue Packard sedan, white leather seats."

I snorted. "The Easter Bunny bring it? No one makes cars that look like that!"

"You got enough money, you can always find someone to make you anything you want," she said. She talked like a woman who knew.

"So your little brother did all right for himself, and pretty fast, too. The pair of you couldn't have been in this country much longer than me."

"We came over in '38."

I whistled, low and long. "That *is* fast for someone to make good; especially for a johnny-come-lately punk like your brother. I'm impressed. What's his racket?"

"I don't know. He never told me."

I got up and went for the office door. I threw it open and told her: "Get out."

She didn't move a muscle. "It's the truth. The one time I asked, he gave me the brushoff. Said something about being in public relations."

"The kind the cops run you in for when they catch you trying it in Griffith Park?" I would've laughed, but I sort of forgot how.

She stood up. "You said you'd listen. I said I'd tell the truth. So far I'm keeping up my end of the deal."

If she was waiting for an apology, she was going to be twice as gray and wrinkled as me before she got it. Still, I closed the office door. "All right, sweets, you made your point. I'll listen."

She gave me a look like ex-wives give their husbands when the bastards swear the check is in the mail. "Like I said, my brother and I have always been very close, but that doesn't mean we're all over each other's business. Ever since our mother died, we looked out for one another. Daddy never had time for us; he had to earn a living, put food in our mouths. Being a woodchopper's no ball."

"Can the sob story and cut to the chase," I told her.

"I'm not looking for sympathy. I'm a big girl. I can take care of myself."

She had me there. Last time our paths crossed, she almost took care of *me*. Permanently. I went back to my desk and motioned for her to go on.

"Like I said, he calls me a lot, so when I didn't hear from him for two weeks straight, I got worried. I went over to his place, the Chez Moderne apartments."

The Chez Moderne . . . Ritzy name for what was basically a rundown old hotel so far downtown that the cockroaches had to take the streetcar. Not the address I'd expect of the man who owns his own powder blue Packard. I shot her a searching look but it bounced right off. If she'd ever wondered about why her brother drove *that* but lived *there*, she didn't let on.

"I had the extra key, so when no one answered my knock, I let myself in." She shuddered, remembering. "The place looked like an earthquake hit it. Someone had been there before me and they tore it up, top to bottom."

"You sure? Maybe your brother just wasn't a very good house-keeper." Her eyes poured me a double dose of arsenic, straight up, so I stopped trying to pass for one of the Marx Brothers.

"Everything was ruined. Whoever'd done it even sliced up the mattress and ripped the lining out of the drapes. The bathroom floor was wall-to-wall pills, all the empty bottles smashed in the bathtub."

I didn't like to bring up what could be a pretty ugly possibility, but I had to ask: "Any blood?"

She shook her head. "I was thankful for that much. My first instinct was to go to the cops, but when I got home, there was a letter waiting for me. It was from my brother."

I held out my hand, waiting for her to cough it up. I kept on waiting.

"I burned it," she explained.

"How convenient."

"You don't understand: I had to!"

"Why?"

"Because he told me to. He didn't want me getting involved. It was too dangerous. If they got their hands on that letter—"

"Not so fast. Who's 'they'?"

"He didn't name names. The same creeps who wrecked his place, I suppose."

"Tough call. What else did the letter say?"

"It said that he was going away for a few weeks, maybe a few months, on business. He didn't come right out and say so, but he hinted that this was it, the big score, something that was going to put the two of us on Easy Street for the rest of our lives. He said he'd be in touch, and for me to sit tight until I heard from him again."

"Did he say how he'd contact you?"

She shook her head.

"So tell me this, cupcake: If you're such a *good* little girl—keeping your nose out of your brother's business, not asking questions, burning that letter strictly on his say-so—then why are you here? Why aren't you back in your own place, sitting tight like he told you?"

There were tears starting up in her eyes again. "Because he's not the one who wrote that letter."

"Not his handwriting?"

"Nothing that amateurish. But I could tell. Someone dictated every word he wrote; it didn't sound like him at all. That was when I decided to get help. That was when I came to you. Will you help me? Please?"

I wrinkled my nose. Her story smelled worse than Fisherman's Wharf, up Frisco way. This dame was spinning a yarn with more loose ends than Rapunzel's marcel wave and expecting me to buy it. She had brass, but all the nerve in the world can't make up for being stupid. Trying to play me for a fool is *real* stupid.

She'd done that once before, in the Old Country, her and her rotten little brother. I didn't see so good back then—try to find a decent eye doc in the sticks—but so what? There's not much worth looking at in the heart of the Black Forest. You seen one squirrel, you seen 'em all. That was how those brats managed to give me the runaround. Every time I told the punk to stick his finger through the bars of the cage where I had him locked away to fatten up, he'd stick out a chicken bone. The gristle should've tipped me off. Too soon old, too late smart, like they say.

As for her, I had hopes: She was a sweet little thing and I was lonely. If they ever made a movie of my life, the screenwriters'd have to call me an old maid or a career gal or just not the marrying kind because the truth would bring the Hays Office down on their necks faster than a well-oiled guillotine. And before you get all hot under the collar, thinking she was just a kid and I was some kind of monster, let me clue you in on something not everyone knows: She and her brother were no babes in the woods, no matter how they twisted the story later. They might've *looked* like kids, small and scrawny on account of growing up at the Hard Knocks Hotel, but they were both safely past the age of consent when they came nibble-nibbling at my door. And believe me, she let on like she *would* consent any day, if I didn't pull a Betty Crocker on her. So that's why he was in the cage but she had the run of the place. Oh yeah, she played innocent-but-willing-to-learn, and she played it good.

That's why I believed her when she said she didn't know how to tell if the oven was hot enough. That's why I stuck my head in first, to show her how it's done. My head was full of stardust, dreams of her and me in that kitschy little woodland cottage, me with my feet up on the pile of kiddie bones, her by the oven, baking gingerbread, everything strictly *Ladies' Home Journal*.

Next thing I knew, my face was full of live coals. She'd shoved me into the oven, locked the door, freed her brother, and beat it.

I'd be a pretty poor witch if I didn't keep an escape spell on the tip of my tongue at all times. But she didn't know that. By the time I got myself out of the oven and under the pump, drenched but extinguished, those two were long gone. Them and my life's savings in gold.

Like I said, we had a past.

That's why I didn't have any second thoughts about nailing her with the same toad spell I used on the cat. It was sweet: One minute she was standing there trying to work the bunco, the next she was squatting on the floor, brown and lumpy as a bowl of boardinghouse oatmeal.

I picked her up easy and dropped her on the desk, then poured myself another drink. This time I got out some cookies to go with all that milk. One chopper left in my head and wouldn't you know it's a sweet tooth? In between sips and swallows, I told her the score:

"Next time you want to work the old shell game, sister, make sure you've got a real chump on the line. That, or get your story straight. First you act all surprised to see a woman gumshoe, then you say your friend gave you the lowdown on me. And she didn't mention *that* little detail? Next we've got the little matter of your brother's fancy car and his invisible means of support. A smart cookie like you wouldn't grill him for some answers there? I'm not buying. As for that letter you say he sent you, the one you knew he didn't write . . . Why'd you act like it was the real McCoy when it came to doing what he said, burning it, only the next words out of that pretty little mouth of yours were 'I knew it wasn't really his'? Your story's got more holes in it than Dillinger. I think you need a little time to think over what a bad girl you've been. You sit right there while I do some digging on my own. Okay, cupcake?"

I wasn't dumb enough to expect an answer. Toads talk less than Charlie McCarthy when Bergen's in the can. I left her with the empty milk bottle and nabbed her purse from the floor. When I dumped it out on the desk, she jumped off and flopped around my ankles, croaking like crazy, but she couldn't do a damn thing to stop me.

I found what I was looking for inside a little plaid change

purse. It was a piece of onionskin paper, folded up small. *Dear Gretel*, it said. *You were right, Mr. LeGras doesn't really care about me, no matter what he says. I'm just another one of the hired help to him, and now he's come back from San Francisco—one of his "business" trips—with that so-called English valet, Carlisle. English! The closest that dog biscuit's been to England is the seat of Mr. LeGras's tweed pants.*

When I told Mr. LeGras how I felt, he gave me the brushoff, said it was all my imagination, threw me some extra scratch and told me to go out and buy myself a good time. No one treats me like that and gets away with it. I'm getting the hell out of here, but before I go, I'm going to leave Mr. LeGras something to remember me by. Or should I say I'm going to take something?

The black bird.

Yes, that *black bird. The one I told you about, the one you say can't possibly be real. But it is real. Real enough to be the source of Mr. LeGras's fortune. Real enough to do the same for us.*

Think of it, my dearest sister! No more warbling your heart out in cheap dives like the La Zazz for you, and for me, no more faking that a pig like Mr. LeGras is my maiden dream of love.

I looked up from the letter. "The black bird," I said aloud. "That's a step up from stealing gingerbread."

The brown toad gave an inquiring croak from the floor.

"Don't tell me you never heard of the black bird, sugarplum," I told her. "Every two-bit hustler and small-time hoodlum in this town knows about the black bird. You want I should draw you a map or just write you a screenplay? Get your hands on the black bird and you're set for life, and I'm not talking ration books, I'm talking gold; solid gold."

I went back to the letter: *I'm going to make the big touch soon, this week. If I don't, I might wind up plugging Carlisle first, making the snatch second. It's easier for me to hide a bird than a body, ha, ha. Soon as I knock over the bird, I'll get word to you. When that happens, meet me up at the place on Lake Arrowhead and we'll blow this pop stand. I'll be waiting. Love, Hansel.*

I folded the letter and put it back in her purse. "I love the way he keeps calling him *Mister* LeGras," I told her. "Even when he's talking about playing him for a sucker. That's class." I crossed my arms and stared down at her. "So you did like he told you: You waited for word, but the week went by and all you came up with was a goose egg. You went over to his place, maybe thinking he lost his nerve and hadn't done it, maybe scared he *had*, and then decided not to cut you in on the score after all. When you found his place wrecked like that, you must've figured that he *did* pull off the heist, only sloppy. LeGras caught wise before Brother Dear could make his getaway, but *not* before the goof managed to hide the swag. So LeGras hired some muscle to get back his property, probably told them that if they wanted to practice their tap-dancing on the little creampuff's face, he wouldn't mind."

The toad launched a rapid-fire burst of angry croaking, slapping its feet on the linoleum floor. I clucked my tongue.

"Hey, I'll talk about your brother any way I want, angelcake. You think he walks on water? He's still a weasel, a slimy little gunsel who got in too deep and who might be getting in deeper as we speak, courtesy of a pair of cement overshoes. Hard to walk on water then."

The toad made a mournful sound and turned its back to me. Its lumpy little shoulders were working like an oil rig in a dry hole. I didn't know toads could sob. Against my better judgement, I felt like a heel.

"Can the waterworks, sweets," I said, squatting down in front of her. "I'll help you, only not the way you asked. We don't need to find your brother. We need to find the bird."

The toad anted up a croak that was as good as a question. I got her drift. "Because if his place was torn up as bad as you say, I'm willing to bet they were after a clue to where he stashed the bird," I explained. "Maybe they found one, maybe not. If they did, well, it's lights out for Hansel; nothing I can do. But if they didn't—" The toad looked hopeful. "—then he's still alive. LeGras wants his precious tweetie back; he won't let his goons kill the rat until it squeals. If *we* can find the bird before Junior cracks, we've got a bargaining chip that just *might* save the little reptile's bacon."

The toad croaked at me indignantly. I snorted. "Yeah, yeah, so reptiles don't have bacon. You want to play egghead games or you want to save your brother before they send him back to you in a box?" The toad looked sorry for having brought up the whole subject. I patted her on the head and said, "Never mind, honey. Let's hit the bricks. Our next step is back to Junior's place so I can—"

I never got to finish saying what I had in mind. A galaxy of stars exploded inside my head and my next step was sprawled flat on my face on the office floor. That's life: Sometimes it hands you a gingerbread house, sometimes it shoves you headfirst into an oven, and sometimes it's happy to have some gorilla sneak up from behind and bean you with a blackjack.

When I came to, I got a firsthand idea of what Junior's ravaged apartment must've looked like. Someone had torn through my office like a two-headed ogre with a migraine. I pulled myself to my feet using what was left of my desk and surveyed the damage.

There were papers everywhere, not a drawer left in place. My file cabinet was stretched out like a coffin, my chairs were kindling, and something very important was missing from the room:

My client.

I didn't need a crystal ball to tell me what had happened, though I could've used the entrails of a black he-goat to fill in the details. The same goon-or-goons-unknown who had ripped up Junior's digs had come a-calling at my door. They'd probably been tailing Gretel, looking to put the snatch on her. I guess some whiz kid figured that if Junior wouldn't sing to save his own skin, maybe he'd twitter through a scale or two to save his sister's. When she came to see me, all nice and private, they got their chance.

I touched the egg growing out of the back of my skull and winced. "That's no way to treat a lady," I muttered. I crossed to the coat closet, avoiding shards of glass and piles of chocolate-chip crumbs. They'd busted my cookies. Nobody busts my cookies.

Lucky for me my uninvited guests had left my broomstick alone. Probably thought it belonged to the cleaning lady. I appreciate opponents with no imagination; it's no loss to the world when I put them away for good. My head was still spinning, but I'd flown with hangovers that were a damn sight worse. Now I needed just one more thing before I could hit the wild blue yonder . . .

"Here, kitty," I called. "Here, kitty, kitty, kitty! Here, Bogey, come to Mama."

The first thing they teach you in my line of work, even before you get within spitting distance of a magic wand or a cauldron or that plug-ugly black pointy hat, is that you don't go up without a co-pilot. You can't. Cats and witches don't hang out together just for the conversation: We need the beasts to power our brooms.

Witches know that every living thing's a source of potential energy. You ever spend a whole day watching a cat? Most of the time he's curled up asleep in the sun, when he's not feeding his face. All intake, no output; the perfect storage battery. Get enough cats together and you could launch a flock of B-29s.

"Bogey-boy, come on, I need you. Puss, puss, puss. Bogey, I'm *calling* you, you mangy fleabag! Get *over* here, Bogey, I mean it!"

Nothing. That wasn't unusual. You show me the cat who comes when he's called and I'll show you an enchanted prince waiting to be kissed. That, or a sick cat. But I was doing more than just beating my gums: I was using his name as the focus for an attraction-spell. If Bogey was anywhere within the sound of my voice, he'd be dragged in and set down at my feet in two minutes. "Bogey, come *here!*"

Two and a half minutes later, I was worried. Nothing could keep Bogey from responding to my attraction-spell if he were alive. "If anything's happened to him . . ." I gritted my teeth. He was more than just a cat to me: He was my partner. No one takes out my partner and gets away with it.

Suddenly, I heard a weak sound coming from the corner behind my toppled file cabinet. "Bogey, is that you?" If I was the church-going type, I would've wasted time saying a little thanksgiving prayer. Instead, I got right to work, moving the cabinet so he could get out. "Hold on, kitty, Mama's coming."

It wasn't a kitty; it was a toad. I forgot that I'd pulled the old shape-change on him before, when he got on my nerves. I was forgetting a lot of things, mostly thanks to that lump on my head.

"Hold still, kid; this won't take a second." I made with the mystic bushwas to restore him to his original shape. There was a hokey puff of smoke as the spell hit him.

"It's about time!" Gretel snapped at me. Her eyes flashed all around my wrecked office. "Thorough bastards, aren't they? Serves you right. Now, where's my purse? I'm getting out of here." She started pawing through the rubble.

I grabbed her arm and pulled her back. "Not so fast, sugar. Aren't you forgetting a little something?"

"You mean my brother?" she shot back, jerking out of my grasp. "Hardly. He's all I'm gonna be thinking about the whole way to New York City, which is exactly where I'm headed as soon as I find my purse." She went back to digging up the ruins, a regular Schliemann in shantung.

I hauled her back to face me a second time. "Cool your heels, sweetiepie. What's all this about New York?"

"It's the farthest away from here I can get, that's what," she said. "By bus, anyway. Maybe you didn't see the pair of thugs that were just in here—"

"They gave me the bum's rush to Slumberland before they bothered to introduce themselves," I replied with a twisty little smile. It hurt. "So there were two of them, you say?"

She nodded. "Big ones. Ugly, too. A couple of reject heavy-weights from palookaville."

"Names?"

"I heard one call the other Max; that's all I know. Max was the one who slugged you."

"Max, huh?" I made a mental note to give Max a tour of the La Brea tar pits from the bottom up when our paths crossed again.

"Anyway, it turned out they'd been spying on us for a while, probably standing out in the hall, eavesdropping, so they knew what you'd done to me. As soon as you were down, Max's partner said, 'Okay, grab the toad and let's blow!'"

"How did you manage to get away?" I asked.

"As soon as I knew they'd come for me, I hid. That's how come they tore up the place, looking for me. They just happened to find the other toad first." She shrugged. "I guess I'm a lucky girl."

"Sure you are." I pretended like I believed her, but I had a feeling it hadn't gone exactly the way she told it. More likely she'd done something to draw those two goons' attention to where Bogey was hiding, then hopped away fast while they bagged the wrong batrachian. "So, they say anything else?"

"Only that Mr. LeGras would be real glad to get his hands on me. That's when I figured it all out: LeGras was going to use me to make Hansel tell where he hid the black bird."

"I'm surprised you didn't go along quietly," I said. "Why pass up a chance to help your darling little brother? You the same girl who was just telling me how close the two of you are?"

She looked away. "Not close enough for me to want to share the same grave. Even if they'd managed to grab me, bring me to LeGras's place, do . . . things to me, Hansel wouldn't talk. I know him, and he knows LeGras. He used to say that once LeGras squeezes the last drop of juice from a lemon, he throws the peel away."

"Can't say I know a lot of people who save it, sugar," I said.

"You know what I mean! Once Hansel tells LeGras where the bird is, LeGras's got no reason left to keep Hansel alive!"

"So he'll clam up? Even if it means buying a few more hours at the cost of your life?"

"Even if it buys him a few more *minutes*," she replied. "Why the hell you think I'm heading for New York?"

"That would not be advisable."

Both of us turned at the sound of an unfamiliar voice from the doorway.

"Mr. LeGras, I presume?" I said.

"The same. May I come in?"

He asked, but he didn't wait for an answer. He barged into my office like he owned the place. For all I knew, he did. He was a big man, but he moved silently and gracefully. So had the Hindenberg. Our Mr. LeGras would have to watch himself. Offhand, I could name five, six practicing fairy godmothers in the downtown area who'd get one eyeful of that pumpkin-shaped body and try turning him into a coach-and-four. He was impeccably dressed in a dapper white suit and Panama hat, a fresh red carnation in his buttonhole. He balanced his enormous bulk on a pair of obscenely tiny feet in glittering black Oxfords, real Italian leatherwork. A silver-headed mahogany walking stick in his left hand took some of the load off. A pearl-handled revolver in his right put some of the heat on.

He was alone. That did surprise me. I'd expected him to show up backed by the two apes who'd wrecked my office, at least. He was a confident s.o.b., our Mr. LeGras. Maybe he'd make a confident toad. I smiled.

"Pray, put any thoughts of thaumaturgy from your mind at once, *gnädige Hexe*," he said. His voice was deep, with a raspy wheeze that made me want to start smoking cigarettes just so I could quit the habit. "Oh yes, I know you for what you are. A man in my position is not without his sources of, aha, reliable information. Knowledge is power. So too are certain, hrrrumph, connections. They permit one to take the appropriate precautions proper to the immediate circumstance."

He held out his hand. At first I thought that maybe he was cuckoo and wanted me to kiss it, like he was the Pope or something. Then I saw the little jade-and-pearl ring crammed onto his pinky. It gave off a protective aura strong enough to fade the letters in a locked grimoire at fifty paces. Any witch stupid enough to try casting a spell at that boy would have it bounce back in her face and do triple damage.

I forced myself to keep smiling. "I guess you want me to be impressed," I said.

"Your reactions are of startlingly minuscule importance to me, my dear," he replied. "I have done you a kindness by allowing you to perceive the ring's power. In ordinary circumstances, it remains hidden until aroused. You should thank me for sparing you a very nasty—and perhaps fatal—surprise."

"Thanks," I said, deadpan. "I'd offer you a seat and ask you to stay to tea, but your boys took care of my chairs."

He laughed. Everything shook except the gun. "You have a sense of humor. Good, good. I find it much easier to deal with people who see the inherent absurdity of life. They are far less likely to take a foolishly heroic stand on matters that do not, in essence, involve them."

"Oh, I'm no hero, dumpling," I replied. "I'm just a poor old lady who wants to get her pussycat back. Your boys picked him up by mistake."

"So we discovered in short order. The same, hrrm, person who supplied me with this ring perceived our mistake even without bothering to remove the unhappy creature's toad form."

I wondered which of my colleagues was down-and-out enough to take LeGras's money and be his *sorciére de joie*. Then I decided that I was happier not knowing anyone *that* desperate.

"No surprise there," I said. "Bogey's more than my cat, he's my familiar. All us girls in the life can tell another witch's familiar on sight, no matter what shape it's wearing. Bring him back to me and you can have the girl. Hell, you can have her now. Take her. She was just telling me how much she misses her little brother. It'd be cruel to keep them apart."

LeGras laughed again. "Ah! An excellent jape. The Algonquin Round Table is the poorer for your absence. Rest assured, it is my intention to reunite brother and sister with due celerity, to the ultimate benefit of, ahem, all parties concerned."

"How sweet. Well, don't let me keep you."

He didn't take the hint. "I am afraid, my dear, that I have not made myself clear: I have come for the young lady, but prudence dictates that you accompany us as well." He made a discreet but unmistakable motion with his gun.

I don't believe in wasting time on useless arguments, especially when my respected opponent has six hot-lead arguments at his disposal. "Mind if I get my hat?" I asked.

LeGras made me a dancing-school bow. "Not at all, dear lady. Fetch your gloves as well, if you so desire. How I deplore the growing disregard for the proprieties of personal appearance in today's society! The numbers of young women I have seen traipsing about with neither *chapeau* nor chaperone would break your heart."

"You're assuming I've got one." I breezed past him to the closet. I could feel him tracking me with the muzzle of his revolver the whole time, feel his fat little trigger finger itching to punch me a one-way ticket to hell if I tried anything funny.

I'm a witch, not a comedian. I got my hat off the top shelf of the closet and dropped the old butterball a curtsey. "Ready when you are, sweets."

LeGras herded us out of my office, down the hall, and into the wheezy old rattletrap of an elevator. There were four passengers in it plus Steve the shaft-monkey. None of them seemed to notice that the two lovely ladies accompanying the personable fat man were doing so under pearl-handled protest. Le Gras's pet witch probably slapped a no-see-'um charm on his gun.

His car was waiting for us right outside my office building, a Cadillac the color of fresh cream. There was a big goon uglying up the space behind the wheel. I wondered if it was my buddy Max, but the circumstances weren't social so I couldn't ask. LeGras jerked his head, silently ordering us into the back seat. He climbed in after, shut the door, and gave the order: "Home."

I wondered where "home" was. I was betting it was somewhere up in the Hollywood Hills, a popular nesting spot for the cash, flash, and trash crowd. I had the window seat, with Gretel wedged in between me and LeGras. I guess I could've tried something smart, like pulling a Houdini when the car stopped for a traffic light, but I didn't. I knew that if I skipped, Gretel'd be stuck paying the full bill.

Yeah, tell me I'm a sucker. Then tell me something I don't already know.

I like riding in cars. You get places faster when you fly a broomstick, but in cars you don't get bugs in your teeth. I leaned back against the upholstery and closed my eyes. For all I knew this was going to be my last ride; might as well enjoy it. If I was going to die, at least I was wearing a nice hat for the occasion. LeGras didn't know it, but there was a reason I'd grabbed this little beauty out of the closet instead of rummaging through the office wreckage for the hat I'd been wearing earlier. *This* hat was special. *This* hat stood up straight and proud, and not just because I'd asked for extra starch at Ling Po's Genuine Chinese Hand Laundry.

This hat was packing a rod.

I had it all planned: We'd get to LeGras's place and he'd bring us face-to-face with Hansel—unless he handed us over to his goons for some preliminary softening up first. He'd try to make the little gunsel sing, but he'd come up against the biggest case of laryngitis known to man. Then he'd start putting the screws to Gretel. The most he'd get out of that would be some cheap entertainment for the hired help. I had LeGras and his gang of creeps pegged for the type who got their kicks watching a woman get hurt. He'd keep his gun on me the whole time, but not his eyes. He'd have more . . . *amusing* things to look at.

That was when I'd ask if I could take off my hat and stay awhile.

Maybe I couldn't use the wand to hurt *him* while he wore that stupid ring, but I *could* use it to create a distraction, like setting the place on fire, or breaking the water mains, or making Max's head explode like a party balloon full of brains and blood. You know, little things. And in the confusion, I could get Gretel and me the hell out of there, easy as—

"We're here." LeGras's wheezy voice busted up my pretty dreams.

I opened my eyes in time to see the car pull up in front of one of those bijou hideaway hacienda-style mansions. It had a tapestry brick driveway, brutally neat flowerbeds, and an ornamental pond where a quartet of swans paddled around looking bored. Silent film stars used to buy up places like this by the bagful, like penny candy, only to toss them back on the market at a dead loss when the talkies showed no signs of going away. It was tucked into the armpit of a mountain with the nearest neighbor located a body-drop below.

A butler answered the door. He looked like a refugee from a Karloff flick. He bowed slightly to Gretel and me and asked if he could take my hat.

"No thanks, Spooky; it's carrying my personality," I told him.

"It is also carrying a concealed weapon," he replied, slick as a lounge lizard's manicure. "I regret to inform you that all such artifacts are powerless within these walls."

I goggled at him like a sea bass with goiter. LeGras escorted me over the threshold, chortling. "Do not be surprised, madam," he said. "I have long been a collector of esoteric souvenirs. The black bird is merely the, hrrrm, most profitable in a series of the same. I am sure you would agree that any malefactors interested in thieving such items must of necessity be versed in the Darker Arts. With that in mind, it would be unwise not to place certain, ah, protective wards upon my property. Just as your ordinary homeowner might have the double security of a high fence to keep housebreakers out and a vicious dog to deal with any who do get in, I too have diversified my defenses. Some, like Stanton here, detect the presence of uninvited magic or magical appurtenances. Others, like this ring which you have already noted—" He flashed his pinky at me. "—repel outright sorcerous attacks. Now be a good little witch and hand over the hat."

Nobody ever called me a good little witch. Nobody still in need of oxygen. I glared daggers at Stanton, but I gave the big stiff my hat. What choice did I have? He pulled out the hidden rod and held it out for his boss's inspection like a cat proudly puking up mouse guts on the doormat.

"A magic wand," LeGras said, tapping it aside with the nose of his revolver. "How quaint. Thank you, Stanton, you may dispose of it."

"Very good, sir." The butler's hand closed on my rod. There was a grinding sound and the whole thing broke into a million splinters. This Stanton wasn't your everyday butler.

I turned to LeGras. "Zombie or golem?" I asked.

"Golem," he replied. "Zombies do not afford quite so much upper body strength, and one does need to feed them on occasion. Shall we proceed?"

Stanton led the way into the depths of LeGras's house, down a hall and up to a pair of heavy double doors. At a touch of his hands, they rolled into their wall pockets silently, revealing a parlor big enough to host a ball game. It'd have to be for the girlie league, though. Everywhere I looked, I saw chintz, gilding, and froufrou. It was like being trapped inside the brain of a wedding cake designer gone gaga.

In the center of the floor was a plain wood kitchen chair. A man was tied to it. It was Hansel. Big surprise. The thick velvet drapes were drawn tight and there was only a single lamp lit, but I could see him good enough. He'd changed about as much as his sister. The grubby-faced kid who'd been too scrawny to pop into my bakeoven had grown up into a man with the body of a has-been athlete and the face of a cherub.

That cherub should've been more careful about where he flew. He'd obviously glided into the bad part of town where some punk grabbed him by the wing and used his face for a punching bag. I wondered whether Hansel's lips were always that pouty or if they'd just swollen up from the beating. One eye was battered shut, the other squinted sullenly in our direction. If he recognized me, he didn't let on. Then again, seeing as how he was flanked by a couple of burly chaperones, maybe he didn't want to get spanked for talking to strangers.

"How goes it, dear boy?" LeGras exclaimed, sidling up to Hansel. He passed his walking stick and gun to one of the two guard-goons. "Have you taken advantage of my absence to repent the error of your ways?"

"He ain't spilled nothin', Boss," the second ape said.

"Ah." LeGras turned to me and shrugged apologetically. "Dear lady, you must forgive Max. He lacks the benefits of a course in proper English."

Max, huh? Hel-looo, nurse. I did my best to keep a poker face. "I don't know, sweets," I said. "That's pretty bad grammar. Someone ought to teach him a lesson."

"Perhaps. In the meantime, I would prefer to limit my attempts at, ha, pedagogy to this young man." He approached Hansel and stooped over—not without a whole lot of effort—just so he could be at eye level when he wheezed: "Was this the face that launched a thousand ships? No longer, alas. Such a needless waste of beauty when beauty is ethereal at best. You disappoint me deeply, my boy. You might have spared yourself this."

"Save it," Hansel growled. "I didn't talk for these creeps and I'm not talking for you. Think I can't see who *that* is?" He nodded in our direction. I gave Gretel a sidelong look. She was staring at her brother, tears streaming down her cheeks, but unless you were close enough to see them in the dim light, you'd never have known they were there. She didn't make a sound. A pair of granite bookends, those two. "You wasted your time, bringing her here," he went on. "I know I'm a dead man, no matter what. Say I *did* tell you where the black bird's stashed, you want me to believe you'd let me go—me *or* her—like nothing ever happened? Fat chance."

LeGras took that last remark personally. "You would choose to perish knowing your innocent sister must share your fate?"

Hansel grinned, showing off some recently administered gaps in his pearly whites. "Yeah. So? I'd die knowing that you'll never see the black bird again in this lifetime. Who says you can't take it with you?"

LeGras waved one fat hand languidly. "Edgar, my things," he said. The goon who wasn't my pal Max fetched a green tin box from the shadows and set it down on the table holding the lamp. LeGras opened it and took out a pair of black rubber gloves and a neatly folded white cloth. While LeGras pulled the gloves on, Edgar spread the cloth over the tabletop, then reached into the tin box and started laying out the tools.

"Stanton, see to the lady," LeGras directed. The golem butler grabbed Gretel and hauled her forward. Max got another kitchen chair and more rope from somewhere behind the Louis-the-Whatever settee and tied her up like the Sunday roast.

"Never send a boy to do a man's job," LeGras murmured, an ugly little smile on his blobby lips. "You see, lad, the question is no longer *if* you will die but how long you will be about it. You are about to have a demonstration of what awaits you, performed with the kind assistance of your own dear sister." He picked up one of the tools from the white-shrouded table. Lamplight glittered along the edge of the blade like a string of fresh-dipped rock candy.

Hansel went pale. He opened his mouth—nothing came out—then closed it and tightened his jaw. I knew that look. Tough guy.

I've got no use for tough guys. I had to leave my home in the Old Country when the tough guys took over. I know their kind: They're real brave as long as they outnumber you, or when it's someone else's neck on the chopping block. Dig the brown-shirted bastards out of their burrows one by one and they stop barking and start whining, no teeth and all tail.

That's why I spoke up when I did:

"Hey, LeGras, do you *like* to waste time?"

He stopped making goo-goo eyes at the blade and gave me a slow, contemptuous look. "I assure you, madam, I shall proceed with all requisite alacrity." He snapped his fingers. Max made a move for Gretel. She screamed like she was auditioning to play an air raid siren.

I laughed. LeGras raised one stubbly eyebrow. "You take pleasure in the impending misfortunes of others? How . . . unsuitable a character trait in a woman. I can't say I approve."

"I'm not laughing at her," I told him. "I'm laughing at you. You're a fool, LeGras, a fat fool." Legras's driver made a grab for me, but I held up one hand and talked fast: "Call him off, LeGras, or kiss the black bird goodbye."

"Hold, Geoffrey." LeGras's trained gorilla stopped dead in his tracks at the sound of his master's voice. LeGras himself set down his sharp, shiny toy and came over to me. "What are you saying, my good woman? That you have some arcane knowledge that may facilitate our search? That you would be willing to place your sorcerous powers in my service to the end of recovering the bird?"

"Right you are, cupcake."

"And I suppose your price will be their lives?" He didn't even bother looking back at his prisoners, he just shook his head and said, "I am afraid that would be out of the question."

I blew his words away like they were smoke rings. "What do you take me for, a sucker? *Me* bargain for *their* lives? What's the matter, gumdrop, your mama never read you any fairy tales at bedtime? Do you even know who I *am*?"

It was a beautiful thing, watching the little lightbulb go on over LeGras's head. "You mean to say that you are *that* witch? My word, this *is* an honor." He grabbed my hand between both of his and shook it briskly. The rubber gloves squeaked and left my palm all sweaty. Beaming, LeGras babbled on: "How fortuitous. Of course you would never ask for *their* lives in fee. Not after what they put you through, eh? Pardon my previous ignorance, but it is understandable. Anyone who has ever heard your story assumes that you perished in the oven where that graceless *cocotte* left you. Well! This puts quite a different complexion on things."

"I'll say." I got my hand out of his clutches and wiped it dry on my skirt. "You want my powers at your service, you got 'em. Pay me what you paid the gal who conjured up that gangbusters ring of yours. Say, not to cut my own throat or anything—" I gave Max a *Wouldn't you like to try?* leer. "—but if you need magic to trace the bird, how come you don't give your bought-and-paid-for witch a call?"

LeGras made an irritated noise deep in his jowly throat. "The unmannerly hag left my employ some months ago, complaining that I did not show her the respect her art deserved. She is of no further consequence, thanks to you. Sorcerous aid will make the search for my treasure far less tedious. *Can* you locate the black bird for me, my good woman?"

"Depends," I said. "Can you locate my cat?"

"Your . . . cat? Ah! Your cat, of course." LeGras smiled. "More than reasonable. Restore the black bird to me and I promise you that not only shall you have your beloved familiar back, but that you shall also remain on permanent retainer in my employ. You shall find me to be, er, decidedly generous."

"So I hear." I stared at Hansel and made sure to do it so that LeGras got my meaning. "Okay, LeGras, bring me my cat and we'll get started."

"Madam, I beg your pardon but you will only receive your cat after I am again in possession of the black bird. Those are my terms and I promise you, they are not negotiable."

"In that case, I hope you packed a lunch because this job's not going any further without Bogey. I told you, he's my familiar. Do you even know what that *means*? He's the supernatural servant I hired at the price of my soul the minute I got into the life. I give the orders, he carries them out; we're a team."

LeGras curled his lip. "So you are powerless without him?"

"Applesauce!" I snapped my fingers under his nose. "He didn't turn *himself* into a toad, did he? I've got plenty of Moxie on my own, but he boosts my capabilities. It comes in handy for the big jobs. You want someone to dig you a grave, do you give him a spoon or a steamshovel? Bogey's my steamshovel."

"I see." LeGras barked a few commands to his boys. Edgar scuttled out of the parlor quick and came back quicker. He was holding a toad. He would've handed it over to me when his boss stopped him. "Before I allow this charming reunion, *fräulein Hexe*, permit me to remind you that I am still protected." Again with the pinky ring. I was sick of the sight of it. It made that pudgy white finger of his look like a grub wearing a garter belt.

"Think I was going to pull a fast one?" I smirked. "Nothing could be further from my mind."

"Is that why you came into my home carrying a concealed weapon?"

"Which your butler destroyed. I'll send you a bill for the replacement as soon as I'm on your payroll. Look, LeGras, I admit I was thinking about using that rod, but that was before I realized we're playing on the same team. I don't bite the hand that feeds me. Heck, until I get me a decent set of dentures, I'm not biting anything tougher than a slab of gingerbread. All I'm gonna do is restore Bogey to his true form. That okay by you, Boss?"

Boss. LeGras liked the sound of that, I could tell. "By all means." He waved his hand at me like he was the sultan of Turkey ordering a harem girl to dance.

I'd give him a dance.

The spell for the restoration of an enchanted being's true form is short and sweet. I got through it faster than a chorus girl with a playboy's bankroll. Edgar was still holding Bogey when the change hit. One second he had his hands wrapped around a toad, the next he was holding eight-foot-six of bright green demon by the tail. Bogey's head turned slowly, his eyes a trio of pits filled with the fires of Hell, his jaws dribbling sulfurous foam, razor-sharp fangs set in a permanent come-to-Papa leer. He snapped off Edgar's head with a crunch like a little kid biting a lollipop.

Cat shape or true shape, Bogey never did like anyone to pull his tail.

Max was next on Bogey's disassembly line, followed by Geoffrey the driver, followed by Stanton. It took Bogey a couple of tries to swallow the golem, but he managed. I'd probably be up all night, nursing him through the bellyache. I was sorry that I couldn't give my old pal Max a personal thank you for what he'd done to my office and my noggin, but *you* go bother a demon at dinnertime.

LeGras was the last to go. The fat man fell to his knees, waggling his pinky ring at Bogey. "You can't touch me!" he squealed. "I am proof against all magical attacks! It will go ill with you if—"

Bogey made four neat bites out of him, then spit out the ring like it was a watermelon seed. He always was a show-off.

I pocketed the ring and rattled through the spell to return Bogey to feline shape. A demonic familiar has his uses, but a cat takes up less room at the foot of your bed. While Bogey sat there washing up after his feed, I untied Gretel's bonds.

"How—how did you do that?" she gasped, rubbing some circulation back into her hands. "Doesn't that ring—?"

"—work?" I finished for her. "Yeah, it works. But it only repels magical attacks. Nothing magical about a demon turning mortals into chop suey; it's what they do, if you give them half a chance. I gave Bogey a whole one."

"How kind of you," said a prim voice behind me. "That is more than I shall give you."

When you've been in my line of work long enough, you can tell a lot from a voice. I didn't even have to turn around to know that this one belonged to someone young, healthy, British, and armed. The last part was a gimme: He had a gun jabbed into my shortribs hard enough for me to know what caliber.

"Mr. Carlisle, I presume?" I said. I played it cool, but mentally I was kicking my own tail seven ways from Sunday. How could I have forgotten about Carlisle, LeGras's sometime valet and full-time prettyboy? The first rule of a good gumshoe is to keep count of your enemies, their weapons, and how many rounds they've already squeezed off. If you screw up the first one, don't bother about the other two; you'll be too dead to care.

"Correct, madam." I felt the gun ease off some and heard the creak of shoe leather on parquet as he took a step away from me. "Please face me. I dislike shooting anyone in the back unless absolutely necessary."

"Not cricket, huh?" I did what he said, turning around and sizing him up. He was easy on the eyes, I'll give him that, one of those tall, thin, English blonds so pale-skinned that a good blush would probably make his cheeks explode. He had a pickpocket's long, delicate fingers. At the moment one of them was wrapped around the trigger of a .45.

"One must play by the rules, mustn't one?" He waved me aside with the heater, then fixed his eyes on Gretel. They were blue and steely, like his gun. "Free him." He nodded at Hansel.

"That's *it*?" I asked while Gretel attacked her brother's bonds. "'Free him'? You don't want to get in line to slap him around until he tells you where the black bird's stashed?"

Carlisle's laugh was about as warm and human as plate glass shattering. "Do you mean to say you haven't guessed the truth even now? A fine detective you are! I should stick to baking gingerbread if I were you."

"Don't be too hard on the old broad," Hansel said. He was on his feet, one arm around his sister. "She's sharp enough, when love's not making her stupid."

"Besides," Gretel chimed in, smiling like a fallen angel, "it's not like we wanted a *smart* cookie for this job."

The truth dropped on me like a grand piano, and the song it played when it hit was *Variations on a Theme for Suckers*. "You were all in this together from the start," I said. "You knew that if you snatched the bird, LeGras and his goons would hunt you down no matter how far you ran or how long it took. You had to get them out of the way, permanently, so you could lie back and enjoy your loot in peace."

"Precisely," Carlisle said. "But given the fact that Mr. LeGras was so well protected—by physical as well as arcane resources—we stood in need of someone of your particular talents. We knew that if we drew you in, you'd find the way to dispose of him for us. We were right."

I watched as Hansel slipped his other arm around Carlisle's slender waist and gave him a kiss on the cheek, so as not to distract his aim. So all that talk about the two of them being rivals was just a lot of jive cooked up to make me dance to their tune. If I had any more egg on my face I'd be an omelette.

Bogey gave me a worried look and meowed. Carlisle laughed again. "Poor pussy. You'd like to destroy us as well, wouldn't you? But I'm afraid you'll remain a cat for the duration. If your mistress so much as begins to utter her demon-freeing spell, I'll kill her by the third syllable." Bogey's tail drooped. I felt the same way.

"Game, set, and match, Carlisle," I conceded. "Since you've got me licked, do an old lady a favor? Before you rub me out, I mean."

"How can I refuse so elegant a plea? What do you want?"

"The black bird," I said. "I want to know how you managed to hide something that size from LeGras and his goons."

"She really *isn't* a very good detective, is she?" Hansel giggled. "The hell with her and her last requests, she's too stupid to live. Shoot her and let's blow."

"Not so fast." Carlisle could've been the love child of Vincent Price and Leslie Howard, a good-looking bad guy who liked to watch his victims squirm. "It's a not unreasonable request. Let us show her, by all means."

They took me out of the house and down the front walk to the pond. As soon as I locked eyeballs with the swans, I knew. Swans are nasty, evil-tempered creatures with vicious streaks a yard wide. Three of the birds sailing across the water looked like they'd wreck their own nests just to throw an eggnog party, but the fourth . . .

"You bastard," I breathed. "You sharp little bastard."

Carlisle was loving it. " 'The Purloined Letter' never does go out of style. Care for a closer look before you die?"

"Don't bother on my account."

"No bother, my dear," he replied, like we were all sitting down to cucumber sandwiches and Earl Grey tea. "None at all. Hansel, if you would—?"

"*I'm* not wading in there." Hansel pouted like a hell-spawned Shirley Temple. "Bad enough I had to let LeGras's apes work me over and *now* you want me to get my pants wet?"

"Would it be the first time?" I muttered.

Carlisle made an impatient sound. "Very well. Gretel, *you* do it."

"Me?" she squealed. She eyed the birds nervously. The three genuine swans gave her the glad eye, a trio of feathered sharks. "Why do *I* have to? I'm with Hansel: Shoot her now."

Carlisle sighed. "Whether I shoot her now or later, we must retrieve the bird *sometime*. Get it."

Gretel began to whimper. "But I'm scaaared! Those swans *bite*. Can I at least go into the house and get a golf club or something to—?"

Carlisle shifted the gun. "If you don't do as I say, I'll be pleased to teach you the meaning of the word *expendable*, my dear."

Grousing and whining, Gretel kicked off her shoes, stripped off her stockings, hiked up her skirt, and stepped into the pond. "Here, goosey," she called timidly, holding out one hand to the ringer swan. "Here, nice goose-goose-goosey. Come to Mama." The way all four of the birds kept their distance, she might as well have been waving a hatchet. Hansel and Carlisle observed her fruitless efforts at poultry-herding with rising amusement, laughing until the tears ran down their faces.

"Good Lord!" Carlisle exclaimed, gasping for breath. "That girl couldn't get a goose at a stag smoker."

"Let the old doll do it," Hansel suggested. "She wanted to see the black bird so bad, make her work for it."

"A capital notion," Carlisle said. He gestured meaningly with his gun.

As a disgruntled Gretel waded out of the pond, I sloshed in past my ankles. It took me all of twenty seconds to cut the right swan from the flock and herd it onto the grass, much to the astonished whispers of Carlisle and his cronies. I'll tell you a little secret from my long-gone childhood: Before Hansel and Gretel, before the gingerbread cottage, even before I first heard the Black Arts whispering my name, I was a snot-nosed German peasant brat like ten thousand others. And when you're a dirt-poor farmer's daughter, you know the first job they hand you, almost as soon as you can toddle? Goose-girl.

The three of them gazed at the phony swan like it was the answer to the fifty dollar question on *Beat the Band*. Carlisle said a few words over the critter's head: Its neck shortened and its webbed feet went from black to red while its plumage went switcheroo from white to black as a cheating woman's heart. The bird looked around stupidly, honked once, settled down on the grass and laid an egg.

A golden egg.

Gretel pounced on it like a studio head on a starlet, but Hansel got there first and strong-armed her away. "What's the big idea?" she shrilled. "I *earned* this!"

"The hell you did," he countered, shoving her away a second time. "I guess it was *your* face got treated like a tough steak? If anyone earned anything, it's me!" The overconfident little creep bent over to seize the egg. He learned the error of his ways when his adoring sister kicked him in the pants, sending him headfirst into the pond. He got up dripping duckweed and grabbed her by the ankle, dragging her into the water with him. The swans took off, flapping their wings and making enough racket to wake the dead.

"Children, please." Carlisle rolled his eyes like a woman who's wondering whether retroactive birth control isn't such a bad idea after all. "The bird will lay more eggs; there will be enough for all of us, in time."

The pair of them paused in mid-shindy. Hansel glowered at the English prettyboy: "This is between me and my sister."

"Yeah!" Gretel hauled herself out of the muck bottoming the pond and tucked a dripping lock of hair behind one ear. "Don't tell us what to do. You wouldn't even be in on this caper if not for Hansel. He was the one who made sure LeGras got an eyeful of you up in Frisco, but he could've picked any other two-bit swish for the job. We were the brains, you were just the bait. You think you're the only pebble on the beach?"

"No," the limey admitted. He raised the .45. "But I *am* the only one with a gun. And now that I come to think about it, I don't believe I want to share at all."

He sent a bullet whizzing past Gretel's ear. Any closer and you could call the story "Hansel and." Brother and sister exchanged a look, then took to their heels like they had a flock of Zeros on their tail. Carlisle squeezed off a few more shots to speed them on their way. The black bird honked like crazy at the sound of gunfire but stayed put surer than if someone had driven a railroad spike through its foot. Carlisle laughed like a crazy man.

He was anything but.

"Now that's what I call sporting," I remarked. "Aren't you afraid they'll come after you . . . *sister*?"

He quit laughing and flashed me a look like a shiv, sharp and ugly. "How did you know?" His features started to blur at the edges, then to run like cheese on a griddle, but his grip on the .45 was rock-solid.

"Maybe I'm not such a bad shamus after all. *You* were the one who lifted the disguise spell off the black bird. That means *you* had to be the one who slapped it on in the first place." I looked over to where the goose was still trying to take it on the lam, in spite of the invisible tether holding her down. "Pretty impressive sorcery from a sugarpuss-for-hire. That little holding spell you've got on the goose confirms it: You're one of us, sister."

Carlisle's prettyboy looks were all gone by the time I finished. His slender body filled out, his short blond hair went long and gray, and his gigolo get-up flashed into a heap of gypsy-bright glad rags. Me, I prefer to work in traditional black, but it's not like we're unionized.

A witch can wear what she wants.

"You *dare* include me in your pathetic, penny-grubbing witcheries?" my newly-unmasked colleague countered. "You are a petty hireling, I am a mastermind! I used those stupid mortals as my tools: They did the dirty work, I reap the prize. And it was so easy!" She threw back her head and laughed. "Like you, I was a refugee, a despised foreigner in this so-called 'Land of the Free.' *Free!* All things here have a price, all costly. I lived hand-to-mouth on *their* sufferance, accepting the pittance they deemed a 'fair' wage for my services. Bah. I spit on their 'fair' wages."

She did, too. Bogey jumped out of the way. It was all he could do. She'd sold her soul to his Head Office, same as me, so he was powerless to attack her, with or without my say-so: professional courtesy.

I didn't like her spitting on my cat, but there was something I liked even less: She was riding the Red broomstick. If she was so in love with Comrade Stalin's way of doing things, why did she bother coming here when she left the Old Country? Maybe because back then, Iron Joe was in Hitler's pocket deep enough to call him sweetheart? I got a bad feeling in my gut. If they ever got up another witch-hunt in this country, I'd know who to blame.

"There was a better way, I knew it," she went on. "A road to the big score, a clean shot at Easy Street. No more dabbling in love potions and impotence tonics, no."

"Six of one—" I began. She ignored me. She was tuned in to *Life Can Be Bitterful* and she couldn't hear anything else.

"My chance came when LeGras hired me. While in his employ, I discovered he possessed the black bird. I resolved to make it mine, to use it to obtain luxury beyond my wildest dreams."

"Sweet dreams," I remarked. "That must've been when it hit you: You couldn't use your magic to pull off the heist because you set up most of the spell-shielding tools in this dump before you found out about the bird. *That* must've stuck a burr under your saddle."

She ground her teeth together, remembering. "A galling situation, but temporary. It was only a matter of finding the proper cat's-paw for the job."

"Namely Hansel? I'll bet he jumped at the chance to get rich quick. Greedy little bastard."

Her lip curled. "Will it surprise you to learn that the lure of gold was secondary in persuading him? Who would expect a common gunsel who sold his favors to be a romantic at heart? It was simple to disguise myself as Carlisle and seduce him, then open his eyes to the possibility of obtaining a fortune at his former master's expense. I even made him think it was his own idea. Oh, I am brilliant!"

"And still you chased him off like that? After all the two of you meant to each other?" I clicked my tongue. "Flirt."

The look on her face would give Beelzebub a case of frostbite. "He is lucky I let him escape alive, him and his floozy sister. Do you think I ever intended to share *anything* with them?"

"That goose can lay enough gold eggs to satisfy everyone in L.A., if you don't count the boys down at City Hall. What's the matter, Einstein? You can't divide by three?"

"*You* would ask me to retain them as my partners? To *trust* them? *You*?" She sneered. "How long do you think it would be before they decided there was one too many hands in the egg basket and shoved *me* into a bakeoven, hmmm? Perhaps you did not learn from your previous experience with those brats, but I am no such fool. Farewell." She was done with the .45, so she turned it into a hankie and waved bye-bye with it before picking up the goose and starting to go.

"Hold it, sister!" I called after her. "You think you can just walk away from this?"

I'd been dealing with mortals too long; I forgot what it's like to confront one of my own people. I just got my last word out when she turned on me faster than milk on a hot summer day and slammed me with the same lousy immobilization charm she'd used on the black bird. I felt my feet root themselves so firmly to the ground that I knew my ordinary escape spell was useless. A team of hopped-up gophers couldn't dig me free. Unless she ended it or something ended her, I was planted for the duration.

Maybe I couldn't move, but I could still fight. I struck back with my own incantation. It left my fingertips like a bolt of lightning, but it hit her like a splash of cheap cologne.

"My specialty is shielding spells," she said, coolly wiping my splattered sorcery off her face. "Or have you forgotten all I did for LeGras? None of your puny magics can touch me. *Now* will you let me leave in peace, or do I make you regret it?" She didn't bother waiting for an answer. I was beneath her contempt. When she showed me her back, she might as well have slapped my face.

"Aloha," I growled, and whispered the rest of what I had to say.

The black bird exploded in her arms like a honking cherry bomb. Feathers flew everywhere, blood drenched her carnival-colored skirts, and one webbed foot landed smack on top of her head like the latest word in Paris millinery fashion. She whirled on me, shrieking: "*What have you done?! What in seven hells have you done?!*"

It was my turn to gloat and I did it pretty. "Just a little something for the war effort, sugar. *My* war. How long you think it'll be before the cops show up and find me stuck here? Bogey's a sloppy eater. With all the blood he spilled inside that house, they're gonna be asking a lot of questions, like about what happened to LeGras and his buddies. If my neck's got to pay the final bill for your shell game, I'm making sure that you don't get anything out of it except a couple slices of white meat and a belly full of might-have-beens." I slipped my hands into my pockets, casual, and added: "Don't you listen to *The Shadow*, sister? *Crime does not pay.*" I tried to ape Lamont Cranston's creepy laugh; it came out a cackle.

"And fools do not live!" she screeched, her empty hands filling with the biggest damn fireball I'd ever seen in all my years of witchcraft.

That was when I knew I'd bought me some serious trouble. You don't use a fireball unless you mean business, and a witch only means that kind of business when she steps into a no-holds-barred duel-to-the-death of sorcery. Fireball spells contain the power of five hundred thousand sticks of dynamite. Casting one takes so much out of you that you're useless for a week after. On the other hand, one is usually all it takes.

A fireball spell is so much destruction tucked into one little package that it's a good thing only a few witches know how do it. Too bad I'm not one of them.

When she saw me standing there, not even trying to conjure up a fireball of my own, she smiled. For a second I knew how Poland must've felt when the Wehrmacht swept over the border. My last thoughts, just before she pulled back her arm, took aim, and let fly, were: *Thank the Powers there's nothing like this in mortal hands, and I hope there never will be or we can kiss our broomsticks good-bye.*

Then the flames hit me.

＊　　　　＊　　　　＊

I put back the glue brush and smoothed down the edges on the latest newspaper clipping in my scrapbook. The accident was still fresh enough for the dailies to use type so big I could read it without my glasses. The gas company kept yapping about how gas was safe, blaming the whole thing on customer negligence, saying that Mr. LeGras or one of his servants must've done *something* wrong with the pipeline to call up the biggest explosion in the history of the greater L.A. area. They were partly right. LeGras *did* do something wrong, sure enough, but the only pipeline with his name on it was the one that went straight to hell.

Bogey jumped up on my desk and sat on the open scrapbook, forcing me to pay attention to him. He was born a demon, but he's all cat at heart. I'd be peeling gluey newsprint off his tail for hours.

"Want your toy?" I asked. I took the silver chain off my neck and let him swat at the little jade-and-pearl pinky ring dangling from it. While Bogey played ping-pong solitaire, I marvelled how something so small had contained power enough to save my skin. Bogey's too. He'd ducked under my skirts just as the fireball hit.

Hit and bounced straight back onto the one who'd launched it. Thanks to the shielding spell on that little ring—a spell she'd set in place herself—the rogue witch got everything she'd been aiming at me, only tripled. Her own shielding spells couldn't stand up to that. There wasn't enough of her left to grease the wheels of a kiddie car.

"That was a close one," I told the cat. "Too close. When I couldn't take her down with my magic, I knew I'd have to turn her own against her. Too bad I had to blow up the bird, but I had to make her mad enough to want me dead. Lucky I managed to slip this baby on my finger in time or she'd've got her wish."

Bogey caught the ring with a left hook, yanking the chain out of my hand. I let him chew on it awhile. "I'm getting too old for this job," I sighed. "Even a cat can play me for a sucker. Gretel did it too, easy; *too* easy. I *knew* better than to trust her, but still I let her reel me in like a prize marlin. Suckers make lousy detectives. Pretty good corpses, but lousy detectives. Maybe it's time I retired, found a cozy cottage up the coast, got back into the bakery business, a little baby-sitting, six of one—"

My office door flew open with a bang. She was five-foot-six

of danger, half of it legs, the other half fireworks. "I need your help," she said. She had one of those breathy voices that leave you gasping for air like you've just been kissed, long, hard, and professionally.

"It's my stepmother. I—I think she wants me dead."

I nodded her into a chair. When she crossed those gams, my little dream house on the coast went up in a fireball bigger than anything LeGras's pet witch ever threw at me. Oh sure, I knew the odds were stacked against her giving me a tumble, but I do my best work when I've got more stars in my eyes than Graumann's Chinese Theater's got in their cement.

That was when I knew that this was how my life was going to stay, until the day they chucked my broom into the janitor's closet at the L.A. morgue: one case after another, rubbing elbows with the dolls and the deadbeats, the chumps and the chiselers, the gophers, gorillas and goons, with maybe a princess or two thrown in to keep the game interesting. A whole lot of fairy tales and not enough happily-ever-afters.

But hey. That's the way the cookie crumbles. Or the gingerbread.

Alimentary, My Dear Watson

> LAWRENCE SCHIMEL <

THE SCENE WAS UNNERVINGLY FAMILIAR AS I CALLED UPON MY friend Sherlock Holmes to wish him the compliments of the season. He was lounging upon the sofa in his purple dressing gown, his pipe rack within reach upon his right, and the morning papers in a crumpled pile upon the floor where he had dropped them after a thorough study. Save for the fact that it was the day after Christmas rather than the second day past, and that the hat under examination was a sharp-looking top hat rather than a seedy and worn hard-felt type, I would have thought I had stepped back into the events which I chronicled in *The Adventure of the Blue Carbuncle.*

"And where, pray tell, is the goose?" I asked in a loud tone as I entered the room, hoping my attempt at humor might alleviate my uneasiness. "You have not, once again, eaten it before my arrival, I hope."

Holmes set the lens and hat upon a wooden chair beside the sofa and smiled at me warmly. "My dear fellow, it is rabbit this time, rather than the goose of the case you allude to. Mrs. Hudson is preparing it as we speak. Meanwhile, tell me what you can deduce from this."

He offered me his lens and I took the hat from where it hung upon the back of the chair. I recalled all that Holmes had been able to deduce of Henry Baker's identity and situation from that hat and tried my best to extrapolate similarly from the details I noticed upon the one I held. It was an ordinary, if rather large, top hat in all regards, save for a slip of paper tucked under the brim which declared: "N THIS SIZE 10/6 and a small stain where a splash of tea had fallen against it. I pondered these facts, and at last declared, "He was not a very careful man, nor overly concerned with his appearance. He has bought himself a very fashionable hat, yet one which does not fit him properly and dips down over his eyes. Nor, having spilled tea upon his own hat, should he have then ventured forth unconcerned with such a prominent stain upon the velvet had he cared about the image he presented to the world. Unless, of course, there was an afternoon struggle which resulted in the stain, and in his haste to flee, the man simply donned his stained hat. Have we a crime to solve this time, or is this a whimsical inquiry?" I replaced the hat and lens upon the chair and waited for Holmes' judgment of my surmises.

"Very good, Watson. You are losing your timidity in drawing inferences. However, one can also tell that the man is short in stature, since the angle of the stain indicates that the hat was being worn at the time it was acquired, rather than lying beside him upon the table or a chair waiting to be spilled upon. Therefore your conclusion that a struggle occurred is most probable. Only, the man did not retrieve his hat when he fled, since we have it before us. It was found in the residence of one Mr. Charles Dodgson, who is presently missing. Will you accompany me for a visit to his residence this afternoon?"

I nodded my assent.

"Good, then sit and share a bit of rabbit before we go. I hear Mrs. Hudson upon the stair."

"The police declared that insufficient time had passed to warrant an investigation," Holmes informed me as we walked to Dodgson's apartments, "but on the implorings of his landlady, Mrs. Bugle, and for the sake and safety of his young niece, Alice, who lived with him, I consented. I must confess, I was intrigued by the puzzle she presented: though he had had no callers, she found the unusual hat, which you have already examined, in his study, a large crack in the looking glass, though she heard no sound of either a struggle or of glass breaking, and the white rabbit of which we partook just recently, lying on the floor of the study, its neck wrung."

We had arrived at Dodgson's apartments, and I mulled over the information Holmes had given me as Mrs. Bugle admitted us and led us up to the study, where she introduced us to Dodgson's niece, Alice. As is quite common for young girls, she had set up a tea party for some imaginary friends of hers, with whom she had been conversing as we entered. She stroked a large grey cat, who sat in her lap.

"That's a handsome watch you've got," Holmes remarked to the girl. "Was it your uncle's?"

The girl pulled it out of her pocket to display. "My uncle's? No, it belonged to the March Hare."

As if a premonition, my stomach began to growl at the mention of the rabbit, and I could not help wondering if we had just eaten the girl's favorite pet.

"You realize that it is set fifteen minutes ahead of the hour," Holmes continued, while looking about the table where the tea service was set.

"Yes," the girl answered, "he was always late, and thus had set his watch ahead in an attempt to arrive at the proper time."

"Did the March Hare also wear this?" Holmes asked, showing her the hat Mrs. Bugle had brought to him.

"Aha!" she said, when she saw it. "So that's where his hat disappeared to. That belongs to the Mad Hatter. He's been frantic over it since yesterday afternoon, when he left it here. It's his only hat."

"He came to tea with you?"

"It's the only way to get him to come, you understand, and he had to come, so they could help me. They had to bring it with them."

"It?" asked Holmes, pointing to a little bottle that rested on the table. A paper label round its neck bore the words DRINK ME in large letters. The girl nodded.

"And what would this do?" Holmes inquired.

"It makes one smaller."

Holmes did not bat an eye at this outlandish remark. "Is there an antidote?"

"There is," the girl replied, and pointed to a cake in a glass box beneath the table. Bending closer to observe it further, I noticed it bore the words EAT ME written upon it in currants.

"I see," said Holmes, who proceeded to dip his finger into the bottle and taste thereof. He shrunk noticeably, around two or three inches, and all his clothing accordingly.

"Curiouser and curiouser," Holmes declared after the transformation had taken place. He looked thoughtful a moment, considering the finger he had just tasted, then continued, "It has a sort of mixed flavour of cherry tart, custard, pineapple, roast turkey, and toffee."

"And also hot buttered toast."

"Yes," Holmes agreed, "and also hot buttered toast. And why did the March Hare and the Mad Hatter need to bring it to you?"

The girl looked between Holmes and myself, her lower lip trembling. Trustingly, she decided to place her confidence in Holmes. Looking back to him, she began, "At night he would climb into bed with me and touch me and—" She broke down into such a fit of crying that she was soon surrounded by a puddle of tears. I cannot explain it, since she must have cried more water than her body could possibly have contained to produce such a puddle. But Holmes and I both witnessed it.

I wanted to reach out and comfort the child, but, especially in view of the circumstances for her tears, forbore. Holmes steered the discussion onto a different matter. "That's a lovely cat you have."

"Dinah?" The girl blew her nose delicately on the sleeve of her dress and patted at her eyes to dry her tears. "Why, yes, she is. Such a capital one for catching mice, and oh, I wish you could see her after the birds! Why, she'll eat a little bird as soon as look at it!"

"Or a man," Holmes asked, "shrunk down to the size of a mouse?"

Dinah gave a large smile, and slowly vanished, beginning with the end of her tail and ending with her grin, which remained some time after the rest of her had disappeared.

Holmes took these unusual occurrences in much calmer stride than myself. "You might," he even ventured to remark, when we were back at Baker Street, "write in your notes that he died of consumption, if you're willing to interpret the term loosely." He smiled, turned away from me, and began an alchemical distillation of the contents of that mysterious cake, in order to determine how much he should consume to return him to his proper height. I saw no evidence that his humor was an attempt to alleviate uneasiness, as my own earlier attempts had been. I was amazed at his lack of ponderings or attempts to explain the many inexplicable events we had witnessed that day. Justice had been done in the girl's favor, he had declared, and was content, evidently, to let the case rest, solved if unexplainable.

I shook my head and stared at his back a moment while he worked. *At this rate,* I thought to myself as I began to prepare my notes, *he'll have me believe in no less than six impossible things before breakfast!*

Fox Tails

> RICHARD PARKS <

I WAS JUST OUTSIDE OF KYOTO, CLOSE ON THE TRAIL OF A FOX spirit, when the ghost appeared. It manifested as a giant red lantern with a small mouth and one large eye, and blocked access to a bridge I needed to cross. While it was true that ghosts made the best informants, their sense of timing could be somewhat lacking.

"I have information, Yamada-san," it said.

"I'm not looking for information. I'm looking for a fox," I said and started to brush past it.

"A silver fox with two tails? Sometimes appears as a human female named Kuzunoha?"

The lantern suddenly had my full attention. "I'm listening."

"You're chasing a *youkai* pretending to be Lady Kuzunoha. You really do not want to catch it, if you get my meaning."

I did. As monsters went, *youkai* ran the gamut from "mildly annoying" to "slurp your intestines like hot noodles." By the time you knew which sort you were dealing with, it was usually too late.

"How do I know you're telling me the truth?"

The lantern looked disgusted. "The other *rei* said you were smart, Yamada-san. How? You can follow that illusion until it gets tired of the game and eats you. Or we can reach an agreement. That is up to you." The lantern pretended to look away, unconcerned, but having only the one eye made it very difficult to glance at someone sideways without him knowing it.

"You're saying you know where Lady Kuzunoha is? What do you want in exchange?"

"Two bowls, plus prayers for my soul at the temple of your choice."

"One bowl, and I haven't been inside a temple since I was seven. I'm not going to start on your account."

I knew it would all come down to just how hungry the ghost was, but I wasn't worried—I'd already spotted the drool. It was staining the lantern's paper. The thing grumbled something about miserly bastards, but gave in.

"Very well, but do it properly."

"Always," I said. "Now tell me where I can find Lady Kuzunoha."

The ghost knew I was good for it. Information was the lifeblood of any nobleman's proxy, and only a fool would cheat an informant once a deal was agreed. I wasn't a fool . . . most of the time.

"Lady Kuzunoha is in Shinoda Forest."

I sighed deeply. "I don't appreciate you wasting my time, *rei*. My patron already had the place searched! She's not there."

"If the idiot hadn't sent his army he might have found her. She had more of a romantic rendezvous in mind, ne? If you're really looking for her, that's where she is. Go there yourself if you don't believe me."

"All right, but remember—I may not be intimate with temples but I do have contacts. If you're lying to me, I'll come back with a tinderbox and a priest who specializes. Do you understand me?"

"She's there, I tell you. Now honor our bargain."

I reached inside my robe and pulled out a bag of uncooked rice already measured out. I took a pair of wooden chopsticks and shoved them point first through the opening of the bag and held the offering in the palms of my hands before the lantern.

"For the good of my friend . . . uh, what's your name?"

"Seita."

"—Seita-san."

The bag floated out of my hands and shriveled like a dead leaf in a winter's wind. In a moment the pitiful remnants of the offering drifted to the ground in front of the bridge and the lantern let out a deep sigh of contentment.

"Quality stuff," it said. "I hope we can do business again."

"Maybe, if your story proves true and Lady Kuzunoha doesn't send any more *youkai* after me."

"But Lady Kuzunoha didn't . . . ahh, please forget I said that." For a moment I thought the lantern was just looking for another offering, but that wasn't it. The thing was actually scared, and there aren't many things short of an exorcist that will scare a ghost.

"If she didn't send it, who did?"

Just before it winked out like a snuffed candle, the lantern whispered, "Yamada-san, there isn't that much rice in Kyoto."

The servant who had come to my home the day before claimed to be from Lord Abe no Yasuna. At first I didn't believe him, but I wasn't so prosperous that I could chance turning down work. I also couldn't risk the potential insult to Lord Abe if the servant was telling the truth; even the Emperor would think twice before courting the Abe family's displeasure.

Like most members of the Court, the Abe family's ancestral lands were elsewhere, but they kept a palatial residence within the city to be close to the seat of power. Courtiers and supplicants waited two deep within the walled courtyard, but the servant ushered me right through. I didn't miss the raised eyebrows and muttering that followed in our wake. It didn't bother me; I was used to it.

Technically I was of noble birth since the minor lordling who was my father lowered himself to acknowledge me. Yet I had no inheritance, no regular patron, and no political connections, so the main difference between someone such as myself and your typical peasant farmer was that the farmer knew where his next meal was coming from. Yet, if it hadn't been for that accident of birth, people like Abe no Yasuna wouldn't deal with me in the first place, so I guess I should count my blessings. One of these days I'll get around to it.

I was ushered in to the Abe family reception hall. "Throne room" would have been a better description, and not too far from the truth. The Abe family counted more than a few actual royalty in their family tree, including the occasional emperor. The man himself was there, waiting for me. He was tall and imposing, probably no more than forty. Handsome, I would say. There was a peppering of gray in his black hair, but no more than that. He seemed distracted. Kneeling at a discreet distance was an older lady. At first glance I assumed she was a servant, but then I got a better look at her kimono, not to mention her face, and saw the family resemblance. It was unusual for a noblewoman to greet male guests save behind a screen, but perhaps the circumstances were unusual. I suspected they might be.

I bowed low. "You sent for me, lord?"

He studied me intently for several seconds before speaking. "Yamada no Goji. Your reputation for effectiveness . . . and discretion, precedes you. I trust it is deserved."

It was all I could do to keep from smiling. A delicate matter. Good—delicate matters paid the best. "I am at my lord's service."

Lord Abe turned to the kneeling woman. "Mother, I need to speak with Yamada-san alone. Boring business."

"Family business," said the old woman dryly as she rose, "but do as you will. It seems you must, these days."

Mother. Now I understood. I had heard of Abe no Akiko by reputation, as had nearly everyone in Kyoto. She had been a famous beauty in her day and, judging from what I could see of her now, that day was not long past. She also had a reputation for being a fierce advocate of her family's position at court and was rumored to have put more than one rival out of the game permanently. Still, that wasn't an unusual rumor for any courtier who'd lasted more than a few seasons. More to the point, she wasn't the one who had summoned me

Lord Abe was silent for a few moments, either collecting his thoughts or making sure his mother was out of earshot; I couldn't tell which.

"Have you ever been married, Yamada-san?" he said finally.

"I have not, lord."

"I was, for a while, to a lovely woman named Kuzunoha. I rather enjoyed it, but love and happiness are illusions, as the scriptures say."

I was beginning to get the drift. "Pardon my impertinence, but when did she leave?"

Lord Abe looked grim. "Two days ago."

"And you wish for me to find her?"

Lord Abe hesitated. "The matter is a bit more complicated than that, as I'm sure you've already guessed. Please follow me."

Despite Lord Abe's confidence, I hadn't guessed much about the situation at all, beyond the obvious. Wives left husbands for numerous reasons, and vice versa, and this wouldn't be the first time I'd been sent after one or the other. Lord Abe's position was such that he had apparently been able to keep the matter quiet; I'd certainly heard nothing of it. Still, the situation was unfortunate but not a real scandal. I followed as Lord Abe led through a small partition leading to a tiny room behind the dais where Lord Abe had received me. We came to a screen that opened onto another courtyard, and beyond that was the roofed wall that surrounded the entire residence complex. There was another gate visible.

Lord Abe stopped at the screen. It took me a few seconds to realize that he wasn't looking beyond it but *at* it. Someone had written a message on the *shoji* screen in flowing script. It was a poem of farewell, but, despite its obvious beauty, that was not what got my attention. It was Lady Kuzunoha's confession, clearly stated, that she was not a woman at all but a fox spirit he had once rescued on the grounds of the Inari Shrine and that she could no longer remain with Lord Abe as his wife. The poem ended: "If you would love me again, find me in Shinoda Forest." The poem was signed "Reluctant Kuzunoha."

"My lord, are you certain this is your wife's script?"

"Without question. She always had the most beautiful calligraphy. She could copy any text of the *sutras* exactly, but when writing as herself her own style is distinctive."

That his wife had left him was one thing. That his wife was a fox was quite another. Pretending to be a human woman was a fox spirit's favorite trick, and Lord Abe wouldn't be the first man to be fooled by one. At the least, that could be somewhat embarrassing, and, in the rarified circles of court where favor and banishment were never separated by more than a sword's edge, "somewhat" could be enough to tip the scale.

"She knew I didn't allow servants in here, so none have seen this but my mother and myself. I will destroy the door," Lord Abe said, "for obvious reasons, but I did want you to see it first. I have already sealed the document granting you authority to act on my behalf in this matter." He pulled the scroll out of a fold of his robe and handed it to me.

I took the scroll but couldn't resist the question. "What matter, Lord Abe? Pardon my saying so, but if this confession is true, then you are well rid of her. Fox spirits are dangerous creatures."

That was an understatement if there ever was. One Chinese emperor had barely avoided being murdered by a fox masquerading as a concubine, and one poor farmer spent a hundred years watching a pair of fox-women playing Go for what he thought was an afternoon. They were tricksters at the best of times and often far worse.

"It wasn't like that," Lord Abe said quietly. "Kuzunoha loved me. I do not know what drove her to leave or to make this confession, but I was never in danger from her."

"You want me to find her, then?" I had to ask. There were at least as many fools among the nobility as elsewhere, and there was always someone who thought the rules didn't apply to him. I was more than a little relieved to discover that Lord Abe was not that stupid.

He shook his head. His expression had not changed, but his eyes were moist and glistening. "Lady Kuzunoha is correct that we cannot be together now, but she should not have asked me to give up Doshi as well."

"Doshi?"

"My son, Yamada-san. She took my . . . our son."

I was beginning to see what he meant by "complicated."

"I take it you've already searched Shinoda Forest?" That was an easy supposition to make. I already knew what he'd found, otherwise I wouldn't be there.

He sighed. "I should have gone personally, but I did not trust myself to let Kuzunoha go if I ever held her again. My mother suggested we send my personal retainers and in my weakness I agreed. They searched thoroughly, and I lost two good men to an ogre in the process. There was no sign of either Kuzunoha or Doshi." He looked at me. "That is your task, Yamada-san. I want you to find my son and return him to me."

"Again I must ask your pardon, lord, but is this wise? The boy will be half fox himself. Isn't there a danger?"

His smile was so faint one might have missed it, but I did not. "There's always a danger, Yamada-san. If we are fortunate we get to decide which ones we choose to face. I want my son back."

"By any means required?"

"Do not harm Lady Kuzunoha. With that one exception, do what you must."

At least my goal was clear enough. I didn't for one moment think it was going to be easy.

✳   ✳   ✳

Another advantage of being of the noble class was that it entitled you to carry weapons openly, and Shinoda Forest was not a place you wanted to go empty-handed. The place had a deserved reputation for being the haunt of fox spirits and worse; most bandits even avoided the place, and any bandit who didn't was *not* the sort you wanted to meet. Yet here I was, for the princely sum of five imported Chinese bronze coins and one *kin* of uncooked rice a day, plus reasonable expenses. You can be sure I counted that payment to the red lantern ghost as "reasonable."

There was a path. Not much of one, but I stuck to it. There was a danger in keeping to the only known path in a wood full of monsters, not to mention it might make finding Lady Kuzunoha even more difficult, but I kept to the path anyway. Getting lost in Shinoda Forest would have done neither me nor my patron much good.

Even so, once you got past the fact that the woods were full of things that wanted to kill you, it was a very beautiful place. There was a hint of fall in the air; the maple leaves were beginning to shade into red, contrasting with the deep green of the rest of the wood. The scent was earthy but not unpleasant. It had been some time since I'd been out of the city and I was enjoying the scent and sounds of a true forest. Too much so, perhaps, otherwise I would never have been caught so easily.

I hadn't walked three paces past a large stone when the world went black. When I woke up, I almost wished I hadn't: my head felt like two *shou* of plum wine crammed into a one *shou* cask. For a moment I honestly thought it would explode. After a little while, the pain eased enough for me to open my eyes. It was early evening, though of which day I had no idea. I was lying on my side, trussed like a deer on a carrying pole, and about ten feet from a campfire. Sitting beside that campfire were two of the biggest, most unpleasant-looking men it had ever been my misfortune to get ambushed by. They were both built like stone temple guardians, and their arms were as thick as my legs. Otherwise there wasn't much to separate them, save one was missing an ear and the other's nose had been split near the tip. One look at them and my aching brain only had room for one question:

Why am I still alive?

I must have moaned with the effort of keeping my eyes open, since one of the bandits glanced in my direction and grunted.

"He's awake. Good. I thought you'd killed him. You know an ogre likes 'em fresh."

There was my answer, though it went without saying that I didn't care for it. Maybe I could get a better one. "You two gentlemen work for an ogre?"

"Don't be stupid," said Missing Ear. "The ogre is just a bonus. Our employer wants you dead, and, since you're dead either way, we sell you to the ogre that lives in this forest. That's good business."

He clearly wasn't the brightest blade in the rack, but I couldn't fault his mercantile instincts. "So who are you working for?"

"You're dead. What do you care?"

"If I'm going to die, I'd like to know why. Besides, if I'm good as dead it's not like I'll be telling anyone."

"Well if you must know—oww!" Missing Ear began, but then Split Nose leaned over and rapped him sharply on the back of his skull.

"You know what *she* said about talking too much," he said. "What if she found out? Do you want her angry at you? I'd sooner take my chances with the ogre."

Her. At this point there didn't seem to be much question as to whom they meant.

Missing Ear rubbed his head. He had a sour look on his face, but what his companion had said to him apparently sank in. "No. That would be . . . bad."

"So far we've done everything like she said. The ogre will see our fire soon and come for this fool, and that's that. We can get out of this demon-blighted place."

"You two are making a big mistake. I'm acting as proxy for Lord Abe. An insult to me is an insult to him." It wasn't much, but it was all I had. I was still surprised at the bandits' reaction. They glanced at each other and burst out laughing.

"We know why you're here, *baka*," said Split Nose when he regained his composure. "Now be a well-behaved meal and wait for the ogre."

The bandits obviously knew more about this matter than I did. It was also obvious that they had searched me before they tied me up. I could see my pack near the campfire and my *tachi* leaning against a boulder only a few feet away. It was the only decent material object I owned, a gift from the grateful father of a particularly foolish young man whose good name I was able to salvage. It was a beautiful sword, with sharkskin-covered grip and scabbard both dyed black. The *tsuba* was of black iron and the blade, I had occasion to know, was sharp enough to shave with. If only I could reach it, I could demonstrate that virtue on my captors, but it was impossible. As close as the *tachi* was, it might as well have been in Mongolia for all the good of it. Try as I might, I could not get free of the ropes. I flashed back on something Lord Abe had said.

"*Love and happiness are both illusions.*"

To which I could add that life was fleeting and illusory itself. I might not have been much for the temple, but the priests had that much right. The best I could hope for now was that the ogre was more hungry than cruel; then at least he would be quick.

There was a very faint rustling in the undergrowth. At first I thought it was the ogre coming for his supper, but then I couldn't quite imagine something that large moving so quietly. A light flared and I assumed someone had lit a torch, but the flame turned blue and then floated over the campsite and disappeared. Then, almost on cue, thirteen additional blue fires kindled in the darkness just beyond the campfire.

Yurrei . . . ? Oh, hell.

Ghosts were just like *youkai* in one important respect—there were ghosts, and then there were ghosts. Some, like the red lantern ghost Seita, were reasonable folk once you got to know them. Some, however, tended to be angry at everything living. Judging from the *onibi* and balefire I was seeing now, all three of us were pretty much stew for the same pot. Split Nose and Missing Ear knew it too. The pair of them had turned whiter than a funeral kimono, and for a moment they actually hugged each other, though Split Nose managed to compose himself enough to rap Missing Ear's skull again.

"You idiot! You made camp in a graveyard!"

"Wasn't no graveyard here!" Missing Ear protested, but Split Nose was already pointing back toward me.

"What's that, then?"

I was having some trouble moving my head, but I managed to see what they were seeing, not ten feet away on the far side of me. It was a stone grave marker, half-covered in weeds and vines, but still visible enough even in the firelight.

When I looked back at the bandits the ghost was already there, hovering about two feet off the ground. It might have been female; it was wearing a funeral white kimono but the way its kimono was tied was about as feminine as the specter got. Its mouth was three feet wide and full of sharp teeth, its eyes were as big as soup bowls and just as bulging. One of its hands was tucked within the kimono, but the other, pointing directly at the cowering bandits, bore talons as long as knives.

YOU HAVE DISTURBED ME. PREPARE TO DIE. The ghost's voice boomed like thunder, and the blue fires showed traces of red.

"Mercy!" cried Split Nose. "It was a mistake!"

YES. NOW PREPARE TO ATONE!

"Mercy!" they both cried again and bowed low.

The revenant seemed to consider. BOW LOWER, DOGS.

They did so. Then came two flashes of silver, and the bandits slumped over into a heap. In an instant the balefires went out, and the ghost floated down to earth, and then she wasn't a ghost at all but a woman carrying a sword.

My sword.

I glanced at the boulder and saw that the *tachi* was missing, though its scabbard still leaned against the stone. The gravestone was gone, but by this time I expected that. Fox spirits were masters of illusion. The woman turned to face me.

I had never seen a more beautiful woman in my life. A master painter could not have rendered a face more perfect, or hair so long and glossy black that it shone like dark fire. She seemed little more than a delicate young woman, but the ease with which she handled my sword and the twitching bodies of the two bandits said otherwise. She walked over to me without a second glance at the carnage behind her.

"Lady Kuzunoha?" I made it sound like a question, but really it wasn't.

"Who are you?" she demanded.

"My name is Yamada no Goji. Lord Abe sent me."

"I've heard of you, Yamada-san. Well, then. Let's get this over with."

She raised the sword again, and I closed my eyes. I would have said a prayer if I could have thought of one. All I could manage was the obvious.

This is my death . . .

I heard the angry whoosh of the blade as it cut through the air. It took me several long seconds to realize that it hadn't cut through *me*. Not only was I still alive, but my hands were free. Another whoosh and my legs were free as well, though both arms and legs were too numb from the ropes to be of much use to me at first. While I struggled to get to my feet, Lady Kuzunoha calmly walked back to the bandits and took a wrapping cloth from one of their pouches which she used to methodically clean the blade. I had just managed to sit up when she returned the long sword to its scabbard and tossed it at my feet.

"I wouldn't advise staying here too long, Yamada-san," she said. "The ogre will be here soon."

"I'm afraid he's going to be disappointed," I said.

She shook her head, and she smiled. "Oh, no. Those two are still alive. We foxes know much of the nature of the spine and where to break it. They'll die soon enough, but probably not before they're eaten. The fools would have been eaten in either case, of course. Ogres don't make bargains with meat."

Her words were like cold water. If they couldn't totally negate the effect her beauty was having on me, at least they reminded me that I wasn't dealing with a human being. An important point that I had best remember. I got to my feet a little unsteadily.

"My thanks for saving me, Kuzunoha-sama," I said, "but I'm afraid that I have some business with you yet."

"So I assumed. The path is about fifteen paces ahead of you. Stay on it until you reach the river. You'll be able to hear a waterfall," she said. "I'll be waiting for you there."

Lady Kuzunoha moved quickly away from me. In a moment her image shimmered, and I saw her true form, a silver fox bearing the second tail that betrayed her spirit nature. She ran swiftly and was soon out of sight. I gathered my belongings and hobbled along the way she had gone as best I could.

I wasn't clear on a lot of things, not the least of which was why Lady Kuzunoha had bothered to save my life. After all, if she knew who sent me, then she knew why I had come and, if she'd been willing to surrender the boy in the first place, she could have arranged that easily enough while Lord Abe's men searched the wood. And if she *wasn't* willing to give up the child, why not just kill me? It's not as if I could have done anything to stop her, and if I had any doubts of either her ability or will in that regard, I had the wretched bandits' example to prove otherwise.

A lot of things didn't make sense, and if I wanted any answers

I'd have to go much deeper into Shinoda Forest to get them. Part of me wondered if I might be better off taking my chances with the ogre. Then I heard a large crashing noise in the forest back the way I'd come and decided not. I picked up the pace as much as the headache and my tingling limbs allowed.

I'd been careless once and was lucky to be alive. This time as I moved down the path, I had my sword out and ready. I wasn't sure how much good it would do me against what I'd likely face, but the grip felt comforting in my hand.

I came to the place Lady Kuzunoha described and followed the sound of rushing water. A cold-water stream rushing down the adjacent hill formed a twelve-foot waterfall into the river's rocky shallows. Lady Kuzunoha was in human form again. She stood directly underneath the rushing water, her slim fingers pressed together in an attitude of prayer, her long black hair flowing over her body like a cloak. Her hair was the only thing covering her. For a little while I forgot to breathe.

I knew Lady Kuzunoha's human form was an actual transformation and not simply illusion, else she would never have been able to bear a human child, but I also knew it was not her true form. Knowing this did not help me at all. The only thing that did was the sharp and clear memory of what she had done to those two hapless bandits; that was *my* cold waterfall. That left the question of why Lady Kuzunoha needed one.

When I finally managed to look away, I noticed Lady Kuzunoha's kimono neatly folded on top of a flat stone nearby. I'm still not sure why I turned away. Maybe it was my common sense, warning me of danger. Or maybe I had come to the reluctant—and relieved—conclusion that this little show was not being staged for my benefit. Lady Kuzunoha was preparing herself for something, but I didn't have clue one as to what that might be.

There was a small clearing nearby; I waited there. Lady Kuzunoha finally emerged, now fully dressed, her hair still wet but combed out and orderly. If anything she appeared more winsome than before. She looked sad but resolute as she approached the center of the clearing. In her sash she had tucked one of those slim daggers that highborn ladies tended to carry both as self-defense and a symbol of rank. She knelt beside me, looking away.

"I'm ready," she said. She drew the dagger and put the naked blade across her thighs.

I frowned. Maybe Seita the ghost was right about me, since what came out of my mouth then wasn't very intelligent. "I don't understand. Ready for what, Lady Kuzunoha?"

It was as if she hadn't even heard me. "I would send my love a poem but words are useless now. You may take back whatever proofs your master requires. Now stand ready to assist me."

The light dawned. The waterfall was a purification rite, which would explain the prayer but not much else. "You think I'm here to kill you!"

Lady Kuzunoha looked up at me. "Do not mock me, Yamada-san. I saved your life, and I think I'm due the courtesy of the truth. Did Lord Abe send you or not?"

"I have his writ and seal if you doubt me. But I am no assassin, whatever you may have heard of me."

Now Lady Kuzunoha looked confused. "But . . . what else? I cannot return. He knows that."

If Lady Kuzunoha was confused, I was doubly so, but at least I had the presence of mind to reach down and take the knife away from her. "First of all, assuming I *had* been sent to harm you, will you please explain why you're being so cooperative?"

She frowned. "Did my husband not explain the circumstances of our first meeting?"

"He didn't have to—I saw your message. You said that he rescued you from hunters . . . before he knew that you and the silver fox were one and the same, I mean."

"There was even more to it that he didn't know, Yamada-san. You see, I was already in love with Lord Abe, from the day his procession rode past Shinoda Forest three years ago. I came to the Inari Shrine in the first place because I knew he would be there. He already owned my heart, but from that day forward he owned my life as well. If now he requires that of me, who am I to deny my love what is his by right?"

Now it was starting to make some sense. No one had ever claimed that self-sacrifice was a fox trait, but I knew love made people do silly things, and it was clear even to a lout like me that Lady Kuzunoha, fox spirit or no, was still deeply in love with her husband. I had suspected that Lord Abe was deluding himself on that point, but now I knew better.

"If Lord Abe didn't know you were a fox, why did you leave him?"

"I didn't want to," Lady Kuzunoha said, sadly. "I tried so hard... You know what I am, Yamada-san. The body I wear now is real, but it is a sort of mask. Sometimes the mask slips; that's unavoidable. Yet it was happening to me more and more. In my foolishness I thought I would be spared this, but the burden of pretending to be something I am not became too much, even for his sake. It was only a matter of time before my true nature would be revealed and my husband and his family shamed. I could no longer take that risk. I am a fraud, but I was honest with my husband about why I had to leave. He did not come himself, so I assume he hates me now."

"He doesn't hate you, Lady Kuzunoha. He understands your reasons and accepts them, though he is very sad as you might imagine."

Lady Kuzunoha rose to her feet with one smooth motion. "Then why did my lord not come himself? Why did he send his warriors? Why did he send *you*?"

"My patron said he did not trust himself to let you go if he ever held you again. I can not fault him in this."

She actually blushed slightly at the compliment, but pressed on. "You didn't answer my other question."

"He sent his retainers and me for the same reason: we were looking for Doshi."

"My son? But why?"

"To bring him home, Lady. Lord Abe lost you. He didn't want to lose his son too. Maybe that's selfish of him, but I think you can understand how he feels."

"But I do *not* understand," Lady Kuzunoha said, and now the gentle, sad expression she had worn since leaving the waterfall was nowhere to be seen. She looked into my eyes and my knees shook. "Yamada-san, are you telling me that my son is missing?"

I fought the urge to back away. "But... you didn't take him?"

"I...? Of course not! Doshi's blood may be mostly fox, but in Shinoda Forest that's not enough. He could never have made a home in my world! Doshi belongs with his father."

I took a deep breath. "If that's the case, then yes, Lady Kuzunoha— I'm telling you that your son is missing."

I'm not sure what I expected, but Lady Kuzunoha merely held out her hand. "Please return my dagger, Yamada-san. I promise not to use it on myself... or you."

I gave the knife back, carefully. "Do you have someone else in mind?"

Her smile was the stuff of nightmares. "That remains to be seen."

I had more questions, but Lady Kuzunoha was in no mood to answer them, and I knew better than to test my luck. She was kind enough to see me safely out of the forest before she disappeared, but it was clear she had other matters on her mind besides my well-being. I, on the other hand, could think of little else.

The bandit was right to call you a fool. You had no idea of how big a mess you were in.

The *youkai* that Seita had warned me about should have been my first clue. Still, if Lord Abe had sent me chasing wild foxfire, there still might be time to get on the right trail. I didn't like where I thought it was going to lead, but I had given my word, and that was the only thing worth more to me than my sword. I just hoped it didn't have to mean more than my life.

When I got back into Kyoto, the first thing I did was track down Kenji. It wasn't that hard. He was at one of his favorite drinking establishments near the Demon Gate. Technically it was the Northeast Gate, but since that was the direction from which demons and evil spirits were supposed to enter, the name stuck. Naturally someone like Kenji would keep close to such a place. He said it was good for business.

Business looked a little slow. For one thing, Kenji was drinking very cheap sake. For another, he was in great need of a barber; his head looked like three days' growth of beard. I found a cushion on the opposite side of his table and made myself comfortable. Kenji looked at me blearily. He had one of those in-between faces, neither old nor young, though I happened to know he was pushing fifty. He finally recognized me.

"Yamada-san! How is my least favorite person?"

"Terrible, you'll be pleased to know. I need a favor."

He smiled like a little drunken Buddha. "Enlightenment is free but in this world all favors have a price. What do you want?"

"I need to seal the powers of a fox spirit, at least temporarily. Is this possible?"

He whistled low. "When all is illusion all things are possible. Still, you're wading in a dangerous current, Yamada-san."

"This I know. Can you help me or not?"

Kenji seemed to pause in thought and then rummaged around inside his robe, which, like him, was in need of a bath. He pulled out a slip of paper that was surprisingly clean considering from where it had come. He glanced at it, then nodded. "This will do what you want, but the effect is temporary. Just how temporary depends on the spiritual powers of the animal. Plus you'll have to place it on the fox directly."

"How many bowls?"

"Rice? For this? Yamada-san, I'll accept three good bronze, but only because it's you."

Reluctantly I counted out the coins. "Done, but this better not be one of your worthless fakes for travelers and the gullible."

He sat up a little straighter. "Direct copy from the Diamond Sutra, Yamada-san. I was even sober when I did it."

"I hope so, since if this doesn't work and somehow I survive, I'll be back to discuss it. If it does work, I owe you a drink."

He just smiled a ragged smile. "Either way, you know where to find me."

I did. Whatever Kenji's numerous faults as a priest and a man, at least he was consistent. I carefully stashed the paper seal and headed for Lord Abe's estate. I wasn't sure how much time I had left, but I didn't think there was a lot.

There was less than I knew.

Before I even reached the gate at the Abe estate, I saw a lady traveling alone. She was veiled, of course. Her wide-brimmed *boshi* was ringed with pale white mesh that hung down like a curtain, obscuring her features. I couldn't tell who it was but her bearing, her clothes, even the way she moved betrayed her as a noble. A woman of that class traveling unescorted was unusual in itself, but more unusual was the fact that no one seemed to notice. She passed a gang of rough-looking workmen who didn't even give her a second glance.

Once, the density of the crowd forced her to brush against a serving girl who looked startled for a moment as she looked around, then continued her errand, frowning. The woman, for her part, kept up her pace.

They can't see her.

At that point I realized it was too late to keep watch at the Abe estate. I kept to the shadows and alleyways as best I could, and I followed. I could move quietly at need and I was as careful as I could be without losing sight of her; if she spotted me, she'd know that fact long before I did. I kept with her as the buildings thinned out and she moved up the road leading out of the city.

She's going to the Inari Shrine.

Mount Inari was clearly visible in the distance, and the woman kept up her pace without flagging until she had reached the grounds of the shrine. Its numerous red *torii* were like beacons, but she took little notice of the shrine buildings themselves and immediately passed on to the path leading up to the mountain.

Hundreds of bright red gates donated by the faithful over the years arched over the pathway, giving it a rather tunnellike appearance. I didn't dare follow directly behind her now; one backward glance would have betrayed me. I moved off the path and kept to the edge of the wood that began immediately behind the shrine buildings. It was easy now to see why hunters might frequent the area; the woods went on for miles around the mountainside. There were fox statues as well, since foxes were the messengers of the God of Rice; they were depicted here in stone with message scrolls clamped in their powerful jaws. The wooden *torii* themselves resembled gates, and I knew that's what they were, symbolic gates marking the transition from the world of men to the world of the spirits, and this was the true destination of my veiled lady. I didn't want to follow her further but I knew there was no real choice now; to turn back meant failure or worse. Going on might mean the same, if I was wrong about what was about to happen.

The woman left the path where the woods parted briefly to create a small meadow. I hid behind a tree, but it was a useless gesture.

"You've followed me for quite some time, Yamada-san. Please do me the courtesy of not skulking about any longer."

I recognized the voice. Not that there was any question in my mind by then, but there was no point in further concealment. I stepped into the clearing. "Greetings, Lady Akiko."

Lady Abe no Akiko untied her veil and removed her *boshi*. She was showing her age just a little more in the clear light of day, though she was still very handsome. "Following me was very rude, Yamada-san. My son will hear of it."

"Perhaps there is a way we can avoid that unpleasantness, Lady, if not all unpleasantness. You're here about your grandson, aren't you?"

She covered her mouth with her fan to indicate that she was smiling. "Of course. Family matters have always been my special concern."

Someone else entered the clearing. Another woman, dressed and veiled in a manner very similar to Akiko. "You said you'd come alone," the newcomer said. It sounded like an accusation.

"It was not my doing that he is here," Lady Akiko said. "And it will make no difference. Surely you can see that?"

"Perhaps." The newcomer removed her *boshi*, but her voice had already announced her. Lady Kuzunoha. She glared at me as she approached. Now she and Lady Akiko were barely a few paces apart.

"Yamada-san, this no longer concerns you," Lady Kuzunoha said.

"I respectfully disagree. My responsibility ends only when Lord Abe's son is found."

Lady Akiko glared at her former daughter-in-law. "And this . . . this *vixen* who betrayed my son knows where he is! Do you deny it?"

"Of course not," Lady Kuzunoha said haughtily. "I know exactly where my son is. As do you."

Lady Akiko practically spat out the words. "Yes! With the person who took him!"

"Yes," Lady Kuzunoha said grimly. She drew her dagger. "Let us settle this!"

"Pitiful fool!"

It turned out that Lady Akiko already had her dagger unsheathed, concealed in the sleeve of her kimono. She lashed out and Lady Kuzunoha gasped in pain. She clutched her hand as her dagger fell uselessly into the grass. In a moment Akiko had Kuzunoha's arms pinned at her sides and her dagger at the young woman's throat.

"One doesn't survive so long at court without learning a few tricks. Or, for that matter, giving your enemies a sporting chance. Now prove the truth of my words, worthless vixen! Tell me before this witness where Lord Abe's son is, and do not try any of your fox tricks else I'll kill you where you stand!"

"You will not taste my blood that easily, old woman."

The fight was far from over. Lady Kuzunoha's power was gathering around her like a storm; the air fairly crackled with it. Lady Akiko held her ground, but the hand holding the knife was shaking, and I knew it took her a great effort to keep the blade pointed at Lady Kuzunoha's throat.

"Tell Yamada-san where Doshi is if you want to live!" Lady Akiko said. "And no lies!"

"Why would he believe anything I say," Lady Kuzunoha said calmly, "if he does not believe what I have told him before now?"

I knew that, in a few seconds, anything I did would be too late. I stepped forward quickly, pulling out Kenji's seal as I did so. Both women watched me intently as I approached. "Lady Kuzunoha, do you know what this is?" She nodded, her face expressionless.

Lady Akiko wasn't expressionless at all. Her look was pure triumph. "Yamada-san, you are more resourceful than I thought. I will recommend to my son that he double your fee."

I gave her a slight bow. "I am in Lord Abe's service." I concentrated then on Lady Kuzunoha. "If you know what this is, then you know what it can do to you. Do you truly know where your son is?"

She looked resigned. "I do."

"That's all I need. Please prepare yourself."

Lady Kuzunoha went perfectly still in Lady Akiko's grip but before either of them could move again, I darted forward and slapped the seal on Lady Akiko's forehead.

"Yamada-sarrrr!!!"

My name ended in a snarl of rage, but Lady Akiko had time to do nothing else before the transformation was complete. In Lady Akiko's place was an old red fox vixen with three tails. Lady Kuzunoha stood frozen, blinking in surprise.

There was no more time to consider. My sword was in my hands just as the fox gathered itself to spring at Lady Kuzunoha's throat. My shout startled it, and it sprang at me instead. My first slash caught it across the chest, and it yipped in pain. My second stroke severed the fox's head from its body. The fox that had been Abe no Akiko fell in a bloody heap, twitching.

I had seen Lady Kuzunoha butcher two men with barely a thought, but she looked away from the remains of her former mother-in-law with a delicacy that surprised me. "I-I still had some hope that it would not come to this. That was foolish of me."

"She didn't leave me much choice."

Lady Kuzunoha shook her head. "No, your life was already worthless to her. Doubly so since you knew her secret. Speaking of that, how *did* you know?"

I started to clean my sword. "Lady Kuzunoha, I have just been forced to take a rather drastic step in the course of my duties. I'll answer your questions if you will answer mine. Agreed?"

She forced herself to look at Lady Akiko's body. "There is no reason to keep her secrets now."

"Very well. There were two things in particular. Someone put me on the trail of a *youkai* that was pretending to be you. Once I knew that you didn't send either it or those bandits, that left the question of who did. More to the point, you told me that Doshi was *mostly* fox, remember?"

She actually blushed. "Careless of me. I did not intend..."

I smiled grimly. "I know, and at first I thought you'd simply misspoken. But, assuming you had not, for Doshi to be more than merely half fox meant his father was at least part fox himself. How could this be? The simplest reasonable answer was Lady Akiko. Did Lord Abe know about his mother? Or himself?"

"No to both. Fortunately his fox blood was never dominant. Lady Akiko and I knew about each other all along, of course. She opposed the marriage but couldn't reveal me without revealing herself. We kept each other's secret out of necessity until..."

"Until Doshi was born?"

She nodded, looking unhappy. "I knew by then I couldn't stay, but I thought my son's position was secure. I was in error. There was too much fox in him, and Lady Akiko was afraid his fox nature would reveal itself, and disgrace the family. The position of the Abe family was always her chief concern."

"If the boy was such a danger, why didn't she just smother him in his sleep?"

Lady Kuzunoha looked genuinely shocked. "Murder her own grandson? Really, Yamada-san ... Besides, it's easy enough to dedicate an unwanted child to some distant temple with no questions about his origin. In preparation, Lady Akiko had him hidden within the shrine complex; the Abe family is their foremost patron, so it was easy to arrange. Once I knew my son was missing it took me a while to follow his trail and to arrange a meeting."

"Duel, you mean."

She looked away. "Just so. While I may have hoped otherwise, it was destined that either I or Lady Akiko would not leave this clearing alive. Her solution to the problem of Doshi was quite elegant, but you were an obstacle to that solution and, once you found me, so was I."

"Which explains why she went to so much trouble trying to prevent me from finding you in the first place. Was she correct then? Won't Doshi be a danger to the family now?"

"Yes," said Lady Kuzunoha frankly. "Yet my husband already knows that. Perhaps not how *great* a risk, I concede, but I don't think that would deter him. Do you?"

I finished cleaning my sword and slid it back into its scabbard. "No, but as grateful as he's going to be at the return of his son, Lord Abe is going to be considerably less so when I explain what happened to his mother, proxy or no."

Lady Kuzunoha covered her mouth as she smiled. "Yamada-san, perhaps there is an 'elegant solution' to this as well. For now, kindly produce my lord's proxy seal and we'll go fetch my son."

That proved easily done. The presence of both the seal and Lady Kuzunoha herself was more than enough to send one of the shrine priests scurrying ahead of us to a small outbuilding near a *koi* pond. There we found Doshi in the care of a rather frightened wet nurse. Lady Kuzunoha paid off the poor woman generously, thanked her for her solicitude, and sent her on her way. The baby looked up, lifting its little arms and gurgling happily, as Lady Kuzunoha smiled down at him.

"Probably time you were weaned, my son." She turned to me. "Please take him, Yamada-san. You'll need to get him back to his father quickly; he'll have to make his own arrangements for Doshi's care. I will give you some writing to take to my husband before you leave."

I hesitated. "Don't . . . don't you wish to hold your son? This may well be your last chance."

She smiled a sad smile. "Thank you for that offer, but I can only echo the words of my lord in this, Yamada-san: If I held him again, what makes you think I could let him go?"

I had no answer to that, but I did have one last question. "One thing still bothers me: you were unable to maintain the deception of being human, but Lady Akiko had been in the family much longer than you. How did she manage?"

Lady Kuzunoha laughed softly. "Yamada-san, as I told you before: the mask will slip, and we cannot control when or how. For me, my right hand would turn into a paw without warning. For Lady Akiko, it was her scent."

I blinked. "Scent?"

She nodded. "Her true scent, as a fox. But the human nose is a poor tool at best. Those close to her would either miss the scent entirely or at worst mistake it for . . . something else," she finished, delicately. "Lady Akiko was simply luckier than I was."

That may have been so, but Lady Akiko's luck had finally run out. I was afraid that mine was about to do the same.

Lord Abe received me in his private chambers after I placed his infant son back in the care of his servants.

"Yamada-san, I am in your debt," he said. "I-I trust Lady Kuzunoha was not . . . difficult?"

From my kneeling position, I touched my forehead to the floor. "That relates to a matter I need to speak of. Lady Kuzunoha was quite reluctant, as you can imagine, but I was impertinent enough to acquire the assistance of Lady Akiko in this. They spoke, mother to mother, and Lady Akiko persuaded her."

"I see."

I could tell that he didn't see at all, but the die was already cast. I produced the scroll Lady Kuzunoha had supplied. "Lady Akiko told me of the . . . differences, between your wife and herself. That her intense desire to protect the family's name had perhaps blinded her to Lady Kuzunoha's virtues. To atone for this—and other burdens—she has decided to renounce the world and join a temple as a nun. She also sent a personal message to you."

Lord Abe was a Gentleman of the Court, whatever else he might be. He concealed his shock and surprise very well. He took the scroll I offered and unrolled it in silence. He remained intent on what was written there for several moments longer than would have been required to actually read the words. I tried not to hold my breath.

"My mother's script," he said, almost to himself. "Perfect." He looked down at me, his expression unreadable. "I don't suppose my mother revealed to you which temple she had chosen to join?"

I bowed again. "She did not so confide in me, my lord, though I had the impression it was quite far from here. She seemed to feel that was for the best. She hoped you would understand."

He grunted. "Perhaps she is right about both. Well then, Yamada-san. I've lost both my wife and my mother, but I have not yet lost all. It seems I must be content with that."

I breathed a little easier once I'd been paid and was safely off the grounds. I wasn't sure how much of my story Lord Abe really believed, but if he didn't realize full well that Lady Kuzunoha had written that message, I'm no judge of men. Perhaps that was another choice he made. As for myself, I chose to be elsewhere for a good long time. Hokkaido sounded best; I'd heard that it's very sparsely populated and only a little frozen at this time of the year. But first I went to meet Kenji by the Demon Gate, since I'd given my word and now I owed him a drink.

I owed myself several more.

A Case of Identity

> RANDALL GARRETT <

THE PAIR OF MEN-AT-ARMS STROLLED ALONG THE RUE KING JOHN II, near the waterfront of Cherbourg, and a hundred yards south of the sea. In this district, the Keepers of the King's Peace always traveled in pairs, each keeping one hand near the truncheon at his belt and the other near the hilt of his smallsword. The average commoner was not a swordsman, but sailors are not common commoners. A man armed only with a truncheon would be at a disadvantage with a man armed with a cutlass.

The frigid wind from the North Sea whipped the edges of the Men-at-Arms' cloaks, and the light from the mantled gas lamps glowed yellowly, casting multiple shadows that shifted queerly as the Armsmen walked.

There were not many people on the streets. Most of them were in the bistros, where there were coal fires to warm the outer man and fiery bottled goods to warm the inner. There had been crowds in the street on the Vigil of the Feast of the Circumcision, nine days before, but now the Twelfth Day of Christmas had passed and the Year of Our Lord 1964 was in its second week. Money had run short and few could still afford to drink.

The taller of the two officers stopped and pointed ahead. "Ey, Robert. Old Jean hasn't got his light on."

"Hm-m-m. Third time since Christmas. Hate to give the old man a summons."

"Aye. Let's just go in and scare the Hell out of him."

211

"Aye," said the shorter man. "But we'll promise him a summons next time and keep our promise, Jack."

The sign above the door was a weather-beaten dolphin-shaped piece of wood, painted blue. The Blue Dolphin.

Armsman Robert pushed open the door and went in, his eyes alert for trouble. There was none. Four men were sitting around one end of the long table at the left, and Old Jean was talking to a fifth man at the bar. They all looked up as the Armsmen came in. Then the men at the table went on with their conversation. The fifth customer's eyes went to his drink. The barkeep smiled ingratiatingly and came toward the two Armsmen.

"Evening, Armsmen," he said with a snaggle-toothed smile. "A little something to warm the blood?" But he knew it was no social call.

Robert already had out his summons book, pencil poised. "Jean, we have warned you twice before," he said frigidly. "The law plainly states that every place of business must maintain a standard gas lamp and keep it lit from sunset to sunrise. You know this."

"Perhaps the wind—" the barkeep said defensively.

"The wind? I will go up with you and we will see if perhaps the wind has turned the gas cock, ey?"

Old Jean swallowed. "Perhaps I did forget. My memory—"

"Perhaps explaining your memory to my lord the Marquis next court day will help you to improve it, ey?"

"No, no! Please, Armsman! The fine would ruin me!"

Armsman Robert made motions with his pencil as though he were about to write. "I will say it is a first offense and the fine will be only half as much."

Old Jean closed his eyes helplessly. "Please, Armsman. It will not happen again. It is just that I have been so used to Paul—he did everything, all the hard work. I have no one to help me now."

"Paul Sarto has been gone for two weeks now," Robert said. "This is the third time you have given me that same excuse."

"Armsman," said the old man earnestly, "I will not forget again. I promise you."

Robert closed his summons book. "Very well. I have your word? Then you have my word that there will be no excuses next time. I will hand you the summons instantly. Understood?"

"Understood, Armsman! Yes, of course. Many thanks! I will not forget again!"

"See that you don't. Go and light it."

Old Jean scurried up the stairway and was back within minutes. "It's lit now, Armsman."

"Excellent. I expect it to be lit from now on. At sunset. Good night, Jean."

"Perhaps a little—?"

"No, Jean. Another time. Come, Jack."

The Armsmen left without taking the offered drink. It would be ungentlemanly to take it after threatening the man with the law. The Armsman's Manual said that, because of the sword he is privileged to wear, an Armsman must be a gentleman at all times.

"Wonder why Paul left?" Jack asked when they were on the street again. "He was well paid, and he was too simple to work elsewhere."

Robert shrugged. "You know how it is. Wharf rats come and go. No need to worry about him. A man with a strong back and a weak mind can always find a bistro that will take care of him. He'll get along."

Nothing further was said for the moment. The two Armsmen walked on to the corner, where the Quai Sainte Marie turned off to the south.

Robert glanced southwards and said: "Here's a happy one."

"Too happy, if you ask me," said Jack.

Down the Quai Sainte Marie came a man. He was hugging the side of the building, stumbling toward them, propping himself up by putting the flat of his palms on the brick wall one after the other as he moved his feet. He wore no hat, and, as the wind caught his cloak, the two Men-at-Arms saw something they had not expected. He was naked.

"Blind drunk and freezing," Jack said. "Better take him in."

They never got the chance. As they came toward him, the stumbling man stumbled for the last time. He dropped to his knees, looked up at them with blind eyes that stared past them into the darkness of the sky, then toppled to one side, his eyes still open, unblinking.

Robert knelt down. "Sound your whistle! I think he's dead!"

Jack took out his whistle and keened a note into the frigid air.

"Speak of the Devil," Robert said softly. "It's Paul! He doesn't smell drunk. I think . . . *God!*" He had tried to lift the head of the fallen man and found his palm covered with blood. "It's soft," he said wonderingly. "The whole side of his skull is crushed."

In the distance, they heard the clatter of hoofs as a mounted Sergeant-at-Arms came at a gallop toward the sound of the whistle.

Lord Darcy, tall, lean-faced, and handsome, strode down the hall to the door bearing the arms of Normandy and opened it.

"Your Highness sent for me?" He spoke Anglo-French with a definite English accent.

There were three men in the room. The youngest, tall, blond Richard, Duke of Normandy and brother to His Imperial Majesty, John IV, turned as the door opened. "Ah. Lord Darcy. Come in." He gestured toward the portly man wearing episcopal purple. "My Lord Bishop, may I present my Chief Investigator, Lord Darcy. Lord Darcy, this is his lordship, the Bishop of Guernsey and Sark."

"A pleasure, Lord Darcy," said the Bishop, extending his right hand.

Lord Darcy took the hand, bowed, kissed the ring. "My Lord Bishop." Then he turned and bowed to the third man, the lean, graying Marquis of Rouen. "My Lord Marquis."

Then Lord Darcy faced the Royal Duke again and waited expectantly.

The Duke of Normandy frowned slightly. "There appears to be some trouble with my lord the Marquis of Cherbourg. As you know, My Lord Bishop is the elder brother of the Marquis."

Lord Darcy knew the family history. The previous Marquis of Cherbourg had had three sons. At his death, the eldest had inherited the title and government. The second had taken Holy Orders, and the third had taken a commission in the Royal Navy. When the eldest had died without heirs, the Bishop could not succeed to the title, so the Marquisate went to the youngest son, Hugh, the present Marquis.

"Perhaps you had better explain, My Lord Bishop," said the Duke. "I would rather Lord Darcy had the information firsthand."

"Certainly, Your Highness," said the Bishop. He looked worried, and his right hand kept fiddling with the pectoral cross at his breast.

The Duke gestured toward the chairs. "Please, my lords—sit down."

The four men settled themselves, and the Bishop began his story. "My brother the Marquis," he said after a deep breath, "is missing."

Lord Darcy raised an eyebrow. Normally, if one of His Majesty's Governors turned up missing, there would be a hue and cry from one end of the Empire to the other—from Duncansby Head in Scotland to .the southernmost tip of Gascony—from the German border on the east to New England and New France, across the Atlantic. If my lord the Bishop of Guernsey and Sark wanted it kept quiet, then there was—there had *better* be!—a good reason.

"Have you met my brother, Lord Darcy?" the Bishop asked.

"Only briefly, my lord. Once, about a year ago. I hardly know him."

"I see."

The Bishop fiddled a bit more with his pectoral cross, then plunged into his story. Three days before, on the tenth of January, the Bishop's sister-in-law Elaine, Marquise de Cherbourg, had sent a servant by boat to St. Peter Port, Guernsey, the site of the Cathedral Church of the Diocese of Guernsey and Sark. The sealed message which he was handed informed My Lord Bishop that his brother the Marquis had been missing since the evening of the eighth. Contrary to his custom, My Lord Marquis had not notified My Lady Marquise of any intention to leave the castle. Indeed, he implied that he had intended to retire when he had finished with certain Government papers. No one had seen him since he entered his study. My lady of Cherbourg had not missed him until next morning, when she found that his bed had not been slept in.

"This was on the morning of Thursday the ninth, my lord?" Lord Darcy asked.

"That is correct, my lord," said the Bishop.

"May I ask why we were not notified until now?" Lord Darcy asked gently.

My Lord Bishop fidgeted. "Well, my lord . . . you see . . . well, My Lady Elaine believes that . . . er . . . that his lordship, my brother, is not . . . er . . . may not be . . . er . . . quite right in his mind."

There! thought Lord Darcy. He got it out! My lord of Cherbourg is off his chump! Or, at least, his lady thinks so.

"What behavior did he display?" Lord Darcy asked quietly.

The Bishop spoke rapidly and concisely. My lord of Cherbourg had had his first attack on the eve of St. Stephen's Day, the 26th of December, 1963. His face had suddenly taken on a look of utter idiocy; it had gone slack, and the intelligence seemed to fade from his eyes. He had babbled meaninglessly and seemed not to know where he was—and, indeed, to be somewhat terrified of his surroundings.

"Was he violent in any way?" asked Lord Darcy.

"No. Quite the contrary. He was quite docile and easily led to bed. Lady Elaine called in a Healer immediately, suspecting that my brother may have had an apoplectic stroke. As you know, the Marquisate supports a chapter of the Benedictines within the walls of Castle Cherbourg, and Father Patrique saw my brother within minutes.

"But by that time the attack had passed. Father Patrique could detect nothing wrong, and my brother simply said it was a slight dizzy spell, nothing more. However, since then there have been three more attacks—on the evenings of the second, the fifth, and the seventh of this month. And now he is gone."

"You feel, then, My Lord Bishop, that his lordship has had another of these attacks and may be wandering around somewhere . . . ah . . . *non compos mentis*, as it were?"

"That's exactly what I'm afraid of," the Bishop said firmly.

Lord Darcy looked thoughtful for a moment, then glanced silently at His Royal Highness, the Duke.

"I want you to make a thorough investigation, Lord Darcy," said the Duke. "Be as discreet as possible. We want no scandal. If there is anything wrong with my lord of Cherbourg's mind, we will have the best care taken, of course. But we must find him first." He glanced at the clock on the wall. "There is a train for Cherbourg in forty-one minutes. You will accompany My Lord Bishop."

Lord Darcy rose smoothly from his chair. "I'll just have time to pack, Your Highness." He bowed to the Bishop. "Your servant, my lord." He turned and walked out the door, closing it behind him.

But instead of heading immediately for his own apartments, he waited quietly outside the door, just to one side. He had caught Duke Richard's look.

Within, he heard voices.

"My Lord Marquis," said the Duke, "would you see that My Lord Bishop gets some refreshment? If your lordship will excuse me, I have some urgent work to attend to. A report on this matter must be dispatched immediately to the King my brother."

"Of course, Your Highness; of course."

"I will have a carriage waiting for you and Lord Darcy. I will see you again before you leave, my lord. And now, excuse me."

He came out of the room, saw Lord Darcy waiting, and motioned toward another room nearby. Lord Darcy followed him in. The Duke closed the door firmly and then said, in a low voice:

"This may be worse than it appears at first glance, Darcy. De Cherbourg was working with one of His Majesty's personal agents trying to trace down the ring of Polish *agents provocateurs* operating in Cherbourg. If he's actually had a mental breakdown and they've got hold of him, there will be the Devil to pay."

Lord Darcy knew the seriousness of the affair. The Kings of Poland had been ambitious for the past half century. Having annexed all of the Russian territory they could—as far as Minsk to the north and Kiev to the south—the Poles now sought to work their way westward, toward the borders of the Empire. For several centuries, the Germanic states had acted as buffers between the powerful Kingdom of Poland and the even more powerful Empire. In theory, the Germanic states, as part of the old Holy Roman Empire, owed fealty to the Emperor—but no Anglo-French king had tried to enforce that fealty for centuries. The Germanic states were, in fact, holding their independence because of the tug-of-war between Poland and the Empire. If the troops of King Casimir IX tried to march into Bavaria, for instance, Bavaria would scream for Imperial help and would get it. On the other hand, if King John IV tried to tax so much as a single sovereign out of Bavaria, and sent troops in to collect it, Bavaria would scream just as loudly for Polish aid. As long as the balance of power remained, the Germanies were safe.

Actually, King John had no desire to bring the Germanies into the Empire forcibly. That kind of aggression hadn't been Imperial policy for a good long time. With hardly any trouble at all, an Imperial army could take over Lombardy or northern Spain. But with the whole New World as Imperial domain, there was no need to add more of Europe. Aggression against her peaceful neighbors was unthinkable in this day and age.

As long as Poland had been moving eastward, Imperial policy had been to allow her to go her way while the Empire expanded into the New World. But that eastward expansion had ground to a halt.

King Casimir was now having trouble with those Russians he had already conquered. To hold his quasi empire together, he had to keep the threat of external enemies always before the eyes of his subjects, but he dared not push any farther into

Russia. The Russian states had formed a loose coalition during the last generation, and the King of Poland, Sigismund III, had backed down. If the Russians ever really united, they would be a formidable enemy.

That left the Germanic states to the west and Roumeleia to the south. Casimir had no desire to tangle with Roumeleia, but he had plans for the Germanic states.

The wealth of the Empire, the basis of its smoothly expanding economy, was the New World. The importation of cotton, tobacco, and sugar—to say nothing of the gold that had been found in the southern continent—was the backbone of the Imperial economy. The King's subjects were well-fed, well-clothed, well-housed, and happy. But if the shipping were to be blocked for any considerable length of time, there would be trouble.

The Polish Navy didn't stand a chance against the Imperial Navy. No Polish fleet could get through the North Sea without running into trouble with either the Imperial Navy or that of the Empire's Scandinavian allies. The North Sea was Imperial-Scandinavian property, jointly patrolled, and no armed ship was allowed to pass. Polish merchantmen were allowed to come and go freely—after they had been boarded to make sure that they carried no guns. Bottled up in the Baltic, the Polish Navy was helpless, and it wasn't big enough or good enough to fight its way out. They'd tried it once, back in '39, and had been blasted out of the water. King Casimir wouldn't try that again.

He had managed to buy a few Spanish and Sicilian ships and have them outfitted as privateers, but they were merely annoying, not menacing. If caught, they were treated as pirates—either sunk or captured and their crews hanged—and the Imperial Government didn't even bother to protest to the King of Poland.

But King Casimir evidently had something else up his royal sleeve. Something was happening that had both the Lords of the Admiralty and the Maritime Lords on edge. Ships leaving Imperial ports—Le Havre, Cherbourg, Liverpool, London, and so on—occasionally disappeared. They were simply never heard from again. They never got to New England at all. And the number was more than could be accounted for either by weather or piracy.

That was bad enough, but to make things worse, rumors had been spreading around the waterfronts of the Empire. Primarily the rumors exaggerated the dangers of sailing the Atlantic. The

word was beginning to spread that the mid-Atlantic was a dangerous area—far more dangerous than the waters around Europe. A
sailor worth his salt cared very little for the threats of weather;
give a British or a French sailor a seaworthy ship and a skipper
he trusted, and he'd head into the teeth of any storm. But the
threat of evil spirits and black magic was something else again.

Do what they would, scientific researchers simply could not
educate the common man to understand the intricacies and limita-
tions of modern scientific sorcery. The superstitions of a hundred
thousand years still clung to the minds of ninety-nine percent of
the human race, even in a modern, advanced civilization like the
Empire. How does one explain that only a small percentage of
the population is capable of performing magic? How to explain
that all the incantations in the official grimoires won't help a
person who doesn't have the Talent? How to explain that, even
with the Talent, years of training are normally required before it
can be used efficiently, predictably, and with power? People had
been told again and again, but deep in their hearts they believed
otherwise.

Not one person in ten who was suspected of having the Evil
Eye really had it, but sorcerers and priests were continually being
asked for counteragents. And only God knew how many people
wore utterly useless medallions, charms, and anti-hex shields
prepared by quacks who hadn't the Talent to make the spells
effective. There is an odd quirk in the human mind that makes
a fearful man prefer to go quietly to a wicked-looking, gnarled
"witch" for a countercharm than to a respectable licensed sorcerer
or an accredited priest of the Church. Deep inside, the majority
of people had the sneaking suspicion that evil was more powerful than good and that evil could be counteracted only by more
evil. Almost none of them would believe what scientific magical
research had shown—that the practice of black magic was, in the
long run, more destructive to the mind of the practitioner than
to his victims.

So it wasn't difficult to spread the rumor that there was Something Evil in the Atlantic—and, as a result, more and more sailors
were becoming leery of shipping aboard a vessel that was bound
for the New World.

And the Imperial Government was absolutely certain that the
story was being deliberately spread by agents of King Casimir IX.

Two things had to be done: The disappearances must cease, and the rumors must be stopped. And my lord the Marquis of Cherbourg had been working toward those ends when he had disappeared. The question of how deeply Polish agents were involved in that disappearance was an important one.

"You will contact His Majesty's agent as soon as possible," said Duke Richard. "Since there may be black magic involved, take Master Sean along—incognito. If a sorcerer suddenly shows up, they—whoever they may be—might take cover. They might even do something drastic to de Cherbourg."

"I will exercise the utmost care, Your Highness," said Lord Darcy.

The train pulled into Cherbourg Station with a hiss and a blast of steam that made a great cloud of fog in the chill air. Then the wind picked up the cloud and blew it to wisps before anyone had stepped from the carriages. The passengers hugged their coats and cloaks closely about them as they came out. There was a light dusting of snow on the ground and on the platform, but the air was clear and the low winter sun shone brightly, if coldly, in the sky.

The Bishop had made a call on the teleson to Cherbourg Castle before leaving Rouen, and there was a carriage waiting for the three men—one of the newer models with pneumatic tires and spring suspension, bearing the Cherbourg arms on the doors, and drawn by two pairs of fine greys. The footmen opened the near door and the Bishop climbed in, followed by Lord Darcy and a short, chubby man who wore the clothing of a gentleman's gentleman. Lord Darcy's luggage was put on the rack atop the carriage, but a small bag carried by the "gentleman's gentleman" remained firmly in the grasp of his broad fist.

Master Sean O Lochlainn, Sorcerer, had no intention of letting go of his professional equipment. He had grumbled enough about not being permitted to carry his symbol-decorated carpetbag, and had spent nearly twenty minutes casting protective spells around the black leather suitcase that Lord Darcy had insisted he carry.

The footman closed the door of the carriage and swung himself aboard. The four greys started off at a brisk trot through the streets of Cherbourg toward the Castle, which lay across the city, near the sea.

Partly to keep My Lord Bishop's mind off his brother's troubles and partly to keep from being overheard while they were on the train, Lord Darcy and the Bishop had tacitly agreed to keep their conversation on subjects other than the investigation at hand. Master Sean had merely sat quietly by, trying to look like a valet—at which he succeeded very well.

Once inside the carriage, however, the conversation seemed to die away. My lord the Bishop settled himself into the cushions and gazed silently out of the window. Master Sean leaned back, folded his hands over his paunch and closed his eyes. Lord Darcy, like my lord the Bishop, looked out the window. He had only been in Cherbourg twice before, and was not as familiar with the city as he would like to be. It would be worth his time to study the route the carriage was taking.

It was not until they came to the waterfront itself, turned, and moved down the Rue de Mer toward the towers of Castle Cherbourg in the distance, that Lord Darcy saw anything that particularly interested him.

There were, he thought, entirely too many ships tied up at the docks, and there seemed to be a great deal of goods waiting on the wharves to be loaded. On the other hand, there did not seem to be as many men working as the apparent volume of shipping would warrant.

Crews scared off by the "Atlantic Curse," Lord Darcy thought. He looked at the men loafing around in clumps, talking softly but, he thought, rather angrily. Obviously sailors; out of work by their own choice and resenting their own fears. Probably trying to get jobs as longshoremen and being shut out by the Longshoremen's Guild.

Normally, he knew, sailors were considered as an auxiliary of the Longshoremen's Guild, just as longshoremen were considered as an auxiliary of the Seamen's Guild. If a sailor decided to spend a little time on land, he could usually get work as a longshoreman; if a longshoreman decided to go to sea, he could usually find a berth somewhere. But with ships unable to find crews, there were fewer longshoremen finding work loading vessels. With regular members of the Longshoremen's Guild unable to find work, it was hardly odd that the Guild would be unable to find work for the frightened seamen who had caused that very shortage.

The unemployment, in turn, threw an added burden on the

Privy Purse of the Marquis of Cherbourg, since, by ancient law, it was obligatory upon the lord to take care of his men and their families in times of trouble. Thus far, the drain was not too great, since it was spread out evenly over the Empire; my lord of Cherbourg could apply to the Duke of Normandy for aid under the same law, and His Royal Highness could, in turn, apply to His Imperial Majesty, John IV, King and Emperor of England, France, Scotland, Ireland, New England and New France, Defender of the Faith, et cetera.

And the funds of the Imperial Privy Purse came from all over the Empire.

Still, if the thing became widespread, the economy of the Empire stood in danger of complete collapse.

There had not been a complete cessation of activity on the waterfront, Lord Darcy was relieved to notice. Aside from those ships that were making the Mediterranean and African runs, there were still ships that had apparently found crews for the Atlantic run to the northern continent of New England and the southern continent of New France.

One great ship, the *Pride of Calais*, showed quite a bit of activity; bales of goods were being loaded over the side amid much shouting of orders. Close by, Lord Darcy could see a sling full of wine casks being lifted aboard, each cask bearing the words: "Ordwin Vayne, Vintner," and a sorcerer's symbol burnt into the wood, showing that the wine was protected against souring for the duration of the trip. Most of the wine, Lord Darcy knew, was for the crew; by law each sailor was allowed the equivalent of a bottle a day, and, besides, the excellence of the New World wines was such that it did not pay to import the beverage from Europe.

Further on, Lord Darcy saw other ships that he knew were making the Atlantic run loading goods aboard. Evidently the "Atlantic Curse" had not yet frightened the guts out of all of the Empire's seamen.

We'll come through, Lord Darcy thought. In spite of everything the King of Poland can do, we'll come through. We always have.

He did not think: *We always will.* Empires and societies, he knew, died and were replaced by others. The Roman Empire had died to be replaced by hordes of barbarians who had gradually evolved the feudal society, which had, in turn, evolved the modern system. It was, certainly, possible that the eight-hundred-year-old Empire that had been established by Henry II in the twelfth century might some day collapse as the Roman Empire had—but it had already existed nearly twice as long, and there were no threatening hordes of barbarians to overrun it nor were there any signs of internal dissent strong enough to disrupt it. The Empire was still stable and still evolving.

Most of that stability and evolution was due to the House of Plantagenet, the House which had been founded by Henry II after the death of King Stephen. Old Henry had brought the greater part of France under the sway of the King of England. His son, Richard the Lion-Hearted, had neglected England during the first ten years of his reign, but, after his narrow escape from death from the bolt of a crossbowman at the Siege of Chaluz, he had settled down to controlling the Empire with a firm hand and a wise brain. He had no children, but his nephew, Arthur, the son of King Richard's dead brother, Geoffrey, had become like a son to him. Arthur had fought with the King against the treacheries of Prince John, Richard's younger brother and the only other claimant to the throne. Prince John's death in 1216 left Arthur as the only heir, and, upon old Richard's death in 1219, Arthur, at thirty-two, had succeeded to the Throne of England. In popular legend, King Arthur was often confused with the earlier King Arthur of Camelot—and for good reason. The monarch who was known even today as Good King Arthur had resolved to rule his realm in the same chivalric manner—partly inspired by the legends of the ancient Brittanic leader, and partly because of his own inherent abilities.

Since then, the Plantagenet line had gone through nearly eight centuries of trial and tribulation; of blood, sweat, toil, and tears; of resisting the enemies of the Empire by sword, fire, and consummate diplomacy to hold the realm together and to expand it.

The Empire had endured. And the Empire would continue to endure only so long as every subject realized that it could not endure if the entire burden were left to the King alone. *The Empire expects every man to do his duty.*

And Lord Darcy's duty, at this moment, was greater than the simple duty of finding out what had happened to my lord the Marquis of Cherbourg. The problem ran much deeper than that.

His thoughts were interrupted by the voice of the Bishop.

"There's the tower of the Great Keep ahead, Lord Darcy. We'll be there soon."

It was actually several more minutes before the carriage-and-four drew up before the main entrance of Castle Cherbourg. The door was opened by a footman, and three men climbed out, Master Sean still clutching his suitcase.

My Lady Elaine, Marquise de Cherbourg, stood in her salon above the Great Hall, staring out the window at the Channel. She could see the icy waves splashing and dancing and rolling with almost hypnotic effect, but she saw them without thinking about them.

Where are you, Hugh? she thought. *Come back to me, Hugh. I need you. I never knew how much I'd need you.* Then there seemed to be a blank as her mind rested. Nothing came through but the roll of the waves.

Then there was the noise of an opening door behind her. She turned quickly, her long velvet skirts swirling around her like thick syrup. "Yes?" Her voice seemed oddly far away in her ears.

"You rang, my lady." It was Sir Gwiliam, the seneschal.

My Lady Elaine tried to focus her thoughts. "Oh," she said after a moment. "Oh, yes." She waved toward the refreshment table, upon which stood a decanter of Oporto, a decanter of Xerez, and an empty decanter. "Brandy. The brandy hasn't been refilled. Bring some of the Saint Coeurlandt Michele '46."

"The Saint Coeurlandt Michele '46, my lady?" Sir Gwiliam blinked slightly. "But my lord de Cherbourg would not—"

She turned to face him directly. "My lord of Cherbourg would most certainly not deny his lady his best Champagne brandy at a time like this, Sieur Gwiliam!" she snapped, using the local pronunciation instead of standard Anglo-French, thus employing a mild and unanswerable epithet. "Must I fetch it myself?"

Sir Gwiliam's face paled a little, but his expression did not change. "No, my lady. Your wish is my command."

"Very well. I thank you, Sir Gwiliam." She turned back to the window. Behind her, she heard the door open and close.

Then she turned, walked over to the refreshment table, and looked at the glass she had emptied only a few minutes before.

Empty, she thought. Like my life. Can I refill it?

She lifted the decanter of Xerez, took out the stopple, and, with exaggerated care, refilled her glass. Brandy was better, but until Sir Gwiliam brought the brandy there was nothing to drink but the sweet wines. She wondered vaguely why she had insisted on the best and finest brandy in Hugh's cellar. There was no need for it. Any brandy would have done, even the Aqua Sancta '60, a foul distillate. She knew that by now her palate was so anesthetized that she could not tell the difference.

But where was the brandy? Somewhere. Yes. Sir Gwiliam.

Angrily, almost without thinking, she began to jerk at the bellpull. Once. Pause. Once. Pause. Once . . .

She was still ringing when the door opened.

"Yes, my lady?"

She turned angrily—then froze.

Lord Seiger frightened her. He always had.

"I rang for Sir Gwiliam, my lord," she said, with as much dignity as she could summon.

Lord Seiger was a big man who had about him the icy coldness of the Norse home from which his ancestors had come. His hair was so blond as to be almost silver, and his eyes were a pale iceberg blue. The Marquise could not recall ever having seen him smile. His handsome face was always placid and expressionless. She realized with a small chill that she would be more afraid of Lord Seiger's smile than of his normal calm expression.

"I rang for Sir Gwiliam," my lady repeated.

"Indeed, my lady," said Lord Seiger, "but since Sir Gwiliam seemed not to answer, I felt it my duty to respond. You rang for him a few minutes ago. Now you are ringing again. May I help?"

"No . . . No . . ." What could she say?

He came into the room, closing the door behind him. Even twenty-five feet away, My Lady Elaine fancied she could feel the chill from him. She could do nothing as he approached. She couldn't find her voice. He was tall and cold and blondly handsome—and had no more sexuality than a toad. Less—for a toad must at least have attraction for another toad—and a toad was at least a living thing. My lady was not attracted to the man, and he hardly seemed living.

He came toward her like a battleship—twenty feet—fifteen . . .

She gasped and gestured toward the refreshment table. "Would you pour some wine, my lord? I'd like a glass of the . . . the Xerez."

It was as though the battleship had been turned in its course, she thought. His course toward her veered by thirty degrees as he angled toward the table.

"Xerez, my lady? Indeed. I shall be most happy."

With precise, strong hands, he emptied the last of the decanter into a goblet. "There is less than a glassful, my lady," he said, looking at her with expressionless blue eyes. "Would my lady care for the Oporto instead?"

"No . . . No, just the Xerez, my lord, just the Xerez." She swallowed. "Would you care for anything yourself?"

"I never drink, my lady." He handed her the partially filled glass.

It was all she could do to take the glass from his hand, and it struck her as odd that his fingers, when she touched them, seemed as warm as anyone else's.

"Does my lady really feel that it is necessary to drink so much?" Lord Seiger asked. "For the last four days . . ."

My lady's hand shook, but all she could say was: "My nerves, my lord. My nerves." She handed back the glass, empty.

Since she had not asked for more, Lord Seiger merely held the glass and looked at her. "I am here to protect you, my lady. It is my duty. Only your enemies have anything to fear from me."

Somehow, she knew that what he said was true, but—

"Please. A glass of Oporto, my lord."

"Yes, my lady."

He was refilling her glass when the door opened.

It was Sir Gwiliam, bearing a bottle of brandy. "My lady, my lord, the carriage has arrived."

Lord Seiger looked at him expressionlessly, then turned the same face on My Lady Elaine. "The Duke's Investigators. Shall we meet them here, my lady?"

"Yes. Yes, my lord, of course. Yes." Her eyes were on the brandy.

The meeting between Lord Darcy and My Lady Elaine was brief and meaningless. Lord Darcy had no objection to the aroma of fine brandy, but he preferred it fresh rather than secondhand. Her recital of what had happened during the days immediately preceding the disappearance of the Marquis was not significantly different from that of the Bishop.

The coldly handsome Lord Seiger, who had been introduced as secretary to the Marquis, knew nothing. He had not been present during any of the alleged attacks.

My lady the Marquise finally excused herself, pleading a headache. Lord Darcy noted that the brandy bottle went with her.

"My Lord Seiger," he said, "her ladyship seems indisposed. Whom does that leave in charge of the castle for the moment?"

"The servants and household are in the charge of Sir Gwiliam de Bracy, the seneschal. The guard is in the charge of Captain Sir Androu Duglasse. I am not My Lord Marquis' Privy Secretary; I am merely aiding him in cataloguing some books."

"I see. Very well. I should like to speak to Sir Gwiliam and Sir Androu."

Lord Seiger stood up, walked over to the bellpull and signaled. "Sir Gwiliam will be here shortly," he said. "I shall fetch Sir Androu myself." He bowed. "If you will excuse me, my lords."

When he had gone, Lord Darcy said: "An impressive looking man. Dangerous, too, I should say—in the right circumstances."

"Seems a decent sort," said My Lord Bishop. "A bit restrained ... er ... stuffy, one might say. Not much sense of humor, but sense of humor isn't everything." He cleared his throat and then went on. "I must apologize for my sister-in-law's behavior. She's overwrought. You won't be needing me for these interrogations, and I really ought to see after her."

"Of course, my lord; I quite understand," Lord Darcy said smoothly.

My Lord Bishop had hardly gone when the door opened again and Sir Gwiliam came in. "Your lordship rang?"

"Will you be seated, Sir Gwiliam?" Lord Darcy gestured toward a chair. "We are here, as you know, to investigate the disappearance of my lord of Cherbourg. This is my man, Sean, who assists me. All you say here will be treated as confidential."

"I shall be happy to cooperate, your lordship," said Sir Gwiliam, seating himself.

"I am well aware, Sir Gwiliam," Lord Darcy began, "that you have told what you know to My Lord Bishop, but, tiresome as it may be, I shall have to hear the whole thing again. If you will be so good as to begin at the beginning, Sir Gwiliam ..."

The seneschal dutifully began his story. Lord Darcy and Master Sean listened to it for the third time and found that it differed only in viewpoint, not in essentials. But the difference in viewpoint was important. Like My Lord Bishop, Sir Gwiliam told his story as though he were not directly involved.

"Did you actually ever see one of these attacks?" Lord Darcy asked.

Sir Gwiliam blinked. "Why . . . no. No, your lordship, I did not. But they were reported to me in detail by several of the servants."

"I see. What about the night of the disappearance? When did you last see My Lord Marquis?"

"Fairly early in the evening, your lordship. With my lord's permission, I went into the city about five o'clock for an evening of cards with friends. We played until rather late—two or two-thirty in the morning. My host, Master Ordwin Vayne, a well-to-do wine merchant in the city, of course insisted that I spend the night. That is not unusual, since the castle gates are locked at ten and it is rather troublesome to have a guard unlock them. I returned to the castle, then, at about ten in the morning, at which time my lady informed me of the disappearance of My Lord Marquis."

Lord Darcy nodded. That checked with what Lady Elaine had said. Shortly after Sir Gwiliam had left, she had retired early, pleading a slight cold. She had been the last to see the Marquis of Cherbourg.

"Thank you, sir seneschal," Lord Darcy said. "I should like to speak to the servants later. There is—"

He was interrupted by the opening of the door. It was Lord Seiger, followed by a large, heavy-set, mustached man with dark hair and a scowling look.

As Sir Gwiliam rose, Lord Darcy said: "Thank you for your help, Sir Gwiliam. That will be all for now."

"Thank you, your lordship; I am most anxious to help."

As the seneschal left, Lord Seiger brought the mustached man into the room. "My lord, this is Sir Androu Duglasse, Captain of the Marquis' Own Guard. Captain, Lord Darcy, Chief Investigator for His Highness the Duke."

The fierce-looking soldier bowed. "I am at your service, m' lord."

"Thank you. Sit down, Captain."

Lord Seiger retreated through the door, leaving the captain with Lord Darcy and Master Sean.

"I hope I can be of some help, y' lordship," the captain said.

"I think you can, Captain," Lord Darcy said. "No one saw my lord the Marquis leave the castle, I understand. I presume you have questioned your guards."

"I have, y' lordship. We didn't know m' lord was missing until next morning, when m' lady spoke to me. I checked with the men who were on duty that night. The only one to leave after five was Sir Gwiliam, at five oh two, according to the book."

"And the secret passage?" Lord Darcy asked. He had made it a point to study the plans of every castle in the Empire by going over the drawings in the Royal Archives.

The captain nodded. "There is one. Used during times of siege in the old days. It's kept locked and barred nowadays."

"And guarded?" Lord Darcy asked.

Captain Sir Androu chuckled. "Yes, y' lordship. Most hated post in the Guard. Tunnel ends up in a sewer, d'ye see. We send a man out there for mild infractions of the rules. Straightens him out to spend a few nights with the smell and the rats, guarding an iron door that hasn't been opened for years and couldn't be opened from the outside without a bomb—or from the inside, either, since it's rusted shut. We inspect at irregular intervals to make sure the man's on his toes."

"I see. You made a thorough search of the castle?"

"Yes. I was afraid he might have come down with another of those fainting spells he's had lately. We looked everywhere he could have been. He was nowhere to be found, y' lordship. Nowhere. He must have got out somewhere."

"Well, we shall have to—" Lord Darcy was interrupted by a rap on the door.

Master Sean, dutifully playing his part, opened it. "Yes, your lordship?"

It was Lord Seiger at the door. "Would you tell Lord Darcy that Henri Vert, Chief Master-at-Arms of the City of Cherbourg, would like to speak to him?"

For a fraction of a second, Lord Darcy was both surprised and irritated. How had the Chief Master-at-Arms known he was here? Then he saw what the answer must be.

"Tell him to come in, Sean," said Lord Darcy.

Chief Henri was a heavy-set, tough-looking man in his early fifties who had the air and bearing of a stolid fighter. He bowed. "Lord Darcy. May I speak to your lordship alone?" He spoke Anglo-French with a punctilious precision that showed it was not his natural way of speaking. He had done his best to remove the accent of the local *patois*, but his effort to speak properly was noticeable.

"Certainly, Chief Henri. Will you excuse us, Captain? I will discuss this problem with you later."

"Of course, your lordship."

Lord Darcy and Master Sean were left alone with Chief Henri.

"I *am* sorry to have interrupted, your lordship," said the Chief, "but His Royal Highness gave strict instructions."

"I had assumed as much, Chief Henri. Be so good as to sit down. Now—what has happened?"

"Well, your lordship," he said, glancing at Master Sean, "His Highness instructed me over the teleson to speak to no one but you." Then the Chief took a good look and did a double take. "By the Blue! Master Sean O Lochlainn! I didn't recognize you in that livery!"

The sorcerer grinned. "I make a very good valet, eh, Henri?"

"Indeed you do! Well, then, I may speak freely?"

"Certainly," said Lord Darcy. "Proceed."

"Well, then." The Chief leaned forward and spoke in a low voice. "When this thing came up, I thought of you first off. I must admit that it's beyond me. On the night of the eighth, two of my men were patrolling the waterfront district. At the corner of Rue King John II and Quai Sainte Marie, they saw a man fall. Except for a cloak, he was naked—and if your lordship remembers, that was a very cold night. By the time they got to him, he was dead."

Lord Darcy narrowed his eyes. "How had he died?"

"Skull fracture, your lordship. Somebody'd smashed in the right side of his skull. It's a wonder he could walk at all."

"I see. Proceed."

"Well, he was brought to the morgue. My men both identified him as one Paul Sarto, a man who worked around the bistros for small wages. He was also identified by the owner of the bistro where he had last worked. He seems to have been feeble-minded, willing to do manual labor for bed, board, and spending money. Needed taking care of a bit."

"Hm-m-m. We must trace him and find out why his baron had not provided for him," said Lord Darcy. "Proceed."

"Well, your lordship . . . er . . . there's more to it than that. I didn't look into the case immediately. After all, another killing on the waterfront—" He shrugged and spread his hands, palms up. "My sorcerer and my chirurgeon looked him over, made the usual tests. He was killed by a blow from a piece of oak with a square corner—perhaps a two-by-two or something like that. He was struck about ten minutes before the Armsmen found him. My chirurgeon says that only a man of tremendous vitality could have survived that long—to say nothing of the fact that he was able to walk."

"Excuse me, Henri," Master Sean interrupted. "Did your sorcerer make the FitzGibbon test for post-mortem activation?"

"Of course. First test he made, considering the wound. No, the body had not been activated after death and made to walk away from the scene of the crime. He actually died as the Armsmen watched."

"Just checking," said Master Sean.

"Well, anyway, the affair might have been dismissed as another waterfront brawl, but there were some odd things about the corpse. The cloak he was wearing was of aristocratic cut—not that of a commoner. Expensive cloth, expensive tailoring. Also, he had bathed recently—and, apparently, frequently. His toe- and fingernails were decently manicured and cut."

Lord Darcy's eyes narrowed with interest. "Hardly the condition one would expect of a common laborer, eh?"

"Exactly, my lord. So when I read the reports this morning, I went to take a look. This time of year, the weather permits keeping a body without putting a preservation spell on it."

He leaned forward, and his voice became lower and hoarser. "I only had to take one look, my lord. Then I had to take action and call Rouen. My lord, it is the Marquis of Cherbourg himself!"

Lord Darcy rode through the chilling wintry night on a borrowed horse, his dark cloak whipping around the palfrey's rump in the icy breeze. The chill was more apparent than real. A relatively warm wind had come in from the sea, bringing with it a slushy rain; the temperature of the air was above the freezing point—but not much above it. Lord Darcy had endured worse cold than this, but the damp chill seemed to creep inside his clothing, through his skin, and into his bones. He would have preferred a dry cold, even if it was much colder; at least, a dry cold didn't try to crawl into a man's cloak with him.

He had borrowed the horse from Chief Henri. It was a serviceable hack, well-trained to police work and used to the cobbled streets of Cherbourg.

The scene at the morgue, Lord Darcy thought, had been an odd one. He and Sean and Henri had stood by while the morgue attendant had rolled out the corpse. At first glance, Lord Darcy had been able to understand the consternation of the Chief Master-at-Arms.

He had only met Hugh of Cherbourg once and could hardly be called upon to make a positive identification, but if the corpse was not the Marquis to the life, the face was his in death.

The two Armsmen who had seen the man die had been asked separately, and without being told of the new identification, still said that the body was that of Paul Sarto, although they admitted he looked cleaner and better cared for than Paul ever had.

It was easy to see how the conflict of opinion came about. The Armsmen had seen the Marquis only rarely—probably only on state occasions, when he had been magnificently dressed. They could hardly be expected to identify a wandering, nearly nude man on the waterfront as their liege lord. If, in addition, that man was immediately identified in their minds with the man they had known as Paul Sarto, the identification of him as my lord the Marquis would be positively forced from their minds. On the other hand, Henri Vert, Chief Master-at-Arms of the City of Cherbourg, knew My Lord Marquis well and had never seen nor heard of Paul Sarto until after the death.

Master Sean had decided that further thaumaturgical tests could be performed upon the deceased. The local sorcerer—a mere journeyman of the Sorcerer's Guild—had explained all the tests he had performed, valiantly trying to impress a Master of the Art with his proficiency and ability.

"The weapon used was a fairly long piece of oak, Master. According to the Kaplan-Sheinwold test, a short club could not have been used. On the other hand, oddly enough, I could find no trace of evil or malicious intent, and—"

"Precisely why I intend to perform further tests, me boy," Master Sean had said. "We haven't enough information."

"Yes, Master," the journeyman sorcerer had said, properly humbled.

Lord Darcy made the observation—which he kept to himself—that if the blow had been dealt from the front, which it appeared to have been, then the killer was either left-handed or had a vicious right-hand backswing. Which, he had to admit to himself, told him very little. The cold chill of the unheated morgue had begun to depress him unduly in the presence of the dead, so he had left that part of the investigation to Master Sean and set out on his own, borrowing a palfrey from Chief Henri for the purpose.

The winters he had spent in London had convinced him thoroughly that no man of intelligence would stay anywhere near a cold seacoast. Inland cold was fine; seacoast warmth was all right. But this—!

Although he did not know Cherbourg well, Lord Darcy had the kind of mind that could carry a map in its memory and translate that map easily into the real world that surrounded him. Even a slight inaccuracy of the map didn't bother him.

He turned his mount round a corner and saw before him a gas lamp shielded with blue glass—the sign of an outstation of the Armsmen of Cherbourg. An Armsman stood at attention outside.

As soon as he saw that he was confronted by a mounted nobleman, the Man-at-Arms came to attention. "Yes, my lord! Can I aid you, my lord?"

"Yes, Armsman, you can," Lord Darcy said as he vaulted from the saddle. He handed the reins of the horse to the Armsman. "This mount belongs to Chief Henri at headquarters." He showed his card with the ducal arms upon it. "I am Lord Darcy, Chief Investigator for His Royal Highness the Duke. Take care of the horse. I have business in this neighborhood and will return for the animal. I should like to speak to your Sergeant-at-Arms."

"Very good, my lord. The sergeant is within, my lord."

After speaking to the sergeant, Lord Darcy went out again into the chill night.

It was still several blocks to his destination, but it would have been unwise to ride a horse all the way. He walked two blocks through the dingy streets of the neighborhood. Then, glancing about to make fairly certain he had not been followed or observed, he turned into a dark alley. Once inside, he took off his cloak and reversed it. The lining, instead of being the silk that a noble-man ordinarily wore, or the fur that would be worn in really cold weather, was a drab, worn, brown, carefully patched in one place. From a pocket, he drew a battered slouch hat of the kind normally worn by commoners in this area and adjusted it to his head after carefully mussing his hair. His boots were plain and already covered with mud. Excellent!

He relaxed his spine—normally his carriage was one of military erectness—and slowly strolled out of the other end of the alley.

He paused to light a cheap cigar and then moved on toward his destination.

"*Aaiiy?*" The blowsy-looking woman in her mid-fifties looked through the opening in the heavy door. "What might you be wanting at this hour?"

Lord Darcy gave the face his friendliest smile and answered in the *patois* she had used. "Excuse me, Lady-of-the-House, but I'm looking for my brother, Vincent Coudé. Hate to call on him so late, but—"

As he had expected, he was interrupted.

"We don't allow no one in after dark unless they's identified by one of our people."

"As you shouldn't, Lady-of-the-House," Lord Darcy agreed politely. "But I'm sure my brother Vincent will identify me. Just tell him his brother Richard is here. Ey?"

She shook her head. "He ain't here. Ain't been here since last Wednesday. My girl checks the rooms every day, and he ain't been here since last Wednesday."

Wednesday! thought Lord Darcy. Wednesday the eighth! The night the Marquis disappeared! The night the body was found only a few blocks from here!

Lord Darcy took a silver coin from his belt pouch and held it out between the fingers of his right hand. "Would you mind going up and taking a look? He might've come in during the day. Might be asleep up there."

She took the coin and smiled. "Glad to; glad to. You might be right; he might've come in. Be right back."

But she left the door locked and closed the panel.

Lord Darcy didn't care about that. He listened carefully to her footsteps. Up the stairs. Down the hall. A knock. Another knock.

Quickly, Lord Darcy ran to the right side of the house and looked up. Sure enough, he saw the flicker of a lantern in one window. The Lady-of-the-House had unlocked the door and looked in to make sure that her roomer was not in. He ran back to the door and was waiting for her when she came down.

She opened the door panel and said sadly: "He still ain't here, Richard."

Lord Darcy handed her another sixth-sovereign piece. "That's all right, Lady-of-the-House. Just tell him I was here. I suppose he's out on business." He paused. "When is his rent next due?"

She looked at him through suddenly narrowed eyes, wondering whether it would be possible to cheat her roomer's brother out of an extra week's rent. She saw his cold eyes and decided it wouldn't.

"He's paid up to the twenty-fourth," she admitted reluctantly. "But if he ain't back by then, I'll be turning his stuff out and getting another roomer."

"Naturally," Lord Darcy agreed. "But he'll be back. Tell him I was here. Nothing urgent. I'll be back in a day or so."

She smiled. "All right. Come in the daytime, if y' can, Friend Richard. Thank y' much."

"Thank y' yourself, Lady-of-the-House," said Lord Darcy. "A good and safe night to y'." He turned and walked away.

He walked half a block and then dodged into a dark doorway.

So! Sir James le Lein, agent of His Majesty's Secret Service, had not been seen since the night of the eighth. That evening was beginning to take on a more and more sinister complexion.

He knew full well that he could have bribed the woman to let him into Sir James' room, but the amount he would have had to offer would have aroused suspicion. There was a better way.

It took him better than twenty minutes to find that way, but eventually he found himself on the roof of the two-story rooming house where Sir James had lived under the alias of Vincent Coudé.

The house was an old one, but the construction had been strong. Lord Darcy eased himself down the slope of the shingled roof to the rain gutters at the edge. He had to lie flat, his feet uphill toward the point of the roof, his hands braced against the rain gutter to look down over the edge toward the wall below. The room in which he had seen the glimmer of light from the woman's lantern was just below him. The window was blank and dark, but the shutters were not drawn, which was a mercy.

The question was: Was the window locked? Holding tight to the rain gutter, he eased himself down to the very edge of the roof. His body was at a thirty-degree angle, and he could feel the increased pressure of blood in his head. Cautiously, he reached down to see if he could touch the window. He could!

Just barely, but he could!

Gently, carefully, working with the tips of the fingers of one hand, he teased the window open. As was usual with these old houses, the glass panes were in two hinged panels that swung inward. He got both of them open.

So far, the rain gutter had held him. It seemed strong enough to hold plenty of weight. He slowly moved himself around until his body was parallel with the edge of the roof. Then he took a good grasp of the edge of the rain gutter and swung himself out into empty air. As he swung round, he shot his feet out toward the lower sill of the window.

Then he let go and tumbled into the room.

He crouched motionlessly for a moment. Had he been heard? The sound had seemed tremendous when his feet had struck the floor. But it was still early, and there were others moving about in the rooming house. Still, he remained unmoving for a good two minutes to make sure there would be no alarm. He was quite certain that if the Lady-of-the-House had heard anything that disturbed her, she would have rushed up the stairs. No sound. Nothing.

Then he rose to his feet and took a special device from the pocket of his cloak.

It was a fantastic device, a secret of His Majesty's Government. Powered by the little zinc-copper couples that were the only known source of such magical power, they heated a steel wire to tremendously high temperature. The thin wire glowed white-hot, shedding a yellow-white light that was almost as bright as a gas-mantle lamp. The secret lay in the magical treatment of the steel filament. Under ordinary circumstances, the wire would burn up in a blue-white flash of fire. But, properly treated by a special spell, the wire was passivated and merely glowed with heat and light instead of burning. The hot wire was centered at the focus of a parabolic reflector, and merely by shoving forward a button with his thumb, Lord Darcy had at hand a light source equal to—and indeed far superior to—an ordinary dark lantern. It was a personal instrument, since the passivation was tuned to Lord Darcy and no one else.

He thumbed the button and a beam of light sprang into existence.

The search of Sir James le Lein's room was quick and thorough. There was absolutely nothing of any interest to Lord Darcy anywhere in the room.

Naturally Sir James would have taken pains to assure that there would not be. The mere fact that the housekeeper had a key would have made Sir James wary of leaving anything about that would have looked out of place. There was nothing here that would have identified the inhabitant of the room as anyone but a common laborer.

Lord Darcy switched off his lamp and brooded for a moment in the darkness. Sir James was on a secret and dangerous mission for His Imperial Majesty, John IV. Surely there were reports, papers, and so on. Where had Sir James kept the data he collected? In his head? That was possible, but Lord Darcy didn't think it was true.

Sir James had been working with Lord Cherbourg. Both of them had vanished on the night of the eighth. That the mutual vanishing was coincidental was possible—but highly improbable. There were too many things unexplained as yet. Lord Darcy had three tentative hypotheses, all of which explained the facts as he knew them thus far, and none of which satisfied him.

It was then that his eyes fell on the flowerpot silhouetted against the dim light that filtered in from outside the darkened room. If it had been in the middle of the window sill, he undoubtedly would have smashed it when he came in; his feet had just barely cleared the sill. But it was over to one side, in a corner of the window. He walked over and looked at it carefully in the dimness. Why, he asked himself, would an agent of the King be growing an African violet?

He picked up the little flowerpot, brought it away from the window, and shone his light on it. It looked utterly usual.

With a grim smile, Lord Darcy put the pot, flower and all, into one of the capacious pockets of his cloak. Then he opened the window, eased himself over the sill, lowered himself until he was hanging only by his fingertips, and dropped the remaining ten feet to the ground, taking up the jar of landing with his knees.

Five minutes later, he had recovered his horse from the Armsman and was on his way to Castle Cherbourg.

The monastery of the Order of Saint Benedict in Cherbourg was a gloomy-looking pile of masonry occupying one corner of the great courtyard that surrounded the castle. Lord Darcy and Master Sean rang the bell at the entrance gate early on the morning of Tuesday, January 14th. They identified themselves to the doorkeeper and were invited into the Guests' Common Room to wait while Father Patrique was summoned. The monk would have to get the permission of the Lord Abbot to speak to outsiders, but that was a mere formality.

It was a relief to find that the interior of the monastery did not share the feeling of gloom with its exterior. The Common Room was quite cheerful and the winter sun shone brightly through the high windows.

After a minute or so, the inner door opened and a tall, rather pale man in Benedictine habit entered the room. He smiled pleasantly as he strode briskly across the room to take Lord Darcy's hand. "Lord Darcy, I am Father Patrique. Your servant, my lord."

"And I yours, Your Reverence. This is my man, Sean."

The priest turned to accept the introduction, then he paused and a gleam of humor came into his eyes. "Master Sean, the clothing you wear is not your own. A sorcerer cannot hide his calling by donning a valet's outfit."

Master Sean smiled back. "I hadn't hoped to conceal myself from a perceptive of your Order, Reverend Sir."

Lord Darcy, too, smiled. He had rather hoped that Father Patrique would be a perceptive. The Benedictines were quite good in bringing out that particular phase of Talent if a member of their Order had it, and they prided themselves on the fact that Holy Father Benedict, their founder in the early part of the sixth century, had showed that ability to a remarkable degree long before the Laws of Magic had been formulated or investigated scientifically. To such a perceptive, identity cannot be concealed without a radical change in the personality itself. Such a man is capable of perceiving, *in toto*, the personality of another; such men are invaluable as Healers, especially in cases of demonic possession and other mental diseases.

"And now, how may I help you, my lord?" the Benedictine asked pleasantly.

Lord Darcy produced his credentials and identified himself as Duke Richard's Chief Investigator.

"Quite so," said the priest. "Concerning the fact that my lord the Marquis is missing, I have no doubt."

"The walls of a monastery are not totally impenetrable, are they, Father?" Lord Darcy asked with a wry smile.

Father Patrique chuckled. "We are wide open to the sight of God and the rumors of man. Please be seated; we will not be disturbed here."

"Thank you, Father," Lord Darcy said, taking a chair. "I understand you were called to attend my lord of Cherbourg several times since last Christmas. My lady of Cherbourg and my lord the Bishop of Guernsey and Sark have told me of the nature of these attacks—that, incidentally, is why this whole affair is being kept as quiet as possible—but I would like your opinion as a Healer."

The priest shrugged his shoulders and spread his hands a little. "I should be glad to tell you what I can, my lord, but I am afraid I know almost nothing. The attacks lasted only a few minutes each time and they had vanished by the time I was able to see My Lord Marquis. By then, he was normal—if a little puzzled. He told me he had no memory of such behavior as my lady reported. He simply blanked out and then came out of it, feeling slightly disoriented and a little dizzy."

"Have you formed no diagnosis, Father?" Lord Darcy asked.

The Benedictine frowned. "There are several possible diagnoses, my lord. From my own observation, and from the symptoms reported by My Lord Marquis, I would have put it down as a mild form of epilepsy—what we call the *petit mal* type, the 'little sickness.' Contrary to popular opinion, epilepsy is not caused by demonic possession, but by some kind of organic malfunction that we know very little about.

"In *grand mal*, or 'great sickness' epilepsy, we find the seizures one normally thinks of as being connected with the disease—the convulsive 'fits' that cause the victim to completely lose control of his muscles and collapse with jerking limbs and so on. But the 'little sickness' merely causes brief loss of consciousness—sometimes so short that the victim does not even realize it. There is no collapse or convulsion; merely a blank daze lasting a few seconds or minutes."

"But you are not certain of that?" Lord Darcy asked.

The priest frowned. "No. If my lady the Marquise is telling the truth—and I see no reason why she should not, his behavior during the . . . well, call them seizures . . . his behavior during the seizures was atypical. During a typical seizure of the *petit mal* type, the victim is totally blank—staring at nothing, unable to speak or move, unable to be roused. But my lord was not that way, according to my lady. He seemed confused, bewildered, and very stupid, but he was not unconscious." He paused and frowned.

"Therefore you have other diagnoses, Father?" Lord Darcy prompted.

Father Patrique nodded thoughtfully. "Yes. Always assuming that My Lady the Marquise has reported accurately, there are other possible diagnoses. But none of them quite fits, any more than the first one does."

"Such as?"

"Such as attack by psychic induction."

Master Sean nodded slowly, but there was a frown in his eyes.

"The wax-and-doll sort of thing," said Lord Darcy.

Father Patrique nodded an affirmative. "Exactly, my lord—although, as you undoubtedly know, there are far better methods than that—in practice."

"Of course," Lord Darcy said brusquely. In theory, he knew, the simulacrum method was the best method. Nothing could be more powerful than an exact duplicate, according to the Laws of Similarity. The size of the simulacrum made little difference, but the accuracy of detail did—including internal organs.

But the construction of a wax simulacrum—aside from the artistry required—entailed complications which bordered on the shadowy area of the unknown. Beeswax was more effective than mineral wax for the purpose because it was an animal product instead of a mineral one, thus increasing the similarity. But why did the addition of sal ammoniac increase the potency? Magicians simply said that sal ammoniac, saltpeter, and a few other minerals increased the similarity in some unknown way and let it go at that; sorcerers had better things to do than grub around in mineralogy.

"The trouble is," said Father Patrique, "that the psychic induction method nearly always involves physical pain or physical illness—intestinal disorders, heart trouble, or other glandular disturbances. There are no traces of such things here unless one considers the malfunction of the brain as a glandular disorder—and even so, it should be accompanied by pain."

"Then you discount that diagnosis, too?" asked Lord Darcy.

Father Patrique shook his head firmly. "I discount none of the diagnoses I have made thus far. My data are far from complete."

"You have other theories, then."

"I do, my lord. Actual demonic possession."

Lord Darcy narrowed his eyes and looked straight into the eyes of the priest. "You don't really believe that, Reverend Sir."

"No," Father Patrique admitted candidly, "I do not. As a perceptive, I have a certain amount of faith in my own ability. If more than one personality were inhabiting my lord's body, I am certain I would have perceived the ... er ... other personality."

Lord Darcy did not move his eyes from those of the Benedictine. "I had assumed as much, Your Reverence," he said. "If it were a case of multiple personality, you would have detected it, eh?"

"I am certain I would have, my lord," Father Patrique stated positively. "If my lord of Cherbourg had been inhabited by another personality, I would have detected it, even if that other personality had been under cover." He paused, then waved a hand slightly. "You understand, Lord Darcy? Alternate personalities in a single human body, a single human brain, can hide themselves. The personality dominant at any given time conceals to the casual observer the fact that other—different—personalities are present. But the ... the *alter egos* cannot conceal themselves from a true perceptive."

"I understand," Lord Darcy said.

"There was only one personality in the ... the *person*, the *brain*, of the Marquis of Cherbourg at the time I examined him. And that personality was the personality of the Marquis himself."

"I see," Lord Darcy said thoughtfully. He did not doubt the priest's statement. He knew the reputation Father Patrique had among Healers. "How about drugs, Father?" he asked after a moment. "I understand that there are drugs which can alter a man's personality."

The Benedictine Healer smiled. "Certainly. Alcohol—the essence of wines and beers—will do it. There are others. Some have a temporary effect; others have no effect in single dosages—or, at least, no detectable effect—but have an accumulative effect if the drug is taken regularly. Oil of wormwood, for instance, is found in several of the more expensive liqueurs—in small quantity, of course. If you get drunk on such a liqueur, the effect is temporary and hardly distinguishable from that of alcohol alone. But if taken steadily, over a period of time, a definite personality change occurs."

Lord Darcy nodded thoughtfully, then looked at his sorcerer. "Master Sean, the phial, if you please."

The tubby little Irish sorcerer fished in a pocket with thumb and forefinger and brought forth a small stoppered glass phial a little over an inch long and half an inch in diameter. He handed it to the priest, who looked at it with curiosity. It was nearly filled with a dark amber fluid. In the fluid were little pieces of dark matter, rather like coarse-cut tobacco, which had settled to the bottom of the phial and filled perhaps a third of it.

"What is it?" Father Patrique asked.

Master Sean frowned. "That's what I'm not rightly sure of, Reverend Sir. I checked it to make certain there were no spells on it before I opened it. There weren't. So I unstoppered it and took a little whiff. Smells like brandy, with just faint overtones of something else. Naturally, I couldn't analyze it without having some notion of what it was. Without a specimen standard, I couldn't use Similarity analysis. Oh, I checked the brandy part, and that came out all right. The liquid is brandy. But I can't identify the little crumbs of stuff. His lordship had an idea that it might be a drug of some kind, and, since a Healer has all kinds of *materia medica* around, I thought perhaps we might be able to identify it."

"Certainly," the priest agreed. "I have a couple of ideas we might check right away. The fact that the material is steeped in brandy indicates either that the material decays easily or that the essence desired is soluble in brandy. That suggests several possibilities to my mind." He looked at Lord Darcy. "May I ask where you got it, my lord?"

Lord Darcy smiled. "I found it buried in a flowerpot."

Father Patrique, realizing that he had been burdened with all the information he was going to get, accepted Lord Darcy's statement with a slight shrug. "Very well, my lord; Master Sean and I will see if we can discover what this mysterious substance may be."

"Thank you, Father." Lord Darcy rose from his seat "Oh—one more thing. What do you know about Lord Seiger?"

"Very little. His lordship comes from Yorkshire . . . North Riding, if I'm not mistaken. He's been working with my lord of Cherbourg for the past several months—something to do with books, I believe. I know nothing of his family or anything like that, if that is what you mean."

"Not exactly," said Lord Darcy. "Are you his Confessor, Father? Or have you treated him as a Healer?"

The Benedictine raised his eyebrows. "No. Neither. Why?"

"Then I can ask you a question about his soul. What kind of man is he? What is the oddness I detect in him? What is it about him that frightens my lady the Marquise in spite of his impeccable behavior?" He noticed the hesitation in the priest's manner and went on before Father Patrique could answer. "This is not idle curiosity, Your Reverence. I am investigating a homicide."

The priest's eyes widened. "Not . . . ?" He stopped himself. "I see. Well, then. Granted, as a perceptive, I know certain things about Lord Seiger. He suffers from a grave illness of the soul. How these things come about, we do not know, but occasionally a person utterly lacks that part of the soul we call 'conscience,' at least insofar as it applies to certain acts. We cannot think that God would fail to provide such a thing; therefore theologists ascribe the lack to an act of the Devil at some time in the early life of the child—probably prenatally and, therefore, before baptism can protect the child. Lord Seiger is such a person. A psychopathic personality. Lord Seiger was born without an ability to distinguish between 'right' and 'wrong' as we know the terms. Such a person performs a given act or refrains from performing it only according to the expediency of the moment. Certain acts which you or I would look upon with abhorrence he may even look upon as pleasurable. Lord Seiger is—basically—a homicidal psychopath."

Lord Darcy said, "I thought as much." Then he added dryly, "He is, I presume, under restraint?"

"Oh, of course; of course!" The priest looked aghast that anyone should suggest otherwise. "Naturally such a person cannot be condemned because of a congenital deficiency, but neither can he be allowed to become a danger to society." He looked at Master Sean. "You know something of *Geas* Theory, Master Sean?"

"Something," Master Sean agreed. "Not my field, of course, but I've studied a little of the theory. The symbol manipulation's a little involved for me, I'm afraid. Psychic Algebra's as far as I ever got."

"Of course. Well, Lord Darcy, to put it in layman's terms, a powerful spell is placed upon the affected person—a *geas*, it's called—which forces him to limit his activities to those which are not dangerous to his fellow man. We cannot limit him too much, of course, for it would be sinful to deprive him entirely of his free will. His sexual morals, for instance, are his own—but he cannot use force. The extent of the *geas* depends upon the condition of the individual and the treatment given by the Healer who performed the work."

"It takes an extensive and powerful knowledge of sorcery, I take it?" Lord Darcy asked.

"Oh, yes. No Healer would even attempt it until he had taken his Th.D. and then specialized under an expert for a time. And there are not many Doctors of Thaumaturgy. Since Lord Seiger is a Yorkshireman, I would venture to guess that the work was done by His Grace the Archbishop of York—a most pious and powerful Healer. I, myself, would not think of attempting such an operation."

"You can, however, tell that such an operation has been performed?"

Father Patrique smiled. "As easily as a chirurgeon can tell if an abdominal operation has been performed."

"Can a *geas* be removed? Or partially removed?"

"Of course—by one equally as skilled and powerful. But I could detect that, too. It has not been done in Lord Seiger's case."

"Can you tell what channels of freedom he has been allowed?"

"No," said the priest. "That sort of thing depends upon the fine structure of the *geas*, which is difficult to observe without extensive analysis."

"Then," said Lord Darcy, "you cannot tell me whether or not there are circumstances in which his *geas* would permit him to kill? Such as, for instance . . . er . . . self-defense?"

"No," the priest admitted. "But I will say that it is rare indeed for even such a channel as self-defense to be left open for a psychopathic killer. The *geas* in such a case would necessarily leave the decision as to what constituted 'self-defense' up to the patient. A normal person knows when 'self-defense' requires killing one's enemy, rendering him unconscious, fleeing from him, giving him a sharp retort, or merely keeping quiet. But to a psychopathic killer, a simple insult may be construed as an attack which requires 'self-defense'—which would give him permission to kill. No Healer would leave such a decision in the hands of the patient" His face grew somber. "Certainly no sane man would leave that decision to the mind of a man like Lord Seiger."

"Then you consider him safe, Father?"

The Benedictine hesitated only a moment. "Yes. Yes, I do. I do not believe him capable of committing an antisocial act such as that. The Healer took pains to make sure that Lord Seiger would be protected from most of his fellow men, too. He is almost incapable of committing any offense against propriety; his behavior is impeccable at all times; he cannot insult anyone; he is almost incapable of defending himself physically except under the greatest provocation.

"I once watched him in a fencing bout with my lord the Marquis. Lord Seiger is an expert swordsman—much better than my lord the Marquis. The Marquis was utterly unable to score a touch upon Lord Seiger's person; Lord Seiger's defense was far too good. *But*—neither could Lord Seiger score a touch upon my lord. He couldn't even try. His brilliant swordsmanship is purely and completely defensive." He paused. "You are a swordsman yourself, my lord?" It was only half a question; the priest was fairly certain that a Duke's Investigator would be able to handle any and all weapons with confidence.

He was perfectly correct. Lord Darcy nodded without answering. To be able to wield a totally defensive sword required not only excellent—superlative—swordsmanship, but the kind of iron self-control that few men possessed. In Lord Seiger's case, of course, it could hardly be called *self*-control. The control had been imposed by another.

"Then you can understand," the priest continued, "why I say that I believe he can be trusted. If his Healer found it necessary to impose so many restrictions and protections, he would most certainly not have left any channel open for Lord Seiger to make any decision for himself as to when it would be proper to kill another."

"I understand, Father. Thank you for your information. I assure you it will remain confidential."

"Thank you, my lord. If there is nothing else . . . ?"

"Nothing for the moment, Reverend Father. Thank you again."

"A pleasure, Lord Darcy. And now, Master Sean, shall we go to my laboratory?"

An hour later, Lord Darcy was sitting in the guest room which Sir Gwiliam had shown him to the day before. He was puffing at his Bavarian pipe, filled with a blend of tobacco grown in the Southern Duchies of New England, his mind working at high speed, when Master Sean entered.

"My lord," said the tubby little sorcerer with a smile, "the good Father and I have identified the substance."

"Good!" Lord Darcy gestured toward a chair. "What was it?"

Master Sean sat down. "We were lucky, my lord. His Reverence *did* have a sample of the drug. As soon as we were able to establish a similarity between our sample and his, we identified it as a mushroom known as the Devil's Throne. The fungus is dried, minced, and steeped in brandy or other spirit. The liquid is then decanted off and the minced bits are thrown away—or, sometimes, steeped a second time. In large doses, the drugged spirit results in insanity, convulsions, and rapid death. In small doses, the preliminary stages are simply mild euphoria and light intoxication. But if taken regularly, the effect is cumulative—first, a manic, hallucinatory state, then delusions of persecution and violence."

Lord Darcy's eyes narrowed. "That fits. Thank you. Now there is one more problem. I want positive identification of that corpse. My Lord Bishop is not certain that it is his brother; that may just be wishful thinking. My Lady Marquise refuses to view the body, saying that it could not possibly be her husband—and that is *definitely* wishful thinking. But *I* must know for certain. Can you make a test?"

"I can take blood from the heart of the dead man and compare it with blood from My Lord Bishop's veins, my lord."

"Ah, yes. The Jacoby transfer method," said Lord Darcy.

"Not quite, my lord. The Jacoby transfer requires at least two hearts. It is dangerous to take blood from a living heart. But the test I have in mind is equally as valid."

"I thought blood tests were unreliable between siblings."

"Well, now, as to that, my lord," Master Sean said, "in theory there is a certain very low probability that brother and sister, children of the same parents, would show completely negative results. In other words, they would have zero similarity in that test.

"Blood similarity runs in a series of steps from zero to forty-six. In a parent-child relationship, the similarity is always exactly twenty-three—in other words, the child is always related half to one parent and half to the other.

"With siblings, though, we find variations. Identical twins, for instance, register a full forty-six-point similarity. Most siblings run much less, averaging twenty-three. There is a possibility of two brothers or two sisters having only one-point similarity, and, as I said, my lord, of a brother and sister having zero similarity. But the odds are on the order of one point seven nine million million to one against it. Considering the facial similarity of My Lord Bishop and My Lord Marquis, I would be willing to stake my reputation that the similarity would be substantially greater than zero—perhaps greater than twenty-three."

"Very well, Master Sean. You have not failed me yet; I do not anticipate that you ever will. Get me that data."

"Yes, my lord. I shall endeavor to give satisfaction." Master Sean left suffused with a glow of mixed determination and pride.

Lord Darcy finished his pipe and headed for the offices of Captain Sir Androu Duglasse.

The captain looked faintly indignant at Lord Darcy's question. "I searched the castle quite thoroughly, y' lordship. We looked everywhere that M' Lord Marquis could possibly have gone."

"Come, Captain," Lord Darcy said mildly, "I don't mean to impugn your ability, but I dare say there are places you didn't search simply because there was no reason to think my lord of Cherbourg would have gone there."

Captain Sir Androu frowned. "Such as, my lord?"

"Such as the secret tunnel."

The captain looked suddenly blank. "Oh," he said after a moment. Then his expression changed. "But surely, y' lordship, you don't think . . ."

"I don't *know*, that's the point. My lord *did* have keys to every lock in the castle, didn't he?"

"All except to the monastery, yes. My Lord Abbot has those."

"Naturally. I think we can dismiss the monastery. Where else did you not look?"

"Well . . ." The captain hesitated thoughtfully. "I didn't bother with the strongroom, the wine cellar, or the icehouse. I don't have the keys. Sir Gwiliam would have told me if anything was amiss."

"Sir Gwiliam has the keys, you say? Then we must find Sir Gwiliam."

Sir Gwiliam, as it turned out, was in the wine cellar. Lord Seiger informed them that, at Lady Elaine's request, he had sent the seneschal down for another bottle of brandy. Lord Darcy followed Captain Sir Androu down the winding stone steps to the cellars.

"Most of this is used as storage space," the captain said, waving a hand to indicate the vast, dim rooms around them. "All searched very carefully. The wine cellar's this way, y' lordship."

The wine-cellar door, of heavy, reinforced oak, stood slightly ajar. Sir Gwiliam, who had evidently heard their footsteps, opened it a little more and put his head out. "Who is it? Oh. Good afternoon, my lord. Good afternoon, Captain. May I be of service?"

He stepped back, opening the door to let them in.

"I thank you, Sir Gwiliam," said Lord Darcy. "We come partly on business and partly on pleasure. I have noticed that my lord the Marquis keeps an excellent cellar; the wines are of the finest and the brandy is extraordinary. Saint Coeurlandt Michele '46 is difficult to come by these days."

Sir Gwiliam looked rather sad. "Yes, your lordship, it is. I fear the last two cases in existence are right here. I now have the painful duty of opening one of them." He sighed and gestured toward the table, where stood a wooden case that had been partially pried open. A glance told Lord Darcy that there was nothing in the bottles but brandy and that the leaden seals were intact.

"Don't let us disturb you, Sir Gwiliam," Lord Darcy said. "May we look around?"

"Certainly, your lordship. A pleasure." He went back to work on opening the brandy case with a pry bar.

Lord Darcy ran a practiced eye over the racks, noting labels and seals. He had not really expected that anyone would attempt to put drugs or poison into bottles; My Lady Elaine was not the only one who drank, and wholesale poisoning would be too unselective.

The wine cellar was not large, but it was well stocked with excellent vintages. There were a couple of empty shelves in one corner, but the rest of the shelves were filled with bottles of all shapes and sizes. Over them lay patinas of dust of various thicknesses. Sir Gwiliam was careful not to bruise his wines.

"His lordship's choices, or yours, Sir Gwiliam?" Lord Darcy asked, indicating the rows of bottles.

"I am proud to say that My Lord Marquis has always entrusted the selection of wines and spirits to me, your lordship."

"I compliment both of you," Lord Darcy said. "You for your excellent taste, and his lordship for recognizing that ability in you." He paused. "However, there is more pressing business."

"How may I help you, my lord?" Having finished opening the case, he dusted off his hands and looked with a mixture of pride and sadness at the Saint Coeurlandt Michele '46. Distilled in 1846 and aged in the wood for thirty years before it was bottled, it was considered possibly the finest brandy ever made.

Quietly, Lord Darcy explained that there had been several places where Captain Sir Androu had been unable to search. "There is the possibility, you see, that he might have had a heart attack—or some sort of attack—and collapsed to the floor."

Sir Gwiliam's eyes opened wide. "And he might be there yet? God in Heaven! Come, your lordship! This way! I have been in the icehouse, and so has the chef, but no one has opened the strongroom!"

He took the lead, running, with Lord Darcy right behind him and Sir Androu in the rear. It was not far, but the cellar corridors twisted oddly and branched frequently.

The strongroom was more modern than the wine cellar; the

door was of heavy steel, swung on gimbaled hinges. The walls were of stone and concrete, many feet thick.

"It's a good thing the captain is here, your lordship," the seneschal said breathlessly as the three men stopped in front of the great vault door. "It takes two keys to open it. I have one, the captain has the other. My Lord Marquis, of course, has both. Captain?"

"Yes, yes, Gwiliam; I have mine here."

There were four keyholes on each side of the wide door. Lord Darcy recognized the type of construction. Only one of the four keyholes on each side worked. A key put into the wrong hole would ring alarms. The captain would know which hole to put his own key in, and so would Sir Gwiliam—but neither knew the other's proper keyhole. The shields around the locks prevented either man from seeing which keyhole the other used. Lord Darcy could not tell, even though he watched. The shields covered the hands too well.

"Ready, Captain?" Sir Gwiliam asked.

"Ready."

"Turn."

Both men turned their keys at once. The six-foot-wide door clicked inside itself and swung open when Sir Gwiliam turned a handle on his side of the door.

There was a great deal worthy of notice inside—gold and silver utensils; the jeweled coronets of the Marquis and Marquise; the great Robes of State, embroidered with gold and glittering with gems—in short, all the paraphernalia for great occasions of state. In theory, all this belonged to the Marquis; actually, it was no more his than the Imperial Crown jewels belonged to King John IV. Like the castle, it was a part of the office; it could be neither pawned nor sold.

But nowhere in the vault was there any body, dead or alive, nor any sign that there had ever been one.

"Well!" said Sir Gwiliam with a sharp exhalation. "I'm certainly glad of that! You had me worried, your lordship." There was a touch of reproach in his voice.

"I am as happy to find nothing as you are. Now let's check the icehouse."

The icehouse was in another part of the cellars and was unlocked.

One of the cooks was selecting a roast. Sir Gwiliam explained that he unlocked the icehouse each morning and left the care of it with the Chief of the Kitchen, locking it again each night. A careful search of the insulated, ice-chilled room assured Lord Darcy that there was no one there who shouldn't be.

"Now we'll take a look in the tunnel," Lord Darcy said. "Have you the key, Sir Gwiliam?"

"Why . . . why, yes. But it hasn't been opened for years! Decades! Never since I've been here, at any rate."

"I have a key, myself, y' lordship," said the captain. "I just never thought of looking. Why would he go there?"

"Why, indeed? But we must look, nevertheless."

A bell rang insistently in the distance, echoing through the cellars.

"Dear me!" said Sir Gwiliam. "My lady's brandy! I quite forgot about it! Sir Androu has a key to the tunnel, my lord; would you excuse me?"

"Certainly, Sir Gwiliam. Thank you for your help."

"A pleasure, my lord." He hurried off to answer the bell.

"Did you actually expect to find My Lord Marquis in any of those places, your lordship?" asked Sir Androu. "Even if my lord had gone into one of them, would he have locked the door behind him?"

"I did not expect to find him in the wine cellar or the ice-house," Lord Darcy said, "but the strongroom presented a strong possibility. I merely wanted to see if there were any indications that he had been there. I must confess that I found none."

"To the tunnel, then," said the captain.

The entrance was concealed behind a shabby, unused cabinet. But the cabinet swung away from the steel door behind it with oiled smoothness. And when the captain took out a dull, patinaed key and opened the door, the lock turned smoothly and effortlessly.

The captain looked at his key, now brightened by abrasion where it had forced the wards, as though it were imbued with magic. "Well, I'll be cursed!" he said softly.

The door swung silently open to reveal a tunnel six feet wide and eight high. Its depths receded into utter blackness.

"A moment, m' lord," said the captain. "I'll get a lamp." He walked back down the corridor and took an oil lamp from a wall bracket.

The two of them walked down the tunnel together. On either side, the niter-stained walls gleamed whitely. The captain pointed down at the floor. "Somebody's been using this lately," he said softly.

"I had already noticed the disturbed dust and crushed crystals of niter," Lord Darcy said. "I agree with you."

"Who's been using the tunnel, then, y' lordship?"

"I am confident that my lord the Marquis of Cherbourg was one of them. His . . . er . . . confederates were here, too."

"But why? And how? No one could have got out without my guard seeing them."

"I am afraid you are right, my good Captain." He smiled. "But that doesn't mean that the guard would have reported to you if his liege lord told him not to . . . eh?"

Sir Androu stopped suddenly and looked at Lord Darcy. "Great God in Heaven! And I thought—!" He brought himself up short.

"You thought *what*? Quickly, man!"

"Y' lordship, a new man enlisted in the Guard two months ago. Came in on m'lord's recommendation. Then m' lord reported that he misbehaved and had me put him on the sewer detail at night. The man's been on that detail ever since."

"Of course!" Lord Darcy said with a smile of triumph. "He would put one of his own men on. Come, Captain; I must speak to this man."

"I . . . I'm afraid that's impossible, y' lordship. He's down as a deserter. Disappeared from post last night. Hasn't been seen since."

Lord Darcy said nothing. He took the lantern from the captain and knelt down to peer closely at the footprints on the tunnel floor.

"I should have looked more closely," he muttered, as if to himself. "I've taken too much for granted. Ha! Two men—carrying something heavy. And followed by a third." He stood up. "This puts an entirely different complexion on the matter. We must act at once. Come!" He turned and strode back toward the castle cellar.

"But— What of the rest of the tunnel?"

"There is no need to search it," Lord Darcy said firmly. "I can assure you that there is no one in it but ourselves. Come along."

In the shadows of a dingy dockside warehouse a block from the pier where the Danzig-bound vessel, *Esprit de Mer*, was tied up, Lord Darcy stood, muffled in a long cloak. Beside him, equally muffled in a black naval cloak, his blond hair covered by a pulled-up cowl, stood Lord Seiger, his quite handsome face expressionless in the dimness.

"There she is," Lord Darcy said softly. "She's the only vessel bound for a North Sea port from Cherbourg. The Rouen office confirms that she was sold last October to a Captain Olsen. He claims to be a Northman, but I will be willing to wager against odds that he's Polish. If not, then he is certainly in the pay of the King of Poland. The ship is still sailing under Imperial registry and flying the Imperial flag. She carries no armament, of course, but she's a fast little craft for a merchant vessel."

"And you think we will find the evidence we need aboard her?" Lord Seiger asked.

"I am almost certain of it. It will be either here or at the warehouse, and the man would be a fool to leave the stuff there now—especially when it can be shipped out aboard the *Esprit de Mer*."

It had taken time to convince Lord Seiger that it was necessary to make this raid. But once Lord Darcy had convinced him of how much was already known and verified everything by a teleson call to Rouen, Lord Seiger was both willing and eager. There was a suppressed excitement in the man that showed only slightly in the pale blue eyes, leaving the rest of his face as placid as ever.

Other orders had had to be given. Captain Sir Androu Duglasse had sealed Castle Cherbourg; no one—no one—was to be allowed out for any reason whatever. The guard had been doubled during the emergency. Not even My Lord Bishop, My Lord Abbot, or My Lady Marquise could leave the castle. Those orders came, not from Lord Darcy, but from His Royal Highness the Duke of Normandy himself.

Lord Darcy looked at his wrist watch. "It's time, my lord," he said to Lord Seiger. "Let's move in."

"Very well, my lord," Lord Seiger agreed.

The two of them walked openly toward the pier.

At the gate that led to the pier itself, two burly-looking seamen stood lounging against the closed gate. When they saw the two cloaked men approaching, they became more alert, stepping away from the gate, toward the oncoming figures. Their hands went to the hilts of the scabbarded cutlasses at their belts.

Lord Seiger and Lord Darcy walked along the pier until they were within fifteen feet of the advancing guards, then stopped.

"What business have ye here?" asked one of the seamen.

It was Lord Darcy who spoke. His voice was low and cold. "Don't address me in that manner if you want to keep your tongue," he said in excellent Polish. "I wish to speak to your captain."

The first seaman looked blank at being addressed in a language he did not understand, but the second blanched visibly. "Let me handle this," he whispered in Anglo-French to the other. Then, in Polish:

"Your pardon, lord. My messmate here don't understand Polish. What was it you wanted, lord?"

Lord Darcy sighed in annoyance. "I thought I made myself perfectly clear. We desire to see Captain Olsen."

"Well, now, lord, he's given orders that he don't want to see no one. Strict orders, lord."

Neither of the two sailors noticed that, having moved away from the gate, they had left their rear unguarded. From the skiff that had managed to slip in under the pier under cover of darkness, four of the Marquis' Own silently lifted themselves to the deck of the pier. Neither Lord Darcy nor Lord Seiger looked at them.

"Strict orders?" Lord Darcy's voice was heavy with scorn. "I dare say your orders do not apply to Crown Prince Sigismund himself, do they?"

On cue, Lord Seiger swept the hood back from his handsome blond head.

It was extremely unlikely that either of the two sailors had ever seen Sigismund, Crown Prince of Poland—nor, if they had, that they would have recognized him when he was not dressed for a state occasion. But certainly they had heard that Prince Sigismund was blond and handsome, and that was all Lord Darcy needed. In actuality, Lord Seiger bore no other resemblance, being a good head taller than the Polish prince.

While they stood momentarily dumbfounded by this shattering revelation, arms silently encircled them, and they ceased to wonder about Crown Princes of any kind for several hours. They were rolled quietly into the shadows behind a pile of heavy bags of ballast.

"Everyone else all set?" Lord Darcy whispered to one of the Guardsmen.

"Yes, my lord."

"All right. Hold this gate. Lord Seiger, let's go on."

"I'm right with you, my lord," said Lord Seiger.

Some little distance away, at the rear door of a warehouse just off the waterfront, a heavily armed company of the Men-at-Arms of Cherbourg listened to the instructions of Chief Master-at-Arms Henri Vert.

"All right. Take your places. Seal every door. Arrest and detain anyone who tries to leave. Move out." With a rather self-important feeling, he touched the Duke's Warrant, signed by Lord Darcy as Agent for His Highness, that lay folded in his jacket pocket.

The Men-at-Arms faded into the dimness, moving silently to their assigned posts. With Chief Henri remained six Sergeants-at-Arms and Master Sean O Lochlainn, Sorcerer.

"All right, Sean," said Chief Henri, "go ahead."

"Give us a little light from your dark lantern, Henri," said Master Sean, kneeling to peer at the lock of the door. He set his black suitcase on the stone pavement and quietly set his corthainn-wood magician's staff against the wall beside the door. The Sergeants-at-Arms watched the tubby little sorcerer with respect.

"Ho*ho*," Master Sean said, peering at the lock. "A simple lock. But there's a heavy bar across it on the inside. Take a little work, but not much time." He opened his suitcase to take out two small phials of powder and a thin laurel-wood wand.

The Armsmen watched in silence as the sorcerer muttered his spells and blew tiny puffs of powder into the lock. Then Master Sean pointed his wand at the lock and twirled it counterclockwise slowly. There was a faint sliding noise and a *snick!* of metal as the lock unlocked itself.

Then he drew the wand across the door a foot above the lock. This time, something heavy slid quietly on the other side of the door.

With an almost inaudible sigh, the door swung open an inch or so.

Master Sean stepped aside and allowed the sergeants and their chief to enter the room. Meanwhile, he took a small device from his pocket and checked it again. It was a cylinder of glass two inches in diameter and half an inch high, half full of liquid. On the surface of the liquid floated a tiny sliver of oak that would have been difficult to see if the top of the glass box had not been a powerful magnifying lens. The whole thing looked a little like a pocket compass—which, in a sense, it was.

The tiny sliver of oak had been recovered from the scalp of the slain man in the morgue, and now, thanks to Master Sean's thaumaturgical art, the little sliver pointed unerringly toward the piece of wood whence it had come.

Master Sean nodded in satisfaction. As Lord Darcy had surmised, the weapon was still in the warehouse. He glanced up at the lights in the windows of the top floor of the warehouse. Not only the weapon, but some of the plotters were still here.

He smiled grimly and followed the Armsmen in, his corthainn-wood staff grasped firmly in one hand and his suitcase in the other.

Lord Darcy stood with Lord Seiger on one of the lower decks of the *Esprit de Mer* and looked around. "So far, so good," he said in a low voice. "Piracy has its advantages, my lord."

"Indeed it does, my lord," Lord Seiger replied in the same tone.

Down a nearby ladder, his feet clad in soft-soled boots, came Captain Sir Androu, commander of the Marquis' Own. "So far, so good, m' lords," he whispered, not realizing that he was repeating Lord Darcy's sentiments. "We have the crew. All sleeping like children."

"All the crew?" Lord Darcy asked.

"Well, m' lord, all we could find so far. Some of 'em are still on shore leave. Not due back 'til dawn. Otherwise, I fancy this ship would have pulled out long before this. No way to get word to the men, though, eh?"

"I have been hoping so," Lord Darcy agreed. "But the fact remains that we really don't know how many are left aboard. How about the bridge?"

"The Second Officer was on duty, m' lord. We have him."

"Captain's cabin?"

"Empty, m' lord."

"First Officer's?"

"Also empty, m' lord. Might be both ashore."

"Possibly." There was a distinct possibility, Lord Darcy knew, that both the captain and the first officer were still at the warehouse—in which case, they would be picked up by Chief Henri and his men.

"Very well. Let's keep moving down. We still haven't found what we're looking for." And there will be one Hell of an international incident if we don't find it, Lord Darcy told himself. His Slavonic Majesty's Government will demand all sorts of indemnities, and Lady Darcy's little boy will find himself fighting the aborigines in the jungles of New France.

But he wasn't really terribly worried; his intuition backed up his logic in telling him that he was right.

Nevertheless, he mentally breathed a deep sigh of relief when he and Lord Seiger found what they were looking for some five or six minutes later.

There were four iron-barred cells on the deck just above the lowest cargo hold. They faced each other, two and two, across a narrow passageway. Two bosuns blocked the passageway.

Lord Darcy looked down the tween-decks hatch and saw them. He had gone down the ladders silently, peeking carefully below before attempting to descend, and his caution had paid off. Neither of the bosuns saw him. They were leaning casually against the opposite bulkheads of the passageway, talking in very low voices.

There was no way to come upon them by stealth, but neither had a weapon in hand, and there was nothing to retreat behind for either of them.

Should he, Lord Darcy wondered, wait for reinforcements? Sir Androu already had his hands full for the moment, and Lord Seiger would not, of course, be of any use. The man was utterly incapable of physical violence.

He lifted himself from the prone position from which he had been peeking over the hatch edge to look below, and whispered to Lord Seiger. "They have cutlasses. Can you hold your own against one of them if trouble comes?"

For answer, Lord Seiger smoothly and silently drew his rapier. "Against both of them if necessary, my lord," he whispered back.

"I don't think it will be necessary, but there's no need taking chances at this stage of the game." He paused. Then he drew a five-shot .42 caliber handgun from his belt holster. "I'll cover them with this."

Lord Seiger nodded and said nothing.

"Stay here," he whispered to Lord Seiger. "Don't come down the stairs . . . sorry, the *ladder* . . . until I call."

"Very well, my lord."

✳   ✳   ✳

Lord Darcy walked silently up the ladder that led to the deck above. Then he came down again, letting his footfalls be heard.

He even whistled softly but audibly as he did so—an old Polish air he happened to know.

Then, without breaking his stride, he went on down the second ladder. He held his handgun in his right hand, concealed beneath his cloak.

His tactics paid off beautifully. The bosuns heard him coming and assumed that he must be someone who was authorized to be aboard the ship. They stopped their conversation and assumed an attitude of attention. They put their hands on the hilts of their cutlasses, but only as a matter of form. They saw the boots, then the legs, then the lower torso of the man coming down the ladder. And still they suspected nothing. An enemy would have tried to take them by surprise, wouldn't he?

Yes.

And he did.

Halfway down the steps, Lord Darcy dropped to a crouch and his pistol was suddenly staring both of them in the face.

"If either of you moves," said Lord Darcy calmly, "I will shoot him through the brain. Get your hands off those blade hilts and don't move otherwise. Fine. Now turn around. *V-e-r-r-ry slowly.*"

The men obeyed wordlessly. Lord Darcy's powerful hand came down twice in a deft neck-chop, and both men dropped to the floor unconscious.

"Come on down, my lord," said Lord Darcy. "There will be no need for swordplay."

Lord Seiger descended the ladder in silence, his sword sheathed.

There were two cell doors on either side of the passageway; the cells themselves had been built to discipline crewmen or to imprison sailors or passengers who were accused of crime on the high seas while the ship was in passage. The first cell on the right had a dim light glowing within it. The yellowish light gleamed through the small barred window in the door.

Both Lord Darcy and Lord Seiger walked over to the door and looked inside.

"That's what I was looking for," Lord Darcy breathed.

Within, strapped to a bunk, was a still, white-faced figure. The face was exactly similar to that of the corpse Lord Darcy had seen in the morgue.

"Are you sure it's the Marquis of Cherbourg?" Lord Seiger asked.

"I refuse to admit that there are *three* men who look that much alike," Lord Darcy whispered dryly. "Two are quite enough. Since Master Sean established that the body in the morgue was definitely *not* related to my lord of Guernsey and Sark, *this* must be the Marquis. Now, the problem will be getting the cell door open."

"I vill open idt for you."

At the sound of the voice behind them, both Lord Darcy and Lord Seiger froze.

"To qvote you, Lord Darcy, 'If either of you moves, I vill shoodt him through the brain,'" said the voice. "Drop de gun, Lord Darcy." As Lord Darcy let his pistol drop from his hand, his mind raced.

The shock of having been trapped, such as it had been, had passed even before the voice behind him had ceased. Shock of that kind could not hold him frozen long. Nor was his the kind of mind that grew angry with itself for making a mistake. There was no time for that.

He had been trapped. Someone had been hidden in the cell across the passageway, waiting for him. A neat trap. Very well; the problem was, how to get out of that trap.

"Bot' of you step to de left," said the voice. "Move away from de cell port. Dat's it. Fine. Open de door, Ladislas."

There were two men, both holding guns. The shorter, darker of the two stepped forward and opened the door to the cell next to that in which the still figure of the Marquis of Cherbourg lay.

"Bot' of you step inside," said the taller of the two men who had trapped the Imperial agents.

There was nothing Lord Seiger and Lord Darcy could do but obey.

"Keep you de hands high in de air. Dat's fine. Now listen to me, and listen carefully. You t'ink you have taken dis ship. In a vay, you have. But not finally. I have you. I have de Marquis. You vill order your men off. Odervise, I vill kill all of you—vun adt a time. Understand? If I hang, I do not die alone."

Lord Darcy understood. "You want your crew back, eh, Captain Olsen? And how will you get by the Royal Navy?"

"De same vay I vill get out of Cherbourg harbor, Lord Darcy," the captain said complacently. "I vill promise release. You vill be able to go back home from Danzig. Vot goodt is any of you to us now?"

None, except as hostages, Lord Darcy thought. What had happened was quite clear. Somehow, someone had managed to signal to Captain Olsen that his ship was being taken. A signal from the bridge, perhaps. It didn't matter. Captain Olsen had not been expecting invaders, but when they had come, he had devised a neat trap. He had known where the invaders would be heading.

Up to that point, Lord Darcy knew, the Polish agents had planned to take the unconscious Marquis to Danzig. There, he would be operated on by a sorcerer and sent back to Cherbourg—apparently in good condition, but actually under the control of Polish agents. His absence would be explained by his "spells," which would no longer be in evidence. But now that Captain Olsen knew that the plot had been discovered, he had no further use for the Marquis. Nor had he any use for either Lord Darcy or Lord Seiger. Except that he could use them as hostages to get his ship to Danzig.

"What do you want, Captain Olsen?" Lord Darcy asked quietly.

"Very simply, dis: You vill order de soldiers to come below. Ve vill lock dem up. Ven my men vake up, and de rest of de crew come aboard, ve vill sail at dawn. Ven ve are ready to sail, all may go ashore except you and Lord Seiger and de Marquis. Your men vill tell de officials in Cherbourg vhat has happened and vill tell dem dat ve vill sail to Danzig unmolested. Dere, you vill be set free and sent back to Imperial territory. I give you my vord."

Oddly, Lord Darcy realized that the man meant it. Lord Darcy knew that the man's word was good. But was he responsible for the reactions of the Polish officials at Danzig? Was he responsible for the reactions of Casimir IX? No. Certainly not.

But, trapped as they were—

And then a hoarse voice came from across the passageway, from the fourth cell.

"Seiger? Seiger?"

Lord Seiger's eyes widened. "Yes?"

Captain Olsen and First Officer Ladislas remained unmoved. The captain smiled sardonically. "Ah, yes. I forgot to mention your so-brave Sir James le Lein. He vill make an excellent hostage, too."

The hoarse voice said: "They are traitors to the King, Seiger. Do you hear me?"

"I hear you, Sir James," said Lord Seiger.

"Destroy them," said the hoarse voice.

Captain Olsen laughed. "Shut up, le Lein. You—"

But he never had time to finish.

Lord Darcy watched with unbelieving eyes as Lord Seiger's right hand darted out with blurring speed and slapped aside the captain's gun. At the same time, his left hand drew his rapier and slashed out toward the first officer.

The first officer had been covering Lord Darcy. When he saw Lord Seiger move, he swung his gun toward Lord Seiger and fired. The slug tore into the Yorkshire nobleman's side as Captain Olsen spun away and tried to bring his own weapon to bear.

By that time, Lord Darcy himself was in action. His powerful legs catapulted him toward First Officer Ladislas just as the point of Lord Seiger's rapier slashed across Ladislas' chest, making a deep cut over the ribs. Then Ladislas was slammed out into the passageway by Lord Darcy's assault.

After that, Lord Darcy had too much to do to pay any attention to what went on between Lord Seiger and Captain Olsen. Apparently oblivious to the blood gushing from the gash on his chest, Ladislas fought with steel muscles. Darcy knew his own strength, but he also knew that this opponent was of nearly equal strength. Darcy held the man's right wrist in a vise grip to keep him from bringing the pistol around. Then he smashed his head into Ladislas' jaw. The gun dropped and spun away as both men fell to the deck.

Lord Darcy brought his right fist up in a smashing blow to the first officer's throat; gagging, the first officer collapsed.

Lord Darcy pushed himself to his knees and grabbed the unconscious man by the collar, pulling him half upright.

At that second, a tongue of steel flashed by Lord Darcy's shoulder, plunged itself into Ladislas' throat, and tore sideways. The first officer died as his blood spurted fountainlike over Lord Darcy's arm.

After a moment, Lord Darcy realized that the fight was over. He turned his head.

Lord Seiger stood nearby, his sword red. Captain Olsen lay on the deck, his life's blood flowing from three wounds—two in the chest, and the third, like his first officer's, a slash across the throat.

"I had him," Lord Darcy said unevenly. "There was no need to cut his throat."

For the first time, he saw a slight smile on Lord Seiger's face.

"I had my orders, my lord," said Seiger, as his side dripped crimson.

With twelve sonorous, resounding strokes, the great Bell of the Benedictine Church of Saint Denys, in the courtyard of Castle Cherbourg, sounded the hour of midnight. Lord Darcy, freshly bathed and shaved and clad in his evening wear, stood before the fireplace in the reception room above the Great Hall and waited patiently for the bell to finish its tally. Then he turned and smiled at the young man standing beside him. "As you were saying, Your Highness?"

Richard, Duke of Normandy, smiled back. "Even royalty can't drown out a church bell, eh, my lord?" Then his face became serious again. "I was saying that we have made a clean sweep. Dunkerque, Calais, Boulogne . . . all the way down to Hendaye. By now, the English Armsmen will be picking them up in London, Liverpool, and so on. By dawn, Ireland will be clear. You've done a magnificent job, my lord, and you may rest assured that my brother the King will hear of it."

"Thank you, Your Highness, but I really—"

Lord Darcy was interrupted by the opening of the door. Lord Seiger came in, then stopped as he saw Duke Richard.

The Duke reacted instantly. "Don't bother to bow, my lord. I have been told of your wound."

Lord Seiger nevertheless managed a slight bow. "Your Highness is most gracious. But the wound is a slight one, and Father Patrique has laid his hands on it. The pain is negligible, Highness."

"I am happy to hear so." The Duke looked at Lord Darcy. "By the way . . . I am curious to know what made you suspect that Lord Seiger was a King's Agent. I didn't know, myself, until the King, my brother, sent me the information I requested."

"I must confess that I was not certain until Your Highness verified my suspicions on the teleson. But it seemed odd to me that de Cherbourg would have wanted a man of Lord Seiger's . . . ah . . . peculiar talents merely as a librarian. Then, too, Lady Elaine's attitude . . . er, your pardon, my lord—"

"Perfectly all right, my lord," said Lord Seiger expressionlessly. "I am aware that many women find my presence distasteful—although I confess I do not know why."

"Who can account for the behavior of women?" Lord Darcy said. "Your manners and behavior are impeccable. Nonetheless, My Lady Marquise found, as you say, your presence distasteful. She must have made this fact known to her husband the Marquis, eh?"

"I believe she did, my lord," said Lord Seiger.

"Very well," said Lord Darcy. "Would My Lord Marquis, who is notoriously in love with his wife, have kept a *librarian* who frightened her? No. Therefore, either Lord Seiger's purpose here was much more important—or he was blackmailing the Marquis. I chose to believe the former." He did not add that Father Patrique's information showed that it was impossible for Lord Seiger to blackmail anyone.

"My trouble lay in not knowing who was working for whom. We knew only that Sir James was masquerading as a common working man, and that he was working with My Lord Marquis. But until Your Highness got in touch with His Majesty, we knew nothing more. I was working blind until I realized that Lord Seiger—"

He stopped as he heard the door open. From outside came Master Sean's voice: "After you, my lady, my lord, Sir Gwiliam."

The Marquise de Cherbourg swept into the room, her fair face an expressionless mask. Behind her came My Lord Bishop and Sir Gwiliam, followed by Master Sean O Lochlainn.

Lady Elaine walked straight to Duke Richard. She made a small curtsy. "Your presence is an honor, Your Highness." She was quite sober.

"The honor is mine, my lady," replied the Duke.

"I have seen my lord husband. He is alive, as I knew he was. But his mind is gone. Father Patrique says he will never recover. I must know what has happened, Your Highness."

"You will have to ask Lord Darcy that, my lady," the Duke said gently. "I should like to hear the complete story myself."

My lady turned her steady gaze on the lean Englishman. "Begin at the beginning and tell me everything, my lord. I must know."

The door opened again, and Sir Androu Duglasse came in. "Good morning, Y' Highness," he said with a low bow. "Good morning, m' lady, y' lordships, Sir Gwiliam, Master Sean." His eyes went back to Lady Elaine. "I've heard the news from Father

Patrique, m' lady. I'm a soldier, m' lady, not a man who can speak well. I cannot tell you of the sorrow I feel."

"I thank you, Sir Captain," said my lady, "I think you have expressed it very well." Her eyes went back to Lord Darcy. "If you please, my lord . . ."

"As you command, my lady," said Lord Darcy. "Er . . . Captain, I don't think that what I have to say need be known by any others than those of us here. Would you watch the door? Explain to anyone else that this is a private conference. Thank you. Then I can begin." He leaned negligently against the fireplace, where he could see everyone in the room.

"To begin with, we had a hellish plot afoot—not against just one person, but against the Empire. The 'Atlantic Curse.' Ships sailing from Imperial ports to the New World were never heard from again. Shipping was dropping off badly, not only from ship losses, but because fear kept seamen off trans-Atlantic ships. They feared magic, although, as I shall show, pure magic had nothing to do with it.

"My lord the Marquis was working with Sir James le Lein, one of a large group of King's Agents with direct commissions to discover the cause of the 'Atlantic Curse.' His Majesty had correctly deduced that the whole thing was a Polish plot to disrupt Imperial economy.

"The plot was devilish in its simplicity. A drug, made by steeping a kind of mushroom in brandy, was being used to destroy the minds of the crews of trans-Atlantic ships. Taken in small dosages, over a period of time, the drug causes violent insanity. A ship with an insane crew cannot last long in the Atlantic.

"Sir James, working with My Lord Marquis and other agents, tried to get a lead on what was going on. My Lord Marquis, not wanting anyone in the castle to know of his activities, used the old secret tunnel that leads to the city sewers in order to meet Sir James.

"Sir James obtained a sample of the drug after he had identified the ringleader of the Polish agents. He reported to My Lord Marquis. Then, on the evening of Wednesday, the eighth of January, Sir James set out to obtain more evidence. He went to the warehouse where the ringleader had his headquarters."

Lord Darcy paused and smiled slightly. "By the by, I must say that the details of what happened in the warehouse were supplied to me by Sir James. My own deductions only gave me a part of the story.

"At any rate, Sir James obtained entry to the second floor of the warehouse. He heard voices. Silently, he went to the door of the room from which the voices came and looked in through the ... er ... the keyhole. It was dark in the corridor, but well-lit in the room.

"What he saw was a shock to him. Two men—a sorcerer and the ringleader himself—were there. The sorcerer was standing by a bed, weaving a spell over a third man, who lay naked on the bed. One look at the man in the bed convinced Sir James that the man was none other than the Marquis of Cherbourg himself!"

Lady Elaine touched her fingertips to her lips. "Had he been poisoned by the drug, my lord?" she asked. "Was that what had been affecting his mind?"

"The man was not your husband, my lady," Lord Darcy said gently. "He was a double, a simple-minded man in the pay of these men.

"Sir James, of course, had no way of knowing that. When he saw the Marquis in danger, he acted. Weapon in hand, he burst open the door and demanded the release of the man whom he took to be the Marquis. He told the man to get up. Seeing he was hypnotized, Sir James put his own cloak about the man's shoulders and the two of them began to back out of the room, his weapon covering the sorcerer and the ringleader.

"But there was another man in the warehouse. Sir James never saw him. This person struck him from behind as he backed out the door.

"Sir James was dazed. He dropped his weapon. The sorcerer and the ringleader jumped him. Sir James fought, but he was eventually rendered unconscious.

"In the meantime, the man whom Sir James attempted to rescue became frightened and fled. In the darkness, he tumbled down a flight of oaken stairs and fractured his skull on one of the lower steps. Hurt, dazed, and dying, he fled from the warehouse toward the only other place in Cherbourg he could call home—a bistro called the Blue Dolphin, a few blocks away. He very nearly made it. He died a block from it, in the sight of two Armsmen."

"Did they intend to use the double for some sort of impersonation of my brother?" asked the Bishop.

"In a way, my lord. I'll get to that in a moment.

"When I came here," Lord Darcy continued, "I of course knew nothing of all this. I knew only that my lord of Cherbourg was missing and that he had been working with His Majesty's Agents. Then a body was tentatively identified as his. If it *were* the Marquis, who had killed him? If it were not, what was the connection? I went to see Sir James and found that he had been missing since the same night. Again, what was the connection?

"The next clue was the identification of the drug. How could such a drug be introduced aboard ships so that almost every man would take a little each day? The taste and aroma of the brandy would be apparent in the food or water. Obviously, then, the wine rations were drugged. And only the vintner who supplied the wine could have regularly drugged the wine of ship after ship.

"A check of the Shipping Registry showed that new vintners had bought out old wineries in shipping ports throughout the Empire in the past five years. All of them, subsidized by the Poles, could underbid their competitors. They made good wine and sold it cheaper than others could sell it. They got contracts. They didn't try to poison every ship; only a few of those on the Atlantic run—just enough to start a scare while keeping suspicion from themselves.

"There was still the problem of what had happened to My Lord Marquis. He had not left the castle that night. And yet he had disappeared. But how? And why?

"There were four places that the captain had not searched. I dismissed the icehouse when I discovered that people went in and out of it all day. He could not have gone to the strongroom because the door is too wide for one man to use both keys simultaneously—which must be done to open it. Sir Gwiliam had been in and out of the wine cellar. And there were indications that the tunnel had also had visitors."

"Why should he have been in any of those places, my lord?" Sir Gwiliam asked. "Mightn't he have simply left through the tunnel?"

"Hardly likely. The tunnel guard was a King's Agent. If the Marquis had gone out that night and never returned, he would have reported the fact—not to Captain Sir Androu, but to Lord Seiger. He did not so report. Ergo, the Marquis did not leave the castle that night."

"Then what happened to him?" Sir Gwiliam asked.

"That brings us back to the double, Paul Sarto," said Lord Darcy. "Would you explain, Master Sean?"

"Well, my lady, gentle sirs," the little sorcerer began, "My Lord Darcy deduced the use of magic here. This Polish sorcerer—a piddling poor one, he is, too; when I caught him in the warehouse, he tried to cast a few spells at me and they were nothing. He ended up docile as a lamb when I gave him a dose of good Irish sorcery."

"Proceed, Master Sean," Lord Darcy said dryly.

"Beggin' your pardon, my lord. Anyway, this Polish sorcerer saw that this Paul chap was a dead ringer for My Lord Marquis and decided to use him to control My Lord Marquis—Law of Similarity, d' ye see. You know the business of sticking pins in wax dolls? Crude method of psychic induction, but effective if the similarity is great enough. And what could be more similar to a man than his double?"

"You mean they used this poor unfortunate man as a wax doll?" asked the Marquise in a hushed voice.

"That's about it, your ladyship. In order for the spells to work, though, the double would have to have very low mind power. Well, he did. So they hired him away from his old job and went to work on him. They made him bathe and wear fine clothes, and slowly took control of his mind. They told him that he was the Marquis. With that sort of similarity achieved, they hoped to control the Marquis himself just as they controlled his simulacrum."

My Lady Elaine looked horrified. "*That* caused his terrible attacks?"

"Exactly, your ladyship. When My Lord Marquis was tired or distracted, they were able to take over for a little while. A vile business no proper sorcerer would stoop to, but workable."

"But what did they do to my husband?" asked the Lady of Cherbourg.

"Well, now your ladyship," said Master Sean, "what do you suppose would happen to his lordship when his simulacrum got his skull crushed so bad that it killed the simulacrum? The shock to his lordship's mind was so great that it nearly killed him on the spot—*would* have killed him, too, if the similarity had been better established. He fell into a coma, my lady."

Lord Darcy took up the story again. "The Marquis dropped where he was. He remained in the castle until last night, when the Polish agents came to get him. They killed the King's Agent on guard, disposed of the body, came in through the tunnel, got the Marquis, and took him to their ship. When Captain Sir Androu told me that the guard had 'deserted,' I knew fully what had happened. I knew that My Lord Marquis was either in the vintner's warehouse or in a ship bound for Poland. The two raids show that I was correct."

"Do you mean," said Sir Gwiliam, "that my lord lay in that chilly tunnel all that time? How horrible!"

Lord Darcy looked at the man for long seconds. "No. Not *all* that time, Sir Gwiliam. No one—especially not the Polish agents—would have known he was there. He was taken to the tunnel after he was found the next morning—in the wine cellar."

"Ridiculous!" said Sir Gwiliam, startled. "I'd have seen him!"

"Most certainly you would have," Lord Darcy agreed. "And most certainly you *did*. It must have been quite a shock to return home after the fight in the warehouse to find the Marquis unconscious on the wine cellar floor. Once I knew you were the guilty man, I knew you had given away your employer. You told me that you had played cards with Ordwin Vayne that night; therefore I knew which vintner to raid."

White-faced, Sir Gwiliam said, "I have served my lord and lady faithfully for many years. I say you lie."

"Oh?" Lord Darcy's eyes were hard. "Someone had to tell Ordwin Vayne where the Marquis was—someone who *knew* where he was. Only the Marquis, Sir Androu, and *you* had keys to the tunnel. I saw the captain's key; it was dull and filmed when I used it. The wards of the old lock left little bright scratches on it. He hadn't used it for a long time. Only *you* had a key that would let Ordwin Vayne and his men into that tunnel."

"Pah! Your reasoning is illogical! If My Lord Marquis were unconscious, someone could have taken the key off him!"

"Not if he was in the tunnel. Why would anyone go there? The tunnel door was locked, so, even, if he *were* there, a key would have to have been used to find him. But if he had fallen in the tunnel, he would still have been there when I looked. There was no reason for you or anyone else to unlock that tunnel—*until* you were looking for a place to conceal My Lord Marquis' unconscious body!"

"Why would he have gone to the wine cellar?" Sir Gwiliam snapped. "And why lock himself in?"

"He went down to check on some bottles you had in the wine

cellar. Sir James' report led him to suspect you. Warehouses and wineries are subjected to rigorous inspection. Ordwin Vayne didn't want inspectors to find that he was steeping mushrooms in brandy. So the bottles were kept *here*—the safest place in Cherbourg. Who would suspect? The Marquis never went there. But he did suspect at last, and went down to check. He locked the door because he didn't want to be interrupted. No one but you could come in, and he would be warned if you put your key in the lock. While he was there, the simulacrumized Paul fell and struck his head on an oaken step. Paul died. The Marquis went comatose.

"When I arrived yesterday, you had to get rid of the evidence. So Vayne's men came and took the bottles of drug and the Marquis. If further proof is needed, I can tell you that we found the drug on the ship, in restoppered bottles containing cheap brandy and bits of mushroom. *But the bottles were labeled Saint Coeurlandt Michele '46!* Who else in Cherbourg but you would have access to such empty bottles?"

Sir Gwiliam stepped back. "Lies! All lies!"

"No!" snapped a voice from the door. "Truth! All truth!"

Lord Darcy had seen Captain Sir Androu silently open the door and let in three more men, but no one else had. Now the others turned at the sound of the voice.

Sitting in a wheelchair, looking pale but still strong, was Hugh, Marquis of Cherbourg. Behind him was Sir James le Lein. To one side stood Father Patrique.

"What Lord Darcy said is true in every particular," said my lord the Marquis in an icy voice.

Sir Gwiliam gasped and jerked his head around to look at my lady the Marquise. "You said his mind was gone!"

"A small lie—to trap a traitor." Her voice was icy.

"Sir Gwiliam de Bracy," said Sir James from behind the Marquis, "in the King's Name, I charge you with treason!"

Two things happened almost at once. Sir Gwiliam's hand started for his pocket. But by then, Lord Seiger's sword, with its curious offset hilt, was halfway from its sheath. By the time Sir Gwiliam had his pistol out, the sword had slashed through his jugular vein. Sir Gwiliam had just time to turn and fire once before he fell to the floor.

Lord Seiger stood there, looking down at Sir Gwiliam, an odd smile on his face.

For a second, no one spoke or moved. Then Father Patrique rushed over to the fallen seneschal. He was too late by far. With all his Healing power, there was nothing he could do now.

And then the Marquise walked over to Lord Seiger and took his free hand. "My lord, others may censure you for that act. I do not. That monster helped send hundreds of innocent men to insanity and death. He almost did the same for my beloved Hugh. If anything, he died too clean a death. I do not censure you, my lord. I thank you."

"I thank you, my lady. But I only did my duty." There was an odd thickness in his voice. "I had my orders, my lady."

And then, slowly, like a deflating balloon, Lord Seiger slumped to the floor.

Lord Darcy and Father Patrique realized at the same moment that Sir Gwiliam's bullet must have hit Lord Seiger, though he had shown no sign of it till then.

Lord Seiger had had no conscience, but he could not kill or even defend himself of his own accord. Sir James had been his decision-maker. Lord Seiger had been a King's Agent who would kill without qualm on order from Sir James—and was otherwise utterly harmless. The decision was never left up to him, only to Sir James.

Sir James, still staring at the fallen Lord Seiger, said: "But . . . how could he? I didn't tell him to."

"Yes, you did," Lord Darcy said wearily. "On the ship. You told him to destroy the traitors. When you called Sir Gwiliam a traitor, he acted. He had his sword halfway out before Sir Gwiliam drew that pistol. He would have killed Sir Gwiliam in cold blood if the seneschal had never moved at all. He was like a gas lamp, Sir James. You turned him on—and forgot to shut him off."

Richard, Duke of Normandy, looked down at the fallen man. Lord Seiger's face was oddly unchanged. It had rarely had any expression in life. It had none now.

"How is he, Reverend Father?" asked the Duke.

"He is dead, Your Highness."

"May the Lord have mercy on his soul," said Duke Richard.

Eight men and a woman made the Sign of the Cross in silence.

The Case of the Skinflint's Specters

> ➤ BRIAN M. THOMSEN ❮

MARLEY WAS DEAD, TO BEGIN WITH. THERE IS NO DOUBT WHATEVER about that. The register of his burial was signed by the clergyman, the clerk, the undertaker, and the chief mourner. Scrooge signed it.

Old Marley was as dead as a doornail . . . but that was seven years ago, and besides, I hadn't been hired to investigate Marley. Scrooge was the subject of my investigation, and after a month of tracking down lost leads, ancient archives, and absent-minded former acquaintances, I now had a dossier in front of me that could have been called "Everything you always wanted to know about Ebenezer Scrooge but couldn't care less about."

I was waiting for my mysterious unnamed client to come by, "he" who had earned my loyalty by paying in advance provided that no questions were asked, and that the information could be picked up no later than early Christmas Eve morn.

It was just past dawn on December twenty-fourth, and I was waiting to fill my half of the bargain so that I could go off on my usual holiday bender down in the sin dens of Whitechapel.

My name is Malcolm Chandler, Mouse to my friends, and I'm your typical down-on-my-luck Victorian gumshoe, who'd probably be spending Christmas in the poorhouse if my client hadn't come through with enough of an advance to settle a few way overdue debts to some reputable establishments which had in the

271

past shown a certain willingness to donate the services of some of their less fortunate debtors to the local treadmill (as well as a few other creditors who enjoyed the sound of kneecaps shattering). Money is good, honestly-earned or otherwise, and quite necessary for one's general well-being since London had become so tough on its debtors.

I sipped from my mug of early morning grog, and hoped that my client arrived shortly. It wasn't as if I had any Christmas shopping to do or anything. It's just that I enjoyed the concept of a case closed, and as soon as I had handed over this file that was the concept to be imprinted.

The warmth of my draught awakened the slumbering little gray cells that had been dormant since I closed the file the night before. They had the uncanny knack of asking my senses the most awkward questions at the most awkward times.

"Mouse," said the gray cells. "Mr. Scrooge is a singularly uninteresting character. Why would anyone need to know his life story?"

"Shut up," I said.

"Why would the selfsame person be willing to pay so much for the aforementioned information, particularly from a down-on-his-luck gumshoe like you?"

"Because I'm good, and you get what you pay for," I replied.

"The gentleman on Baker's Street with his physician companion is better."

"Shut up!" I insisted, just managing to stifle my outburst before my client entered the office.

Regaining my composure, I quickly jumped to my feet, and offered my hand to help my benefactor off with his cloak. He quickly denied the offer, saying, "The file. Do you have it?"

"Right here, my lord," I offered in my classiest tone, pointing to the sheaf of pages on my desk.

The client picked up the folder, and quickly began skimming through the material. As he skimmed, I scanned. I couldn't help noticing that he was dressed almost purposely to disguise his build and obscure his face. His cloak was long and drawn across the bottom half of his face like some sort of Rumanian count out for a good evening. A gentleman's silk topper covered his crown, and a muffler succeeded in obscuring the territory between his cloak and the hat. Even while he was rifting through the pages, he managed to carefully balance his masks like a sheik in a sandstorm.

He must have sensed my eyes boring into him, because he quickly looked up and said, "Fine. Your services are appreciated and no longer necessary," and then, reaching into his pocket, he extracted a coin purse, and lobbed it onto the desk, saying, "Consider this an added bonus. Now forget everything you've learned over the past few weeks. Forget Scrooge, forget me. In fact, you and I have never met."

"I don't even know your name," I added.

"Exactly, and let's keep it that way," and with that he was gone.

Any other day of the year, I would probably have just left the office at that point and headed off to the sin pits, but since I probably would not be making it back before the New Year given my current state of flush, and wishing to avoid the unnecessary difficulties that ensue when one trips over debris, I decided to give my office a slight once-over before leaving. (My underpaid secretary, Victoria of the elegant legs, had gone home to Wales for the holidays.)

After removing and disposing of several left-behind corset stays from some former business acquaintances, a few tobacco-stained IOUs, and a Hogarth pinup, I came across a business card of a certain F.S. Rogers, Esquire.

Since I didn't know anyone called F.S. Rogers, Esquire or otherwise, I was fairly certain that he must have been my mysterious employer.

Rogers . . . the name rang a bell, but I couldn't figure out why . . . in fact, this further tickled my curiosity to the point where I quickly found myself muffled and mittened against the cold, and off down the street to the address on the card.

No sooner did I arrive within half a block of my destination than I recognized my former employer heading off in the opposite direction. Doing a quick 180, I took off in hot pursuit at a discreet distance.

I soon found myself in the theatrical lowlife section of town where the division between actresses and harlots, and actors and con men depended on one's income for a given week. My quarry ran into a rundown tavern called The Charley D, where he quickly joined three equally bundled and obscured figures at a table.

I took a seat at the bar, yet well within earshot, being careful not to remove my muffler or turn down my collar so as to give my presence away.

"Mighty cold out," said Bumble the bartender.

"Sure is, guvner," I replied, watching the four figures remove their long coats.

"What'll it be?" he asked.

"A spot of brandy, and an extra shilling if you can tell me who that gentleman is with that motley trio."

"Sure. That's Mr. Rogers, a regular patron of the arts he is."

Bumble fetched my brandy and returned to serving the rest of the bar while I set my efforts to spying.

The three figures my former employer was conversing with were an odd lot. On his left was a strangely androgynous, almost childlike, albino who was no taller than five one. Next to him, or her (or whatever, it took all types in the theater world) was a burly bear of a fellow who could have just as easily made a living on the loading dock or in the wrestling arena. Every few minutes the tavern's conversation would be interrupted by his boisterous laugh that threatened to shake the bottles down off the shelves and the inebriated off their perches. The third was a tall yet somewhat emaciated fellow who could have won the best-looking cadaver contest at any local poorhouse. All three listened to my former employer intently.

"All of the information is in these notes," he said, and then, focusing on the wan one, he continued: "Remember, you are the past. Bring up all about that horrible Christmas season he had at boarding school, adding details like how he loved the Arabian Nights, and such. Then move into his apprenticeship under Fez-ziwig. Dick Wilkins was his old crony, and Belle was the girl that got away."

"Yessir," the wan one replied in an asexual lilt.

"And you," he continued, moving on to the bearish fellow, "remember to cover his current life. All of the facts on that guy Cratchit's family will do the trick. Play up that brat Tim, the one with the gimp. The old buzzard has to wallow in guilt and regret."

"What about the nephew?" the bear asked. "This guy named Fred."

"Oh, yeah," my former employer agreed. "Cover him, too."

Turning to the walking corpse, he finished with: "You don't say anything. Just show him those pictures and try to look creepy . . . like death warmed over."

"Is that all?" the cadaver inquired.

"That's it. You already have your cloaks. White for past, green for present, and black for—"

"Yet to come," the cadaver interrupted.

"Whatever. Just remember to show up starting at twelve, one of you on each hour. No later than that or the drug that will be mixed in his dinner will have worn off. By morning, he'll be a raving lunatic, and by New Year's, Bedlam's latest inmate."

"And bonuses all around," added the bear.

"Here, here!" the group replied.

From my tavern stool observation post I was horrified. It was clear that they were using the research I had carefully gathered to drive an admittedly unlikable yet innocent man insane.

The question was why, but it quickly all clicked in place.

The nephew Fred, the son of Scrooge's sister Fantine.

Fantine's married name was Rogers.

How could I have been so blind? Fred Rogers, Scrooge's nephew, was my former employer.

I was so busy flagellating myself for my stupidity, that I didn't even hear the bear come up behind me and put me in a choke hold.

I passed out as the weight of a thousand curses of stupidity came crashing down.

I came to, what must have been hours later. I was trussed up like a holiday goose, in the back area of some storeroom. Above me I heard the voices of a crowd at play, a Christmas party of some sort. My head hurt, and the more I struggled the more exhausted I became.

After an enormous effort I finally managed to work the trusses off my ankles, freeing my legs from their bondage.

Then I passed out again, the stupid singsong of a holiday round beating through my skull.

My rest was disturbed by a lantern bearer, who doused my face with a glass of holiday cheer.

"Stupid detective," a voice behind the light scolded. "All of the party guests have gone home, and now I must deal with you."

"I guess so, Fred," I said, and then added with false bravado, "and, by the way, seasons greetings."

"I was afraid you had put it all together, Mr. Chandler. That's why I had Barnaby escort you here. You may not remember. You were quite unconscious at the time."

"Barnaby the bear," I offered.

"You could have been enjoying the holiday right now, but no. You had to be nosy."

"And you had to be greedy," I countered "You're Scrooge's only heir. God knows he's not going to give it to charity. Couldn't you just wait? His days are obviously numbered at this point."

"With any luck, tonight's little dramatic recital will have taken care of that already. The best case is that his ticker gives out, at which point I inherit the firm. The worst case is he goes crazy, at which point I take control of the firm and he goes to the loony bin. I win either way."

Somewhere in the distance the bells of Christmas dawn tolled.

"There! A new day is dawning. Scrooge & Marley will now be Fred Rogers and Company," he laughed, and then added, taking a gun from out of his pocket, "and you are the only flaw in a perfect plan. A flaw that will be taken care of now."

The gun was trained on me, and I was about to kiss my arse good-bye, when a ghostly bellow shook the cellar.

"I don't think so," the unearthly voice cried, accompanied by shaking chains, and the sounds of ledgers and coin boxes dropping. "It's still *my* business."

Taking advantage of this otherworldly occurrence that had temporarily distracted my former employer, I barreled forward into Fred's midsection, knocking him down, and beat a hasty escape up the cellar stairs and out a nearby servants' exit.

I heard a scream that sounded like Fred's voice, but kept on running.

I finally reached my office, where I eventually worked my hands loose from their bonds.

Exhausted, I locked the door and passed out from fatigue, and the beatings my body had taken.

The rest of the facts of the case are rather sketchy. Scrooge got up Christmas morning, and was a changed man . . . maybe crazy, but at least for the better, and not in a way that he could be committed. He became a regular humanitarian, helped out his clerk, and signed over all of his estate to charity.

Fred Rogers was found cringing in his cellar, claiming that a dead man was trying to kill him. He was Bedlam's first inmate of the New Year.

What can I say? It was poetic justice.

Nosing around, I later heard that the word on the street was that Scrooge had joked about being visited by four spirits on Christmas Eve.

Four? I thought. But Fred had only hired three stooges to be ghosts. Who could the fourth have been?

The following year on Christmas Eve, I had once again managed to drink myself into a stupor and wound up sleeping it off in the office.

When I came to, I felt strange ... as if I had been visited by someone the night before.

On the floor leading to my desk were scratches that could have been left by chains that had been dragged across it bit by bit.

On top of my desk was an envelope with a fifty-pound banknote. There was also a short written note attached.

It read: *"For your trouble of last holiday season. JM."*

JM, I thought, who could it be? Then it dawned on me.

... but Jacob Marley was dead, and there was and is no doubt about that. I decided not to think about it, put the fifty pounds in my pocket, and made a New Year's resolution to cut back on my drinking real soon now.

The Black Bird

> DAVID BARR KIRTLEY <

THE BLACK BIRD ON THE MANTELPIECE SPOKE. IT SAID, "NEVERMORE."

Spade looked up from cleaning his pistol. The bird, a black-lacquered falcon statuette, sat motionless. Spade placed the pistol on his desk, pushed back the brim of his hat, and approached the bird.

"You talk?" Spade said.

The bird watched him evenly with two small, black eyes. "Yes," it answered. Its voice was eerily familiar and echoed through the silent office.

"How?" Spade demanded. "You're just a statue."

The bird's lacquered beak moved as if it were alive. "Sounds like a mystery to me," it said.

Spade confidently lit a cigarette. "Well, I'm good with mysteries. I just solved one."

"You didn't solve squat." The bird sneered.

Spade blinked. He had solved the case. The black bird was a fake—a decoy. They had scraped away a bit of its lacquered exterior and instead of priceless jewels they had found nothing but worthless lead. "What do you mean?" asked Spade suspiciously.

"You never did find the real falcon," said the bird. "Don't you wonder where it is?"

Spade shrugged. "The Russian has it, probably. Let Gutman and the others go after it if they want. They'll never find it."

"Wrong," said the bird. "The Russian doesn't have it. In fact, it's right around here somewhere."

Spade studied the bird carefully. "All right." He sat back down. "I'm listening."

"This is a real mystery." The bird shook its head. "Not like your usual work—which is always about who killed who, or who's banging whose wife. That's not a mystery, Spade. That's hardly even a puzzle."

Spade frowned.

"Real mysteries," the bird continued, "like, why do we exist? What's the nature of truth? Is there a higher power? They don't have solutions. That's what makes them mysteries."

Spade broke in. "Okay, so where's the real falcon?"

The bird sighed. "It's so obvious. I would think you would have figured it out by now. You're a detective, after all."

"Tell me."

"Didn't you ever read *The Purloined Letter*? The best place to hide something is in plain view, where no one will think to look for it."

Spade frowned. He walked across the room and lifted the black bird off the mantelpiece. It watched him, and chuckled as he turned it all around. Spade went back to his desk, brushed off the cigarette ash, and placed the bird in front of him. He flicked open his pocketknife and began scraping off more of the black lacquer. Underneath, of course, was nothing but lead.

"You're getting warmer," said the bird.

Spade opened his drawer and took out an iron file. He scraped away at the bird's leaden neck.

The bird chuckled. "Oh. You're getting even warmer now."

Lead filings flaked away. Spade scraped deeper and deeper. Finally, something began to emerge beneath the lead. Spade took a deep breath and blew, sending filings flying away into the smoky air.

Beneath the lacquer and the lead, the bird was made of gold and jewels, which glowed and sparkled even in the dim light of Spade's office. "Congratulations," the bird cried. "You solved the mystery!"

Spade got up and closed the buff-curtained windows.

A faint hint of ammonia drifted up from the courtyard.

"You're rich," the bird chanted. "You did it! Case solved."

"Something's not right here," Spade said.

He took up his pocketknife again, and poked the largest jewel.

The tip of the knife sank in a few centimeters, as if the jewel were made out of chocolate. Carefully, Spade started scraping it away altogether. Beneath, there was something else.

"Oh boy," said the bird. "Now you've done it. The plot thickens!"

Spade scraped away at more of the jewels.

"I should warn you," the bird intoned ominously, "if you keep digging into this matter, you may not like what you find."

Spade ignored him.

"Of course," the bird continued, "people in mysteries always say that, don't they? And does it ever happen? No way. The hero goes right ahead, catches the killer, and gets the girl. He gets his picture in the paper, and a handshake from the mayor. So go ahead, Spade. Don't listen to me. Keep digging. Everything will probably turn out all right in the end."

Spade carefully scraped away at the bird's throat. The faux jewels fell away like dry scabs. Beneath lay an intricate network of tiny machinery, cogs, and flashing lights.

"What's this?" Spade asked.

"Microcircuitry," the bird explained. "That's what allows me to talk."

"There's no such thing," Spade said.

"Well," the bird exclaimed. "Look who knows so much! Just because you've never seen microcircuitry before, you presume it can't possibly exist. What a fool. Read Hume some time, why don't you?"

Spade poked at the microcircuitry with his pocketknife. "What is all this?"

"Computers," the bird said. "Machines. That's what it's all about, Spade. Everything's a machine in one sense or another—your body, the universe. One day, you'll probably be replaced by a machine. Who knows?"

"I don't think so." Spade shook his head.

"Sound improbable? Why don't you try scraping away at your own outer layer? You might be surprised at what you find."

Spade absently ran a fingernail over the skin on his forearm.

"Leave well enough alone," the bird said. "Just this once."

"I think there's something else," Spade said. He began to scrape away at the microcircuitry. "A deeper layer."

The circuits popped and sparked and fell away. The tiny motors broke and oozed hydraulic fluid. The lights went dark.

"You're out of your league, Spade," the bird said. "Why don't you go back to murder, adultery, that sort of thing. That's more up your alley."

"I've broken the machines," Spade observed, "but you're still talking."

The bird nodded reluctantly. "Perhaps it isn't the microcircuitry after all."

The last layer of twisted metal mechanics flaked away. Beneath was a soft, porous surface.

"Looks like skin," Spade said.

"Maybe," said the bird.

Spade scraped away at the falcon's head. Its beak cracked off and fell away onto the floor. Spade carved away at its head, its eyes, and throat.

"It's a face!" he exclaimed, as the shape gradually took form.

"Oh. It gets better," said the bird.

"It's my face," said Spade finally.

A living, miniature version of his own face stared back at him from the carved portion of the black bird's head. Two brown, living eyes regarded him.

"So you see," said the bird, with its miniature human face, "this is how I can talk. I'm actually alive, after all."

Spade realized with a start why the bird's voice sounded so familiar. It was his own. "Why do you look like me?" Spade asked.

The bird sighed. "Because our perception of things, mysteries for example, are filtered through our own consciousness. If you keep digging for truth, eventually all you find is yourself."

"There must be something deeper," Spade insisted.

"I wouldn't count on it," said the bird.

Spade held the pocketknife towards the miniature face. The eyes regarded it nervously. "Spade? What are you doing?"

Sam Spade had never failed to solve a mystery, and he didn't intend to start now. "I want the truth," he said. With an unsteady hand he began to scrape away the flesh of the miniature face's cheek. A viscous, transparent fluid oozed out. Spade cut deeper. He began to scrape away at the falcon's throat.

"That's the jugular vein," the bird whispered hoarsely. "You might want to be careful around that."

"Will it kill you?" Spade asked.

"No," the bird answered.

Spade sliced it. A thick line of blood billowed forth, splattering dark spots across the desk. Spade gasped. "Blood?"

"Blood," the bird confirmed. "That's as deep as you're going to get."

Spade put down the knife and frowned. "That's the answer to your mystery? Blood?"

"I never said there was an answer." The bird scowled. "Quite the opposite, in fact."

Spade looked disgusted. "That's not a mystery."

"Au contraire," said the bird, "that is a true mystery. Real quests for the truth usually end in fits of self-destruction and bitter disappointment."

"I'm not finished yet," Spade said.

"Oh no? What's left to do? You've already—" The bird paused. "Uh-oh, Spade," it added, "looks like you're bleeding."

"What?" Spade stuck his hand to his throat, and it came away sticky and soaked with wet blood. He leapt to his feet, ran across the room, and leaned towards the mirror.

"I told you it wouldn't kill me," said the bird. "Beyond that, who's to say?"

Blood oozed from a gory section of Spade's cheek, and a deep gash ran across his throat. Spade seized a cloth to staunch the flow of blood out of his neck, but it soaked through instantly.

He spun around, and looked at the bird.

"I said you might not like what you found," the bird said, almost apologetically, "but you didn't listen."

Spade sank to his knees, his blood dripping wide, wet spots across the carpet.

"No girl for you," the bird scolded. "No handshake from the mayor." It hopped down off Spade's desk and slowly walked across the carpet towards him. "I told you that you were out of your league." The bird shook its head ruefully. "I said to stay away from real mysteries, but would you listen? You've learned your lesson now, though."

Spade's neck collapsed and his forehead struck against the carpet.

Spade watched warily as the bird loomed closer and closer, speaking with its identical, bleeding face. Finally, it stood over him, casting a dark shadow across his eyes.

"Nevermore," it answered, chuckling. "Nevermore!"

The Enchanted Bunny

➤ DAVID DRAKE ◄

JOE JOHNSON GOT INTO THE LITTLE CAR OF THE AIRPORT'S PEOPLE
Mover, ignoring the synthesized voice that was telling him to
keep away from the doors. Joe was trying to carry his attaché
case—stuffed with clothes as well as papers, since he'd used it for
an overnight bag on this quick trip to see the Senator—and also
to read the wad of photocopy the Senator had handed Joe in front
of the terminal "to glance through on the flight back."

The Senator hadn't wanted to be around when Joe read the
new section. He must have thought Joe wouldn't be pleased at
the way he'd handled the Poopsi LaFlamme Incident.

The Senator was right.

Joe sat down on a plastic-cushioned seat. At least the car was
empty except for Joe and the swarthy man—was he an Oriental?—
the swarthy Oriental at the far end. When Joe flew in the day
before, he'd shared the ride to the main concourse with a family
of seven, five of whom—including the putative father—were playing catch with a Nerf ball.

The doors closed. The People Mover said something about the
next stop being the Red Concourse and lurched into gentle motion.

Joe flipped another page of the chapter over the paper clip
holding it by the corner. *It was about that time that I met a
Miss LaFlamme, a friend of my wife Margaret, who worked, as I
understand it, as a dancer of some sort....*

Good God Almighty! Did the Senator—did the *ex*-Senator,

285

who was well known to be broke for a lot of the reasons that could make his memoirs a best-seller—really think he was going to get away with this?

The publishers hadn't paid a six-figure advance for stump speeches and homilies. They'd been promised scandal, they *wanted* scandal—

And the Senator's rewrite man, Joe Johnson, wanted scandal, too, because his two-percent royalty share was worth zip, zilch, *zero* if *The Image of a Public Man* turned out to be bumpf like this.

". . . stopping at the Red Concourse," said the synthesized voice. The car slowed, smoothly but abruptly enough that the attaché case slid on Joe's lap and he had to grab at it. More people got on.

Joe flipped the page.

—*helping Miss LaFlamme carry the bags of groceries to her suite. Unfortunately, the elevator*—

The People Mover shoop-shooped into motion again. Joe tightened his grip on the case. One of the new arrivals in the car was a crying infant.

Joe felt like crying also. Senator Coble had been *told* about the sort of thing that would go into the book. He'd *agreed*.

An elevator repairman at Poopsi LaFlamme's hotel had lifted the access plate to see why somebody'd pulled the emergency stop button between floors. He'd had a camera in his pocket. That had been the Senator's bad luck at the time; but the photo of two goggle-eyed drunks, wearing nothing but stupid expressions as they stared up from a litter of champagne bottles, would be *great* for the back jacket. . . .

Except apparently the Senator thought everybody—and particularly his publishers—had been living on a different planet when all that occurred.

"In a moment, we will be stopping at the Blue Concourse," said the People Mover dispassionately.

Joe flipped the page. *Unfortunately, pornographic photographs, neither of whose participants looked in the least like myself or Miss LaFlamme, began to circulate in the gutter press*—

And the Washington *Post.* And *Time* magazine. And—

The car halted. The people who'd boarded at the previous stop got off.

Joe flipped the page. —*avoided the notoriety inevitable with legal proceedings, because I remembered the words of my sainted mother, may she smile on me from her present home with Jesus.* "Fools' names," she told me, "and fools' faces, are always found in public—"

Damn! Joe's concourse!

The People Mover's doors were still open. Joe jumped up.

The paper clip slipped and half the ridiculous nonsense he'd been reading spewed across the floor of the car.

For a moment, Joe hesitated, but he had plenty of time to catch his plane. He bent and began picking up the mess.

The draft might be useless, but it wasn't something Joe wanted to leave lying around either. The swarthy man—maybe a Mongolian? He didn't look like any of the Oriental races with which Joe was familiar—watched without expression.

The car slowed and stopped again. Joe stuffed the papers into his attaché case and stepped out. He'd cross to the People Mover on the opposite side of the brightly-lighted concourse and go back one stop.

There were several dozen people in the concourse: businessmen, family groups, youths with backpacks and sports equipment that they'd have the dickens of a time fitting into the overhead stowage of the aircraft on which they traveled. Nothing unusual—

Except that they were all Japanese.

Well, a tourist group; or chance; and anyway, it didn't matter to Joe Johnson. . . .

But the faces all turned toward him as he started across the tile floor. People backed away. A little boy grabbed his mother's kimono-clad legs and screamed in abject terror.

Joe paused. A pair of airport policemen began running down the escalator from the upper level of the concourse. Joe couldn't understand the words they were shouting at him.

The policemen wore flat caps and brass-buttoned frock coats, and they were both drawing the sabers that clattered in patent-leather sheaths at their sides.

Joe hurled himself back into the People Mover just as the doors closed. He stared out through the windows at the screaming foreign crowd. He was terrified that people would burst in on him before the car started to move—

Though the faces he saw looked as frightened as his own must be.

The People Mover's circuitry shunted it into motion. Joe breathed out in relief and looked around him. Only then did he realize that he wasn't in the car he'd left.

There were no seats or any other amenities within the vehicle. The walls were corrugated metal. They'd been painted a bilious hospital-green at some point, but now most of their color came from rust.

Scratched graffiti covered the walls, the floor, and other scribblings. The writing wasn't in any language Joe recognized.

Joe set his attaché case between his feet and rubbed his eyes with both hands. He felt more alone than he ever had before in his life. He must have fallen and hit his head; but he wasn't waking up.

The car didn't sound as smooth as a piece of electronics any more. Bearings squealed like lost souls. There was a persistent slow jarring as the flat spot in a wheel hit the track, again and again.

The People Mover—if that's what it was now—slowed and stopped with a sepulchral moan. The door didn't open automatically. Joe hesitated, then gripped the handle and slid the panel sideways.

There wasn't a crowd of infuriated Japanese waiting on the concourse. There wasn't even a concourse, just a dingy street, and it seemed to be deserted.

Joe got out of the vehicle. It was one of a series of cars which curved out of sight among twisted buildings. The line began to move again, very slowly, as Joe watched transfixed. He couldn't tell what powered the train, but it certainly wasn't electric motors in the individual cars.

There was a smell of sulphur in the air, and there was very little light.

Joe looked up. The sky was blue, but its color was that of a cobalt bowl rather than heaven. There seemed to be a solid dome covering the city, because occasionally a streak of angry red crawled across it. The trails differed in length and placement, but they always described the same curves.

The close-set buildings were three and four stories high, with peak roofs and many gables. The windows were barred, and none of them were lighted.

Joe swallowed. His arms clutched the attaché case to his chest. The train clanked and squealed behind him, moving toward some unguessable destination. . . .

Figures moved half a block away: a man was walking his dogs on the dim street. Claws or heel taps clicked on the cracked concrete.

"Sir?" Joe called. His voice sounded squeaky. "Excuse me, sir?"

They were very big dogs. Joe knew a man who walked a pet cougar, but these blurred, sinewy forms were more the size of tigers.

There was a rumbling overhead like that of a distant avalanche. The walker paused. Joe looked up.

The dome reddened with great blotches. *Clouds*, Joe thought—and then his mind coalesced the blotches into a single shape, a human face distorted as if it were being pressed down onto the field of a photocopier.

A face that must have been hundreds of yards across.

Red, sickly light flooded down onto the city from the roaring dome. The two "dogs" reared up onto their hind legs. They had lizard teeth and limbs like armatures of wire. The "man" walking them was the same as his beasts, and they were none of them from any human universe.

A fluting *Ka-Ka-Ka-Ka-Ka* came from the throats of the demon trio as they loped toward Joe.

Joe turned. He was probably screaming. The train clacked past behind him at less than a walking pace. Joe grabbed the handle of one of the doors. The panel slid a few inches, then stopped with a rusty shriek.

Joe shrieked louder and wrenched the door open with a convulsive effort. He leaped into the interior. For a moment, he was aware of nothing but the clawed hand slashing toward him.

Then Joe landed on stiff cushions and a man's lap, while a voice said, "Bless me, Kiki! The wizard we've been looking for!"

"I beg your pardon," said Joe, disentangling himself from the other man in what seemed to be a horse-drawn carriage clopping over cobblestones.

It struck Joe that he'd never heard "I beg your pardon" used as a real apology until now; but that sure wasn't the *only* first he'd racked up on this trip to Atlanta.

The other man in the carriage seemed to be in his late teens. He was dressed in a green silk jumper with puffed sleeves and breeches, high stockings, and a fur cloak.

A sword stood upright with the chape of its scabbard between the man's feet. The weapon had an ornate hilt, but it was of a serviceable size and stiffness. Joe rubbed his nose, where he'd given himself a good crack when he hit the sword.

A tiny monkey peeked out from behind the youth's right ear, then his left, and furiously. The animal wore a miniature fur cloak fastened with a diamond brooch.

The monkey's garment reminded Joe that wherever he was, it wasn't Atlanta in the summertime. The carriage had gauze curtains rather than glazing over the windows. Joe shivered in his cotton slacks and short-sleeved shirt.

"I'm Delendor, Master Sorcerer," the youth said. "Though of course you'd already know that, wouldn't you? May I ask how you choose to be named here in Hamisch?"

Kiki hopped from Delendor's shoulder to Joe's. The monkey's body was warm and smelled faintly of stale urine. It crawled around the back of Joe's neck, making clicking sounds.

"I'm Joe Johnson," Joe said. "I think I am. God."

He clicked open the latches of his attaché case. Everything inside was as he remembered it, including the dirty socks.

Kiki reached down, snatched the pen out of Joe's shirt pocket, and hurled it through the carriage window at the head of a burly man riding a donkey in the opposite direction.

The man shouted, "Muckin' bassit!"

Joe shouted, "Hey!"

Delendor shouted, "Kiki! For shame!"

The monkey chirped, leaped, and disappeared behind Delendor's head again.

"I *am* sorry," Delendor said. "Was it valuable? We can stop and . . . ?"

And discuss things with the guy on the donkey, Joe thought. "No thanks, I've got enough problems," he said aloud. "It was just a twenty-nine-cent pen, after all."

Though replacing it might be a little difficult.

"You see," Delendor continued, "Kiki's been my only friend for eight years, since father sent my sister Estoril off to Glenheim to be fostered by King Belder. I don't get along very well with my brothers Glam and Groag, you know . . . them being older, I suppose."

"Eight years?" Joe said, focusing on a little question because he sure-hell didn't want to think about the bigger ones. "How long do monkeys live, anyway?"

"Oh!" said Delendor. "I don't—I'd rather not think about that." He wrapped his chittering pet in his cloak and held him tightly.

Joe flashed a sudden memory of himself moments before, clutching his attaché case to his chest and praying that he was somewhere other than in the hell which his senses showed him. At least Kiki was alive....

"Estoril's visiting us any day now," Delendor said, bubbly again. Kiki peeked out of the cloak, then hopped to balance on the carriage window. "It'll be wonderful to see her again. And to find a great magician to help me, too! My stars must really be in alignment!"

"I'm not a magician," Joe said in a dull voice.

Reaction was setting in. He stared at the photocopied chapter of the Senator's memoirs. *That* sort of fantasy he was used to.

"After you help me slay the dragon," Delendor continued, proving that he hadn't been listening to Joe, "I'll get more respect. And of course we'll save the kingdom."

"Of course," muttered Joe.

Kiki reached out the window and snatched the plume from the helmet of a man in half-armor who carried a short-hafted spontoon. The spontoon's ornate blade was more symbol than weapon. The man bellowed.

"Kiki!" Delendor cried. "Not the Civic Guard!" He took the plume away from his pet and leaned out the window of the carriage as the horses plodded along.

"Oh," said the guardsman—the cop—in a changed voice as he trotted beside the vehicle to retrieve his ornament. "No harm done, Your Highness. Have your little joke."

"Ah ..." Joe said. "Ah, Delendor? Are you a king?"

"Of course not," Delendor said in surprise. "My father, King Morhaven, is still alive."

He pursed his lips. "And anyway, both Glam and Groag are older than I am. Though that wouldn't *prevent* father..."

Joe hugged his attaché case. He closed his eyes. The carriage was unsprung, but its swaying suggested that it was suspended from leather straps to soften the rap of the cobblestones.

God.

"Now," the prince went on cheerfully, "I suppose the dragon's the important thing ... but what I *really* want you to do is to find my enchanted princess."

Joe opened his eyes. "I'm not ..." he began.

But there wasn't any point in repeating what Delendor wouldn't listen to anyway. For that matter, there was nothing unreasonable about assuming that a man who plopped out of midair into a moving carriage was a magician.

The prince opened the locket on his neck chain and displayed it to Joe. The interior could have held a miniature painting—but it didn't. It was a mirror, and it showed Joe his own haggard face.

"I've had the locket all my life," Delendor said, "a gift from my sainted mother. It was the most beautiful girl in the world—and as I grew older, so did the girl in the painting. But only a few weeks ago, I opened the locket and it was a *rabbit,* just as you see it now. I'm sure she's the princess I'm to marry, and that she's been turned into a bunny by an evil sorcerer."

Delendor beamed at Joe. "Don't you think?"

"I suppose next," Joe said resignedly, "you're going to tell me about your wicked stepmother."

"I beg your pardon!" snapped the prince, giving the phrase its usual connotations.

Delendor drew himself up straight and closed the locket. "My mother Blumarine was a saint! Everyone who knew her says so. And when she died giving birth to me, my father never *thought* of marrying a third time."

"Ah," said Joe. "Look, sorry, that's not what I meant." It occurred to him that Delendor's sword was too respectable a piece of hardware to be only for show.

"I'm not sure what father's first wife was like," the prince went on, relaxing immediately. "But I think she must have been all right. Estoril more than balances Glam and Groag, don't you think?"

"I, ah," Joe said. "Well, I'll take your word for it."

"They say that Mother had been in love with a young knight in her father's court," Delendor went on. "Her father was King Belder of Glenheim, of course. But they couldn't marry until he'd proved himself—which he tried to do when the dragon appeared in Glenheim that time. And it almost broke Mother's heart when the dragon ate the young man. King Belder married her to my father at once to take her, well, her mind off the tragedy, but they say she never really recovered."

Kiki leaned out of the window and began chittering happily. Delendor stroked his pet's fur and said, "Yes, yes, we're almost home, little friend."

He beamed at Joe once more. "That's why it's so important

for me to slay the dragon now that it's reappeared, you see," the prince explained. "As a gift to my sainted mother. And *then* we'll find my enchanted princess."

Joe buried his face in his hands. "Oh, God," he muttered.

Something warm patted his thumb. Kiki was trying to console him.

The measured hoofbeats echoed, then the windows darkened for a moment as the carriage passed beneath a masonry gateway. Joe pushed the curtain aside for a better look.

They'd driven into a flagged courtyard in the center of a three-story stone building. The inner walls glittered with hundreds of diamond-paned windows. Servants in red and yellow livery bustled about the coach, while other servants in more prosaic garb busied themselves with washing, smithing, carpentry—and apparently lounging about.

"The Palace of Hamisch," Delendor said with satisfaction.

Joe nodded. A real fairytale palace looked more practical—and comfortable—than the nineteenth-century notion of what a fairytale palace should be.

A real fairy-tale palace. God 'elp us.

The carriage pulled up beneath a porte cochere. Servants flung open the doors with enthusiasm to hand out the prince and his companion.

Joe didn't know quite how to react. He let a pair of liveried youths take his hands, but the whole business made him feel as though he were wearing a corsage and a prom dress.

Kiki jumped from Delendor's right shoulder to his left and back again. Joe noticed that each of the nearest servants kept a hand surreptitiously close to his cap.

The carriage clucked into motion. There was a stable on the opposite side of the courtyard.

"Your Highness," said the fiftyish man whose age and corpulence marked him as the palace major domo, "your father and brothers have been meeting in regard to the, ah, dragon; and King Morhaven specifically asked that when you arrived, you be sent—"

"Is my sister here yet?" Delendor interrupted.

"Yes," said the major domo, "the Princess Estoril has been placed in her old rooms in—"

As the carriage swung into the stables, the driver turned and smirked over his shoulder at Joe. He was the swarthy maybe-Mongolian who'd shared Joe's car in Atlanta.

"*Hey!*" Joe bawled as he took a long stride. His foot slipped on the smooth flagstones and he fell on his arse.

The coach disappeared into the stables.

Instead of making another attempt to run after the man, Joe stood and used the attention that his performance had just gained him to demand, "Prince! Your Highness, that is. Who was driving us?"

Delendor blinked. "How on earth would I know?" he said. "I just called for a coach, of course."

The nods of all the servants underscored a statement as obviously true as the fact the sun rose in the east.

Did the sun here rise in the east?

"Well, anyway, Clarkson," the prince went on, turning again to the major domo, "find a room for my friend here in my wing. I'll go see Estoril at once."

"Ah, Your Highness," the major domo replied with the fixed smile of an underling caught in the middle. "Your father did specifically ask that—"

"Oh, don't worry about that, Clarkson!" Delendor threw over his shoulder as he strode into the palace. "My friend Joe here is a mighty magician. He and I will take care of the dragon, never fear!"

Clarkson watched as his master disappeared, then sized up Joe. "No doubt . . ." the major domo said neutrally. "Well, we're used to His Highness' enthusiasms, aren't we?"

Joe nodded, though he was pretty sure that the question wasn't one which Clarkson expected him to answer.

Joe's room was on the third floor, overlooking the courtyard. Its only furnishings were a bed frame and a cedar chest. There were two casement windows and, in one corner against the outer wall, a fireplace which shared a flue with the room next door.

The fire wasn't set, and the room was colder than Hell.

Clarkson watched with glum disdain as a housekeeper opened the cedar chest with a key hanging from her belt. She handed out feather comforters to lower-ranking maids. They spread them over the bed frame in what looked like a warm, if not particularly soft, arrangement.

"Why isn't the fire laid?" the major domo demanded peevishly. "And there should be a chamberpot, you *know* what happens when there isn't a chamberpot. And on the courtyard side, too!"

"I don't know where the girl's gotten to," the housekeeper said with a grimace. "I'm sure it'll be seen to shortly, sir."

"Ah," Joe said. "Ah, Clarkson? I wonder if you could find me some warmer clothes? A fur coat would be perfect."

The major domo stared at Joe disdainfully. "That's scarcely my affair," he said. "I suppose you can talk to the chamberlain. Or to the prince, no doubt."

Enough was enough.

Joe set his attaché case down and stood with his hands on his hips.

"Oh?" he said, letting the past hour of terror and frustration raise his voice into real anger. "Oh? It doesn't matter to you, then? Well, Clarkson, does it matter to you if you spend the rest of eternity as a fat green frog in the castle moat?"

The maids and housekeeper scurried out of the room, their mouths forming ovals of silent horror. Clarkson's face set itself in a rictus. "Yes, of course, milord," he muttered through stiff lips. "Yes, of course, I'll take care of that immediately."

The major domo dodged through the door like a caroming pinball, keeping as far from Joe as he could. He bowed, spreading his arms—and grabbed the handle to pull the door closed behind him.

Which left Joe alone, as cold as fear and an all-stone room could make a man.

He stared out one of the diamond-paned windows. It was clean enough, but there was frost on both sides of the glass. Maybe one of the half-seen figures in the rooms across the courtyard was the maybe-Mongolian, who'd maybe brought Joe—

His door opened and banged shut again behind a slip of a girl in drab clothing. She shot the flimsy bolt and ran two steps toward the cedar chest before she realized Joe had turned from the window and was watching her in amazement.

Joe thought she was going to scream, but she choked the sound off by clapping both her hands over her own mouth. Through her fingers she whimpered, "Please help me! Please hide me!"

"Coo-ee!" called a man's deep voice from the hallway.

"Here chick-chick-chickee!" boomed another man.

A fist hammered Joe's door. "Better not make us come in for you, chickie," the first voice warned.

Great.

"Sure," Joe whispered.

The girl was short and rail-thin. Mousy brown hair trailed out from beneath her mobcap. She started for the chest again.

Joe grabbed her by the shoulder. "Not there," he said, raising his voice a little because the banging on the door had become louder and constant. He threw back the top comforter.

"*There,*" he explained, pointing. She gave him a hopeful, terrified look and flattened herself crossways on the bed.

Joe folded the thick feather quilt over her. Then he slid up one of the windows—it couldn't possibly make the room colder—and drew open the bolt just as the door panel started to splinter inward under the impacts of something harder than a hand.

Two black-bearded men, built like NFL nose guards, forced their way into the room. They'd been hammering the door with their sword pommels.

Delendor's weapon had looked serviceable. The swords *this* pair carried would have been two-handers—in hands smaller than theirs.

They didn't even bother to look at Joe. "Where are you, bitch?" one shouted. "We were just gonna show you a good time, but by god it'll be the *last* time fer you now!"

"Look, I'm here as a guest of—" Joe began.

"*There* we go!" the other intruder boomed as his eyes lighted on the cedar chest as the only hiding place in the room.

He kicked the chest with the toe of his heavy leather boot. "Come out, come out, wherever you are!" he shouted.

His fellow rammed his big sword through the top of the cedar chest and splinteringly out the back. Its point sparked on the stone flooring.

Both men stabbed repeatedly at the fragile wood until it was quite obvious that the chest was empty.

They'd thought she was inside that, Joe realized. His body went cold. He'd already put his case down. Otherwise his nerveless hands would've dropped it.

"We saw 'er come in, so she musta got out the . . ." one of the men said. He peered through the open casement. There was no ledge, and the walls were a smooth, sheer drop to the flagstone courtyard.

The two men turned toward Joe simultaneously. They held their bare swords with the easy naturalness of accountants keying numbers into adding machines.

"And just who the hell are you, boyo?" asked the one who'd first stabbed the cedar chest.

In what seemed likely to be his last thought, Joe wondered whether the FAA kept statistics on the number of air travelers who were hacked to death by sword-carrying thugs.

"He's the magician who's going to help your royal brother slay the dragon, Groag," said a cold voice from the doorway.

Which would make the other thug Glam; and no, they didn't show much family resemblance to Delendor.

Joe turned. The brothers had jumped noticeably when the newcomer spoke; and anyway, turning his back on Glam and Groag wouldn't make them *more* likely to dismember him.

"I'm Joe Johnson," he said, holding out his hand to be shaken. "I'm glad to see you."

Classic understatement.

The newcomer was tall, gray, and fine-featured. He wore black velvet robes, rather like academic regalia—though heavier, which this damned unheated building made a good idea. He stared at Joe's hand for a moment, then touched it in an obvious attempt to puzzle out an unfamiliar form of social interchange.

"My name is Ezekiel," he said. "I—"

"I think we'll go now," muttered Glam, bouncing off the door-jamb in much the fashion that the major domo had done minutes earlier. Groag followed him on the same course. Joe noticed that the brothers had sheathed their swords.

The room returned to normal size with Glam and Groag out of it. There were *some* advantages to being mistaken for a magician.

"Ah, thanks," Joe said. "I, ah . . . didn't like the way things were going."

"They're not bad lads," Ezekiel said with what seemed to be his universal air of cool detachment. "A little headstrong, perhaps. But I couldn't have you turning the king's elder sons into . . . frogs, I believe I heard?"

He raised a quizzical eyebrow.

Joe shrugged. Before he spoke—before he decided *what* to say—a train of servants streamed into the room, carrying furs; charcoal and kindling with which they laid a fire; and a chamberpot.

"I suppose," Ezekiel pressed, "you have your apparatus with you? You don't—" he paused "—plan to deal with the dragon unaided, do you?"

"I was wondering," Joe temporized, "if you could tell me something about this dragon?"

Ezekiel blinked. "I'm not sure what it is you want to know," he said reasonably enough. "It's a dragon more than thirty yards long and invulnerable to weapons except at one point on its body . . . which no one in recorded history has discovered."

He smiled coldly. "It digs a burrow deep in the rock and sleeps twenty years of twenty-one, which is good . . . but in the year the beast wakes, it does quite enough damage to ruin a kingdom for a generation. Glenheim has barely recovered from the most recent visitation . . . and this time, the creature has chosen to devour a path through Hamisch. As no doubt your friend Prince Delendor has explained."

The servants were leaving with as much dispatch as they'd arrived. They carried out the scraps of cedar chest with a muttered promise of a replacement.

The fire burned nicely and might even have warmed the room, except that the window was still open. Joe shut it.

"Delendor was too occupied with seeing his sister to give me much of the background," he said neutrally.

Ezekiel's face twisted with disgust, the first emotion he'd shown since he arrived. "Prince Delendor's affection for his sister is, I'm sorry to say, unnatural," he said. "The king was well advised to send Estoril away when he did."

His lips pursed, shutting off the flow of excessively free words. "I wish you luck with your difficult task," Ezekiel concluded formally. "It's of course an honor to meet so powerful a colleague as yourself."

He left the room, and Joe closed the door behind him.

Joe took a deep breath. Well, he was still alive, which he wouldn't've bet would be the case a few minutes ago.

"Ah," he said to the bed. "You can come out now."

The folded comforter lay so flat that for an instant Joe thought the girl had been spirited away—which fit the way other things had been happening, though it wouldn't've improved his mood.

"Oh, bless you, sir," said her muffled voice as the feathers humped. The girl slipped out and stood before him again.

She wasn't really a girl. Her face was that of a woman in her mid-twenties, maybe a few years younger than Joe. Her slight form and, even more, her air of frightened diffidence made her look much younger at a glance.

"I'll . . ." she said. "I think it's safe for me to leave now. Bless—"

"Wait a darn minute!" Joe said. He put out his arm to stop her progress toward the door, then jerked back—furious with himself—when he saw the look of terror flash across her face.

"Look," he said, "I'd just like to know your name—"

"Mary, sir," she said with a deep curtsey. When she rose, she was blushing.

"For *God*'s sake, call me Joe!" he said, more harshly than he'd meant.

Joe cleared his throat. His new fur garments were stacked in a corner. He donned a cloak as much to give his hands something to do as for the warmth of it. "And, ah," he said, "maybe you can give me a notion of what's going on? I mean—"

He *didn't* mean Glam and Groag, as Mary's expression of fear and distaste suggested she thought he did.

Joe understood the brothers well enough. They were jocks in a society which put even fewer restrictions on jock behavior than did a college dorm.

"No, no," Joe said, patting her thin shoulder. "Not that. Just tell me if what Ezekiel said about the dragon's true. And who *is* Ezekiel, anyway?"

"Why, he's the royal sorcerer," Mary said in amazement. "And a very powerful one, though nowhere near as powerful as you, Master Joe. It would take Ezekiel weeks to turn somebody into a frog, and I'm sure he doesn't know how to deal with the dragon."

"Oh, boy," Joe said. From the look behind Ezekiel's eyes when they talked, the magician had been contemplating the start of a multiweek project that would leave him with one fewer rival—and the moat with one more frog.

"I'm sure he must really hate you, Master Joe," Mary said, confirming Joe's guess. "Of course, Ezekiel doesn't really like anybody, though he does things for Glam and Groag often enough."

Does this palace even have a moat?

"Look, Mary," he said "is Delendor the only guy trying to kill this dragon, then? Isn't there an army or—you know, something?"

"Well, many brave knights have tried to slay the dragon over the years," Mary said, frowning at the unfamiliar word "army." "And sometimes commoners or even peasants have attacked the beast, but that didn't work either. So now there's . . . well, Glam and Groag say they've been spying out the dragon's habits, but I don't think anybody *really* wants to get near it."

A look of terrible sadness crossed the woman's face. "Except for Prince Delendor. He's serious. Oh, Master Joe, you *will* save him, won't you?"

Joe smiled and patted the woman's shoulder again. "We'll see what we can do," he said.

But dollars to doughnuts, there was damn-all a freelance writer *could* do about this problem.

Joe waited in his room; at first in the expectation that Delendor would be back shortly . . . and later, because Joe didn't have anyplace better to go. Anyway, the scatterbrained youth *might* still arrive.

Joe carried the *Fasti* to read on the airplane. Ovid's erudite myths and false etymologies had at least as much bearing on this world as they did on the one from which the People Mover had spirited Joe away.

After an hour or so, Joe snagged the first servant to pass in the hallway and asked for an armchair. What he got was solid, cushionless, and not particularly comfortable—but it arrived within fifteen minutes of Joe's request. The men carrying the chair panted as if they'd run all the way from the basement with it.

The frog story seemed to have gotten around.

But nobody else came to Joe's room until a servant summoned him to dinner in the evening.

"It's so brave of you to return to Hamisch to show solidarity when the dragon threatens, Estoril," said Delendor. "Most people are fleeing the other way."

Kiki sat on the prince's head. When Delendor leaned forward to see his sister past his two huge brothers and King Morhaven, the youth and monkey looked like a totem pole.

Estoril was black-haired, like Glam and Groag, but her fine features were at least as lovely as Delendor's were boyishly handsome.

"Or into the city," said the king gloomily. "We're going to have

a real sanitation problem soon, especially because of the herds
of animals."

"I don't think that will be a serious difficulty, Your Highness,"
said Ezekiel, beside Estoril at the far end of the table from Joe.
"The creature demolished the walls of Glenheim within minutes
on its previous appearance . . . and, as I recall, made short work
of the cattle sheltering there."

"Well," said Delendor brightly, "*that* won't be a problem here,
because I'm going to slay the dragon. Right, Joe?"

"Actually," said Estoril, giving Delendor a look that Joe couldn't
fathom, "my visiting now had nothing to do with the dragon.
Katya—that was Blumarine's old nurse—died. In her last hours,
she told me some things that . . . well, I thought I'd visit again."

Ezekiel took a sip of wine that Joe thought could double as
antifreeze. "I met Katya once," he said. "She was a wise woman
of some power. Did *you* know her, Joe?" the magician added
sharply.

Joe choked on a mouthful of stewed carrot.

"Uh-uh," he managed to mumble without spraying. The meal
ran to grilled meat and boiled vegetables, both of which would
have been okay if they'd been taken off the heat within an hour
or so of being thoroughly cooked.

Estoril turned. Joe couldn't see her face, but there was steel in
her voice as she said, "According to Katya, Blumarine herself was
a powerful magician. Was that the case, Master Ezekiel?"

"My mother?" Delendor blurted in amazement.

"My understanding, dear Princess," Ezekiel said in a deliberately
condescending voice, "is that your stepmother may have been a
student of wisdom; but that if she ever practiced the craft, it was
on the most rarified of levels. At any rate—"

The magician paused to drink the rest of his wine with apparent satisfaction. "At any rate," he went on, "it's certain that she
couldn't prevent the young knight with whom she was romanti-
cally linked from being killed and eaten by the dragon."

The table waited in frozen silence.

"I believe," Ezekiel concluded, "that his name was Delendor,
too, was it not, Princess?"

King Morhaven hid his own face in his winecup. Glam and
Groag chuckled like pools of bubbling mud.

The hell of embarrassment was that it only afflicted decent—or at least partially-decent—people. "I wonder if any of you can tell me," Joe said loudly to change the subject, "about the kind of guns you have here?"

Everyone stared at him. "Guns?" the king repeated.

Well, they'd been speaking English until now. "I mean," Joe explained, "the things that shoot, you know, bullets?"

This time it was Delendor who said, "Bullets?"

Ezekiel sneered.

Right, back to words of one syllable. After all, Joe had worked with the Senator. . . . "What," said Joe, "do you use to shoot things at a distance?"

"Distance" was two syllables.

"Arbalests, of course," said Morhaven. He pointed to a servant and ordered, "You there. Bring Master Joe an arbalest."

"Or you can throw rocks," Delendor noted happily. "I met a peasant who was very clever that way. Knocked squirrels right out of trees."

"From what I've been told," Joe said, "I doubt that slinging pebbles at your dragon is going to do a lot of good."

"What?" Groag said to Delendor in honest horror. "You're going to throw rocks at the dragon instead of facing it with your sword?"

The servant was returning to the table, carrying a massive crossbow that looked as though it weighed twenty pounds.

And that meant, just possibly, that Joe *could* arrange for Delendor to kill the dragon!

"Why, that's disgusting!" Glam added, echoing Groag's tone. "Even for a little shrimp like you!"

"Hang on—" Joe said. Everybody ignored him.

"I said nothing of the sort!" Delendor spluttered, his voice rising an octave. "How dare you suggest that I'd act in an unknightly fashion?"

Joe snapped his fingers and shouted, "Wait a minute!"

The room fell silent. Servants flattened. Delendor's brothers flinched as if ready to duck under the table to preserve themselves from frogness.

"Right," said Joe in a normal voice. "Now, the problem isn't knightly honor, it's the dragon. Is that correct?"

Morhaven and all three of his sons opened their mouths to object. Before they could speak, Estoril said, "Yes, that *is* correct."

She looked around the table. Her eyes were the color of a sunlit glacier. The men closed their mouths again without speaking.

"Right," Joe repeated. "Now, I know you've got charcoal. Do you have sulphur?"

The proportions were seventy-five, fifteen, ten. But Joe couldn't for the life of him remember whether the fifteen was charcoal or sulphur.

Everyone else at the table looked at Ezekiel. The magician frowned and said, "Yes, I have sulphur in my laboratory. But I don't see—"

"Wait," said Joe, because this was the kicker, the make-or-break. He swallowed. "Do you have potassium nitrate here? Saltpeter? I think it comes from . . ."

Joe *thought* it came from under manure piles, but unless the locals had the stuff refined, he was damned if he could find it himself. He wasn't a chemist, he just had slightly misspent his youth.

"Yes . . ." Ezekiel agreed. "I have a store of saltpeter."

"Then, by god, I *can* help you kill this dragon!" Joe said in a rush of heady triumph. "No problem!"

Reality froze him. "Ah . . ." he added. "That is, if Master Ezekiel helps by providing materials and, ah, equipment for my work?"

"And *I'll* slay—" Delendor began.

"Father," Estoril interjected with enough clarity and volume to cut through her brother's burbling, "Delendor is after all rather young. Perhaps Glam or—"

"What?" roared Glam and Groag together.

"What?" shrilled Delendor as he jumped to his feet. Kiki leaped from the prince's head and described a cartwheel in the air. "I *demand* the right to prove myself by—"

"*Silence!*" boomed King Morhaven. He stood, and for the first time Joe was reminded that the hunched, aging man *was* a monarch.

The king pointed at Delendor and dipped his finger. The youth subsided into his chair as if Morhaven had thrown a control lever.

King Morhaven transferred his gaze and pointing finger to Joe. "You," he said, "will prepare your dragon-killing magic." He turned. "And you, Ezekiel," he continued, "will help your colleague in whatever fashion he requires."

The magician—the real magician—nodded his cold face. "I hear and obey, Your Highness," he said.

Morhaven turned majestically again. "Delendor," he said, "your sister is correct that you are young; but the task is one at which seasoned heroes have failed in ages past. You have my permission to try your skill against the monster."

The king's face looked haggard, but there was no denying the authority in his voice as he added, "And if you succeed in saving the kingdom, my son, then there can be only one suitable recompense."

Joe blinked. If he understood correctly (and there couldn't be much doubt about what Morhaven meant), then the king had just offered the crown to his youngest son for slaying the dragon.

No wonder everybody was staring in amazement as King Morhaven seated himself again.

The regal gesture ended with a thump and a startled gasp from the king as his fanny hit the throne six inches below where it had been when he stood.

Kiki, chirruping happily, ran for the door. The monkey dragged behind him the thick cushion he'd abstracted from the throne while Morhaven was standing.

Joe, wearing an ankle-length flannel nightgown (at home he slept nude; but at home he didn't sleep in a stone icebox), had just started to get into bed when there was a soft rapping on his door.

He straightened. The fireplace held only the memory of an orange glow, but it was enough for him to navigate to the door past the room's few objects.

"Yes?" he whispered, standing to the side of the stone jamb in memory of the way the brothers' swords had ripped the cedar chest.

"Please, sir?" responded a tiny voice he thought he recognized.

Joe opened the door. Mary, a thin wraith, slipped in and shoved the door closed before Joe could.

"Please, sir," she repeated. "If you could hide me for a few nights yet, I'd be ever so grateful."

"What?" Joe said. "Mary, for Pete's sake! I'd like to help, but there's nowhere—"

And as she spoke, the obvious thought struck him dumb. *No! She was the size of an eight-year-old, she was as helpless as an eight-year old, and the very thought—*

Ick!

"Oh, Master Joe, I'll sleep at the foot of your bed," Mary explained. "I'll be ever so quiet, I promise. I'm just so afraid."

With excellent reason, Joe realized. If the dragon was half as real and dangerous as Glam and Groag, then this place was long overdue for the invention of gunpowder.

And anyway, there wasn't much time to spend thinking about the situation, unless he wanted them both to freeze.

"Right," Joe said. "We'll, ah—"

But the girl—the woman!—had already eeled between the upper and lower comforters, lying crosswise as she'd hidden this afternoon. Joe got in more gingerly, keeping his knees bent.

"Ah, Mary?" he said after a moment.

"Joe sir?"

"Could King Morhaven make Delendor his successor under, ah, your constitution?"

"Oh, yes!" the muffled voice responded. "And wouldn't it be wonderful? But only when Delendor shows what a hero he is. Oh, Master Joe, sir, you're a gift from heaven to all Hamisch!"

"Or something," muttered Joe. But now that he'd thought of gunpowder, he was pretty confident.

Arnault, the royal armorer, was a husky, sooty man wearing a leather apron. His forearms were the size of Joe's calves; blisters from flying sparks gave them an ulcerated look.

"Yaas, master?" he rumbled in a voice that suggested that he was happier in his forge than being summoned to the new magician's laboratory.

Joe wasn't thrilled about the laboratory either. He was using the palace's summer kitchen, built in a corner of the courtyard and open on all sides to vent the heat of the ovens and grills during hot weather.

The weather now was cold enough that Joe wore fur mittens to keep the brass mortar and pestle from freezing his hands. On the other hand, the light was good; there was plenty of work space . . . and if something went wrong, the open sides would be a real advantage.

"Right," said Joe to the armorer. "I want you to make me a steel tube about three feet long and with a bore of . . ." *Forty-five caliber? No, that might be a little tricky.*

Joe cleared his throat. "A bore of about a half inch. Somewhere around that, it doesn't matter precisely so long as it's the same all the way along."

"Whazat?"

"And, ah," Joe added, beaming as though a display of confidence would banish the utter confusion from the armorer's face, "make sure the tube's walls are thick. Maybe you could use a wagon axle or something."

After all, they wouldn't have to carry the gun far.

"What?" the armorer repeated.

"I thought you wanted the tube to be steel, Joe," said Estoril. "Or was that one of the paradoxes of your craft?"

There were at least a hundred spectators, mostly servants. They crowded the sides of the summer kitchen to goggle at the magical preparations. He'd ordered them away half a dozen times, but that just meant the mass drew back a few yards into the courtyard . . . and drifted inward as soon as Joe bent over his paraphernalia again.

Of course, Joe could demand a closed room and bar himself in it until he'd finished the process—or blown himself to smithereens. That still didn't seem like the better choice.

Joe didn't even bother telling the members of the royal family to leave him alone. But if he had to do this over, he'd keep a couple frogs in his coat pockets and let them out at strategic times. . . .

The spectators weren't the immediate problem, though.

"Right," Joe said with his chirpy face on. "How thick are your axles here?"

"Waal," said the armorer, "they's aboot—" He mimed a four-inch diameter with his hands.

"But they're wooden!" said Delendor. "Ah, aren't they?" He looked around at the other spectators.

Ezekiel nodded silently. Joe thought he saw the magician's mouth quirk toward a smile.

"Right," said Joe. "Wood."

He swallowed. "Well, all I meant was that you need to get a round steel rod about this thick"—he curled his middle finger against the tip of his thumb, making a circle of about two inches in diameter—"and a yard long. Then—"

"Naow," said the armorer.

"No?" Joe translated aloud. His control slipped. "Well, why the hell *not*, then?"

"Whaar's a body t' foind so much stale, thaan?" the armorer demanded. "Is a body t' coot the edge fram avery sword in the kingdom, thaan?"

The big man's complexion was suffusing with blood and rage, and Joe didn't like the way the fellow's hands knotted about one another. The armorer wouldn't have to strangle a man in the normal fashion. He could just grab a victim's head and give a quick jerk, like a hunter finishing a wounded pheasant. . . .

"And after you have provided Arnault with the billet of steel, Master Joe," Ezekiel interjected—and thank goodness for the sardonic magician for a change, because he directed Arnault's smoldering eyes away from Joe. "Then I think you'll have to teach him your magical technique of boring the material."

The armorer didn't deign to nod.

"Right," said Joe, as though the false word were a catechism. Black gloom settled over his soul.

Joe didn't know anything about metalworking. If he *had* some background in metallurgy, he still wouldn't know how to adapt modern techniques to things Arnault could accomplish . . . which seemed to mean hammering bars into rough horseshoe shapes.

"Perhaps Arnault could weld a bundle of iron rods into a tube?" Estoril suggested. "About a yard long, you said?"

"Yaas, loidy," agreed the armorer with a massive nod.

"*No!*" gasped Joe.

Even Joe could visualize the blackened mass of weak spots and open holes that would result from somebody trying to weld a tube on a hand forge. Arnault wouldn't be making a gun, it'd be a bomb!

Joe's face cleared while the others stared—or glowered, in the cases of Arnault and Delendor's brothers—at him. "Estoril," he said, "you're brilliant! Now, how fast does this dragon move?"

"Yes, not only beautiful but wise beyond imagining," Delendor said, turning toward the princess. "I—"

"Del!" Estoril snapped, glancing fiercely toward Delendor, then looking away as if to emphasize that she'd never seen him before in her life.

"For the most part, not very quickly," Ezekiel answered. Joe had already noticed that the magician was carrying out the spirit as well as the letter of King Morhaven's orders. "And it sleeps for long periods."

He smiled again. You didn't have to know Ezekiel for long to know what kind of news would cause him to smile.

"When the beast chooses to run, though," Ezekiel went on, "it can catch a galloping horse ... as I understand *Sir* Delendor of Glenheim learned in times past."

Joe stared at Ezekiel and thought, *You cruel son of a bitch.*

Ezekiel scared him, the way looking eye-to-eye at a spider had scared him once. There wasn't anything in the magician that belonged in human society, despite the man's undoubted brains and knowledge.

"Right," said Joe as though he still thought he was speaking to a human being. "Would the dragon go around, say, a cast-iron kettle—" *Did they have cast-iron kettles?* "—if it had a fuze burning to it?"

"The dragon walks through walls of fire," Delendor said. "I don't think we'll be able to burn it, Joe."

He sounded doubtful. Doubtful about his choice of a magician, Joe suspected.

"We won't try," Joe said in sudden confidence. "We'll blow the thing to hell and gone!"

His enthusiasm—the foreign wizard's enthusiasm—drew a gasp of delight and wonder from the assembled crowd; except, noticeably, from Ezekiel and Delendor's brothers.

"Now," said Joe, "we'll need to test it. What do you use for pipes here?"

"Poipes?" said Arnault.

"You know," Joe explained. "Water pipes."

"Pipes for water?" said Delendor. "Why, we have wells. Don't you have wells in your own country, Joe?"

"I have tubing drawn of lead, left over from my clepsydra," said Ezekiel.

He held up his index finger. "The outer size is this," he explained, "and the inner size"—he held up the little finger of the same hand—"is this."

"Perfect!" Joe said, wondering what a clepsydra was. "Great! Fetch me a six-inch length, that'll be enough, and I'll get back to making something to fill it with. Boy, that dragon's going to get his last surprise!"

Ezekiel stayed where he was, but Joe had more important things to deal with than enforcing instantaneous obedience. He hadn't gotten very far with his gunpowder, after all.

Joe had made gunpowder when he was in grade school, but he'd never been able to make it correctly because of the cost. Now it *had* to be right, but cost didn't matter.

Charcoal was easy, then as now. As a kid, he'd ground up a charcoal briquette, using the face of a hammer and a saucepan abstracted from the kitchen.

Here, Ezekiel provided a mortar and a pestle whose sides sloped to a concave grinding surface which mated with the mortar's convex head, both of brass. Pieces of natural charcoal (which looked disconcertingly like scraps of burned wood) powdered more cleanly than briquettes processed with sawdust had done.

Joe poured the black dust into one of Ezekiel's screw-stoppered brass jars. He didn't bother wiping the pestle clean, because after all, he was going to mix all the ingredients at some point anyway.

Lumps of sulphur powdered as easily as bits of dried mud. Sulphur had been a cheap purchase at the drugstore also. The only complicating factor was that you didn't want to buy the jar of sulphur from the same druggist as sold you the saltpeter.

Saltpeter was the rub. Saltpeter was expensive, and it was supposed to provide seventy-five percent of the bulk of the powder; so Joe and his friends had changed the formula. It was as simple as that.

After all, they weren't trying to shoot a knight out of his armored saddle—or blow a dragon to kingdom come. They just wanted spectacular fireworks. Mixing the ingredients in equal parts gave a lot more hiss and spatter from a small jar of saltpeter than the "right" way would have done.

With his powdered sulphur in a second jar, Joe got to work on the saltpeter.

Ezekiel's store of the substance amounted to several pounds, so far as Joe could judge the quantity in the heavy brass container. He didn't know precisely how much gunpowder it was going to take to blow up a dragon, but this ought to do the job.

The saltpeter crystals were a dirty yellow-white, like the teeth of Glam and Groag. They crushed beneath the mortar with a faint squeaking, unlike the crisp, wholesome sound the charcoal had made.

The spectators were getting bored. Kiki had snatched a hat and was now more the center of interest than Joe was. Servants formed a ring about the little animal and were making good-natured attempts to grab him as he bounced around them, cloak fluttering.

The spectators who weren't watching the monkey had mostly broken up into their own conversational groups. Delendor and his sister murmured about old times, while Glam and Groag discussed the fine points of unlacing a deer.

It had bothered Joe to feel that he was some sort of a circus act. He found that it bothered him more to think that he was a *boring* circus act, a tumbler whom everybody ignored while the lion tamer and trapeze artists performed in the other rings.

Almost everybody ignored him. As Joe mixed his test batch of powder—three measures of saltpeter and a half measure each of charcoal and sulphur (because he still couldn't for the life of him remember which of the pair was supposed to be fifteen percent and which ten)—he felt Ezekiel's eyes on his back. The magician's gaze was cold and veiled, like a container of dry ice.

And Ezekiel wasn't quite the only one watching with unabated interest as Joe went on with the procedure. Joe lifted his head to stretch his cramped shoulders. In a third-floor room across the courtyard—Joe's room, he thought, though he couldn't be sure—was a wan white face observing at a safe distance from Glam and Groag.

Mary's features were indistinct, but Joe felt the poor kid's concern.

He went back to mixing his ingredients. He felt better for the glimpse at the window.

"All right, Ezekiel," Joe said loudly to call *everybody's* attention back to him. "I'll need the tube now."

Ezekiel smiled and extended his hand with the length of lead pipe in it.

Joe was sure Ezekiel hadn't left the summer kitchen. The piece could have been concealed in the magician's sleeve all the time, but that left the question of how he'd known what Joe would want before Joe himself knew.

Being thought to be a magician in this culture was fine. Knowing a *real* magician was rather like knowing a real Mafioso. . . .

"Right," said Joe, staring at the pipe and thinking about the possible remainder of his life—unless he could find a People Mover going in the opposite direction. "Right . . ."

Time for that later. He needed to close one end of the pipe before he filled it with powder. He could use Ezekiel's mortar to pound the soft metal into a seam, but that wasn't the job for which the piece of lab equipment had been designed.

Besides, the mortar's owner was watching.

"Arnault," Joe said briskly to the master armorer. "I need to close the end of this pipe. Do you have a hammer with you?"

"This poipe . . . ?" Arnault said, reaching out for the piece. When the armorer frowned, wrinkles gave his face almost the same surface as his cracked, stained leather apron.

He took the piece between his right thumb and index finger. When he squeezed, the metal flattened as if between a hammer and anvil.

Joe blinked. Arnault returned the pipe to him. The flattened end was warm.

Arnault didn't speak, but a smile of pride suffused his whole pitted, muscular being.

"Ah," said Joe. "Thank you."

Joe looked at the pipe he held, the glass funnel set out in readiness, and the brass container of gunpowder. Either the cold or the shock of everything that'd been happening made his brain logy, because it took ten seconds of consideration before he realized that he was going to need a third hand. He glanced at the crowd.

Ezekiel was used to this type of work; Delendor was the guy whose life and career most depended on the job—

And Joe, for different reasons, didn't trust either one of them. "Estoril?" he said. "Princess? Would you please hold this tube vertical while I pour the powder into it?"

Joe's eyes had scanned the window across the courtyard before settling back on the princess; but that was a silly thought and unworthy of him, even in his present state.

Estoril handled the pipe with the competence Joe already knew to expect from her. The spout of the funnel fit within the lead cylinder, so he didn't have to tell her not to worry if some of the gunpowder dribbled down.

The brass powder container was slick, heavy, and, when Joe

took off his glove for a better grip, shockingly cold. He shook the jar as carefully as he could, dribbling a stream of the dirty-yellow gunpowder into the funnel and thence the pipe.

It sure didn't look black. Maybe he should've used more charcoal after all?

Drifting grains of sulphur gave the air a brimstone hint that reminded Joe of the immediately-previous stop on what had begun as a People Mover.

The tube was nearly full. Joe put down the items he held and took the tube from Estoril. "Arnault," he said, holding the almost-bomb to the armorer, "I'd like you to close this down to a little hole in the end. Can you do that?"

Arnault stared at the piece. It looked tiny in his hand. "Right," he said. "Doon to a coont haar."

Joe pursed his lips. "A little larger than that, I think," he said. "About the size of a straw."

Though, thinking about the sort of women who would willingly consort with the master armorer, Arnault's description might have been quite accurate.

Granted that lead wasn't armor plate, it was still amazing to watch Arnault force the tube into the desired shape between the tips of his thumbs and index fingers. When he handed the result back, Joe couldn't imagine a machine shop back home improving on the job.

Nothing left to do but to complete the test.

Joe had been planning to take the bomb outside the walls of the palace, but now he had a better idea. The summer kitchen's three ovens were solid masonry affairs; and this was, after all, only a little bomb. . . .

Joe arranged it at the back of the center oven.

"Now, I want all of you to keep to the sides," Joe said, his voice deepened and multiplied by the cavity. When he straightened, he found everybody was staring at him from wherever they'd been standing before . . . except that Delendor and his brothers had moved up directly behind "the magician" to stare into the oven.

Ezekiel grinned.

Joe stuck his thumbs in his ears and waggled his fingers. "Back!" he shouted.

Kiki's four limbs gripped Delendor's head, completely hiding the youth's face. Glam and Groag hurtled into the crowd like elephants charging butt-first, doing a marvelous job of clearing the area in front of the oven.

"Right," said Joe, breathing heavily. "Now, if you'll all just keep it that way while I set the fuze."

From what he remembered, you were supposed to make your fuze by soaking string in a solution of gunpowder and letting it dry—or some damned thing. For this purpose, a bare train of powder would do well enough.

Joe dribbled a little pile of the foul-looking stuff at the base of the bomb, then ran the trail out to the mouth of the oven. Granted that he wasn't being graded on aesthetics, he still sure wished his black powder looked back.

"Now—" he said with his hand raised for a flourish.

Oops.

Joe screwed down the top on the powder container and set it carefully on the ground to the side of the bank of ovens. All he needed was for a spark to get into *that*.

"Now," Joe repeated as the crowd watched him. "I'm going to light the fuze and—"

And neither he, not any of the people around him, had a match.

"Ah," he said, changing mental direction again. "Would somebody bring me a candle or—something, you know? I want to light the fuze."

"You want to light it *now*?" asked Ezekiel.

Joe nodded. He didn't understand the emphasis. "Ah, yeah," he said. "Is there some reason—"

Ezekiel snapped his fingers. Something that looked like a tiny—no, it had to have been a spark—popped from his pointing index finger. The spark flicked the end of the train of gunpowder.

"Get back!" Joe shouted, waving his arms as he scrambled aside also. "Get clear, y'all!"

Ezekiel was smiling at him in cold satisfaction.

The pops and splutters of burning gunpowder echoed from the oven. Stinking white smoke oozed out of the door and hung in the cold air like a mass of raw cotton, opaque and evil-looking.

Joe put his hands over his ears and opened his mouth to help equalize pressure against the coming blast. He wished he'd remembered to warn the locals that the bang would—

There was a pop. A stream of orange-red sparks spurted through the open oven door. Joe heard a whanging sound from within, a

whee!—and the would-be bomb came sailing straight up the flue
of the oven. It mounted skyward on a trail of white smoke and
a rain of molten lead.

The crowd scattered, screaming in justified terror. Delendor
picked up his sister and ran for the nearest doorway in a cloud
of skirts. Even Ezekiel fled, though he did so with more judgment than any of the others: he flung himself into one of the
cold ovens.

The rocket began to curve as the wall of the lead tube melted
unevenly. The only two people still watching it were Joe, in utter
dismay; and Arnault, who stared out from the haze of his smoldering hair with a rapturous look on his face.

The rocket punched through one of the third-floor windows
across from Joe's room. There was a faint *pop* from within. The
remainder of the damaged window shivered outward into the
courtyard.

Maybe a boxcar load of this "gunpowder" would daze a dragon.
But probably not.

Arnault turned to Joe. The armorer's spark-lighted beard had
gone out, but a wreath of hideous stench still wrapped him. "Moy,
but yoor a cooning baastaard!" Arnault bellowed happily as he
hugged Joe to him.

Joe squealed. His mother had always told him that if he persisted in playing with gunpowder he'd surely be killed, though
he doubted she'd expected him to be crushed in an elephantine
expression of joy. . . .

Arnault threw open his arms. Joe sprawled on the flagstones.
He took a deep breath of the cold, sulphurous air and began
coughing it out again.

Ezekiel crawled from the oven. His face was livid where it wasn't
smudged with soot. For a moment, the magician stared upward
toward the missing window, a gap in the array of diamond-paned
reflections. A tiny wisp of smoke came out of the opening.

"You may think you're clever, destroying my laboratory that
way!" he cried to Joe. "But it won't help your protege against the
dragon, you know. And *that's* what you're sworn to do!"

The magician turned and strode toward the door into the palace. His robes were flapping. The wisp of smoke from his room
became a column. As Ezekiel reached the doorway, he flung
dignity to the winds and began to run up the stairs.

Delendor reappeared, looking flushed and joyful. "Wow!" the prince said. "That's tremendous, Joe! My mother's spirit certainly led me right. Why, that dragon won't have a chance!"

"I'm glad you feel that way," said Joe as he got to his feet.

Joe's belly felt cold. What he'd done was sure-hell impressive . . . but it proved that he couldn't make gunpowder that would explode.

And that meant that Delendor was a dead duck.

There was a faint tap on Joe's door.

"Sure, come in," he mumbled without looking away from the window. The sun was still above the horizon, but in the shadowed courtyard beneath, servants and vehicles moved as if glimpsed through the water of a deep pool.

Mary slipped into the room. For a moment she poised beside the door, ready to flee. Then she asked, "Master Joe, am I disturbing you? If you need to plan all the little details of how you'll destroy the dragon, then I—"

Joe turned. The room was almost dark. The charcoal fire gave little light, and the low sun had to be reflected many times to reach Joe's leading-webbed windows.

"I *can't* destroy the dragon!" he said savagely. "I can't kill it, and I can't go home. And none of it's any fault of mine that *I* can see!"

Mary cowered back against the door. Her eyes were on Joe's face but her thin fingers fumbled to reopen the door.

"Aw, child, don't do that . . ." he said, reaching out—then grimacing in self-disgust when he saw her wince at the gesture. "Look," he said, "I'm just frustrated that . . . well, that I made things worse."

Mary began fussing with the fire, adding small bits of charcoal from the terra cotta container beside the fireplace. "And so now you want to leave?" she asked.

"I always wanted to leave," Joe said. He tried to keep the force of his emotion out of his voice. "Mary, I never wanted to *come* here, it just happened. But it doesn't look like I'll ever be able to leave, either."

"But Joe," she said, lifting her big frightened eyes to his, "only a great magician could have done what you did this morning. I don't see why you think you're failing."

"Because I'm not a chemist," Joe explained.

He turned away from the pain in the maid's expression. The courtyard was still deeper in shadow. "Because I'm not much of anything, if you want to know the truth. I did the only thing I know how to do—from when I was a kid. And that's not going to help a damned bit if the dragon's half what everybody tells me it is."

Mary touched the hem of Joe's cloak diffidently. "I think you're something," she said.

"What I am," said Joe, "is the guy who told Delendor he'd fix it so he'd kill the dragon. Which was a lie. And Delendor's a decent kid who deserved better 'n that."

A four-horse carriage drove out of the stables across the courtyard. The streets would be pitch dark soon, so the lanterns on the vehicle's foreposts were lighted. They waked glimmers of vermilion lacquer and gilt on the carriage's polished sides.

"I'm sure you'll find a—" Mary began.

The carriage driver looked up at Joe's window. *Great god almighty! It was the Mongolian!*

Joe spun to his door. He had barely enough control to jiggle the latch open—it was simple but not of a present-day familiar type—instead of breaking off the slender handle that lifted the bar. His shoes skidded as he ran to the nearest staircase, but he managed not to fall.

At the back of Joe's mind was the knowledge that somebody— fate, the Mongolian, sunspots, *whatever*—might be playing with him. He could reach the courtyard and find that the coach had driven out the main gate and into the city . . . or simply had disappeared.

But Joe had to try. He should've had better sense to begin with than to think he could do any good in a world with dragons and real sorcerers. Since he'd screwed things up even worse, the only honorable course was to get himself the hell out of the way at the first chance that was offered.

Sure, that was honorable. And besides, it was survivable.

This was a servants' staircase, helical with stone steps that were just as slick as the floors. There wasn't any namby-pamby nonsense about stair railings, either. By god, there were things Joe knew that he could teach these people . . .

Unfortunately, none of those things included dragon-slaying methods; and nobody in Hamisch was going to be much interested in staircase and bathroom designs from the guy who got Prince Delendor killed.

Joe swept down on a trio of maids. They flattened to the curving walls in terror when "the new magician" galloped past them.

The two long flights took him—well, Joe didn't know how long it took him. He knew if he slipped, he'd knock himself silly for sure; and he suspected that was just the sort of joke the Mongolian had in mind to torment a perfectly innocent ghostwriter.

He reached the ground floor between the laundry room and the buttery. A liveried servant dozed on a chair beside the courtyard door. Joe slammed past him, startling the man shriekingly awake as though the morning's rocket had been set off again between his coattails.

The carriage waited in the twilit courtyard. The swarthy driver smirked past the coach lamp toward Joe. Vague voices drifted between the stone walls, and concertina music came from somewhere in the servants' quarters.

Joe put his foot on the carriage step and gripped the silver door latch. It was warmer than the surrounding air, but it wouldn't have stopped Joe if he'd thought the cold metal would flay the skin from his palm.

"Stop, Master Joe!" somebody wailed.

The carriage door started to swing open. Joe looked over his shoulder.

Mary had followed him down the stairs. Her eyes were streaming tears.

Her arms held out to him the attaché case he'd abandoned when he saw his chance to go home.

Much the way Joe had abandoned Mary and his promise to Delendor.

"Right," said Joe. He hopped down from the carriage step and took the case from the maid.

"I don't think I'll need this for a while," he said to the sobbing woman. "But it may as well stay in my room for now. With me."

The driver clucked something to his horses. The coach began to move in toward the archway, but Joe didn't look back as he guided Mary into the palace.

As a result, Joe didn't see the clawed, skeletally-thin hand that pulled shut the carriage door from the inside.

✳   ✳   ✳

A horde of minuscule demons was sweeping shattered equipment from Ezekiel's workbench. They suddenly froze in place, then formed a flying arrowhead which curved halfway around the laboratory before vanishing into the dimension from which the creatures had come. Their voices made a tiny eeping that persisted several seconds after the demons themselves disappeared.

"What's that?/What happened?" Glam and Groag blurted together in high-pitched voices. Each brother slapped one hand to his swordhilt and covered his face with the other, as though they thought the swarm of demons might flee down their throats—

As indeed the panicky demons might do, and much good the outflung hands would be in that event.

Ezekiel made one attempt to regain control by gesturing. Then he *heard* what the demons were wailing and stepped to an undamaged window—the center of the three casements was boarded up—to glance down into the courtyard.

"Great God!" he muttered as he jumped back again from the glass—and much good a stone wall would be if the *being* below chose to act against Ezekiel.

"What's going on?" Glam demanded in his full, booming voice. He'd regained confidence now that the flying demons were gone, and there seemed to be no room within his thick skull for wonder at what had frightened the horde away.

"I saw a . . ." the magician said. "A being. A being from the 7th Plane."

Groag strode over to the window Ezekiel had vacated and looked out. "You mean Delendor's tame wizard?" he said. "He don't look any great shakes to me."

"Joe Johnson is down there?" Ezekiel asked sharply. "You see him?"

"Yeah, sure I see him," Groag said, testy with his sudden fear and his present, false, assumption of safety. "He's getting into a carr—no, he ain't. He's going—" the big man squinted for a better look in the twilight "—back inside."

Ezekiel swallowed. The lingering smell of brimstone seemed sharper. "What is the—carriage doing?" he asked with as much nonchalance as he could muster.

"Huh?" Groag answered. "It just drove off, out the gate. Why?"

"Whadda ya mean, 7th Plane?" Glam asked. "You mean a demon?"

As though the word had been a summons, one of Ezekiel's pack of demons thrust its head back into the laboratory, then followed with its entire body. The creature was blue and more nearly the size of a gnat than a fly.

The demon gripped a shard of broken alembic and tried to lift the piece with a metallic shimmering of its wings. After it quivered vainly for several seconds, hundreds more of its fellows poured through the hole in the continuum and resumed their duties. Bits and pieces of wreckage rose and vanished.

"Not a demon," the magician said, speaking as much to himself as to the pair of humans with him in his laboratory. "Demons are beings of the 3d Plane, below rather than above ours. The inhabitants of the 7th Plane are—"

"But it's not this Joe character that we're supposed to worry about, then?" Glam interrupted.

"If he communes with creatures of the 7th Plane, then you'd *better* worry about him!" Ezekiel snapped. The magician's vehemence straightened the two hulking princes like a slap. "The—folk of the 7th Plane don't meddle in human affairs, precisely . . . but they offer choices. They have terrible powers, but they won't be guided by humans. *Nobody* deals with them."

"Well then, what—" Groag said, his brow furrowing.

"Except," Ezekiel continued, "that the Princess Blumarine is said to have done so."

"You mean Delendor's mother . . . ?" Glam said in what was for him a considerable mental stretch. "But she's dead. Ain't she?"

"Blumarine couldn't save her beloved knight," Ezekiel said savagely. "And she won't be able to save her son, either. Do you hear?"

He glared around the room. "*Do you hear?*"

The waves of tiny demon wings rose and trembled with the amplitude of the magician's voice.

"Ah, good morning, Joe," said Delendor. "I was just wondering how preparations for my dragon-slaying are coming?"

Joe looked at the prince sourly. "You're up bright and early," he said.

"Well, ah, yes," Delendor agreed, looking around Joe's room with vague interest. "I *do* get up early, you know; and besides, Estoril and I are going on a picnic today."

Mary, wearing a sturdy pair of boots in place of her usual slippers, curtsied. She was blushing furiously. Kiki hopped from the prince's shoulder and chirped at Mary's feet, but the maid seemed unwilling even to admit the monkey was there.

"Ah, you're going on a picnic also, Joe?" Delendor added. His lips pursed. "But with an arbalest?"

"What we're doing," Joe said, "is taking a look at your blasted dragon."

"Really?" said Delendor. "Goodness. Why?"

"Because I haven't got a clue as to what to do about a damned dragon!" Joe snarled. "Because I'm not a magician! But I *might* be able to help if I had the faintest notion of what I'm supposed to be dealing with."

He didn't so much calm as run through the temporary enthusiasm that anger gave him. "And I, well, I'd really like to help things out here. Mary said she'd guide me. Apparently the dragon's pretty close to the city already."

Delendor nodded with his lips still pursed. "Yes," he said, "I wanted to go to the glade north of the walls where we picnicked when we were little, but Clarkson says that's not a good idea. But why the arbalest?"

The youth's expression grew tight and angry. "You're not planning to—"

"No, I'm *not* planning to shoot the dragon with a crossbow!" Joe blazed. "Though I sure as hell would if I thought it'd do a damned bit of good."

"*Oh!*" squealed Mary.

The maid had stuffed rags in her boots to line them down to the size of her tiny feet. Kiki grabbed the end of one and ran around in a circle, attempting to bind Mary's ankles together. Joe snatched at the monkey with his free hand.

Kiki bounded up the wall, off the ceiling, and back onto Delendor's shoulder in an impressive display of acrobatics—and judgment, given the fury that bent Joe's groping hand into a claw.

"Bad, bad monkey!" Delendor chided.

"Look, Delendor," Joe continued in an attempt to sound calm. "I just figured I ought to be armed if I'm going to look for this thing."

"Oh, well," the prince said, his face clearing. "Well, I'll loan you a sword then, Joe. It's more fitting to your position, though I suppose technically a magician isn't a—"

"No, I don't want a sword," Joe interrupted. "I don't know anything about swords except they're long enough to trip me if I need to run . . . as I figure I'll want to, pretty soon now."

"Ah," said Delendor. He didn't look as though he would have approved if he understood. His eyes wandered; focused on Mary, who'd taken off her boot to restuff it; and snapped back to Joe.

"Delendor," Joe said, "I don't know anything about crossbows either. Or guns, if it comes to that. Arnault had to crank this—" he hefted the weapon in his right hand with some difficulty "—up for me."

Joe tried to smile as though he meant it. "Mary," he went on with a nod to the maid, "warned me not to put an arrow in the thing until I was out in open country. It's just a security blanket, but the good lord knows I need some security."

Delendor reached a decision. He nodded enthusiastically. "I understand," he said. "A very noble, if I may say so, undertaking. I'll tell Estoril that we won't be able to picnic today, because I'm going with my magician to view the threat to the kingdom first-hand."

"Ah," Joe said. "Ah, are you really sure you want to do this?"

"I certainly do," the prince responded firmly. "And not only that, but we'll go on foot. The—fate—of Sir Delendor, my namesake, suggests that horses aren't to be trusted in the vicinity of the dragon."

Joe nodded. It just might be, he thought, that Delendor wasn't a complete airhead.

"Well, it's certainly a beautiful day to be out in the country, isn't it?" Delendor gushed. "Bright sun, crisp breeze . . . just cool enough to be bracing."

Joe sneezed. "No people around," he said. "Not a soul."

He looked back over his shoulder. The pennoned turrets on the city walls were still visible every time the road rolled upward. They'd set out on the main turnpike between Glenheim and Hamisch, so there should've been *some* traffic.

Unless the dragon was a lot closer than the farmers from outlying districts, now thronging the streets of Hamisch, had insisted.

It occurred to Joe that the farmers might be more than a little upset about the lack of progress in dealing with the beast that was devastating their lands. If some of the nobles who were supposed to slay such threats could be enticed into proximity to the dragon, then one or the other was going to be killed.

And the farmers might think either result was a good one.

"I don't think we should be walking right up the road," Mary said, echoing Joe's next thought as it formed.

Delendor looked at the brush fringing the sides of the highway, then tapped the road's cobblestone surface with his green leather shoe. The edges of the road were apparently cut back every few years, but at the moment they were a tangle of saplings, bushes, and creepers—thick enough to provide concealment for somebody a few yards in, but not too dense to get through without a machete.

"Well, it might be more comfortable for walking," he said judiciously. "But my sword would catch. I don't think we'll do that."

"We'll do that," said Joe grimly as he forced his way into the brush.

Joe's legs were holding up—they'd walked less than a mile—but his arms were aching with the weight of the crossbow. The nut that held back the thumb-thick cord had a slot in it to grip the nock of the bolt. At least Joe didn't have the bolt falling off every time he let the weapon point down, the way he'd expected.

The bolt—the quarrel—had a thick wood shaft and three wooden feathers. The head was square and steel, with a four-knobbed face instead of a point. It looked dangerous as hell—

And if the dragon had shrugged off showers of similar missiles, as everybody assured Joe the beast had, then the dragon was hell on four legs.

Kiki was having the time of his life, swinging around the three humans. He was so light that the branches of saplings, none of which were more than twelve feet tall, were sufficient to support his cheerful acrobatics.

Delendor, last in the line, had rotated his swordbelt so that the weapon in its scabbard hung behind him like a stiff tail. It didn't get in his way after all.

The prince's tasseled fur cloak, his ruffed tunic, and his ballooning silk breeches, on the other hand, seemed to cling and fray on every thorn. Delendor became increasingly—vocally—irritated about the fact.

"Joe," he called, "this doesn't make any sense at all. We could never escape if the dragon charged us, but the thorns wouldn't slow the beast a bit."

"We couldn't outrun it anyway," Joe said, doggedly forcing his way between a clump of saplings. "All we're trying to do is stay out of sight."

"The dragon stops when it makes a kill," Mary said. "The others will have time to get away while it eats."

The careless, matter-of-fact statement contrasted unpleasantly with the maid's timid voice.

"Well, perhaps in that case I should be in the lead," Delendor suggested. "Because my rank is—*drat*! Where do all these blackberry vines come from?"

If the prince had paid attention to what he was doing rather than to his concept of *noblesse oblige*, he'd've gone around those vines the way his companions had.

"You know," Delendor resumed a moment later, "this makes even less sense than I'd thought. We're making so much noise that we'll never sneak up on the—"

Joe froze with one foot lifted. He hissed, "Hush!"

"—dragon. I've done enough hunting to know—*ulp*!"

Mary had turned and clamped her hand over Delendor's mouth with surprising strength. "Oh, please, Prince!" she whispered. "*Please* obey Master Joe."

Joe put his foot down very carefully. Something that clanked and wheezed like a steam locomotive was coming up the road toward them. There wasn't much doubt about what the something was.

The dragon came around a sweeping bend only fifty yards away. Its color was the red of glowing iron.

The dragon probably wasn't any longer than the thirty-odd yards Ezekiel had claimed for it . . . but seeing a creature of the unimaginably great size was very different from hearing the words spoken.

No wonder the knights—and the crossbowmen—had been unable to harm the thing.

The dragon was covered with bony scutes similar to those of a crocodile, and the beast's general shape was crocodilelike as well: so low-slung that the long jaws almost brushed the cobblestones, with a massive body carried on four short legs. The upper and lower rows of the dragon's teeth overlapped like the spikes of an Iron Maiden.

The dragon's claws sparked on the roadway. Its breath chuffed out a reek of decay which enveloped Joe as he peered from the brush in amazement.

Well, he'd come to look at the dragon to determine what were its weak spots.

There weren't any.

They'd have to get back to Hamisch as fast as they could—making the necessary wide circuit to avoid the dragon. The beast would reach the city in a few tens of minutes, and the only hope of the people inside was to scatter. The walls wouldn't last a—

"*Kikikikiki!*" shrieked the monkey. It hurled a bit of seedpod as it charged the dragon.

"Kiki!" cried Delendor in a voice almost as high-pitched as his pet's. The prince whisked his sword from its sheath and crossed the expanse of brush between himself and the highway in three deerlike leaps.

With Mary running after him, an equally athletic, equally quixotic, demonstration.

"For god's sake!" Joe screamed. He tried to aim his arbalest. A loop of honeysuckle was caught around the right arm of the bow. "Come back! Come back!"

The dragon didn't charge, but its head swung with horrifying speed to clop within a finger's breadth of Kiki. The monkey's cries rose into a sound like an electronic watch alarm.

Kiki hurled himself back into the brush. Delendor continued to run forward, with Mary right behind him—casting doubt on the evolutionary course of intelligence.

"Get down!" Joe cried. "*Don't,* for god's sake—"

He slipped his bow loose of the vines and raised the weapon. He'd fired a rifle a couple times but the crossbow had a knob rather than a shoulder stock.

There weren't any proper sights. Joe tried to aim along the bolt's vertical fin, but the weapon's heavy muzzle wobbled furiously around a six-inch circle. The dragon was only twenty feet away, and Joe was going to miss it if he—

Delendor swung his sword in a swift, glittering arc. It rang on the dragon's snout as though it had struck an anvil. The blade shattered and the hilt, vibrating like a badly-tuned harmonica, flew out of Delendor's hand.

Delendor yelped and lost his footing. He hit the cobblestones butt-first, which was just as well in the short run because the dragon's jaws slammed where the prince's torso had been.

"*Get out of the—*" Joe shrieked.

"Take me!" Mary cried, waving her arms to catch the monster's attention as she stepped on Delendor's swordhilt.

Mary's foot flew in the air. She hit the ground in a flurry of skirts.

The dragon paused, faced with two victims ten feet apart. It opened its jaws wider. The maw was the size of a concert grand with the lid up. The interior of the dragon's mouth was as white as dried bone.

I'll never have a better chance, thought Joe as he squeezed the under-lever trigger of his crossbow. The muzzle dropped as the cord slammed forward.

Joe whanged his bolt into the roadway in an explosion of sparks.

The dragon snorted. It started to—

For Pete's sake, it was arching its short neck, then its back. Its monstrous, clawed forelegs were off the ground—

The sight should've been as ridiculous as that of *Fantasia's* crocodiles doing *The Dance of the Hours* . . . but this close to the creature, it was more like watching an ICBM rising from its silo in preparation to launch.

The dragon was quivering in a tetanic arch, making little whimpering sounds. Its belly plates were red like the scutes of its back and sides, but there were fine lines of yellow skin where the plates met.

There was a hole where the lower jaw joined the first plate covering the underside of the neck. The hole didn't look large, but blood was bubbling furiously out of it.

Joe's quarrel had ricocheted into what might very well be the only vulnerable point in the dragon's armor.

The dragon rose onto the claws of its hind feet. Its tail was stiff. The beast's armor squealed under the strain to which convulsing muscles were subjecting it.

Mary and Delendor sat up, staring at the monster that towered above them. Their legs were splayed, and they supported their torsos on their hands.

"Wow!" said the prince. Joe, fifty feet back in the brush, couldn't come up with anything more suitable for the occasion.

Kiki hopped onto Joe's shoulder. He made what were almost purring sounds as he stroked Joe's hair.

The dragon completed its arc and toppled backwards. It hit the ground with a crash.

Its limbs and tail continued to pummel the ground for hours, like the aftershocks of an earthquake.

Though there were eight yoke of oxen hitched to the sledge, they wheezed and blew with the effort of dragging the dragon's head, upside down, into the palace courtyard. The beast's tongue lolled out to drag the flagstones, striking sparks from them.

Prince Delendor sat astride the stump of the beast's neck. He waved his swordhilt and beamed as he received the boisterous cheers of the crowd.

"Must be the whole city down there," Groag said glumly as he watched from one window of Ezekiel's laboratory.

"Must be the whole *country*," Glam corrected in a similar tone. "'Cept us."

"*Lookit* that!" said Groag.

"Then get out of the way and I will," snapped the magician, tapping Groag on the shoulder and making little shooing motions with his hand. The big prince stepped aside, shaking his head.

The wreckage was gone from the laboratory, but neither the middle window nor the broken glassware had been replaced. A tinge of brimstone from the rocket still clung to the air.

The scene in the courtyard did nothing to improve Ezekiel's humor. King Morhaven was kneeling to Delendor, though the youth quickly dismounted as from a horse and stood Morhaven erect again.

The cheering rattled the laboratory's remaining windows.

"He'll make Delendor co-ruler as a result of this, you know," Ezekiel said. "And heir."

He turned and glared savagely at the two royal brothers. "You *know* that, don't you?"

Glam twisted the toe of his boot against the floor, as though trying to grind something deep into the stone. "Well," he said, "you know . . . You know, if the little prick killed the dragon, I dunno what else the ole man could do. Lookit the *teeth* on that sucker."

"Don't be a bigger fool than God made you!" Ezekiel snarled.

"Delendor didn't have anything to do with killing the dragon. It was that magician of his! That *damned* magician."

He made a cryptic sign. A swarm of twinkling demons whisked out of their own plane. Their tiny hands compressed globes of air into a pair of shimmering lenses.

Ezekiel stared through the alignment, then stepped back. "There," he said to the brothers. "Look at that."

Glam looked through the tubeless telescope, despite an obvious reluctance to put his eye close to the miniature demons who formed it. The lenses were focused on the dragon's neck. The wound there was marked with a flag of blood.

"Well," said Glam as his brother shouldered him aside, "that's where he stabbed the sucker, right?"

"Idiot!" Ezekiel said. "The wound's *square*, from a crossbow bolt. And who do you see carrying a crossbow?"

"Oh-h-h," said the brothers together.

Behind the sledge, almost lost in the crowd that mobbed Delendor, was the prince's magician—carrying a heavy arbalest. A servant girl clung to him, squeezed by the people cheering their master.

"I don' get it," Groag said. "Lotsa guys shot it with crossbows before, din't they? I heard that, anyhow."

"Of course they did, oaf!" said Ezekiel. "This was obviously an enchanted arbalest which struck the one vulnerable part of the dragon's armor—even though a spot on the underside of the beast's throat *couldn't* be hit by a crossbow bolt."

He swung the telescope slightly by tapping the manicured nail of his index finger against the objective lens. Tiny demons popped and crackled at the contact.

Groag glared at the crossbow. "Don' look so special ta me," he said.

"I don' get it," Glam said. "If he got a crossbow ta kill the dragon, then what was all that stuff with the powder and fire t'other morning? Some kinda joke, was it?"

The magician grimaced. "I'm not sure," he admitted, glancing around his laboratory and remembering how it had looked *before* a rocket sizzled through the center window. "But I think . . ."

Ezekiel had been shrinking down into his velvet robes. Now he shook himself and rose again to his full height.

"I think," the magician resumed, "that Joe Johnson has been

brought here from a very great distance by a—7th Plane inhabitant. He initially attempted to use the magic of his own region
here, but the correspondences differed. Rather than work them
out, he found it easier to adapt *our* magic to the task."

"You promised us," said Glam in a dangerous voice, "that there
wouldn't be no problem with Delendor. An' now you say there is."

"I can take care of your brother easily enough," said Ezekiel
in a carefully neutral tone. "But only after Joe Johnson is out of
the way. Do you understand?"

Glam guffawed in a voice that rattled the window even against
the cheering voices below. "You bet we do!" he said. "Cold iron's
proof agin magic, right?"

"Ah, belt up," said his brother, staring through the telescope
again. "You charge in like a bull in a boo-dwa, you just screw
things up. *I'll* handle this one."

As he spoke, Groag marked carefully the servant to whom Joe
Johnson gave his enchanted crossbow.

"And *you* said you weren't a magician!" Delendor crowed.

"Del, careful!" Estoril warned, but the prince had already jumped
into a heel-clicking curvette too energetic for Joe's small room.

The feather in Delendor's peaked cap flattened against the ceiling. Kiki bounded from the prince's shoulder and caromed off
the four walls before cringing against Joe's ankles.

Joe wrapped the quilt around him tighter. Servants had built up
the fire next to which he huddled in his armchair. Despite that
and the quilt, he still felt cold enough that the monkey's warm
body was surprisingly pleasant.

He wondered where Mary had gone—and whether she'd be
back tonight as usual.

He sneezed again.

"Bless you!" said Delendor, slightly more subdued. He sat down
again on the cedar chest beside Estoril. "You know," he bubbled
to the princess, "I just swung, *swish!*"

"I believe I heard that, yes," Estoril said dryly. Joe thought
she winked at him, but he was blowing his nose and couldn't
be sure.

Did Lancelot catch colds while carrying out deeds of derring-do?
More to the point, did Lancelot's faithful servant catch colds?

"I didn't even know that I'd killed it until I saw it topple over backward!" Delendor continued, oblivious to everything but his own—false—memory. "Joe here's magic guided my thrust straight to the monster's throat! Except..."

Delendor's handsome brow furrowed. "You know, I thought I'd *cut* at the dragon instead of thrusting." He brightened again. "Just shows how memory can play tricks on you, doesn't it?"

Joe sneezed.

Maybe now that the dragon was dead, he'd be able to go back home ... though somehow, after the primary colors of life in Hamisch, even the Senator and his shenanigans seemed gray.

"But here, I've been doing all the talking," Delendor said, showing that he had *some* awareness of the world beyond him. "Essie, what was it you came back from Glenheim to tell us?"

Estoril looked at her hands, laid neatly in a chevron on the lap of her lace-fronted dress. "To tell the truth," she began, "I'm not sure...."

"You know," the prince resumed, as though Estoril had finished her thought instead of merely her words, "when Joe arrived here, I really wanted him to find my enchanted princess."

Delendor fumbled within his puff-fronted tunic. "But now that you're back, Essie, I—well, I don't think about it very much."

He opened the oval locket and handed it to Estoril. From the flash of lamplight as the object passed, Joe knew it was still a mirror so far as he was concerned. He roused himself to ask, "Princess, what do *you* see in it?"

Estoril smiled. "My face," she said. "But the locket is very old—and it belonged to Del's mother."

She returned the locket to Delendor. "The Princess Blumarine was a very good woman," she said carefully. "But from what Katya told me, she was very—"

A sort of smile, wry but good-humored, flicked Estoril's mouth. "Powerful would be the wrong word, I think. The Princess Blumarine was very learned. I'm sure that the mirror shows her son whatever he says it does."

Delendor gave her a look of prim horror. "Essie!" he said. "Of *course* I wouldn't lie to you!"

Estoril glanced at the windows. They were again gray traceries of leading that barely illuminated the room. "Master Joe," the princess said, "would you like us to summon lamps?"

"Huh?" said Joe, aroused from his doze. "Oh, no—I mean ...

after you leave, that is, I think I'll just sit here and hope my sinuses decide to drain."

The problem wasn't just the cold breeze—and being out in it all day while the trophy was dragged to the palace. The shock of everything he'd been through today and the past three days had weakened Joe, leaving him prey to a bug.

"Well," said Estoril as she stood up, "we were just leaving."

"We . . . ?" said Delendor, though he hopped to his feet also.

"Are leaving," Estoril repeated. "And we're going to send some hot soup up to Joe."

"Oh, I'm not really—" Joe began.

"Which he will drink *all* of," the princess continued in a tone with as much flexibility as the dragon's armor.

Estoril opened the door and pointed Delendor into the hall; but then she paused. "Master Joe," she said softly, "the kingdom owes its safety to you. And I owe you Delendor's life—"

"Yes, yes," the prince broke in over Estoril's shoulder. "We owe it all to you, Joe."

"I wouldn't want you to think," Estoril continued as though there had been no interruption, "that *we* are unaware of precisely what you've accomplished. Or that we're ungrateful for your tact."

"It wasn't—" Joe said, but there was no way he could explain just what it *was* since he didn't have a clue himself. He started to get up.

"No, stay right there," Estoril ordered in her head nurse/mother persona.

"Kiki?" called Delendor. "*Kiki?*"

The monkey peeked out from between Joe's feet. Kiki had wrapped himself in a corner of the quilt also. After a moment, and with obvious reluctance, the little creature sprang across the cold floor and back on his master's shoulder.

"Remember to drink your soup," Estoril called as she pulled the door closed behind her.

Joe relaxed again. He missed the warmth of Kiki, though. Estoril was quite a lady. Smart and tough, but not cold for all that. She could've made the best ruler of anybody Joe had met yet in Hamisch, but it was obvious that wouldn't happen while there were sons around.

For that matter, Estoril probably couldn't get elected President, either, so long as there was some male boob with a fluent smile and the right connections to run against her.

Delendor wasn't a bad kid, and in a few years he wouldn't be a kid. He'd proved he had guts enough when he charged the dragon—like a damned fool! Maybe with his sister behind to do the thinking for the next while, Delendor could turn out to be a useful king.

Joe wasn't sure whether he was awake or dreaming. The coals in the fireplace were a mass of white ash, but they continued to give off heat.

If he got up and looked through the window behind him, would he really see the head of a dragon in the courtyard? Would he even see a courtyard?

But the warmth was good, and Joe really didn't want to move. Whatever reality was would keep. . . .

Something that sounded like a dropped garbage can came banging its way down the hall. The dragon's claws had sounded like that on the roadway—if there was a dragon, if there was a road. The claws hadn't echoed, but they'd been louder because the beast was so—

Joe's door burst open under the stroke of an armored hand. The latch flew across the room, bar in one direction and bracket in the other. A figure in full armor stood in the doorway with a drawn sword.

"You're in league with sundry devils, magician," the figure boomed in Glam's voice—muffled by coming through the pointed faceplate of a pig's-head basinet. "But your time's come now!"

Joe's skin flushed as though he were coming out of a faint. He jumped to his feet, slinging aside the quilt—

And fell on his face in front of Glam.

A pane of the window behind Joe blasted into the room like storm-blown ice. There was a *blang!* Many times louder than the sound of Glam knocking the door open. Joe twisted, trying unsuccessfully to get his feet back under him in the worst nightmare he'd had since—

Since jumping from that demon-wracked hell into Delendor's carriage, a detached, analytical part of his mind told him.

Glam toppled over on his pointed faceplate. Amazing how much noise a suit of plate armor makes when you drop it to a stone floor. . . .

Delendor, Estoril, and a crowd of servants burst into the room—led by Mary with a lantern and a terrified expression.

"Stop right where you are, Glam!" Delendor shouted. The youth's right hand kept dipping to his empty scabbard. Lack of a sword hadn't kept him from charging Glam as blithely as he had the dragon in the morning.

"Oh, Master Joe," Mary said, kneeling on the stones as Joe managed to rise into a squat. "I saw Glam coming down the hall, so I ran to get help."

"You're all right, then?" Delendor said in amazement. He finally took in the fact that the awkward sprawl on the floor was Glam, not Joe; and that Glam wasn't moving.

Which surprised the hell out of Joe, too, now that he had time to think about it.

"You lot," Estoril ordered, gesturing to a pair of the huskier servants. "Stand the brute up again."

The princess had come running also; and it couldn't have been because she thought Glam in a rage would spare a woman. "Joe, what happened?"

"I'm damned if I know," Joe muttered. "Except that—"

He looked accusingly toward the prince's shoulder. Kiki cowered behind Delendor's head, then peeked over his master's feathered cap.

"—except that I know your little pet tied my shoelaces, Delendor," Joe concluded.

"Then you should thank him, Joe," said Estoril in a voice carefully purged of all emotion. "Because he seems to have saved your life."

She pointed. The fins of a heavy quarrel stood out slightly from the square hole in the center of Glam's breastplate. Crossbows here might not be able to penetrate dragons easily, but they sure punched through steel armor a treat.

Joe looked over his shoulder at the pane missing from the casement. The bolt that blew it out could've been fired from any of a dozen rooms across the courtyard, he supposed; but Joe wasn't in any real doubt as to whose hand had been on the trigger.

Not a bad time to fall on his face.

Delendor swept his hat off and bowed to Joe. The faces of all those who'd come to rescue Joe were suffused with awe.

"Through *iron*," the prince said, speaking for all of them. "What an amazingly powerful magician!"

"I did *not* tell you to kill the foreign magician, Groag," said Ezekiel. He pitched his voice in a compromise between being threatening and keeping anybody in the hall from overhearing.

"And I most particularly didn't tell you—you, a layman!—to attempt using a magician's own weapons against him!"

"B-b-but—" Groag said. His hands clenched into fists the size of deer hams. The tears squeezing from his eyes could have been either from grief for his brother or from rage.

Or from fear. In which case *both* the men in Ezekiel's laboratory were afraid of Joe Johnson.

"Although the thought of using the foreigner's magic against him wasn't a bad one," Ezekiel added mildly, now that he was sure Groag wasn't going to pull him apart with his bare hands.

The magician's workbench had been partly refurbished into a production line. In a large glass vat, minuscule demons swam though a dark sludge. The demons' blue wings and scales sparkled as the creatures rose to the surface in waves, then submerged for another pass, thoroughly mixing the constituents of the thick mass.

Another work-gang of demons lifted tiny shovelsful of the sludge and spread it on a copper plate pierced with thousands of identical holes. Still more demons hovered and blew their hot breath on the bottom of the plate, keeping it just warm to the touch.

Groag stared at the operation for a moment. "Whazat?" he demanded.

"That," said Ezekiel, "was what you would have done if you'd had any sense."

"You din't tell—"

"You didn't ask!" the magician snapped.

He cleared his throat. "It was obvious to me," Ezekiel resumed in the dry, supercilious voice of a haughty lecturer, "that Joe Johnson's flame magic required some amendments to work here. I consulted my sources to learn the secret of those changes. Thus—"

Ezekiel gestured. "The ingredients were correct, though the proportions had to be modified slightly. Most important, they have to be mixed wet so that each *kernel* of powder retains the proper proportion of each ingredient."

Groag leaned to get a better look at the flowing sludge. His nose almost touched the surface. The wave of mixers broke upward just then; one of the demons yanked a hair out of Groag's nostril before resubmerging.

"*Ouch!*"

"After the mixing is complete," Ezekiel continued with a satis-fied smirk, "the material is spread here—" he indicated the plate "—and dried at low heat. When that process is almost complete, my minions will form the material into kernels by extruding it through the holes in the plate."

Groag, covering his nose with his left hand, furrowed his brow and stared at the production line while a thought slowly formed. At last he said, "So what?"

The magician sighed. "Yes," he said, "I rather thought that might be the next question. Well, my boy, I'll show you 'what.'"

He gestured. A squad of demons whisked together the grains of gunpowder which had already been forced through the plate and carried them to a glass bottle of a size to hold a lady's perfume. When the demons were done, there was just enough room left for Ezekiel to insert the stopper firmly into the bottle's neck.

"When this batch is complete," the magician said as he picked up the bottle and walked to one of the undamaged windows, "there will be enough of the material to fill the brass container on the end of the bench."

He slid the casement up in its frame, then set the bottle on the ledge. A cold breeze rushed into the laboratory, making the oil lamps gutter. A glittering demon began to curvette above the bottle like a blowfly over a corpse.

"If you were to take that large container into Joe Johnson's room tomorrow evening while everyone is at dinner," Ezekiel continued as he stepped back, "you could conceal it under the chair in which he sits. And when Joe Johnson returns to his room—"

Ezekiel gestured. The demon shot straight down and reached a tiny arm through the bottle. When Ezekiel snapped his fingers, there was a spark from the demon's hand and the gunpowder detonated with a tremendous crash.

Groag bellowed in fear. Even the magician stepped backward, startled by the vehemence of what he'd achieved. His hand brushed his fine, gray beard and came away sparkling with slivers of glass.

Ezekiel cleared his throat. His ears rang.

He thought his own voice sounded thin as he concluded, "—*that* might happen to our foreign friend!"

✳   ✳   ✳

The lock of Joe Johnson's door hadn't been repaired, so Groag didn't need a key to make a surreptitious entry into the magician's room.

Nobody would remark on Groag's absence at dinner. They'd just assume he was still sulking about the way the old man fawned on Delendor. They'd've been right any other time, too.

They'd see how long that poof Delendor lasted, once his tame magician was splattered all across the walls!

There was a small lamp burning in the room. It provided the only light, now, because Joe Johnson had tacked curtains over his windows. Was the magician afraid of another quarrel flying through the glass?

Groag shuddered under his chain mail even to think of aiming an arbalest at the cunning bastard. He'd been lucky his stupid brother came in the door just then. Otherwise Joe Johnson would probably have turned the bolt around and it'd've been Groag with wooden fins growing out of his chest!

The brass container, its top screwed down tight on the magic powder, was heavy. Its surface was slick, and it kept turning in Groag's hands as though it wanted to slip away from him.

What if Ezekiel's magic *hadn't* been strong enough to counteract the power of the stranger?

Groag looked at the armchair pulled close to the fireplace. Its seat and legs were bare, nothing whatever to cover the shining container.

The comforter in which Joe Johnson wrapped himself was neatly folded on the bed. If Groag moved the quilt, that would be as much a giveaway as the obvious presence of the container itself.

Which left one sure hiding place. Groag stepped to the fireplace and used the poker to scrape a long trench in the pile of charcoal and hot, white ash. He set the magic container into the trench and carefully covered it again.

The mound was higher than it had been, but there was nothing to draw the eye in the few moments between Joe Johnson entering the room and his sitting down directly in front of the fireplace. . . .

Groag straightened, looking pleased. There was a whisper of sound behind him. He turned like a great cat and met the wide, frightened eyes of the little maid who'd just opened the door.

By god, it was the bitch he and Glam had been chasing the other day!

"What are you doing here?" the maid demanded in a squeaky soprano.

"Nothing *you'll* live to tell about!" Groag bellowed. He didn't bother to draw a sword. Instead, he leaped forward with the poker upraised.

There was a flash as red as the fires of Armageddon.

The blast was equally impressive, but Groag didn't live to hear it.

Mary lay on her back, across the hall from where white haze seethed from Joe's doorway.

Joe had left the banquet before the serious drinking began, so he reached the bomb site as quickly as any of the servants. Wind through the window openings drew orange flickers from the fire within; the stench of burning feathers mingled with the brimstone odor of gunpowder.

Joe knelt, cradling Mary's fragile body in his arms. She was unconscious but breathing normally.

Thank god!

Dozens of servants came running from both directions, many of them carrying firebuckets. Joe grabbed a sturdy-looking female, pointed to Mary, and said, "Watch her! I'll be right back!"

He snatched a lamp from a wall bracket and plunged into his room. His feet slipped.

On Groag.

King Morhaven's eldest son had taken most of the blast. The shock wave blew Mary through the open door; Groag had been driven into the stone doorjamb instead.

Joe couldn't be sure whether Groag's clothes had been blown off his body, or whether the body had simply leaked through the fabric after being strained through his chain-link armor. He could be identified by the ornate hilt of his sword.

Confirmation came from the smoldering black beard hairs which clung to the bloodstained wall.

"Joe! Joe!" Delendor shouted as the young prince led a crowd up the stairway from the banquet hall. "Are you all right?"

Servants were tossing buckets of water on the flames, but that was pointless: there was nothing left in the room to save, and the wooden roof beams weren't yet in danger.

Joe grabbed a handful of burning bedding and flung it through one of the window openings. The mass drifted down into the courtyard. Blazing bits of cloth and feathers dribbled away like a slow-motion firework.

Others took over the job, hurling out even the shattered remnants of the bed frame and cedar chest. Nobody seemed to be too concerned about Groag.

Joe wasn't concerned either. He stepped out into the hall again, just as the thundering squadron of nobles from the banquet hall reached the scene.

Most of the nobles. Master Ezekiel wasn't among them.

"Is it . . . ?" King Morhaven called. "Is it . . . ?"

The king knew as well as anybody else did who was likely to be at the bottom of the current problem.

Joe opened his mouth to answer as bluntly as rage made him wish—but you couldn't blame the father for the sons, and anyway, there'd been enough outbursts of one sort and another this night.

"You'd better look for yourself," he said, and he handed Morhaven the lamp. The king, Delendor, and Estoril forced their way into the room through the mob of frantic servants.

"I'll take over now," Joe said as he squatted beside Mary again. A firebucket had been set nearby. He dipped his handkerchief in the water and began to sponge powder blackening and speckles of Groag from the maid's face.

The king came out of Joe's room. He'd aged a decade in a few seconds. Delendor and the princess walked to either side of Morhaven, looking worried and poised to catch him if he collapsed. Even Kiki seemed upset.

Morhaven straightened. "Very well," he said. "Events have forced me to the choice I'd already made. People of Hamisch, my successor shall be my son Delen—"

Estoril put one slim white hand over King Morhaven's mouth. "Father," she said in the shocked silence, "I wasn't sure that I'd ever repeat what Katya told me before she died. I think now that I have to."

"Katya?" Delendor repeated with a puzzled expression.

"Your mother Blumarine's nurse!" the princess snapped. "Don't you remember?"

Which of course Delendor hadn't, but he was used enough to the situation to nod wisely. His monkey aped his motions.

Estoril lowered her hand and looked Morhaven in the eye. "Father," she said. "Your Majesty. Princess Blumarine was secretly married to Sir Delendor. And her son Delendor—isn't your son, Your Majesty."

"Well I'll be!" said Delendor. If there was any emotion besides amazement in his tone, Joe didn't hear it. "Well I'll *be*. Then you're not my sister, Essie?"

"No," Estoril said, "but you *have* a real older sister." She took the locket from around Delendor's neck and snapped it open. "There," she continued. "That's your sister."

"Why," said Delendor. "Why . . . why look, Joe, she isn't a rabbit any more!"

He held the locket down to Joe. Instead of a mirror, it held a miniature painting on ivory of a young woman with lustrous blond hair. She was absolutely beautiful.

"*And*," Delendor added, rising with new excitement in his voice, "that means there's no reason *we* can't be married. Essie, will you be my queen?"

"I think," said Estoril dryly, "that the proper question is, 'Del, will you be my consort?' But I think the answer is yes, either way."

She smiled. There was nothing dry about the affection in her eyes.

The woman in Joe's lap stirred. He looked down, his mouth already forming the words, "Oh, thank god you're all right, Mary—"

She wasn't Mary.

She was the woman in the locket painting.

"Good lord!" Joe blurted. "Who are you?"

The blond woman smiled. If there was a sight more beautiful than her face, it was her face with a smile wrapping it. "I'm Mary, Joe," she said.

Mary tried to sit. She was still dizzy from the explosion; Joe's arm helped her. "You've told my brother, then?" she asked/said to Estoril.

Even Estoril looked surprised. "Yes, and you're . . ."

"I'm your sister, Del," Mary said, "though for your sake and hers, Mother kept it a secret. When the dragon appeared, I wanted to help you—but Katya put a spell on me to hide my likeness to you and prevent me from telling you the truth. She'd promised Blumarine . . . but I came to be near you anyway."

"And I broke the spell," Estoril amplified to Delendor's puzzled expression, "by telling you who your real father was."

Delendor blinked. Then his face cleared and he beamed happily. "Well, anyway," he said, "everything's settled now."

"No," said Joe in a voice that would have chilled him if it hadn't come from his own mouth. "There's one thing yet to be settled. Between me and Ezekiel."

He squeezed Mary's hand as he released her, but the woman didn't occupy a major part of his mind just at the moment.

Joe stood and picked up Groag's sword. The shagreen scabbard had been blown away, and several of the jewels had been knocked out of the hilt, but the weapon was still serviceable.

It would serve.

With the sword in his hand, Joe began jogging down the hall. He was moving at a pace he was sure he could keep up until he reached Ezekiel's laboratory across the building.

Or wherever else the magician ran, this side of Hell.

Joe heard a crash of metal and breaking glass as he neared the last corner between him and the laboratory. When he rounded it, he saw the door of the laboratory open, a satchel dropped on the hallway, still spilling paraphernalia—

And a stairwell door still swinging closed.

Ezekiel had run from the banquet hall to his laboratory to pack the cream of his belongings. When he heard retribution coming, he'd abandoned even those valuables in his haste to escape.

Which he wasn't about to do.

"Hold it right there, Ezekiel!" Joe bellowed as he slammed down the stairs behind the fleeing magician. The long sword in Joe's hand sang and sparked crazily as its point scraped the stairwell. Ezekiel's black robe trailed back around the stone helix, almost close enough to touch, but the unencumbered magician was able to maintain his distance ahead of his pursuer, past the first landing, the second—

Ezekiel banged through the door to the ground floor.

"Stop him!" Joe called to the servant there at the door by the pantry.

The fellow might have tried, but Ezekiel snapped his fingers. The servant froze with his mouth gaping like that of a surfaced carp. He blinked a moment later, but the magician was already past.

Ezekiel wasn't—*puff*—casting spells at Joe—*puff*—because he was sure—*puff*—that Joe was a greater magician than he was.

Ezekiel ran outside. Joe slipped and had to grab the jamb to keep from falling. A four-horse carriage waited in the courtyard.

The driver was a smirking Mongolian.

Ezekiel recognized the 7th Plane inhabitant also. "I'll be back to defeat you yet, Joe Johnson!" the magician screamed over his shoulder. He grabbed the latch and threw open the carriage door.

A clawed, hairy paw closed on Ezekiel's neck and drew him the rest of the way into the conveyance.

Joe stood panting, still clinging to the doorjamb as the coach drew away. It was accelerating faster than horses should have been able to move it.

Something flew out of a side window just as the vehicle disappeared into the arched gateway. It looked like a hand, but Joe didn't feel any need for certainty on the point.

Someone touched Joe's shoulder. He turned to see Mary, the new Mary, with a wistful smile on her face.

"It's over," Joe said to her, all he could manage while he tried to catch his breath.

"Mother—Mother's friends, I suppose—brought you here to save my brother," Mary said. An attempt to make her smile a cheerful one failed miserably. "I suppose you'll go home to your own plane now?"

Joe grunted something that was meant to be laughter.

"I think that was my ride," he said, pointing his thumb in the direction the coach had disappeared.. "Believe me, *I'm* not getting in if it decides to come back again."

Mary wet her full, red lips nervously. "Are you disappointed?" she asked in a whisper.

"Do you remember what the king said upstairs?" Joe asked carefully. "About events making him do what he'd already decided he wanted to?"

Joe dropped the sword so that he could use both his arms to hug Mary.

He had a lot to learn about this world, but some things were just the same as they were back home.

The Adventure of the Pearly Gates

➤ MIKE RESNICK ◄

"... An examination by experts leaves little doubt that a personal contest between the two men ended, as it could hardly fail to end in such a situation, in their reeling over, locked in each other's arms. Any attempt at recovering the bodies was absolutely hopeless, and there, deep down in that dreadful cauldron of swirling water and seething foam, will lie for all time the most dangerous criminal and the foremost champion of the law of their generation ..."
—*The Final Problem*

IT WAS MOST DISCONCERTING. ONE MOMENT I WAS TUMBLING over the falls at Reichenbach, my arms locked around Professor Moriarty, and the next moment I seemed to be standing by myself in a bleak, gray, featureless landscape.

I was completely dry, which seemed not at all surprising, though there was no reason why it should not have been. Also, I had felt my leg shatter against the rocks as we began our plunge, and yet I felt no pain whatsoever.

Suddenly I remembered Moriarty. I looked around for him, but he was nowhere to be seen. There was an incredibly bright light up ahead, and I found myself drawn to it. What happened next I can remember but hazily; the gist of it is that I found myself in, of all places, Heaven. (No one told me that I was in Heaven, but when one eliminates the impossible, whatever remains, however improbable, must be the truth . . . and Professor Moriarty's absence was quite enough to convince me that I was not in Hell.)

How long I remained there I do not know, for there is no means by which one can measure duration there. I only know that I felt I might as well have been in the Other Place, so bored was I with the eternal peace and perfection of my surroundings. It is an admission that would certainly offend all churchmen, but if there is one place in all the cosmos for which I am uniquely unsuited, it is Heaven.

In fact, I soon began to suspect that I was indeed in Hell, for if each of us makes his own Heaven and his own Hell, then my Hell must surely be a place where all my training and all my powers are of no use whatsoever. A place where the game is never afoot, indeed where there is no game at all, cannot possibly qualify as a Paradise for a man such as myself.

When I was bored beyond endurance back on Earth, I had discovered a method of relief, but this was denied me in my current circumstances. Still, it was a craving for cerebral stimulation, not for a seven percent solution of cocaine, that consumed me.

And then, when I was sure that I was facing an eternity of boredom, and was regretting all the chances I had forsaken to commit such sins as might have placed me in a situation where at least I would have had the challenge of escaping, I found myself confronted by a glowing entity that soon manifested itself in the outward form of a man with pale blue eyes and a massive white beard. He wore a robe of white, and above his head floated a golden halo.

Suddenly I, too, took on human shape, and I was amazed to discover that I had not until this very moment realized that I had no longer possessed a body.

"Hello, Mr. Holmes," said my visitor.

"Welcome, Saint Peter," I replied with my newfound voice.

"You know who I am?" he said, surprised. "Your indoctrination period is supposed to be instantly forgotten."

"I remember nothing of my indoctrination period," I assured him.

"Then how could you possibly know who I am?"

"Observation, analysis and deduction," I explained. "You have obviously sought me out, for you addressed me by my name, and since I have evidently been a discorporate being, one of many billions, I assume you have the ability to distinguish between us all. That implies a certain authority. You have taken the body you used when you were alive, and I perceive that the slight indentations on the fingers of your right hand were made by a crude fishing line. You possess a halo while I do not, which therefore implies that you are a saint. Now, who among the many saints was a fisherman and would have some authority in Heaven?"

Saint Peter smiled. "You are quite amazing, Mr. Holmes."

"I am quite bored, Saint Peter."

"I know," he said, "and for this I am sorry. You are unique among all the souls in Heaven in your discontent."

"That is no longer true," I said, "for do I not perceive a certain lack of content upon your own features?"

"That is correct, Mr. Holmes," he agreed. "We have a problem here—a problem of my own making—and I have elected to solicit your aid in solving it. It seems the very least I can do to make your stay here more tolerable to you." He paused awkwardly. "Also, it may well be that you are the one soul in my domain who is capable of solving it."

"Cannot God instantly solve any problem that arises?" I asked.

"He can, and eventually He will. But since I have created this problem, I requested that I be allowed to solve it—or attempt to solve it—first."

"How much time has He given you?"

"Time has no meaning here, Mr. Holmes. If He determines that I will fail, He will correct the problem Himself." He paused again. "I hope you will be able to assist me to redeem myself in His eyes."

"I shall certainly do my best," I assured him. "Please state the nature of the problem."

"It is most humiliating, Mr. Holmes," he began. "For time beyond memory I have been the Keeper of the Pearly Gates. No one can enter Heaven without my approval, and until recently I had never made a mistake."

"And now you have?"

He nodded his head wearily. "Now I have. A *huge* mistake."

"Can't you simply seek out the soul, as you have sought me out, and cast it out?"

"I wish it were that simple, Mr. Holmes," he replied. "A Caligula, a Tamerlaine, an Attila I could find with no difficulty. But this soul, though it is blackened beyond belief, has thus far managed to elude me."

"I see," I said. "I am surprised that five such hideous murders do not make it instantly discernable."

"Then you know?" he exclaimed.

"That you seek Jack the Ripper?" I replied. "Elementary. All of the others you mentioned were identified with their crimes, but the Ripper's identity was never discovered. Further, since the man was mentally unbalanced, it seems possible to me, based on my admittedly limited knowledge of Heaven, that if he feels no guilt, his soul displays no guilt."

"You are everything I had hoped you would be, Mr. Holmes," said Saint Peter.

"Not quite everything," I said. "For I do not understand your concern. If the Ripper's soul displays no taint, why bother seeking him out? After all, the man was obviously insane and not responsible for his actions. On Earth, yes, I would not hesitate to lock him away where he could do no further damage—but here in Heaven, what possible harm can he do?"

"Things are not as simple as you believe them to be, Mr. Holmes," replied Saint Peter. "Here we exist on a spiritual plane, but the same is not true of Purgatory or Hell. Recently, an unseen soul has been attempting to open the Pearly Gates from *this* side." He frowned. "They were made to withstand efforts from without, but not within. Another attempt or two, and the soul may actually succeed. Once possessed of ectoplasmic attributes, there is no limit to the damage he could do in Purgatory."

"Then why not simply let him out?"

"If I leave the gates open for him, we could be overwhelmed by even more unfit souls attempting to enter."

"I see," I said. "What leads you to believe that it *is* the Ripper?"

"Just as there is no duration in Heaven, neither is there location. The Pearly Gates, though quite small themselves, exist in *all* locations."

"Ah!" I said, finally comprehending the nature of the problem. "Would I be correct in assuming that the attempt to break out was made in the vicinity of the souls of Elizabeth Stride, Annie Chapman, Catherine Eddowes, Mary Kelly and Mary Ann Nicholls?"

"His five victims," said Saint Peter, nodding. "Actually, two of them are beyond even *his* reach, but Stride, Chapman and Kelly are in Purgatory."

"Can you bring those three to Heaven?" I asked.

"As bait?" asked Saint Peter. "I am afraid not. No one may enter Heaven before his or her time. Besides," he added, "there is nothing he can do to them in spiritual form. As you yourself know, one cannot even communicate with other souls here. One spends all eternity reveling in the glory of God."

"So *that* is what one does here," I said wryly.

"Please, Mr. Holmes!" he said severely.

"I apologize," I said. "Well, it seems we must set a trap for the Ripper on his next escape attempt."

"Can we be sure he will continue his attempts to escape?"

"He is perhaps the one soul less suited to Heaven than I myself," I assured him.

"It seems an impossible undertaking," said Saint Peter morosely. "He could try to leave at any point."

"He will attempt to leave in the vicinity of his victims," I answered.

"How can you be certain of that?" asked Saint Peter.

"Because those slayings were without motive."

"I do not understand."

"Where there is no motive," I explained, "there is no reason to stop. You may rest assured that he will attempt to reach them again."

"Even so, how am I to apprehend him—or even identify him?" asked Saint Peter.

"Is location *necessarily* meaningless in Heaven?" I asked.

He stared at me uncomprehendingly.

"Let me restate that," I said. "Can you direct the Pearly Gates to remain in the vicinity of the souls in question?"

He shook his head. "You do not comprehend, Mr. Holmes. They exist in all times and places at once."

"I see," I said, wishing I had my pipe to draw upon now that I was in human form. "Can you create a second gate?"

"It would not be the same," said Saint Peter.

"It needn't be the same, as long as it seemed similar to the perception of a soul."

"He would know instantly."

I shook my head. "He is quite insane. His thought processes, such as they are, are aberrant. If you do as I suggest, and place a false gate near the souls of his victims, my guess is that he will not pause to notice the difference. He is somehow drawn to them, and this will be a barrier to his desires. He will be more interested in attacking it than in analyzing it, even if he were capable of the latter, which I am inclined to doubt."

"You're quite sure?" asked Saint Peter doubtfully.

"He is compelled to perform his carnage upon prostitutes. For whatever reason, these seem to be the only souls he can identify as prostitutes. Therefore, it is these that he wishes to attack." I paused again. "Create the false gates. The soul that goes through them will be the one you seek."

"I hope you are correct, Mr. Holmes," he said. "Pride is a sin, but even *I* have a modicum of it, and I should hate to be shamed before my Lord."

And with that, he was gone.

He returned after an indeterminate length of time, a triumphant smile upon his face.

"I assume that our little ruse worked?" I said.

"Exactly as you said it would!" replied Saint Peter. "Jack the Ripper is now where he belongs, and shall never desecrate Heaven with his presence again." He stared at me. "You should be thrilled, Mr. Holmes, and yet you look unhappy."

"I envy him in a way," I said. "For at least he now has a challenge."

"Do not envy him," said Saint Peter. "Far from having a challenge, he can look forward to nothing but eternal suffering."

"I have that in common with him," I replied bitterly.

"Perhaps not," said Saint Peter.

I was instantly alert. "Oh?"

"You have saved me from shame and embarrassment," he said. "The very least I can do is reward you."

"How?"

"I rather thought *you* might have a suggestion."

"This may be Heaven to you," I said, "but it is Hell to me. If you truly wish to reward me, send me to where I can put my abilities to use. There is evil abroad in the world; I am uniquely qualified to combat it."

"You would really turn your back on Heaven to continue your pursuit of injustice, to put yourself at risk on almost a daily basis?" asked Saint Peter.

"I would."

"Even knowing that, should you fall from the path of righteousness—and it is a trickier path than your churches would have you believe—this might not be your ultimate destination?"

"Even so." And privately I thought: *especially* so.

"Then I see no reason why I should not grant your request," said Saint Peter.

"Thank God!" I muttered.

Saint Peter smiled again. "Thank Him yourself—when you think of it. He *does* listen, you know."

Suddenly I found myself back in that infinite gray landscape I had encountered after going over the falls at Reichenbach, only this time, instead of a shining light, I thought I could see a city in the distance . . .

"Holmes!" I cried. "Is it really you? Can it indeed be that you are alive? Is it possible that you succeeded in climbing out of that awful abyss?"

The Seventh Chapter

➤ HARRY TURTLEDOVE ◄

THE SNOW WAS FALLING HARDER NOW. KASSIANOS' MULE, A GOOD stubborn beast, kept slogging forward until it came to a drift that reached its belly. Then it stopped, looking reproachfully back over its shoulder at the priest.

"Oh, very well," he said, as if it could understand. "This must be as Phos wills. That town the herder spoke of can't be far ahead. We'll lay over in—what did he call it?—Develtos till the weather gets better. Are you satisfied, beast?"

The mule snorted and pressed ahead. Maybe it did understand, Kassianos thought. He had done enough talking at it, this past month on the road. He loved to talk, and had not had many people to talk to. Back in Videssos the city, his clerical colleagues told him he was mad to set out for Opsikion so late in the year. He hadn't listened; that wasn't nearly so much fun as talking.

"Unfortunately, they were right," he said. This time, the mule paid him no attention. It had reached the same conclusion a long time ago.

The wind howled out of the north. Kassianos drew his blue robe more tightly about himself, not that that did much good. Because the road from the capital of the Empire to Opsikion ran south of the Paristrian mountains, he had assumed they would shield him from the worst of the weather. Maybe they did. If so, though, the provinces on the other side of the mountains had winters straight from the ice of Skotos' hell.

349

Where was he? For that matter, where was the road? When it ran between leaf-bare trees, it had been easy enough to follow. Now, in more open country, the pesky thing had disappeared. In better weather, that would only have been a nuisance (in better weather, Kassianos reminded himself, it wouldn't have happened). In this blizzard, it was becoming serious. If he went by Develtos, he might freeze before he could find shelter.

He tugged on the reins. The mule positively scowled at him: what was he doing, halting in the cold middle of nowhere? "I need to find the town," he explained. The mule did not look convinced.

He paused a moment in thought. He had never been to Develtos, had nothing from it with him. That made worthless most of the simpler spells of finding he knew. He thought of one that might serve, then promptly rejected it: it involved keeping a candle lit for half an hour straight. "Not bloody likely, I'm afraid," he said.

He thought some more, then laughed out loud. "As inelegant an application of the law of similarity as ever there was," he declared, "but it will serve. Like does call to like."

He dismounted, tied the mule's reins to a bush so it would not wander off while he was incanting. Then, after suitable prayers and passes, he undid his robe and pissed—quickly, because it was very cold.

His urine did not just form a puddle between his feet. Instead, impelled by his magic, it drew a steaming line in the snow toward more like itself, and thus, indirectly, toward the people who made it.

"That way, eh?" Kassianos said, eyeing the direction of the line. "I might have known the wind would make me drift south of where I should be." He climbed back onto his mule, urged it forward. It went eagerly, as if it sensed he knew where he was going again.

Sure enough, not a quarter of an hour later the priest saw the walls of Develtos looming tall and dark through the driving snow. He had to ride around a fair part of the circuit before he came to a gate. It was closed and barred. He shouted. Nothing happened. He shouted again, louder.

After a couple of minutes, a peephole opened. "Who ye be?" the man inside called, his accent rustic. "Show yerself to me and give me your name."

"I am Kassianos, eastbound from Videssos the city," the priest answered. He rode a couple of steps closer, lowered his hood so the guard could see not only his blue robe but also his shaven head. "May I have shelter before I am too far gone to need it?"

He did not hear anyone moving to unlatch the gate. Instead, the sentry asked sharply, "Just the one of you there?"

"Only myself. In Phos' holy name I swear it." Kassianos understood the gate guard's caution. Winter could easily make a bandit band desperate enough to try to take a walled town, and falling snow give them the chance to approach unobserved. A quick rush once the gate was open, and who could say what horrors would follow?

But Kassianos must have convinced the guardsman. "We'll have you inside in a minute, holy sir." The fellow's voice grew muffled as he turned his face away from the peephole. "Come on, Phostis, Evagrios, give me a hand with this bloody bar." Kassianos heard it scrape against the iron-faced timbers of the gate.

One of the valves swung inward. The priest dug his heels into the mule's flanks. It trotted into Develtos. The sentries closed the gate after it, shoved the bar back into place. "Thank you, gentlemen," Kassianos said sincerely.

"Aye, you're about this far from being a snowman, aren't you, holy sir?" said the guard who had been at the peephole. Now Kassianos could see more of him than a suspicious eyeball: he was short and lean, with a knitted wool cap on his head and a sheepskin jacket closed tight over a mail shirt. His bow was a hunter's weapon, not a soldier's. He was, in other words, a typical small-town guardsman.

"Want I should take you to Branas' tavern, holy sir, let you warm yourself up outside and in?" asked one of the other guards. But for a back-and-breast of boiled leather and a light spear in place of a bow, he was as like the first as two peas in a pod. He glanced toward that man, who was evidently his superior. "Is it all right, Tzitas?"

"Aye, go on, Phostis, we'll manage here." Tzitas showed his teeth in a knowing grin. "Just don't spend too much time warming yourself up in there."

"Wouldn't think of it," Phostis said righteously.

"No, you wouldn't; you'd do it," said Evagrios, who'd been quiet till then. Tzitas snorted.

Phostis sent them both a rude gesture. He turned back to the priest. "You come with me, holy sir. Pay these scoffers no mind." He started off down the street. His boots left pockmarks in the snow. Still on muleback, Kassianos followed.

The tavern was less than a hundred yards away. (Nothing in Develtos, come to that, looked to be more than a quarter mile from anything else. The town barely rated a wall.) In that short journey, though, Phostis asked Kassianos about Videssos the city four different times, and told him twice of some distant cousin who had gone there to seek his fortune. "He must have found it, too," Phostis said wistfully, "for he never came back no more."

He might have starved trying, Kassianos thought, but the priest was too kind to say that out loud. Videssos' capital drew the restless and ambitious from all over the Empire, and in such fast company not all could flourish.

Even with Phostis', "Here we are, holy sir," Kassianos could have guessed which building was Branas' from the number of horses and donkeys tied up in front of it. He found space at the rail for his mule, then went in after the sentry.

He shut the door behind him so none of the blessed heat inside would escape. A few quick steps brought him to the fireplace. He sighed in pure animal pleasure as the warmth began driving the ice from his bones. When he put a hand to his face, he discovered he could feel the tip of his nose again. He'd almost forgotten he still owned it.

After roasting a bit longer in front of the flames, Kassianos felt restored enough to find a stool at a table close by. A barmaid came over, looked him up and down. "What'll it be?" she asked, matter-of-fact as if he were carpenter rather than priest.

"Hot red wine, spiced with cinnamon."

She nodded, saucily ran her hand over his shaved pate. "That'll do it for you, right enough." Her hips worked as she walked back to the tapman with his order; she looked over her shoulder at the priest, as if to make sure he was watching her.

His blood heated with a warmth that had nothing to do with the blaze crackling in the fireplace. He willed himself to take no notice of that new heat. Celibacy went with Phos' blue robe. He frowned a little. Even the most shameless tavern wenches knew that. Clerics were men too, and might forget their vows, but he still found an overture as blatant as this girl's startling. Even in the jaded capital, a lady of easy virtue would have been more discreet. The same should have gone double for this back-country town.

The barmaid returned with his steaming mug. As he fumbled in his beltpouch for coppers to pay the score, she told him, "You want to warm up the parts fire and wine don't reach, you let me know." Before he could answer, someone called to her from a table halfway across the room. She hurried off, but again smiled back at Kassianos as she went.

Before he lifted the cup to his lips, he raised his hands to heaven and intoned the usual Videssian prayer before food or drink: "We bless thee, Phos, lord with the great and good mind, by thy grace our protector, watchful beforehand that the great test of life may be decided in our favor." Then he spat in the rushes to show his rejection of Skotos. At last he drank. The cinnamon nipped his tongue like a playful lover. The figure of speech would not have occurred to him a moment before. Now it seemed only too appropriate.

When his mug was empty, he raised a finger. The girl hurried over. "Another, please," he said, setting more coppers on the table.

She scooped them up. "For some silver . . ." She paused expectantly.

"My vows do not allow me carnal union. What makes you think I take them lightly?" he asked. He kept his voice mild, but his eyes seized and held hers. He had overawed unrepentant clerics in the ecclesiastical courts of the capital; focusing his forensic talents on a chit of a barmaid reminded him of smashing some small crawling insect with an anvil. But she had roused his curiosity, if not his manhood.

"The monks hereabouts like me plenty well," she sniffed; she sounded offended he did not find her attractive. "And since you're a man from Videssos the city itself," (news traveled fast, Kassianos thought, unsurprised) "I reckoned you'd surely be freer yet."

Along with its famed riches, the capital also had a reputation in the provinces as a den of iniquity. Sometimes, Kassianos knew, it was deserved. But not in this . . . "You are mistaken," the priest replied. "The monks like you well, you say?"

The girl's eyes showed she suddenly realized the hole she had dug for herself. "I'm not the only one," she said hastily. "There's a good many women they favor here in town, most of 'em a lot more than me."

She contradicted herself, Kassianos noted, but never mind that now. "Are there indeed?" he said, letting some iron come into his voice. "Perhaps you will be so good as to give me their names?"

"No. Why should I?" She had spirit; she could still defy him.

He dropped the anvil. "Because I am Kassianos, *nomophylax*— chief counsel, you might say—to the most holy ecumenical Patriarch Tarasios, prelate of Videssos the city and Videssos the Empire. I was summoned to Opsikion to deal with a troublesome case of false doctrine there, but I begin to think the good god Phos directed me here instead. Now speak to me further of these monks."

The barmaid fled instead. Eyes followed her from all over the taproom, then turned to Kassianos. The big man whose place was behind the bar slowly ambled over to his table. As if by chance, he held a stout club in his right fist. "Don't know what you said to little Laskara, blue-robe," he said casually, "but she didn't much like it."

"And I, friend, did not much like her seeking to lead me astray from my vows, and liked even less her telling me the monks hereabouts are accustomed to ignoring theirs," Kassianos answered. "I do not think the most holy Tarasios, Phos bless him, would like that either. Perhaps if I root out the evil, it will never have to come to his attention."

At the mention of that name, the tapman sat down heavily beside Kassianos, as if his legs no longer wanted to support him. The priest heard him drop the bludgeon among the dried rushes on the floor. "The—Patriarch?" the fellow said hoarsely.

"The very same." Kassianos' eyes twinkled. Most of the time, being *nomophylax* was nothing but drudgery. Sometimes, as now, it was fun. "Suppose you tell me about the lecherous monks you have here. Your Laskara thought I was of the same stripe as they, and tried to sell herself to me."

"Aye, we have a monastery here, dedicated to the holy Tralitzes, Phos bless his memory." The tapman drew the good god's sun-circle over his heart. Kassianos had never heard of the local saint, but that hardly signified: every little town had some patron to commemorate. The tapman went on, "But the monks, lecherous? No, holy sir—they're good men, pious men, every one."

He sounded sincere, and too shaken to be lying so well. "Do they then conform to the rules set down by the holy Pakhomios, in whose memory all monks serve?" Kassianos asked.

"Holy sir, I'm no monk. Far as I know, they do, but I dunno what all these rules and things is." The fellow was sweating, and not from the fireplace's being near.

"Very well, then, hear the seventh chapter of Pakhomios' *Rule*, the chapter entitled 'On Women': 'To ensure the preservation of the contemplative life, no brother shall be permitted to entertain women.'"

"I dunno about any of that," the tapman insisted. With a sudden access of boldness, he went on, "And it's not me you should ought to be going after if you've got somewhat against our monks. You take that up with the abbot—Menas, his name is."

"I shall," Kassianos promised. "Believe me, I shall."

The holy Tralitzes' monastery lay a couple of miles outside Develtos. Monks working in the snowy fields and gardens looked up from their labors as Kassianos rode toward Phos' temple, the largest building of the monastery complex. It was further distinguished from the others by a spire topped with a gilded globe.

An elderly monk came out of the temple, bowed courteously to Kassianos. "Phos be with you, holy sir," he said. "I am Pleuses, porter of the monastery. How may I serve you?"

Kassianos dismounted, returned the bow. "And with you, brother Pleuses. I have come to see your abbot—Menas is his name, is it not? I am Kassianos, *nomophylax* to Tarasios. Would you announce me to the holy abbot?"

Pleuses' eyes widened. He bowed once more. "Certainly, holy sir. Menas will surely be honored to entertain such a distinguished guest." He shouted for a younger brother to take charge of Kassianos' mule, then, bowing a third time, said, "Will you come with me?"

The abbot's residence lay beyond the dormitory that housed the rest of the monks. "Wait here a moment, will you?" Pleuses said at the doorway. He went in and, as promised, quickly returned. "He will see you now."

Kassianos was expecting a leering voluptuary. The sight of Menas came as something of a shock. He was a thin, pleasant-faced man of about forty-five, with laugh lines crinkling the corners of his eyes. Among the codices and scrolls on bookshelves behind him were many, both religious and secular, that Kassianos also esteemed.

The abbot rose, bowed, hurried up to clasp Kassianos' hand. "Phos bless you, holy sir, and welcome, welcome. Will you take wine?"

"Thank you, Father Abbot."

Menas poured with his own hands. While he was doing so, he asked, "May I be permitted to wonder why such an illustrious cleric has chosen to honor our humble monastery with his presence?"

Kassianos' eyes flicked to Pleuses. Menas followed his glance, and dismissed the porter with a few murmured words. The abbot was no fool, Kassianos thought. Well, abbots were not chosen to be fools. The two men performed the usual Videssian ritual over wine, then Menas returned to his own seat and waved Kassianos to the other, more comfortable, chair in the room. The abbot's question still hung in the air.

"Father Abbot," Kassianos began, more carefully than he had intended before meeting Menas, "I came to Develtos by chance a few days ago, compelled by the blizzard to take shelter here. In Branas' tavern, a chance remark led me to believe the monks practiced illegal, immoral cohabitation with women, contrary to the strictures of the seventh chapter of the holy Pakhomios' *Rule*."

"That is not so," Menas said quietly. "We follow the *Rule* in all its particulars."

"I am glad to hear you say that," Kassianos nodded. "But I must tell you that my inquiries since I came here made me think otherwise. And, Father Abbot, they make me believe this not only of your flock but of yourself."

"Having once said that I adhere to Pakhomios' *Rule*, I do not suppose that mere repetition will persuade you I speak truly," Menas said after a moment's thought. He grinned wryly; shaven head and gray-streaked beard or no, it made him look very young. "And, having now once said something you do not believe, I cannot hope you will accept my oath." He spread his hands. "You see my difficulty."

"I do." Kassianos nodded again. He thought better of Menas for not gabbling oaths that, as the abbot pointed out, had to be thought untrustworthy. He had not expected or wanted to think better of Menas. He had wanted to get on with the business of reforming the monastery. Things did not seem as simple as he'd thought. Well, as *nomophylax* he'd had that happen to him often enough.

"I will follow any suggestion you may have on resolving this difficulty," Menas said, as if reading his thoughts.

"Very well, then: I know a decoction under whose influence you will speak truth. Are you willing to drink it down and then answer my questions?"

"So long as you are asking about these alleged misdeeds, certainly."

Menas showed no hesitation. If he was an actor, he was a good one, Kassianos thought. But no one could dissemble under the influence of this potion, no matter how he schooled himself beforehand.

"I shall compound the drug this evening and return to administer it tomorrow morning," the *nomophylax* said. Menas nodded agreement. Kassianos wondered how brash he would be once his lascivious secrets were laid bare.

The abbot peered curiously at the small glass flask. He held it to his nose, sniffed. "Not a prize vintage," he observed with a chuckle. He tossed the drug down, screwed up his face at the taste.

Kassianos admired his effrontery, if nothing else. He waited for a few minutes, watched the abbot's expression go from its usual amused alertness to a fixed, vacant stare. The *nomophylax* rose, passed a hand in front of Menas' face. Menas' eyes did not followed the motion. Kassianos nodded to himself. Sure enough, the decoction had taken hold.

"Can you hear me?" he asked.

"Aye." Menas' voice was distant, abstracted.

"Tell me, then, of all the violations of the holy Pakhomios' *Rule* that have occurred among the monks of this monastery over the past half a year."

Menas immediately began to obey: the drug robbed him of his own will and left him perfectly receptive to Kassianos' question. The *nomophylax* settled back in his chair and listened as Menas spoke of this monk's quarrel with that one, of the time when three brothers got drunk together, of the monk who missed evening prayers four days running, of the one who had refused to pull weeds until he was disciplined, of the one who had sworn at an old man in Develtos, of the monk who had stolen a book but tried to put the blame on another, and on and on, all the petty squabbles to which monasteries, being made up of men, were prone.

Kassianos kept pen poised over parchment, ready to note down every transgression of chapter seven of the *Rule*. Menas talked and talked and talked. The pen stayed poised. Kassianos wrote nothing, for the abbot gave him nothing to write.

Menas, at length, ran dry. Kassianos scowled, ran a hand over his smooth pate. "Do you recall nothing more?" he demanded harshly.

"Nothing, holy sir." Menas' voice was calm; it would not have changed had Kassianos held his hand to the flame flickering in the lamp on the table beside him. The *nomophylax* knew he was deeply under the influence of the potion. He also knew the monks of the monastery of the holy Tralitzes had illicit congress with a great many women of Develtos. His inquiries in the town had left him as certain of that as he was of Phos' eventual victory over Skotos.

Kassianos hesitated before asking his next question. But, having failed with a general inquiry, he saw no choice but to probe specifically at the rot he knew existed: "Tell me of every occasion when the monks of this monastery have transgressed against the seventh chapter of the holy Pakhomios' *Rule*, the chapter which forbids the brethren to entertain women."

Menas was silent. Kassianos wondered if the abbot could somehow be struggling against the decoction. He shook his head—he knew perfectly well it was irresistible. "Why do you not speak?" the *nomophylax* snapped.

"Because I know of no occasion when the monks of this monastery have transgressed against the seventh chapter of the holy Pakhomios' *Rule*, the chapter which forbids the brethren to entertain women."

The rotelike repetition of his words and the tone of the abbot's voice convinced Kassianos that Menas was still drugged. So did the reason he gave for staying quiet before. If someone under this potion had nothing to say in response to a question, he would keep right on saying nothing until jogged by a new one. Which, depressingly, was just what Menas had done.

Kassianos sighed. He neither liked nor approved of paradoxes. Knowing that because of the decoction he was only being redundant, he nevertheless asked, "Do you swear by Phos you have told me the truth?"

"I swear by Phos I have told you the truth," Menas replied.

The *nomophylax* ground his teeth. If Menas swore under the drug that the monks of the monastery of the holy Tralitzes were obeying Pakhomios' *Rule*, then they were, and that was all there was to it. So act as though you believe it, Kassianos told himself. He could not.

He was tempted to walk out of Menas' study and let the abbot try to deal with the monastery's affairs while still in the grip of the potion. He had played that sort of practical joke while a student at the Sorcerers' Collegium. Regretfully, he decided it was beneath the dignity of the Patriarch's *nomophylax*. He sat and waited until he was sure Menas had come around.

"Remarkable," the abbot said when he was himself again. "I felt quite beside myself. Had we been guilty of any transgressions of the sort you were seeking, I would not have been able to keep them from you."

"That, Father Abbot, was the idea," Kassianos said tightly. He knew he should have been more courteous, but could not manage it, not with the feeling something was wrong still gnawing at him. But, not having anything on which to focus his suspicions, he could only rise abruptly and go out into the cold for the ride to Develtos.

He kept asking questions when he got back into town. The answers he got set him stewing all over again. They were not given under the influence of his decoction, but they were detailed and consistent from one person to the next. They all painted the monks of the monastery of the holy Tralitzes as the lechers he had already been led to believe them.

How, then, had Menas truthfully asserted that he and his flock followed Pakhomios' *Rule*?

The question nagged at Kassianos like the beginnings of a toothache for the rest of the day. By this time the snowstorm had long since blown itself out; he could have gone on to Opsikion. It never occurred to him. After taking his evening meal in Branas' taproom, he went up to the cubicle he had rented over it.

There he sat and thought and fumed. Maybe Menas had found

an antidote to his potion. But if he had, it was one that had eluded all the savants at the Sorcerers' Collegium for all the centuries of Videssos' history. That was possible, but not likely. Was it likelier than a deliberate campaign of slander against the abbot's monks? The *nomophylax* could not be sure, but he thought both ideas most improbable. And they were the best ones he had.

He pounded a fist against his knee. "What can Menas be up to, anyway?" he said out loud. Then he blinked, surprised at himself. "Why don't I find out?"

Normally, he would have dismissed the thought with the same automatic discipline he used to suppress the longing of his flesh for women. Spying sorcerously on a man who had proven himself innocent under drugged interrogation went against every instinct Kassianos had. On the other hand, so did believing Menas.

If the abbot is blameless, Kassianos told himself, I'll perform an act of penance to make up for the sin I commit in spying on him like this. Having salved his conscience, the *nomophylax* set about preparing the spell he would need.

The law of similarity was useless to him here, but the law of contagion applied: once in contact, always in contact. Kassianos scraped a bit of skin from the palm of his right hand with a small sharp knife—because that hand had clasped Menas', it still held an affinity for the abbot.

As Kassianos' incantation built, a cloud of smoke grew in his cubicle. It was no ordinary cloud, though, for it formed a rectangle with edges so precise they might have been defined by an invisible picture frame. The analogy pleased Kassianos, for when he spoke a final word of command, the smoke would indeed yield a picture of what Menas was about.

He spoke the word,. The trapped smoke before him roiled, grew still. Color began seeping into it, here and there. The first thing the *nomophylax* clearly made out was the roaring fire in one corner of his magical image. He frowned; the blaze was bigger than any the hearth in the abbot's dwelling could contain.

Of itself, of course, that meant nothing. Menas could have any number of legitimate reasons for not being in his own quarters. Kassianos waited for more of the picture to emerge.

Blue . . . Surely that was the abbot's robe. But it lay on the floor, crumpled and forgotten. Where was Menas, and why had he thrown aside his vestments?

Within moments, Kassianos had his answer. He felt a hot flush rise, not just to his cheeks, but to the very crown of his shaven head. He turned away from the image he had conjured up, yet still he saw body conjoined with body, saw that the man straining atop his eager partner was the abbot Menas.

Kassianos spoke another word, felt his sorcery dissolve. His face remained hot, now with fury rather than embarrassment. So Menas thought he could play him for a fool, eh? He imagined the abbot telling his paramour how he had fooled the fellow from the capital, and both of them laughing as they coupled. That thought only made the *nomophylax*'s rage burn hotter.

Then he caught himself wishing he had not turned his back quite so soon. He had not thought he could be any angrier, but found he was wrong. Before, his anger's flame had extended only to Menas and his still unknown lover. Now it reached out and burned him too.

Kassianos stamped grimly through the snow toward the monastery of the holy Tralitzes. He had left his mule behind on purpose, accepting the walk as the beginning of the penance he would pay for failing to root out the corruption in the monastery at the first try. His footprints left an emphatic trail behind him.

The pale, fitful sun gleamed off the gilded dome topping Phos' temple ahead. Kassianos turned aside before he was halfway there. Scanning the landscape ahead with a hunter's alertness, he spotted a blue-robe strolling toward a small wooden house several hundred yards to one side of the monastery. He was not sure whether hunter's instinct or sorcerer's told him it was Menas, but he knew.

The *nomophylax*'s breath burst from him in an outraged steaming cloud. "Phos grant us mercy! Not content with making a mockery of his vows, the sinner goes to show off his stamina," Kassianos exclaimed, though there was no one to hear him.

The abbot disappeared into the little house. Some men might have hesitated before disturbing the occupants of a trysting place, but not Kassianos. He strode resolutely up to pound on the door, crying, "Menas, you are a disgrace to the robes you wear! Open at once!"

"Oh, dear," Menas said as Kassianos withered him with a glare. "You do take this seriously, don't you?" Now the abbot did not look amused, as he had so often back in his study. He looked frightened. So did the woman around whose shoulder he flung a protective arm.

The night before, her features slack with pleasure, she had seemed only a symbol of Menas' depravity. Now Kassianos had to confront her as a person. She was, he realized slowly, not a whore after all. Perhaps ten years younger than the abbot, she had an open, pretty face, and wore an embroidered linen blouse over a heavy wool skirt: peasant garb, not a courtesan's jewels and clinging silks.

Even without what his magic had let him witness, the way her hand reached up and clutched for Menas' would have told Kassianos everything he needed to know. It told him other things as well, things he had not thought to learn. It had never occurred to him that the cleric's illicit lover might feel all the same things for her man as another woman would for a proper partner.

Because the woman confused him, Kassianos swung his attention back to Menas. "Should I not take your perjury seriously?" he said heavily. "It only adds to the burden of your other sins."

"Perjury? I gave you my oath on Phos, holy sir, under the influence of your own drug, that I truly obey my vows. I do; I am not forsworn."

Kassianos' eyes narrowed. "No? You dare say that, in the company you keep? Hear once again, then, wretch, the seventh chapter of the holy Pakhomios' *Rule*. As you know, it is entitled 'On Women.' I hope you will trust my memory as I quote it: 'To ensure the preservation of the contemplative life, no brother shall be permitted to entertain women.' Standing where you are, with the person whose house this must be, how can you tell me you are no oathbreaker?"

To the amazement of the *nomophylax*, Menas'—companion— burst into laughter. Kassianos stared, thunderstruck. The woman said, "As you guessed, holy sir, this house was my husband's till he died six years ago, and belongs to me now. And so my dear Menas cannot entertain me here. I entertain him, or at least I hope I shall." She smiled smokily up at the worried abbot, stroked his bearded cheek.

Kassianos felt his jaw drop. He became aware that he had not blinked for some time, either. In fact, he realized his expression had to resemble nothing so much as a fresh-caught perch's. Pulling himself together with a distinct effort of will, he said slowly, "That is the most outlandish piece of casuistry I've heard in a lifetime of theological study."

He waited for his pompous wrath to burst forth in a great, furious shout. What came out instead was laughter. And once free, it would not let itself be restrained. Kassianos laughed until tears ran down his face into his beard, laughed until he doubled over. Now Menas and the woman were staring at him rather than the other way around.

Slowly the fit passed. Kassianos straightened, felt the sudden pain of a stitch in his side, ignored it. He wiped his eyes with his sleeve, then, more or less in control of himself, asked Menas, "Your monks are all, hmm, entertained themselves, and do no entertaining?"

"Of course, holy sir." The abbot sounded genuinely shocked. "Did we act otherwise, we would violate our vows."

"Hmm," Kassianos said again. "How long has this, ah, custom existed at the monastery of the holy Tralitzes?"

"Truly, holy sir, I do not know. Since before I entered as a novice, certainly, and before the novitiate of the oldest brothers there at that time, for they knew no different way."

"I see." And, curiously enough, Kassianos did. Develtos was just the sort of back-country town where a spurious practice like this could quietly come into being and then flourish for Phos only knew how long before anyone from the outside world noticed it was there.

Menas must have been thinking along with him, for he asked, "Holy sir, is it not the same everywhere?"

"Hardly." Kassianos' voice was dry. "In fact, I daresay you've found a loophole to appall the holy Pakhomios—and one untold generations of monks have prayed for in vain. I suppose I should congratulate you. Oh, my." He wiped his eyes again.

"Perhaps you should, but I doubt you will," Menas' ladylove observed. "What will you do?"

The *nomophylax* eyed her with respect: no fool here. "Well, an inquisitor's court might fight its way through your logic," he said. Both the woman and Menas looked alarmed. Kassianos went on, "I doubt that will happen, though."

"What then?" Menas asked.

"First, I'd guess, a synod will convene in Videssos the city to

revise the holy Pakhomios' *Rule* so no further, ah, misunderstandings of the seventh chapter will occur. That being accomplished,
word of the corrected *Rule* will be sent to all monasteries in the
Empire—including, I am comfortably certain, this one."

"And what will they do to us for having contravened their
interpretation of the *Rule*?" Menas asked; Kassianos noted the
slight emphasis the abbot put on "interpretation." He smiled to
himself. In Menas' sandals, he would have tried to appear as
virtuous as possible, too.

He answered, "While I cannot speak for the synod, I would
expect it to decree no punishments for what is here a long-
established, even if erroneous, custom. I would also expect, however, that an *epoptes*—a supervising monk—will come out from
the capital to make certain the monastery of the holy Tralitzes
diligently adheres to the seventh chapter as redefined."

Neither Menas nor his companion looked very happy at that.
The *nomophylax* had not thought they would. He went on, "I
mean what I say. If you continue to flout the *Rule* after it is
changed to mean in letter what it does in spirit, you will not
enjoy the consequences."

He had intended to impress them further with the seriousness
of the situation. But the woman said, "Then we will just have to
make the most of the time we have left." She shut the door in
Kassianos' face.

He knew he should be angry. Instead, to his own discomfiture,
he found himself admiring her. He realized with sudden regret
that he had never learned her name. He raised his hand to knock
on that closed door and ask. After a moment, he thought better
of it.

Shaking his head, he turned and slowly started walking back
to Develtos.

The Detective of Dreams

› GENE WOLFE ‹

I WAS WRITING IN MY OFFICE IN THE RUE MADELEINE WHEN Andrée, my secretary, announced the arrival of Herr D_____. I rose, put away my correspondence, and offered him my hand. He was, I should say, just short of fifty, had the high, clear complexion characteristic of those who in youth (now unhappily past for both of us) have found more pleasure in the company of horses and dogs and the excitement of the chase than in the bottles and bordels of city life, and wore a beard and mustache of the style popularized by the late emperor. Accepting my invitation to a chair, he showed me his papers.

"You see," he said, "I am accustomed to acting as the representative of my government. In this matter I hold no such position, and it is possible that I feel a trifle lost."

"Many people who come here feel lost," I said. "But it is my boast that I find most of them again. Your problem, I take it, is purely a private matter?"

"Not at all. It is a public matter in the truest sense of the words."

"Yet none of the documents before me—admirably stamped, sealed, and beribboned though they are—indicates that you are other than a private gentleman traveling abroad. And you say you do not represent your government. What am I to think? What is the matter?"

"I act in the public interest," Herr D_____ told me. "My fortune is not great, but I can assure you that in the event of your

365

success you will be well recompensed; although you are to take it that I alone am your principal, yet there are substantial resources available to me."

"Perhaps it would be best if you described the problems to me?"

"You are not averse to travel?"

"No."

"Very well then," he said, and so saying launched into one of the most astonishing relations—no, *the* most astonishing relation—I have ever been privileged to hear. Even I, who had at first hand the account of the man who found Paulette Renan with the quince seed still lodged in her throat; who had received Captain Brotte's testimony concerning his finds amid the Antarctic ice; who had heard the history of the woman called Joan O'Neal, who lived for two years behind a painting of herself in the Louvre, from her own lips—even I sat like a child while this man spoke.

When he fell silent, I said, "Herr D_____, after all you have told me, I would accept this mission though there were not a *sou* to be made from it. Perhaps once in a lifetime one comes across a case that must be pursued for its own sake; I think I have found mine."

He leaned forward and grasped my hand with a warmth of feeling that was, I believe, very foreign to his usual nature. "Find and destroy the Dream-Master," he said, "and you shall sit upon a chair of gold, if that is your wish, and eat from a table of gold as well. When will you come to our country?"

"Tomorrow morning," I said. "There are one or two arrangements I must make here before I go."

"I am returning tonight. You may call upon me at any time, and I will apprise you of new developments." He handed me a card. "I am always to be found at this address—if not I, then one who is to be trusted, acting in my behalf."

"I understand."

"This should be sufficient for your initial expenses. You may call me should you require more." The cheque he gave me as he turned to leave represented a comfortable fortune.

I waited until he was nearly out the door before saying, "I thank you, Herr Baron." To his credit, he did not turn; but I had the satisfaction of seeing a red flush rising above the precise white line of his collar before the door closed.

Andrée entered as soon as he had left. "Who was that man?

When you spoke to him—just as he was stepping out of your office—he looked as if you had struck him with a whip."

"He will recover," I told her. "He is the Baron H_____, of the secret police of K_____. D_____ was his mother's name. He assumed that because his own desk is a few hundred kilometers from mine, and because he does not permit his likeness to appear in the daily papers, I would not know him; but it was necessary, both for the sake of his opinion of me and my own of myself, that he should discover that I am not so easily deceived. When he recovers from his initial irritation, he will retire tonight with greater confidence in the abilities I will devote to the mission he has entrusted to me."

"It is typical of you, monsieur," Andrée said kindly, "that you are concerned that your clients sleep well."

Her pretty cheek tempted me, and I pinched it. "I am concerned," I replied; "but the Baron will not sleep well."

My train roared out of Paris through meadows sweet with wildflowers, to penetrate mountain passes in which the danger of avalanches was only just past. The glitter of rushing water, sprung from on high, was everywhere; and when the express slowed to climb a grade, the song of water was everywhere too, water running and shouting down the gray rocks of the Alps. I fell asleep that night with the descant of that icy purity sounding through the plainsong of the rails, and I woke in the station of I_____, the old capital of J_____, now a province of K_____.

I engaged a porter to convey my trunk to the hotel where I had made reservations by telegraph the day before, and amused myself for a few hours by strolling about the city. Here I found the Middle Ages might almost be said to have remained rather than lingered. The city wall was complete on three sides, with its merloned towers in repair; and the cobbled streets surely dated from a period when wheeled traffic of any kind was scarce. As for the buildings—Puss in Boots and his friends must have loved them dearly: there were bulging walls and little panes of bull's-eye glass, and overhanging upper floors one above another until the structures seemed unbalanced as tops. Upon one gray old pile with narrow windows and massive doors, I found a plaque informing me that though it had been first built as a church, it had been successively a prison, a customhouse, a private home,

and a school. I investigated further, and discovered it was now
an arcade, having been divided, I should think at about the time
of the first Louis, into a multitude of dank little stalls. Since it
was, as it happened, one of the addresses mentioned by Baron
H_____, I went in.

Gas flared everywhere, yet the interior could not have been
said to be well lit—each jet was sullen and secretive, as if the
proprietor in whose cubicle it was located wished it to light none
but his own wares. These cubicles were in no order; nor could I
find any directory or guide to lead me to the one I sought. A few
customers, who seemed to have visited the place for years, so that
they understood where everything was, drifted from one display
to the next. When they arrived at each, the proprietor came out,
silent (so it seemed to me) as a specter, ready to answer questions
or accept a payment; but I never heard a question asked, or saw
any money tendered—the customer would finger the edge of a
kitchen knife, or hold a garment up to her own shoulders, or
turn the pages of some moldering book; and then put the thing
down again, and go away.

At last, when I had tired of peeping into alcoves lined with
booths still gloomier than the ones on the main concourse outside,
I stopped at a leather merchant's and asked the man to direct me
to Fräulein A_____.

"I do not know her," he said.

"I am told on good authority that her business is conducted
in this building, and that she buys and sells antiques."

"We have several antique dealers here, Herr M_____—"

"I am searching for a young woman. Has your Herr M_____
a niece or a cousin?"

"—handles chairs and chests, largely. Herr O_____, near the
guildhall—"

"It is within this building."

"—stocks pictures, mostly. A few mirrors. What is it you wish
to buy?"

At this point we were interrupted, mercifully, by a woman from
the next booth. "He wants Fräulein A_____. Out of here, and to
your left; past the wigmaker's, then right to the stationer's, then
left again. She sells old lace."

I found the place at last, and sitting at the very back of her booth
Fräulein A_____ herself, a pretty, slender, timid-looking young

woman. Her merchandise was spread on two tables; I pretended to examine it and found that it was not old lace she sold but old clothing, much of it trimmed with lace. After a few moments she rose and came out to talk to me, saying, "If you could tell me what you require? . . ." She was taller than I had anticipated, and her flaxen hair would have been very attractive if it were ever released from the tight braids coiled round her head.

"I am only looking. Many of these are beautiful—are they expensive?"

"Not for what you get. The one you are holding is only fifty marks."

"That seems like a great deal."

"They are the fine dresses of long ago—for visiting, or going to the ball. The dresses of wealthy women of aristocratic taste. All are like new; I will not handle anything else. Look at the seams in the one you hold, the tiny stitches all done by hand. Those were the work of dressmakers who created only four or five in a year, and worked twelve and fourteen hours a day, sewing at the first light, and continuing under the lamp, past midnight."

I said, "I see that you have been crying, Fräulein. Their lives were indeed miserable, though no doubt there are people today who suffer equally."

"No doubt there are," the young woman said. "I, however, am not one of them." And she turned away so that I should not see her tears.

"I was informed otherwise."

She whirled about to face me. "You know him? Oh, tell him I am not a wealthy woman, but I will pay whatever I can. Do you really know him?"

"No." I shook my head. "I was informed by your own police."

She stared at me. "But you are an outlander. So is he, I think."

"Ah, we progress. Is there another chair in the rear of your booth? Your police are not above going outside your own country for help, you see, and we should have a little talk."

"They are not our police," the young woman said bitterly, "but I will talk to you. The truth is that I would sooner to you, though you are French. You will not tell them that?"

I assured her I would not; we borrowed a chair from the flower stall across the corridor, and she poured forth her story.

"My father died when I was very small. My mother opened

this booth to earn our living—old dresses that had belonged to her own mother were the core of her original stock. She died two years ago, and since that time I have taken charge of our business and used it to support myself. Most of my sales are to collectors and theatrical companies. I do not make a great deal of money, but I do not require a great deal, and I have managed to save some. I live alone at Number 877 _____strasse; it is an old house divided into six apartments, and mine is the gable apartment."

"You are young and charming," I said, "and you tell me you have a little money saved. I am surprised you are not married."

"Many others have said the same thing."

"And what did you tell them, Fräulein?"

"To take care of their own affairs. They have called me a manhater—Frau G_____, who has the confections in the next corridor but two, called me that because I would not receive her son. The truth is that I do not care for people of either sex, young or old. If I want to live by myself and keep my own things to myself, is it not my right to do so?"

"I am sure it is; but undoubtedly it has occurred to you that this person you fear so much may be a rejected suitor who is taking revenge on you."

"But how could he enter and control my dreams?"

"I do not know, Fräulein. It is you who say that he does these things."

"I should remember him, I think, if he had ever called on me. As it is, I am quite certain I have seen him somewhere, but I cannot recall where. Still . . ."

"Perhaps you had better describe your dream to me. You have the same one again and again, as I understand it?"

"Yes. It is like this. I am walking down a dark road. I am both frightened and pleasurably excited, if you know what I mean. Sometimes I walk for a long time, sometimes for what seems to be only a few moments. I think there is moonlight, and once or twice I have noticed stars. Anyway, there is a high, dark hedge, or perhaps a wall, on my right. There are fields to the left, I believe. Eventually I reach a gate of iron bars, standing open—it's not a large gate for wagons or carriages, but a small one, so narrow I can hardly get through. Have you read the writings of Dr. Freud of Vienna? One of the women here mentioned once that he had written concerning dreams, and so I got them from the library, and if I were a man I am sure he would say that entering that gate meant sexual commerce. Do you think I might have unnatural leanings?" Her voice dropped to a whisper.

"Have you ever felt such desires?"

"Oh, no. Quite the reverse."

"Then I doubt it very much," I said. "Go on with your dream. How do you feel as you pass through the gate?"

"As I did when walking down the road, but more so—more frightened, and yet happy and excited. Triumphant, in a way."

"Go on."

"I am in the garden now. There are fountains playing, and nightingales singing in the willows. The air smells of lilies, and a cherry tree in blossom looks like a giantess in her bridal gown. I walk on a straight, smooth path; I think it must be paved with marble chips, because it is white in the moonlight. Ahead of me is the *Schloss*—a great building. There is music coming from inside."

"What sort of music?"

"Magnificent—joyous, if you know what I am trying to say, but not the tinklings of a theater orchestra. A great symphony. I have never been to the opera at Bayreuth; but I think it must be like that—yet a happy, quick tune."

She paused, and for an instant her smile recovered the remembered music. "There are pillars, and a grand entrance, with broad steps. I run up—I am so happy to be there—and throw open the door. It is brightly lit inside; a wave of golden light, almost like a wave from the ocean, strikes me. The room is a great hall, with a high ceiling. A long table is set in the middle and there are hundreds of people seated at it, but one place, the one nearest me, is empty. I cross to it and sit down; there are beautiful loaves on the table, and bowls of honey with roses floating at their centers, and crystal carafes of wine, and many other good things I cannot remember when I awake. Everyone is eating and drinking and talking, and I begin to eat too."

I said, "It is only a dream, Fräulein. There is no reason to weep."

"I dream this each night—I have dreamed so every night for months."

"Go on."

"Then he comes. I am sure he is the one who is causing me to dream like this because I can see his face clearly, and remember it when the dream is over. Sometimes it is very vivid for an hour or more after I wake—so vivid that I have only to close my eyes to see it before me."

"I will ask you to describe him in detail later. For the present, continue with your dream."

"He is tall, and robed like a king, and there is a strange crown on his head. He stands beside me, and though he says nothing, I know that the etiquette of the place demands that I rise and face him. I do this. Sometimes I am sucking my fingers as I get up from his table."

"He owns the dream palace, then."

"Yes, I am sure of that. It is his castle, his home; he is my host. I stand and face him, and I am conscious of wanting very much to please him, but not knowing what it is I should do."

"That must be painful."

"It is. But as I stand there, I become aware of how I am clothed and—"

"How are you clothed?"

"As you see me now. In a plain, dark dress—the dress I wear here in the arcade. But the others—all up and down the hall, all up and down the table—are wearing the dresses I sell here. These dresses." She held one up for me to see, a beautiful creation of many layers of lace, with buttons of polished jet. "I know then that I cannot remain; but the king signals to the others, and they seize me and push me toward the door."

"You are humiliated then?"

"Yes, but the worst thing is that I am aware that he knows that I could never drive myself to leave, and he wishes to spare me the struggle. But outside—some terrible beast has entered the garden. I smell it—like the hyena cage at the *Tiergarten*—as the door opens. And then I wake up."

"It is a harrowing dream."

"You have seen the dresses I sell. Would you credit it that for weeks I slept in one, and then another, and then another of them?"

"You reaped no benefit from that?"

"No. In the dream I was clad as now. For a time I wore the dresses always—even here to the stall, and when I bought food at the market. But it did no good."

"Have you tried sleeping somewhere else?"

"With my cousin who lives on the other side of the city. That made no difference. I am certain that this man I see is a real man. He is in my dream, and the cause of it; but he is not sleeping."

"Yet you have never seen him when you are awake?"

She paused, and I saw her bite at her full lower lip. "I am certain I have."

"Ah!"

"But I cannot remember when. Yet I am sure I have seen him—that I have passed him in the street."

"Think! Does his face associate itself in your mind with some particular section of the city?"

She shook her head.

When I left her at last, it was with a description of the Dream-Master less precise than I had hoped, though still detailed. It tallied in almost all respects with the one given me by Baron H_____; but that proved nothing, since the Baron's description might have been based largely on Fräulein A_____'s.

The bank of Herr R_____ was a private one, as all the greatest banks in Europe are. It was located in what had once been the town house of some noble family (their arms, overgrown now with ivy, were still visible above the door), and bore no identification other than a small brass plate engraved with the names of Herr R_____ and his partners. Within, the atmosphere was more dignified—even if, perhaps, less tasteful—than it could possibly have been in the noble family's time. Dark pictures in gilded frames lined the walls, and the clerks sat at inlaid tables upon chairs upholstered in tapestry. When I asked for Herr R_____, I was told that it would be impossible to see him that afternoon; I sent in a note with a sidelong allusion to "unquiet dreams," and within five minutes I was ushered into a luxurious office that must once have been the bedroom of the head of the household.

Herr R_____ was a large man—tall, and heavier (I thought) than his physician was likely to have approved. He appeared to be about fifty; there was strength in his wide, fleshy face; his high forehead and capacious cranium suggested intellect; and his small, dark eyes, forever flickering as they took in the appearance of my person, the expression of my face, and the position of my hands and feet, ingenuity.

No pretense was apt to be of service with such a man, and I

told him flatly that I had come as the emissary of Baron H_____, that I knew what troubled him, and that if he would cooperate with me I would help him if I could.

"I know you, monsieur," he said, "by reputation. A business with which I am associated employed you three years ago in the matter of a certain mummy." He named the firm. "I should have thought of you myself."

"I did not know that you were connected with them."

"I am not, when you leave this room. I do not know what reward Baron H_____ has offered you should you apprehend the man who is oppressing me, but I will give you, in addition to that, a sum equal to that you were paid for the mummy. You should be able to retire to the south then, should you choose, with the rent of a dozen villas."

"I do not choose," I told him, "and I could have retired long before. But what you just said interests me. You are certain that your persecutor is a living man?"

"I know men." Herr R_____ leaned back in his chair and stared at the painted ceiling. "As a boy I sold stuffed cabbage-leaf rolls in the street—did you know that? My mother cooked them over wood she collected herself where buildings were being demolished, and I sold them from a little cart for her. I lived to see her with half a score of footmen and the finest house in Lindau. I never went to school; I learned to add and subtract in the streets—when I must multiply and divide I have my clerk do it. But I learned men. Do you think that now, after forty years of practice, I could be deceived by a phantom? No, he is a man—let me confess it, a stronger man than I—a man of flesh and blood and brain, a man I have seen somewhere, sometime, here in this city—and more than once."

"Describe him."

"As tall as I. Younger—perhaps thirty or thirty-five. A brown, forked beard, so long." (He held his hand about fifteen centimeters beneath his chin.) "Brown hair. His hair is not yet gray, but I think it may be thinning a little at the temples."

"Don't you remember?"

"In my dreams he wears a garland of roses—I cannot be sure."

"Is there anything else? Any scars or identifying marks?"

Herr R_____ nodded. "He has hurt his hand. In my dream, when he holds out his hand for the money, I see blood in it—it is his own, you understand, as though a recent injury had reopened and was beginning to bleed again. His hands are long and slender—like a pianist's."

"Perhaps you had better tell me your dream."

"Of course." He paused, and his face clouded, as though to recount the dream were to return to it. "I am in a great house. I am a person of importance there, almost as though I were the owner; yet I am not the owner—"

"Wait," I interrupted. "Does this house have a banquet hall? Has it a pillared portico, and is it set in a garden?"

For a moment Herr R_____'s eyes widened. "Have you also had such dreams?"

"No," I said. "It is only that I think I have heard of this house before. Please continue."

"There are many servants—some work in the fields beyond the garden. I give instructions to them—the details differ each night, you understand. Sometimes I am concerned with the kitchen, sometimes with livestock, sometimes with the draining of a field. We grow wheat, principally, it seems; but there is a vineyard too, and a kitchen garden. And of course the house must be cleaned and swept and kept in repair. There is no wife; the owner's mother lives with us, I think, but she does not much concern herself with the housekeeping—that is up to me. To tell the truth, I have never actually seen her, though I have the feeling that she is there."

"Does this house resemble the one you bought for your mother in Lindau?"

"Only as one large house must resemble another."

"I see. Proceed."

"For a long time each night I continue like that, giving orders, and sometimes going over the accounts. Then a servant, usually it is a maid, arrives to tell me that the owner wishes to speak to me. I stand before a mirror—I can see myself there as plainly as I see you now—and arrange my clothing. The maid brings rose-scented water and a cloth, and I wipe my face; then I go in to him.

"He is always in one of the upper rooms, seated at a table with his own account book spread before him. There is an open window behind him, and through it I can see the top of a cherry tree in bloom. For a long time—oh, I suppose ten minutes—I stand before him while he turns over the pages of his ledger."

"You appear somewhat at a loss, Herr R_____—not a common condition for you, I believe. What happens then?"

"He says, 'You owe . . .'" Herr R_____ paused. "That is the problem, monsieur, I can never recall the amount. But it is a large sum. He says, 'And I must require that you make payment at once.'

"I do not have the amount, and I tell him so. He says, 'Then you must leave my employment.' I fall to my knees at this and beg that he will retain me, pointing out that if he dismisses me I will have lost my source of income, and will never be able to make payment. I do not enjoy telling you this, but I weep. Sometimes I beat the floor with my fists."

"Continue. Is the Dream-Master moved by your pleading?"

"No. He again demands that I pay the entire sum. Several times I have told him that I am a wealthy man in this world, and that if only he would permit me to make payment in its currency, I would do so immediately."

"That is interesting—most of us lack your presence of mind in our nightmares. What does he say then?"

"Usually he tells me not to be a fool. But once he said, 'That is a dream—you must know it by now. You cannot expect to pay a real debt with the currency of sleep.' He holds out his hand for the money as he speaks to me. It is then that I see the blood in his palm."

"You are afraid of him?"

"Oh, very much so. I understand that he has the most complete power over me. I weep, and at last I throw myself at his feet—with my head under the table, if you can credit it, crying like an infant.

"Then he stands and pulls me erect and says, 'You would never be able to pay all you owe, and you are a false and dishonest servant. But your debt is forgiven, forever.' And as I watch, he tears a leaf from his account book and hands it to me."

"Your dream has a happy conclusion, then."

"No. It is not yet over. I thrust the paper into the front of my shirt and go out, wiping my face on my sleeve. I am conscious that if any of the other servants should see me, they will know at once what has happened. I hurry to reach my own counting room; there is a brazier there, and I wish to burn the page from the owner's book."

"I see."

"But just outside the door of my own room, I meet another servant—an upper-servant like myself, I think, since he is well dressed. As it happens, this man owes me a considerable sum of money, and to conceal from him what I have just endured, I demand that he pay at once." Herr R_____ rose from his chair and began to pace the room, looking sometimes at the painted scenes on the walls, sometimes at the Turkish carpet at his feet. "I have had reason to demand money like that often, you understand. Here in this room.

"The man falls to his knees, weeping and begging for additional time; but I reach down, like this, and seize him by the throat."

"And then?"

"And then the door of my counting room opens. But it is not my counting room with my desk and the charcoal brazier, but the owner's own room. He is standing in the doorway, and behind him I can see the open window, and the blossoms of the cherry tree."

"What does he say to you?"

"Nothing. He says nothing to me. I release the other man's throat, and he slinks away."

"You awaken then?"

"How can I explain it? Yes, I wake up. But first we stand there; and while we do I am conscious of . . . certain sounds."

"If it is too painful for you, you need not say more."

Herr R_____ drew a silk handkerchief from his pocket, and wiped his face. "How can I explain?" he said again. "When I hear those sounds, I am aware that the owner possesses certain other servants, who have never been under my direction. It is as though I have always known this, but had no reason to think of it before."

"I understand."

"They are quartered in another part of the house—in the vaults beneath the wine cellar, I think sometimes. I have never seen them, but I know—then—that they are hideous, vile and cruel; I know too that he thinks me but little better than they, and that as he permits me to serve him, so he allows them to serve him also. I stand—we stand—and listen to them coming through the house. At last a door at the end of the hall begins to swing open. There is a hand like the paw of some filthy reptile on the latch."

"Is that the end of the dream?"

"Yes." Herr R_____ threw himself into his chair again, mopping his face.

"You have this experience each night?"

"It differs," he said slowly, "in some details."

"You have told me that the orders you give the under-servants vary."

"There is another difference. When the dreams began, I woke when the hinges of the door at the passage end creaked. Each night now the dream endures a moment longer. Perhaps a tenth of a second. Now I see the arm of the creature who opens that door, nearly to the elbow."

I took the address of his home, which he was glad enough to give me, and leaving the bank made my way to my hotel.

When I had eaten my roll and drunk my coffee the next morning, I went to the place indicated by the card given me by Baron H_____, and in a few minutes was sitting with him in a room as bare as those tents from which armies in the field are cast into battle. "You are ready to begin the case this morning?" he asked.

"On the contrary. I have already begun; indeed, I am about to enter a new phase of my investigation. You would not have come to me if your Dream-Master were not torturing someone other than the people whose names you gave me. I wish to know the identity of that person, and to interrogate him."

"I told you that there were many other reports. I—"

"Provided me with a list. They are all of the petite bourgeoisie, when they are not persons still less important. I believed at first that it might be because of the urgings of Herr R_____ that you engaged me; but when I had time to reflect on what I know of your methods, I realized that you would have demanded that he provide my fee had that been the case. So you are sheltering someone of greater importance, and I wish to speak to him."

"The Countess—" Baron H_____ began.

"Ah!"

"The Countess herself has expressed some desire that you should be presented to her. The Count opposes it."

"We are speaking, I take it, of the governor of this province?"

The Baron nodded. "Of Count von V_____. He is responsible, you understand, only to the Queen Regent herself."

"Very well. I wish to hear the Countess, and she wishes to talk with me. I assure you, Baron, that we will meet; the only question is whether it will be under your auspices."

The Countess, to whom I was introduced that afternoon, was a woman in her early twenties, deep-breasted and somber-haired, with skin like milk, and great dark eyes welling with fear and (I thought) pity, set in a perfect oval face.

"I am glad you have come, monsieur. For seven weeks now our good Baron H_____ has sought this man for me, but he has not found him."

"If I had known my presence here would please you, Countess, I would have come long ago, whatever the obstacles. You then, like the others, are certain it is a real man we seek?"

"I seldom go out, monsieur. My husband feels we are in constant danger of assassination."

"I believe he is correct."

"But on state occasions we sometimes ride in a glass coach to the *Rathaus*. There are uhlans all around us to protect us then. I am certain that—before the dreams began—I saw the face of this man in the crowd."

"Very well. Now tell me your dream."

"I am here, at home—"

"In this palace, where we sit now?"

She nodded.

"That is a new feature, then. Continue, please."

"There is to be an execution. In the garden." A fleeting smile crossed the Countess's lovely face. "I need not tell you that that is not where the executions are held; but it does not seem strange to me when I dream.

"I have been away, I think, and have only just heard of what is to take place. I rush into the garden. The man Baron H_____ calls the Dream-Master is there, tied to the trunk of the big cherry tree; a squad of soldiers faces him, holding their rifles; their officer stands beside them with his saber drawn, and my husband is watching from a pace or two away. I call out for them to stop, and my husband turns to look at me. I say: 'You must not do it, Karl. You must not kill this man.' But I see by his expression that he believes that I am only a foolish, tenderhearted child. Karl is . . . several years older than I."

"I am aware of it."

"The Dream-Master turns his head to look at me. People tell me that my eyes are large—do you think them large, monsieur?"

"Very large, and very beautiful."

"In my dream, quite suddenly, his eyes seem far, far larger than mine, and far more beautiful; and in them I see reflected the figure of my husband. Please listen carefully now, because what I am going to say is very important, though it makes very little sense, I am afraid."

"Anything may happen in a dream, Countess."

"When I see my husband reflected in this man's eyes, I know—I cannot say how—that it is this reflection, and not the man who stands near me, who is the real Karl. The man I have thought real is only a reflection of that reflection. Do you follow what I say?"

I nodded. "I believe so."

"I plead again: 'Do not kill him. Nothing good can come of it . . .' My husband nods to the officer, the soldiers raise their rifles, and . . . and . . ."

"You wake. Would you like my handkerchief, Countess? It is of coarse weave; but it is clean, and much larger than your own."

"Karl is right—I am only a foolish little girl. No, monsieur, I do not wake—not yet. The soldiers fire. The Dream-Master falls forward, though his bonds hold him to the tree. And Karl flies to bloody rags beside me."

On my way back to the hotel I purchased a map of the city; and when I reached my room I laid it flat on the table there. There could be no question of the route of the Countess's glass coach—straight down the Hauptstrasse, the only street in the city wide enough to take a carriage surrounded by cavalrymen. The most probable route by which Herr R_____ might go from his house to his bank coincided with the Hauptstrasse for several blocks. The path Fräulein A_____ would travel from her flat to the arcade crossed the Hauptstrasse at a point contained by that interval. I need to know no more.

Very early the next morning I took up my post at the inter-section. If my man were still alive after the fusillade Count von V_____ fired at him each night, it seemed certain that he would appear at this spot within a few days, and I am hardened to wait-ing. I smoked cigarettes while I watched the citizens of I_____ walk up and down before me. When an hour had passed, I bought a newspaper from a vendor, and stole a few glances at its pages when foot traffic was light.

Gradually I became aware that I was watched—we boast of reason, but there are senses over which reason holds no authority. I did not know where my watcher was, yet I felt his gaze on me, whichever way I turned. So, I thought, you know me, my friend. Will I too dream now? What has attracted your attention to a mere foreigner, a stranger, waiting for who-knows-what at this corner? Have you been talking to Fräulein A_____? Or to someone who has spoken to her?

Without appearing to do so, I looked up and down both streets in search of another lounger like myself. There was no one—not a drowsing grandfather, not a woman or a child, not even a dog. Certainly no tall man with a forked beard and piercing eyes. The windows then—I studied them all, looking for some movement in a dark room behind a seemingly innocent opening. Nothing.

Only the buildings behind me remained. I crossed to the opposite side of the Hauptstrasse and looked once more. Then I laughed.

They must have thought me mad, all those dour burghers, for I fairly doubled over, spitting my cigarette to the sidewalk and clasping my hands to my waist for fear my belt would burst. The presumption, the impudence, the brazen insolence of the fellow! The stupidity, the wonderful stupidity of myself, who had not recognized his old stories! For the remainder of my life now, I could accept any case with pleasure, pursue the most inept criminal with zest, knowing that there was always a chance he might outwit such an idiot as I.

For the Dream-Master had set up His own picture, and full-length, and in the most gorgeous colors, in His window. Choking and sputtering I saluted it, and then, still filled with laughter, I crossed the street once more and went inside, where I knew I would find Him. A man awaited me there—not the one I sought, but one who understood Whom it was I had come for, and knew as well as I that His capture was beyond any thief-taker's power. I knelt, and there, though not to the satisfaction I suppose of Baron H_____, Fräulein A_____, Herr R_____, and the Count and the Countess von V_____, I destroyed the Dream-Master as He has been sacrificed so often, devouring His white, wheaten flesh that we might all possess life without end.

Dear people, dream on.

The Witch's Murder

➤ DAVE FREER AND ERIC FLINT ◄

BROTHER MASCOLI KNEW THAT HE MADE AN UNIMPRESSIVE FIGURE in his much washed and faded cassock. The monk of the Peterine order of Saint Hypatia was a small man, as plain and unassuming as the wooden cross from around his neck, which he held aloft in an effort to try and cool the mob.

"Burn her!"

The crowd carried pitchforks, kitchen knives, staves and burning brands. If the door they'd been attacking held out for much longer they would probably set fire to the house.

Mascoli clambered awkwardly onto an empty barrel, which allowed him to look over the heads of the mob. The chant that had attracted his attention, and brought him running to the scene as fast as his old legs would carry him, had begun to pick up again. He held up his hands for quiet.

"Brothers! Sisters! Cease! What are you doing?"

"We're here to burn the witch!" said a tall man, with a slight cast to his eye, from the middle of mob. "She's a pagan, a devil-worshipper and a murderess!"

In the villages and small towns along the marshy fringes of the Venetian Lagoon there was a reasonable chance that most of the people were half pagan themselves. This mob was unlikely to be any exception. Not a half a mile outside the town he'd passed a little shrine to two-headed Janus at the crossroads. The two faces of the old idol were weather-etched into mere featureless rounded shapes. But it was well tended, with a fresh offering of flowers. He'd spotted some drops of fresh blood on the ground, near it, and gone to look closely.

If there was blood sacrifice, the church would intervene. But Mascoli had found the true culprit soon enough. A torn bladder, plainly from a fresh blood sausage that had gone awry, discarded on the nearby pathway to a lonely farmhouse. There was a lot of pig-killing at this time of year, as the peasant farmers got ready for the winter. If he hadn't stopped to investigate, he would have reached the small town in daylight, before the mob had assembled.

Yes, they were a half-pagan lot, here. Not that the entire population wouldn't all be in church, and praying devoutly, and taking communion on Sunday. It was just that old ways and beliefs clung among the peasantry. The marshes had been the last redoubt for many people over the centuries, for pagans too. The twisted muddy reed-fringed waterways had hidden many things over the years, including witches and nonhuman creatures. Brother Mascoli knew, well enough, that some of them were black indeed.

He also knew that others were not. They came through the consecrated wards of the water-chapel to visit him, to seek healing.

Another thing struck him. The accent of the accuser had Milanese overtones, if he was any judge. He turned his mild gaze on the man. "And who are you, sir, that make such accusations? You sound a foreigner to these parts."

It must have been the right thing to say, because the crowd hushed. Villages—and this one straddled the divide where locals would proudly call it a town, and outsiders would call it a village—were insular places. Strangers could take generations to integrate completely.

The fellow started, as if surprised that he should even be asked. "I am Dottore Sarbucco. This is my home," there was an infinitesimal pause, "now. I am from Milan, some years back, before I came here seeking quietness and my health. But we are here to deal with this witchwoman! She has murdered Vincente! Killed him by her black arts. Brother, is it not written that you shall not suffer a witch to live? We must haul her hence or roast her in her vile nest before she escapes!"

The crowd yelled its approval.

Mascoli held up his hands for calm again. "Friends, please! The church and the law have their own methods for dealing with those who abuse magic. It is not for us to preempt God's justice."

The monk felt very alone there, perched above sixty villagers. Still, he had been a preacher and healer to the rough canal folk and the nonhuman denizens of the marshes for forty years. He was not about to be cowed. "Go home. Let the Podesta and the priest come to me, and also this woman's accusers. We will try the truth of this matter. There will be no rough justice served here this evening."

"Podesta's drunk," said one of crowd, with a knowing chuckle. "You won't get sense out of him before sext tomorrow."

"And Father Baritto has gone to give the last rites to old Fili," said another. "It's all of five miles to the farm. He'll not be back tonight."

A man came thrusting through the crowd, whacking people aside with a rough crutch. He was not someone Brother Mascoli would want to stand in the way of, at least, not by what one could see in the torchlight. His broad face was marred by several scars and was further adorned by a crooked broken nose. He still had all his teeth, though, and he was grinning.

A path opened in front of him. Plainly, once they realized who was coming through the villagers had no desire to stand in his way.

"Good day, Brother," he said, as if this were a chance meeting in the course of a pleasant evening stroll. "Carlo Palinni at your service. I am newly retired here, from service in the army of Padua. I have a small pension-job as assistant to the Podesta, and the receiver of messages from the Doge's messengers." He grimaced and patted the crutch. "I am not much use as a soldier these days. Can I be of assistance?"

Brother Mascoli eyed him with both relief and trepidation. The man was offering to help but he looked more like a criminal himself. Mascoli had tended those, as he tended the wounds of any who entered his small run-down chapel. That was why he was here now: he'd come from Venice, with a very scanty purse of silver, to buy certain herbs and simples from a woman of this town on the eastern fringe of the lagoon. Winter was creeping in and with the winter fogs came the coughs and chest complaints, especially from the bridge brats. What they needed was food, warmth and a dry place to sleep, but all he had to offer was treatment for the coughs and his prayers. He was never sure how effective the former was.

One of the city's closet Strega—at least, Mascoli was sure that he was a magic user—had pointed him at this source. This very house, on the edge of the village, unless he was mistaken. It meant that there was a genuine likelihood that the woman trapped inside actually was a witch, or at least a worker of magics.

"Can you clarify this situation?" he asked gently.

"I would, but I'm new here myself," said the old soldier. "Very new. I only arrived here the day before yesterday. I heard the noise and came to see. I've already noticed that there's not usually much noise in these parts after dark."

The last was said dryly. The soldier pointed with his crutch. "You. Pox-doctor. Sarbucco. And you. Wine-draper. What's your name again? Lampara. You stay here and tell us what this is all about. We will deal with it. The rest of you go home. Now."

There was something so very final and firm about that "Now" that the edges of the crowd began to melt away into the twilight even as he said it. A few of the crowd stood irresolutely and then suddenly found reason to be elsewhere when they realized that they'd be standing there on their own.

The soldier snagged a pitch-dipped brand from a departing villager. It cast a ruddy light on the two men who remained. Mascoli was sure that he saw someone else lurking in the shadows. The hint of a skirt, perhaps.

The man the soldier had called "pox-doctor" looked absolutely furious. The other, Lampara, looked as if he had sampled too freely of his own wares. Actually, the whole group had reeked of wine. One or two had been reeling drunk as they'd staggered off. That in itself was not necessarily odd, except for the circumstances. It was early and in the middle of the week, with no feast day or holiday in sight.

"Now," said the soldier, grimacing as he straightened his leg and sat down on the step of the house. "What's all this about?"

"Murder!" said the innkeeper Lampara. "And she's the only one who could have done it." His voice shook slightly, and there was no mistaking the genuine horror in it.

"You should not have stopped us," said Sarbucco angrily. "She can reach through walls to kill with black magics. She killed Vincente! She murdered him in a locked room. She is evil to the core."

Brother Mascoli had very keen hearing. He was sure that he heard an outraged sniff at this comment, from somewhere behind him. "We are not murderers. And evil cannot triumph over God and the law," he said tranquilly, although in his heart he knew evil could sometimes defeat the law, at least.

By the brief snort and the shake of his shoulders, the old soldier didn't believe it either.

"Tell us, exactly, what we are dealing with," said Palinni. "And then if needs be we'll haul the suspect out and keep her for the Podesta in the morning. Well, after sext bell."

"You must come and see," said the innkeeper eagerly. "It is my back room. I keep it for . . . uh, private business. It has no windows. Only the one door made of good oak. Three fingers thick at least. And it was locked from the inside, when Vincente began screaming. He screamed her name. Over and over. We all heard him."

Lampara shuddered and crossed himself. "It was very horrible, brother. When we came in he was lying there, facedown in a great pool of blood. Dead!"

"And he was alone in the chamber, Brother," said Sarbucco. "The witch killed him, as surely as I stand here. Half the town must have heard him accuse her, as we tried to break the door down. The testimony of a dying man cannot be denied."

"Well," said the soldier, grunting as he stood up. "There is that. I've known it to be wrong at times, though."

Palinni reached into his pocket and produced a large bunch of keys. A very large bunch for an honest man to just happen to have in his pocket. Then he frowned as he looked at the door. "I should have guessed," he said grumpily. "Not locked. Barred."

He knocked hard on the door. "Come out. They've all gone."

"No. Go away," said the woman behind the door, who had plainly been listening at the crack. There was a thin edge of hysteria in her voice.

"Signora, if you don't open the door they'll burn you out," said the soldier. "I know the ways of the mob. They'll drink some more courage and come back."

"And if I do come out these liars will burn me anyway. I swear I had nothing to do with the death of that fool Vincente Trazzoria. I did not even know he was dead until they came hunting me like a pack of mad dogs. I will die in my own home." There was definitely a sob at the end of her statement.

"Sister," said Mascoli, in the gentle voice he usually kept for treating hurt children. "I am Brother Mascoli, a Sibling of the Order of Saint Hypatia. I prevented the mob from killing you earlier. Surprise was on my side then. It will not be again. Come out, and we will escort you to a place where you can stay safely, at least until you are given a fair trial. If you have truly done no ill, then you have nothing to fear. Magic leaves its own traces and I am skilled at detecting those."

After a moment, there was the sound of a heavy bar being lifted. And then came another pause. "The Podesta may not accept such evidence."

"Accept it or not," growled the soldier. "Come out and down to the cells. That way you will at least live until tomorrow."

The bar was lifted, and the door pushed slightly open. Frightened dark eyes peered at them from around the edge of it, making sure that the mob was not hiding in the darkness.

"Witch," hissed Sarbucco. She spat at his shoes. The innkeeper looked terrified, as if he would like to melt back into the darkness.

"Take her arm," said the soldier to the innkeeper, preventing his hasty departure and pushing him forward with his crutch. "I would, but it is awkward with this thing."

They walked down the dark street, with shutters snapping closed as they went, until they came to the building in the middle of the town which plainly served as the prison, courthouse and residence for such forces of Venice's law as watched over this backwater of her empire. It was, by local standards, quite impressive—two stories, of brick and mortar and with a tiled roof.

The soldier rapped on the door with his crutch. At length it was unlocked and they were faced by a sleepy plump man with blond hair, carrying an arquebus. He blinked at the party. "Signor Carlo?"

"It's not San Marco come back down from heaven," said Palinni. "Let us in, Karg. We've got a prisoner for the cells."

Like most of the Schiopettieri who served as the Republic's police, this one was apparently a German mercenary. Karg swung open the door and let them into the stone-flagged room.

Coming into the light, Brother Mascoli could see their prisoner properly for the first time, and understood why she was suspected of being a witch and trafficking with the devil. She was quite beautiful, in truth; but also, in the back country where women flowered young and were old crones at thirty-five, too old to be considered that attractive by most villagers. Judging by the tiny lines around her eyes, she was at least forty years old. She carried herself far too upright, too, for a commoner. Her dark hair was straight and lustrous, with just one or two strands of white.

"You two, go home," said the old soldier, pointing to the innkeeper and the doctor. "Karg, see the lady to a cell."

Palinni was used to giving orders, Brother Mascoli thought, looking at the man. If he was to have suspected any man of murder, it would be this one. He turned to leave.

"Where are you off to, Brother?" asked Palinni.

"I thought I would fulfil my promise and go to the room where the unfortunate man was murdered, and see if there was any magic used, and if there are traces left as to who might have done it. And then I was going to the church. I wrote to Father Baritto and he promised me a bed. He is away, but perhaps there is a housekeeper . . ."

"Lives alone," supplied Karg. "But the sacristan can let you in. If it is not unlocked. There's not much crime hereabouts."

"Other than murders and witch-burning mobs just as soon as I arrive," said the old soldier. "Well, lead on, Brother. Not too fast. I am a bit slower than I should be on this pin. Lock up after us, Karg."

"Is it wise? The mob may come here," said Mascoli. This place was more of a fortress than the woman's house had been, but one man and one arquebus seemed scanty defense.

"We're only two doors down from the inn. We'll hear if anything happens, and I've never let murder or dead bodies in a pool of blood put me off my supper, which I haven't had yet." Palinni spoke with casual disregard for the finer feelings of his companions. "Let's go. You can tell me how you came here just in time to stop a witch-burning, and I'll see if there is enough copper, and piety, in my purse to buy you supper." He looked critically at the Hypatian monk. "Piety is in short supply, but it's feed you or let a strong breeze blow you away."

Mascoli had resigned himself to a cold night and an empty stomach, being no stranger to either, and he was rather taken aback by the rough kindness behind the comment. This Carlo Palinni was not quite what he'd first taken him to be. He gave orders far too confidently to have been just a foot soldier, although his appearance did not suggest anything else.

"Let us go then, Signor Palinni. I confess it has been some time since I ate. And the sooner we get to the body the better. I am a healer. I have seen many ailments and wounds, and know a little of what could kill a man."

"Better and better. I'll add a glass of wine to the meal." The old soldier was stumping along next to him with quite a turn of speed, despite his comments about how his leg slowed him up.

The inn was crowded, with many of the faces that Mascoli had seen in the mob. That in itself was also unusual, as money for drinking was sparse in villages. But perhaps the excitement had brought them out.

There was a sudden silence as they walked in. It was not hard to guess what the topic of conversation had been.

"Lampara," said Palinni. "Give us two plates of food, and some of that wine of yours. The red from Signor Forli's vineyards, not the rubbish you tried to give me the first night I was here. And you can take us to look at the body while you get the food ready."

"But Signor Carlo," protested Lampara, "I have closed up that part of the inn. There is another door in the passage. I . . . I thought it best that he lay there until Father Baritto gets here. It is the dead. You should not gawk at the dead."

"You fat fraud. You'd sell tickets to your grandmother's funeral," said the soldier genially. "I wonder what gave you this idea."

"The Dottore . . ." He looked at the soldier's face and nodded. "I will get the key."

As he scurried away, Mascoli looked curiously at his companion. "For a man who has barely been in town for two days, you know a remarkable amount about the locals. Who makes the good wine. People's names . . ."

"You learn to be quick about learning both as a soldier. Especially about the wine," said the man, thrusting people aside with his crutch, and heading them towards a nondescript door at the back of the common room.

The innkeeper joined them with a large key and opened it. The passage behind was as black as the very pits of hell. Mascoli took a tallow-dipped rush from a pile in the corner and kindled it from a simple lamp, just wicks thrust into a clay bowl of olive oil, perched in the sconce. They walked down the cool passage, which sloped distinctly.

"This is a cellar?"

"Yes. It was," said Lampara. "But I no longer use it for that purpose. It serves for guests who want a private place away from the common room."

Walking down the cool passage, Brother Mascoli had to wonder just who in such a village would want such privacy? A tryst for lovers seemed unlikely, not if they had to enter through the common room. Such places were often used by conspirators or heretical sects or the practitioners of the kinds of magic that was best not revealed to the sun.

"Who was this Vincente?" he asked. "A local man?"

The innkeeper scowled. "He was born here, yes. But he went off to Venice just as soon as he could find a boat to carry him. He came back after the war with Milan full of big stories about how he'd been a galley oarsman and been to Outremer. His father was dead then and he got the two farms out Fruili way."

"A wealthy man?"

The innkeeper snorted. "Only if you count his debts as wealth. He was a gambler. One doesn't like to speak ill of the dead, but he wasn't even a good gambler. He owed money to nearly everyone. But he said he'd had a good coup." He sighed. "He promised me . . . And now I'll never see my money either."

They came to the broken door. The wood itself had been splintered rather than the heavy old lock.

Mascoli pushed it inwards and lifted the rush to look at the blood on the flagged floor.

He could only look at the blood because there was no body.

There was quite a lot of blood, though.

The innkeeper's eyes widened in horror. "He was dead!" he exclaimed, his voice shaking. "I saw him myself. Half the town saw him. Dottore Sarbucco examined him. Felt for a pulse in his neck. He was dead!"

Palinni was already prowling around the room. "Well, either you were mistaken or someone moved the body. When did you lock the outer door?"

"On my honor, straight after the last person left. I went and hung the key up behind the bar. Magro, you can ask him, he said to me, 'We are going to kill a witch and you still hang the key up.'

"He called me an old woman," added the innkeeper indignantly. "The Dottore told me to lock it. But no one calls him an old woman."

"Magro's a fool. Can't tell a jackass from an old woman," said the soldier. "You hung the key up where everyone in this little town knows you always hang it, I'll wager? In the same place as you've hung it for the last twenty years, belike."

The innkeeper nodded.

"When we leave here, you'll lock it again. This time I'll keep the key."

Palinni turned to Brother Mascoli who was kneeling on the floor next to the small table and the pool of blood. "Well, Hypatian? Praying for the dear departed?" There was a hint of amusement in his voice.

Mascoli shook his head. "Looking at the blood, Signor Carlo. It is not enough, if the man bled to death. Of course he may have bled internally."

"Hmm. It's an odd place for a man to sit alone, for no reason," said Carlo, stumping over to the table. "What was he doing in here?"

The innkeeper tried to look blank but only managed to look evasive. "I do not ask," he said, throwing his hands up. "It is the customer's business."

"Perhaps you should go and wash those hands, Pontius," said Brother Mascoli allowing his thoughts to escape his lips. He would have to do penance for that, but it was obvious something was awry here.

He took four candles from his frayed pouch, and began to carefully set them out at the cardinal points. If some dark magic had left its residue here the wards would provide some protection.

The innkeeper blinked at him. "My name is Paolo, not Pontius."

"Well, Paolo-Pontius," said the soldier, "get along with you and see how that woman of yours is doing with a plate of food for us. How long will you be, master monk?"

"It will take but a short while," said Mascoli, and began to chalk the seven lines of enclosure, chanting from the psalms as he did so. But even as he did it, he knew it for a waste of labor. Nothing more magical than a dried salamander being struck into flame had ever happened down here, he'd warrant. There was none of the faint taint to the air that magic always brought to his nostrils. A smell not unlike that of a tinker's solder, which he had been told that most people were unaware of.

A little while later he knew the definite truth. None of the telltale signs of magical workings were here. But he was still left with the feeling evil had been done in this room.

"He did not die by magic," he said to Carlo and two or three of the tavern louts who had sneaked down the passage to gawk.

Carlo nodded. "I assume that that's why someone removed the body."

Brother Mascoli found himself nodding in reply. He knelt, soaked up a little of the blood onto a shred of linen, and put it into a small bottle in his pouch. He caught the questing gaze of the soldier. "There may be someone with hunting dogs," he explained.

"Clever. I had not thought of that. Of course it will depend on the victim dripping blood. I'll see to it in the morning. Let's get some food into you."

Brother Mascoli followed him to a hot plate of bollo misto. His companion ate too, in silence, as they listened to the inn's patrons telling increasingly grisly stories about what was behind the locked door. The large, simple key, Brother Mascoli noted, Carlo Palinni had carefully put in his pouch. The wine, an inky Barbera, was too like the blood on the floor for comfort. After he had eaten, one of the locals escorted him to the sacristan, who took him to a truckle bed that had been prepared for him.

He knelt, prayed and gratefully lay down on it. He'd walked a long way that day. He could have come all the way by boat, but such a passage was beyond his slender means. There were other, better uses for the little bit of silver he had with him. He was tired, but sleep was far from him. He wondered if it had occurred to anyone, his crippled escort or anyone else, that the missing body implied that the murderer had had at least one accomplice. The woman had not killed the fellow by magic, if she had killed him at all. Troubling thoughts about Carlo Palinni crossed his mind, too, until he drifted into an uneasy sleep.

His rest was disturbed in the gray predawn by someone sitting on the bed. He opened his eyes to find Palinni at the foot of it. "Good morning, my clerical friend," said the soldier, scratching a stubbly scarred chin.

"You are up early." Mascoli rubbed sleep from his eyes.

"And to bed late, too. A few people to talk to, and a large number of fruitless hours spent tapping walls and floors in a cellar."

Mascoli blinked. "I had wondered . . ."

"I thought you might. It was quite obvious that the real murderer might have hidden there and screamed false accusations. Through a thick oak door one screamed voice is much like another. The bad news is that there is no hidden chamber. I am especially good at finding them."

The monk had to wonder why. "He could perhaps have hidden behind the door, and joined the press of onlookers?"

The grizzled old soldier shook his head. "I am before you there. I questioned all of those who were on the scene. Most of them were too full of wine to be holding anything back. Three of them were there at the front, when the door broke. Big fellows all, charging it. They fell into the room—and the door bounced back and closed behind them. They were sweating freely just telling me of it, being in that candle-lit room with the dead man."

"They could have been accomplices . . ."

The soldier shook his head. "I don't think so. Their stories were are slightly different."

"Meaning they lied."

The soldier shook his head. "Meaning they told the truth. If their stories had all been exactly the same, then I would know they'd colluded. The stories were close enough, just slightly different as to the details. No, this Vincente was all alone in that locked room with no secret chambers or exits. It does look like the magic you say could not have happened, did. And what's more, he was known to have had a very public dispute with the woman in the street, two days ago, in which she threatened him with 'consequences.'"

"And what does she say about this?"

"Nothing. She has decided that she will not talk to me. I wondered if she might talk to you."

"Me?"

"You. She trusted you yesterday. And you are not from this little nest of rogues. They'll lie like flat fish to protect each other. I don't trust them at all."

"You are going to a great deal of effort, Carlo Palinni," said

Mascoli, getting up. He was wondering if all of this was true—and if so, why the old soldier was pursuing the matter with such diligence.

"I have my own axe to grind," explained Palinni, with just a hint of implacable grimness on his broad, scarred, and patently untrustworthy visage. "Come down to the cells. Please."

Mascoli nodded. "I will be there, shortly."

In the pale light of dawn the little town looked much like any other fishing village on the marshy fringe of the great lagoon. It smelled a little better though. The wind was blowing across the sandy scrub-covered sandbar from the Adriatic only a few miles away, bringing the salty tang of the open sea with it. Brother Mascoli took a deep lungful of sea air and knocked on the door leading to the cells. The same Schiopettieri, Karg, opened it for him. The plump German did not look as if he had slept. He yawned. "Through here, Brother."

The town had two cells, which was probably more than it needed most of the time. The woman did not look as if she'd slept either.

"Blessings, sister," said Mascoli.

"Spare me the religious prattle. When are they coming to kill me?" There was both pride and fear in her voice. She stood straight and defiant holding onto the bars.

"Sister, I could find no trace of any magic being used in the cellar where this man was killed."

She looked at him, incredulously. And then burst into tears.

Mascoli reached through the bars and took her hand, gently squeezing it. He let her cry for a little while. "It is said that you threatened him."

"I . . . I did it just to frighten him." She sniffed, and then said defiantly, "He called me a *puttana* and fraud on the street. I am used to respect. You may as well know that they believe that I am a witch. Everyone believes it. Even the Podesta, when he's sober enough to believe anything."

"And are you, daughter?" asked Mascoli, calmly.

She sighed and nodded. "Sort of. I suppose. What they might call a witch. They're going to kill me anyway. It is no use pretending. I have done no evil. No black magic or sacrifice, Brother. Or traffic with the Devil. Just remedies and rituals that I learned from my mother, and she learned from her mother. I swear upon my soul. It is just herbs, the old gods, and . . . using their fear. Understanding them. Knowing how people think."

"You abused this gift a little, I think," said Mascoli, gently. "But not to kill."

She shook her head violently. "Not to kill. Never."

"Then we will have to find out just who did kill him."

"And why," said the gravelly voice of the old soldier, from just around the corner. "'Why' usually answers all the questions."

Mascoli sighed. "I suppose eavesdropping is another thing you had to learn in the army."

"It's useful. You know which parades to avoid," Carlo said calmly, stumping towards them. "Now let's get a crust to eat and a glass of wine, and we can talk about the latest development."

He looked at the woman. "Your magical skills are greater than you realized. You made a body vanish last night. Or at least that is what they're saying on the street."

"What?" She peered owlishly at him.

"Vincente's corpse. You made it disappear into thin air."

"And I would stand here behind bars if I had such powers?" she demanded, hands on her hips.

"It does seem a little unlikely, doesn't it?" he said dryly. "But it was a choice of that or admit that you might have an accomplice, or that someone else murdered him. It would seem that this Vincente wasn't a great candidate for resurrection."

She shuddered and held herself. "No. He owed me money, though."

"It seems that he owed everyone money. What did he owe you money for?"

She held her tongue.

"They'll either burn you or hang you, you know," he said conversationally. "You might as well tell us."

"Blue lotos."

It was a mild narcotic, introduced from North Africa to the swamps and cultivated in secret there—unlike the black lotos, its far more powerful and addictive cousin, which was still smuggled in. The blue was illegal, but Brother Mascoli himself had several medicines that contained it. The Venetian authorities turned a blind eye to the blue, but they would hang traffickers in the black.

"Not the black?" asked Carlo mildly, raising an eyebrow.

She shook her head. "It's filth. No one should deal in it."

But then, she would say that.

Carlo nodded. "True. Come, Brother. Karg is bringing something for the lady. We also need to eat a morsel before the huntsman gets here. I hope his dogs are more promising than he is."

The dogs came in a variety of shades and sizes and their barking was obviously not sitting too well with their owner's patently sore head. "Too much new wine. Dottore Sarbucco was celebrating buying a new farm last night. Before the murder," he explained.

"Can the dogs find a blood scent?" asked Mascoli looking at the motley pack.

"They usually do," said the owner laconically. "But that's a boar, or a buck, not a man."

They put the dogs to the blood scent and followed them as they ran off barking down the road. The trail did not lead them very far . . . to a dogfight and a newly butchered hog, being turned into pancetta, salami and some fine hams.

"Fine dogs," said Carlo, feeling his painful knee.

The owner shrugged. "Vincente was a bit of a pig."

Carlo bit his knuckle. "There goes my last throw. We need the body."

They walked back towards the town, more slowly, past an inlet of the lagoon. The road was raised a little above the water on ancient stones from the Roman days. The stones on the water's edge were carved, being plainly part of some old shrine. Time had etched most of the carvings away but Brother Mascoli could make out the form of a triton. It stirred some thoughts in his head. "The murderer didn't have much time to bury a body or take it very far."

"No."

"Maybe he threw it into the water?"

The soldier shrugged. "Very likely, but that would be even harder to find. We could spend a year dragging, especially if they used a boat and dropped him off in the middle of the lagoon. There'd be nothing but eel-gnawed bones in a few days. That woman doesn't have even a few days."

Mascoli looked at the water, and around at the empty landscape of reedy marshland. "You believe that she is innocent?"

"Not as clean as driven snow, but innocent of *this* murder. Mark my words, if we solve this murder mystery, it will be tied to the smuggling of the black lotos."

"You think she is involved in that evil trade?"

Carlo shrugged. "Maybe. But most likely not. She made her money from selling the blue. That I knew before she confessed. But this little village is the entrepôt for the black. I am sure of that."

Brother Mascoli looked doubtfully at his companion. What was he? Why did he know so much about a dark trade? He looked like a rogue, but he did not behave like one. And he seemed to be genuinely trying to solve this murder, even if he was doing it for reasons of his own, and not to save an innocent. That, Brother Mascoli knew, was his duty.

"I have . . . contacts," he said quietly. "Nonhuman ones. They could find the body for us, if it was dumped into the water."

"So I had been told," said the old soldier, with a broad smile. "I sent a messenger to Venice during the night. It appears that you are highly regarded by certain very powerful people, for a humble monk. They gave you a glowing character reference."

Mascoli raised his eyebrows. "The Podesta's assistant and a receiver of messages from the Republic in a place too small to be properly called a town, and you sent messengers during the night? All the way to Venice and back? You are not the common soldier that you pretend to be."

His large companion leaned on his crutch and smiled sardonically. "I give orders too easily for a start. I never said that I was a common soldier. I never said that I was once a condottiere either. I never lie if I can help it. I let my appearance deceive those who wish to be deceived."

"And what are you doing here?" asked Brother Mascoli carefully. Carlo did have an injured knee. But he was still a powerful man, and the water was very close.

"That is for me to know. But for now our purposes run in tandem. Call up your undine friends, Brother. I'll keep watch."

So Brother Mascoli prepared his summonsing. And with a faint mist on the water, they came. Juliette, whom he had treated, healed from a savage cruel gash that would have marred her inhuman beauty if not taken her life, and the triton Androcles. The tritons preferred the open sea, but, well, it was perhaps best not to ask questions about the physical relationships between the creatures. Juliette smiled at them, her teeth like pearls. "Cleaner waters, healer," she said.

"Too brackish for my liking," said Androcles, "but cleaner than the waterways of that cesspit you live in. What can we do for you, healer?"

Mascoli dug in his pouch for the shred of red-brown stained linen in its tiny bottle. "There is blood on this cloth. I want you to find the man it came from, if his body lies in the water."

Androcles took the scrap of cloth and put it into water he scooped into his cupped palm. Then both of them tasted the water. Brother Mascoli knew that they smelled and tasted things many thousands of times more sensitively than humans. They'd found bodies for him before. It helped the grieving widows of fishermen to reach some closure, and bodies were just dead things to nonhumans

The two water denizens looked at each other and then began to laugh.

"Do you mind telling us what is so funny?" asked the soldier, his eyes narrow.

"You've made an error with the sample, Brother," said Juliette. "This blood is not that of a human."

"Fey blood?" asked Mascoli warily. This opened up a whole new and dangerous area.

Carlo ground his teeth. "No, Brother. We've been set up. Pig blood, I'll warrant. Say goodbye to your friends. We need to get back to town."

Carlo walked at a brisk pace for a man with a crutch. "Where are we going?" asked Mascoli, keeping up, but not without effort.

"To the blacksmith. I doubt if there is anyone else in this one-donkey town capable of making a key. We already know where the bastards got the blood. The dogs led us right there."

"Pig blood! You mean . . . ?"

"Yes, Brother," said the soldier. "Fresh blood sausage probably. We haven't been busy trying to find a murderer. We've been busy trying to prevent one. The mob failed him. Now he will let the law—or that useless drunk that passes for it here—do it for him. And I think I now know why, too, and why he tried to do it that way."

"What? I mean who? Why?"

The soldier smiled sharkishly. "You sound confused, Brother. I was too, until I realized just now that I had looked at the wrong motive for the crime. I thought it was a falling out between black lotos smuggler-bosses. That this Vincente had somehow gotten in the way. Instead it was a clever way of getting rid of a thorn in his flesh, that the smuggler-master dared not simply have killed. The locals liked his money—the place is awash with more loose money than you'd ever find in a poor fishing and small market-town. They feared him and obeyed his orders. But they were scared of the witch. They respected her. He was an incomer, and she was thwarting him where she could. She deals with blue Lotos from the swamp. She did not want to lose her customers to the black."

They'd arrived at the smithy, where the smith was hammering away at his trade. He was a burly man, as smiths are wont to be.

"I want to know who you made a key for," said Carlo, not beating about the bush, pointing at him with the crutch.

The smith eyed him truculently. "I don't know what you're talking about." He started to turn back to his work.

Mascoli scarcely saw Carlo move, he was so fast. The crutch speared out and hit the smith in the solar plexus. As the man doubled forward, Carlo twisted the top of the crutch and drew out a long, thin concealed blade. He held it against the man's throat. "Unless you wish to die, don't lie to me. Who else could make a key?"

"They will kill me," said the smith fearfully. But there was resolve behind that fear. He looked at Brother Mascoli, a hasty glance, but something both of them saw. He believed—or perhaps just hoped—that the soldier would not kill him before a man of God.

Mascoli himself was less sure. He did not approve of the violence, but there was a time and place for it. And great evil would come unless they found evidence here. At the very least the Strega woman would die. The flow of black lotos would do more harm by far.

"My friend," he said with gentle firmness. "You know the woman Lucia Bari. I believe her ill sayings were respected." He would do penance for that too. But it was necessary.

The smith nodded. "She could turn cows' milk. Or women barren and cold. Or so my wife believes," he added warily.

He believed too, Mascoli could see. Both were simple herbal matters, hedge magic. But here in this rural swampland, well, little could be more important. A man's life was just his life, but his children were more than that. No wonder she was respected.

"A dying curse is powerful," he said. "I will tell her what you have done."

"I have done nothing to her," protested the smith. "I was not even with the crowd. I came home before the Dottore bought wine for the men in the inn. I would have stayed if I had known," he admitted. "I would do nothing to the Streghira. I swear."

"Yet you made the key for Vincente. So he could escape after he pretended he was dead. And you fear him, and his smuggler friends."

"Vincente? I do not fear Vincente," said the affronted smith. "He owes me money. You say . . . he pretended to be dead? Anyway I did not make the key for him."

"My friend," said Mascoli, "do you think that you will have anything to fear from an outsider and his friends when the truth comes out? That they tried to get the people of this town to murder the Streghira by pretending that she had killed Vincente? Who owed, by the sounds of it, every man in the district money. You made the key for Dottore Sarbucco, did you not?"

Slowly, the man nodded. "But you cannot touch him. He is too powerful."

Carlo slid the blade back into its sheathing crutch. "As an agent of the Signoria di Notte of the Republic of Venice, I think you will find that I can," he said grimly.

The smith's eyes nearly started out of his head.

"You will accompany me back to the cells," said Palinni. "My patrol of Schiopettieri are hidden in the house. We are going to visit the home of Dottore Sarbucco. Even if I cannot find him with black lotos on his hands . . . I think I may find a key, and a certain very alive dead man who was willing to pretend death to escape his debts. That will be enough to persuade the justices in Venice to put Sarbucco away for a considerable length of time, if they will not oblige me by hanging him."

"But his men . . ." said the smith warily.

"He lives about half a mile outside the town. We will have him away in a boat and on his way to Venice before the town even knows."

Brother Mascoli did not accompany them on their raid. Instead he went to the church. He felt a need for prayer, and a little soul searching. He found that his soul was not as offended by his conduct as he'd thought it should be. He was just walking out to greet the newly returned Father Baritto, when he heard a great commotion.

It was Carlo and the plump Schiopettieri Karg, walking on

either side of a man in chains. They were being followed by most of the town. Father Baritto gaped.

Brother Mascoli took him by the arm. "It would appear, Father, that we have witnessed something no man has seen for fifteen hundred years. A man returned from the dead. But this one is no messiah. I think he has just come to pay his debts."

"He owes me money," said Father Baritto.

Later, Mascoli sat and enjoyed some more of the Barbera at the inn with the agent of the Signoria di Notte. It seemed a good wine, now, and not at all like blood.

"So he screamed his lungs out while Sarbucco gathered witnesses, well liquored witnesses, into a suitable mob. Once they started pounding on the door, Vincente broke open the bladder full of pig's blood and lay down in it. I believe that Sarbucco made them all hold back while he certified the man dead. He then had Lampara lock the second door, making sure that no one would find the missing corpse, leaving Vincente to use the spare key to let himself out and take off in the twilight for Sarbucco's house. Of course the deed was supposed to be done, and Lucia dead, by the time morning came and the mob sobered up enough to realize that they'd killed someone they were scared of."

"What are you planning to do with her?" asked Mascoli.

"Leave her to you, I should think," said Carlo with a grin. "You're going to preach at her, aren't you? She's had something of a fright. That should keep her from playing with real danger . . . which the blue lotos is not. And anyone attempting to move black lotos through her patch will suffer severe consequences now, I should think. I gather a few people have left town hastily since she was freed."

"You are not the evil man I thought you might be, Carlo Palinni."

"Not good either. And my name is not Palinni, of course. But you aren't the saint I feared you might be either, Brother. Sometimes we need saints, and sometimes we need a bit of pragmatism. I've been looking for a priest I could speak to with confidence for a while. Will you hear my confession? I've done things with this crutch that weigh on my conscience, and in my line of work a man can die unexpectedly."

Brother Mascoli nodded.